DAYS OF SHATTERED FAITH

ALSO BY ADRIAN TCHAIKOVSKY

THE TYRANT PHILOSOPHERS
City of Last Chances
House of Open Wounds
Days of Shattered Faith

SHADOWS OF THE APT
Empire in Black and Gold
Dragonfly Falling
Blood of the Mantis
Salute the Dark
The Scarab Path
The Sea Watch
Heirs of the Blade
The Air War
War Master's Gate
Seal of the Worm

TALES OF THE APT
Spoils of War
A Time for Grief
For Love of Distant Shores
The Scent of Tears (with Frances Hardinge et al.)

ECHOES OF THE FALL
The Tiger and the Wolf
The Bear and the Serpent
The Hyena and the Hawk

DOGS OF WAR
Dogs of War
Bear Head

CHILDREN OF TIME
Children of Time
Children of Ruin
Children of Memory

FINAL ARCHITECTURE
Shards of Earth
Eyes of the Void
Lords of Uncreation

OTHER FICTION
Cage of Souls
Alien Clay
Service Model
Guns of the Dawn
Spiderlight
Ironclads
Firewalkers
Ogres
Walking to Aldebaran
One Day All This Will Be Yours
And Put Away Childish Things
Saturation Point
The Doors of Eden
Feast and Famine (collection)

DAYS OF SHATTERED FAITH

ADRIAN TCHAIKOVSKY

HEAD of ZEUS

An Ad Astra Book

First published in the United Kingdom in 2024 by Head of Zeus,
part of Bloomsbury Publishing Plc

9 7 5 3 2 4 6 8

A catalogue record for this book is available from the British Library.

ISBN (HB): 9781035901524
ISBN (GOLDSBORO HB): 9781035916887
ISBN (XTPB): 9781035901500
ISBN (E): 9781035901517

Printed and bound in Great Britain by
CPI Group (UK) Ltd, Croydon CRO 4YY

MIX
Paper | Supporting responsible forestry
FSC® C013604

Head of Zeus Ltd
First Floor East
5–8 Hardwick Street
London EC1R 4RG

WWW.HEADOFZEUS.COM

A long time ago now, I played in a LARP entitled Maelstrom, as part of a group of expatriates driven to other shores by a revolution at home. It was a remarkably immersive experience, not for battles for great heroic deeds, but for small moments of everyday living. I played an architect and spent most of the time engaging in petty ambitions, socialising and just generally *being* an ordinary man in a different world. Amongst my companions of the tankard and the fire was one Stefan, chancer, wheeler-dealer and minor noble, whose fellowship contributed a great deal to the fun I had. It seems particularly appropriate, therefore, to dedicate this book to the memory of Stefan's player, my friend James Coote.

About the Author

Adrian Tchaikovsky is a British science fiction and fantasy writer known for a wide variety of work including the Children of Time, Final Architecture, Dogs of War, Tyrant Philosophers and Shadows of the Apt series, as well as standalone books such as *Elder Race*, *Doors of Eden*, *Spiderlight* and many others. His Children of Time series has won the Arthur C. Clarke, Hugo, and BSFA awards, and his other works have won the British Fantasy, British Science Fiction and Sidewise Awards.

Contents

Dramatis Personae

The Palleseen

Sage-Invigilator 'Gil' Angilly – Palleseen Resident in Usmai
Sage-Broker Berkely – Valuations
Sage-Invigilator Palinet – Palleseen Resident in Peor
Sage-Inquirer Dalry – scholar
Fellow-Archivist Annet – scholar
Fellow-Archivist Drathel – Decanter
Fellow-Monitor 'Flint' Postry – Ventures
Fellow-Invigilator Wattery – Demonist
Companion-Invigilator Galversty – Demonist, deceased
Companion-Monitor Steggers – Ventures, Flint's second
Companion-Invigilator Samellers – Diplomatic aide
Cohort-Invigilator Loret – Aide to the Resident
Cohort-Monitor Croskin – Unnatural

The Usmiat Royal Family and Court

His Tranquillity Oparan – Alkhand of Usmai
Kaleithi – his absent wife
Gorbudan – the First Son
Dekamran – the Second Son, the Heir
Premath – the Third Son
Enshili – the Daughter
Sorthist, the 'Serpent's Fang' – brother of the Alkhand, deceased
Follo – Preceptor of the Usrani monks

His Quietude the Grand Moerend Arkanith
Lhisamena – Preceptor of the Tesemer
Coregan – custodian and functionary
Hakoran – Emorandi officer
Dolethi – poet
Teerasla – Tesemer Louse Speaker

Others in Alkhalend

Kakrops – the frog god, a divine being
Tarcomir – Loruthi envoy to Usmai
Hullseer Orhuhst – leader of the Cotto pirates
The Warden of the House of Hard Angles
The Under-warden of the House of Hard Angles
Oathan – Palleseen alchemist at the Fever Lodge
Tally – Jarokiri Surgeon at the Fever Lodge
The Reckoner – Miracle Worker at the Fever Lodge
Happy Jack – of the Fever Lodge, Maric
Kilbery – of the Fever Lodge, Palleseen
Caecelian 'the Viper' – of the Fever Lodge
Kass – Ibaleth queen

Nations and People

Cotto – a coastal, piratical people
Goshumai – a state of the Successor Coast
Janni Despotate – a long-fallen empire reliant on demons
Lor – a powerful mercantile state recently humbled by the Palleseen
Lucibi – a state of the Successor Coast
Moeribandi Empire – a necromantic dominion, now fallen, that once controlled the Successor States
Pallesand – expansionist state exporting perfection

Peor – a state of the Successor Coast aided by Pallesand
Usmai – greatest of the states of the Successor Coast

Places

Alkhalend – the capital and greatest city of Usmai
Constellar Gardens – the gleaming gardens about the House of Tranquillity
The Emora – the wealthy cliffside districts of Alkhalend
The Fever House – the expatriate hospital in the Sand Lanes
The House of Hard Angles – prison in the Sand Lanes of Alkhalend
House of Tranquillity – the Alkhand's Palace
Mantekor – Gorbudan's fortified stronghold
Sand Lanes – the poor districts of Alkhalend
Slate House – the Palleseen consulate building in Alkhalend
The Successor Coast – the region of the former Moeribandi Empire south of the Garmoers
The Successor States – the region formerly under the Moeribandi Sway
Tesemera – the sanctum and chapterhouse of the Tesemer
Water Lanes – the dockside district of Alkhalend
Waygrove – a portal to other worlds near Alkhalend

Things

Alborandi – order of masked monks who tend to the Waygrove
Alkhand – the ruler of Usmai
Clavamachy – a duel with clavars
Clavar – cutting blade used by male Usmiat duellists
Emorandi – noble inhabitants of Alkhalend's Emora
Falx – the two-handed Tesemer sword

Hookloper – Tesemer steed
Hus – strong Cotto liquor
Ibaleth – reptilian creatures from beyond the Waygrove
Kepishi – Usmiat slang for foreigners from overseas
Louse Speaker – a Tesemer elite warrior-monk
Mirror Throne – the throne of Usmai
Moerend – a priest of the old Imperial death cult
Ogrodon – enormous Ibaleth war-beast
Pel – the utilitarian language of Pallesand
Ramaht – the traditional drink of Usmai
Seraphi – troops swearing loyalty to a nation not their own
Skia – the rapier used by female Usmiat duellists
Skiamachy – a duel with skias
Spiribandi – order of monks
Taumachy – the game of pitting animated wooden animals against one another
Tesemer – the Louse Monks, a militant order from beyond the Grove
Usmiri – the language of Usmai
Usrani – order of monks worshipping Kakrops and performing civic duties
White Petal Crown – the crown of Usmai
Windsaw – Tesemer fighting beast

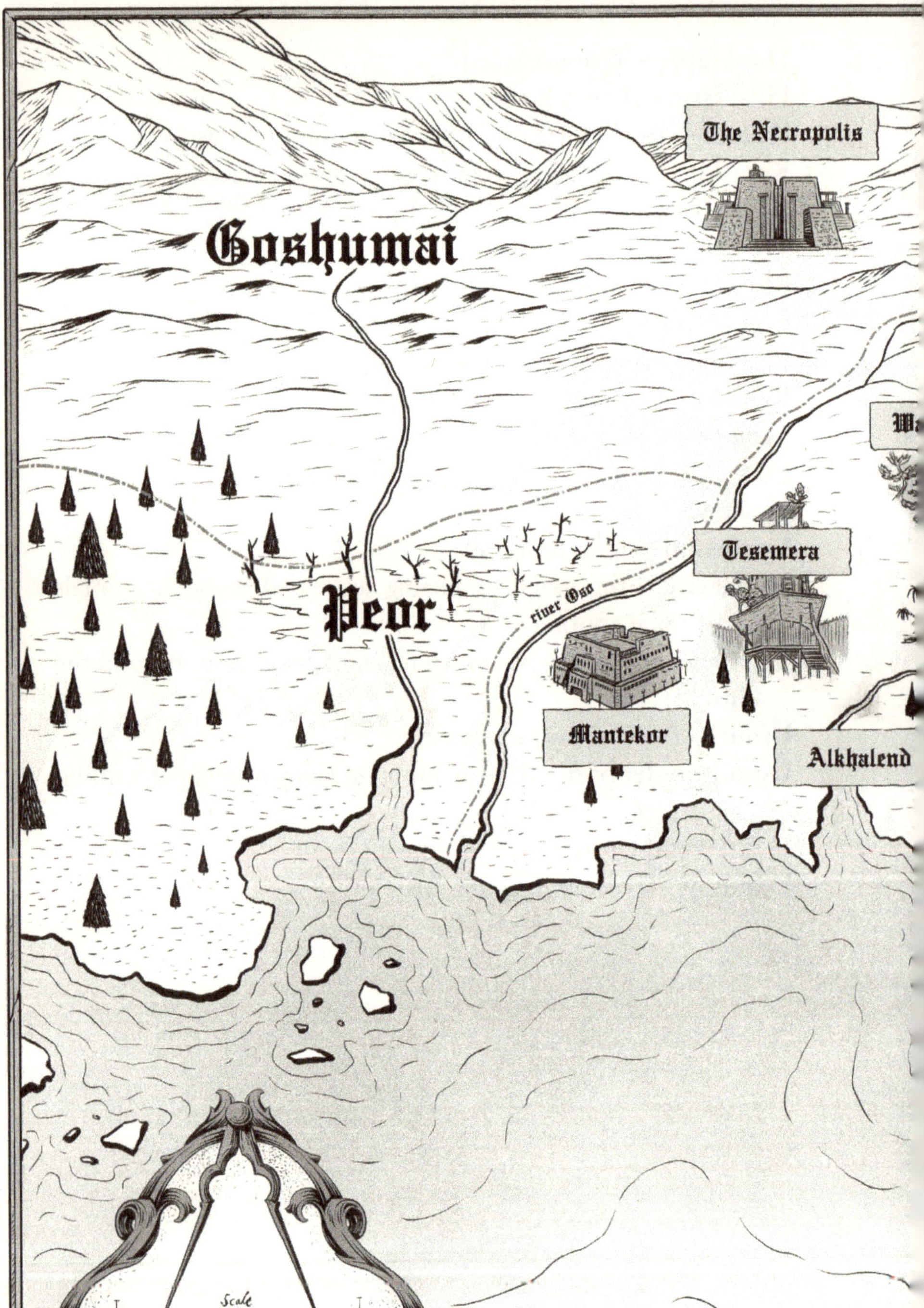
The Necropolis
Goshumai
Tesemera
Peor
river Oso
Mantekor
Alkhalend
Scale

he Successor Steppes
N
The Garmoers
ove
aleth Den
Usmai
Lucibi
The Successor Coast

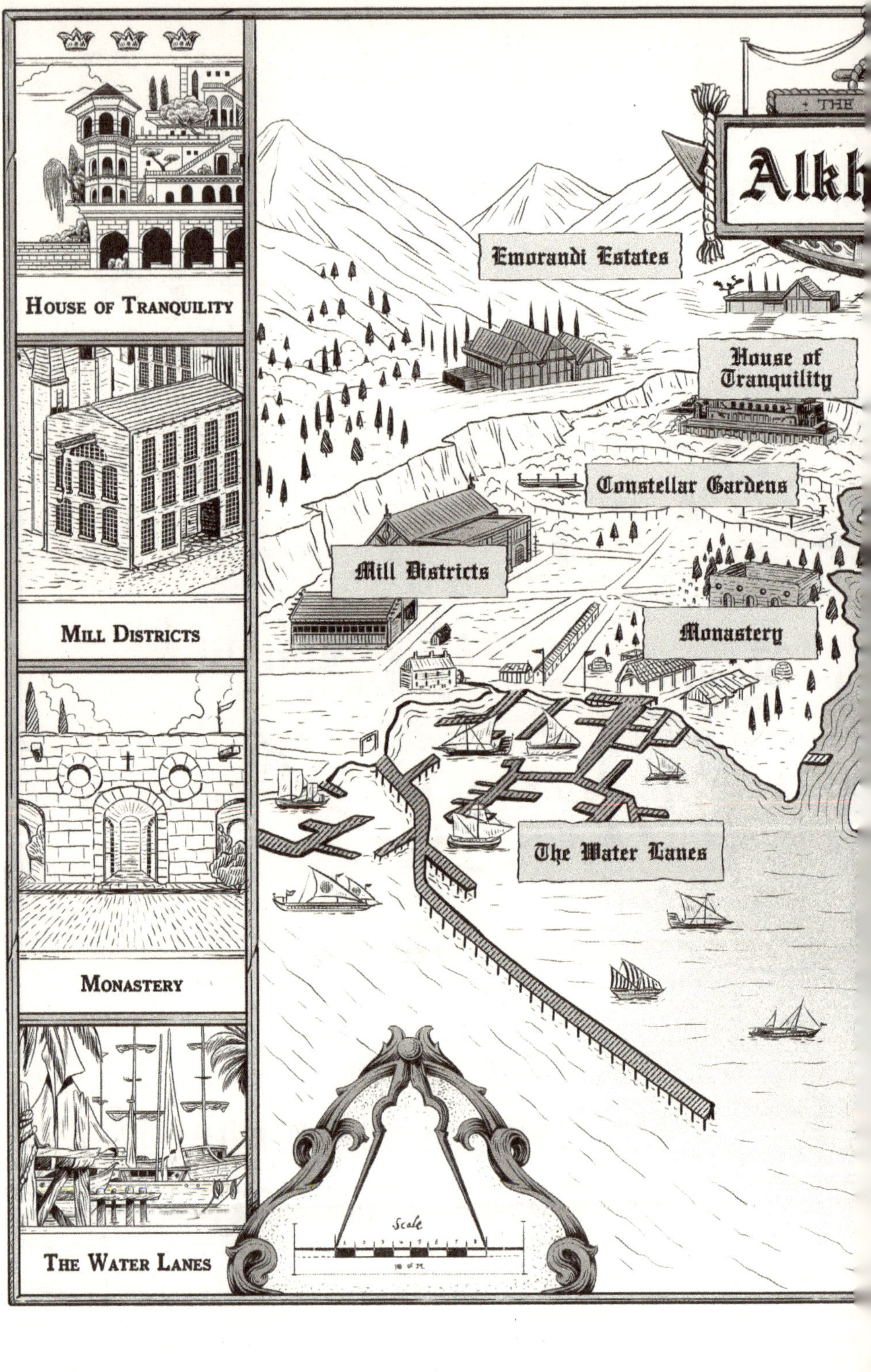
House of Tranquility
Mill Districts
Monastery
The Water Lanes
Emorandi Estates
House of Tranquility
Constellar Gardens
Mill Districts
Monastery
The Water Lanes
Scale

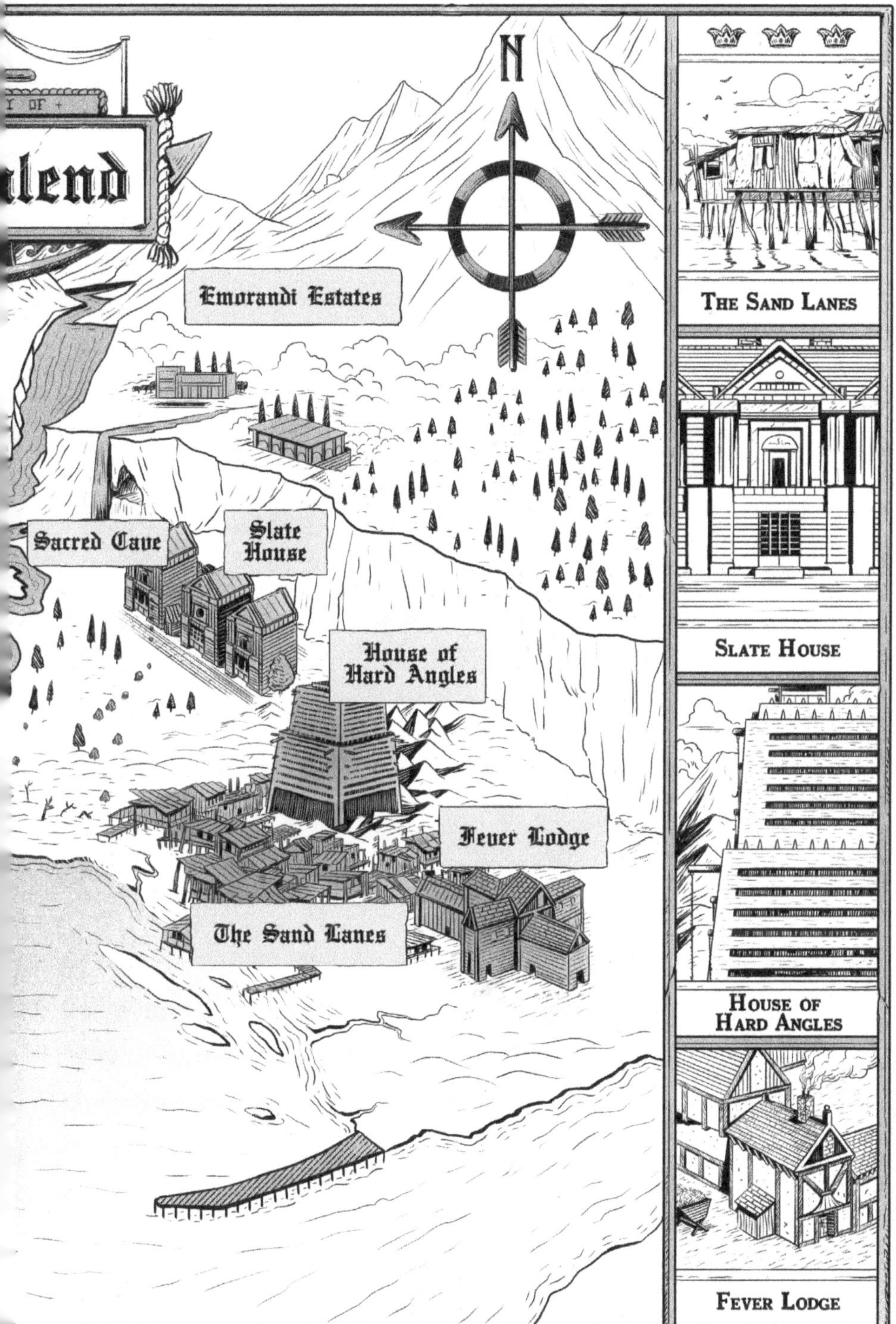

lend
N
Emorandi Estates
Sacred Cave
Slate House
House of Hard Angles
Fever Lodge
The Sand Lanes
THE SAND LANES
SLATE HOUSE
HOUSE OF HARD ANGLES
FEVER LODGE

Fresh Off the Boat

On the ship, as it tacked in past the sea wall, she was in her coffin of a cabin trying, by stub of candle and sequin of mirror, to make herself presentable. Clean shirt, clean face, uniform darned and done up. What does the mirror show her? By the time she's done, and the drum of feet overhead has the character of unloading and disembarking, not just seamanship, all that's visible is a bobbing phantom, a paleness like the face of a drowned woman sinking into dark water. When she makes the deck, evening is shading into night. Of the wonders of Alkhalend – "Oh you must view it from the sea, the waters, the palaces!" – there is nothing. Even the moon has taken the night off. She steps off the gangplank into darkness. And now this.

Loret had spent the voyage braced for pirates. The war with the Loruthi was done but all the boats and fleets and whole pillage-happy coastal fiefdoms were still out there, and hungry as ever. She'd thought she'd be past the threat of them when she stepped onto shore, except what she stepped onto wasn't even the shore. Someone had put a shifting maze of jetties and rafts and boats between her ship and dry land, and then hung it with an inadequate quantity of lanterns that made every step a flirtation with drowning. And she could swim, as even the meanest child of the Archipelago could, but not in a space where great floating weights of wood clashed together like nautical teeth.

The city was only in evidence from its own lamps, and these

were strung upwards as though the whole of Alkhalend had been arrested in the midst of being lifted into the heavens by divine fiat. Not an image that should come readily to a good, god-denying Palleseen girl, but desperation was the prybar that opened foolish minds to divinity, as they'd said back in the phalanstery.

They'd said a lot of things in the phalanstery, in the classes she'd sat through with her mind on her belly, or anything else. Now she wished she'd listened rather better because this place wasn't anywhere she'd wanted to end up.

Alkhalend, the Jewel of the Waters, capital of Usmai, greatest of the Successor States that had once been part of the… she couldn't even remember the name of whatever dead empire had once claimed this part of the world, and then petrified into a little kernel of tombs centuries ago, a receding tide that had left places like Usmai to grapple with their neighbours over who got to wield the big stick. Usmai, Alkhalend; yes, such beauty, yes, so exotic. She'd never wanted to be here. If she'd been curious she could have read a book or something.

And dark, so the beauty and exoticism just became a lot of unfamiliar and unpleasant noises that sounded terrifying.

Then the man, appearing at her elbow. The enormous, tattooed, scarred, terrifying man. Was this what an Usmiat looked like? She rather thought it wasn't. He was seven feet tall and bare chested except for a leather harness. He addressed her in a language she didn't know – one she didn't even know anything *like* – and then in Usmiri, bringing his face down close to hers and making the words slowly. Not like a man who wasn't happy with the language but like a man who thought she was very stupid. And she did speak Usmiri. Or she spoke *some* Usmiri. And had not been practising from her primer on the voyage because someone had assured her that Pel and Usmiri shared a lot of vocabulary and so 'you'll pick it up really quickly'. The man spoke to her now, and she caught only a word that sounded a lot like 'lost'.

She had nodded before realising that, as a lone foreign woman in a shifting maze of docks, admitting to being lost wasn't the wisest thing in the world.

In about nine heartbeats she was on his ship. Or on *a* ship that he felt comfortable just strolling onto. In a room with about a dozen men and women who all looked similarly terrifying. They wore too few clothes and were all of them leanly muscled as though they spent each spare moment cracking nuts with every part of their anatomy. The man who'd found her told everyone who she was in that first language, that seemed gesture as much as word; the language that wasn't *even* the language she had failed at honing over the voyage. They all laughed, probably at her. One woman had teeth that were filed sharp. Some of them were wearing even sharper teeth around their necks. They had great wild mops of hair, unlike the man who'd found her whose head was shaved bald and intricately inked. Then a woman with a dense interweaving of abstract piscine forms tattooed all over her cleavage came in, and she had a tatty Palleseen uniform coat over her shoulders. Which did not, Loret understood, suggest any kind of national sympathy, but instead meant they certainly killed and probably even ate Palleseen nationals. And then wore their clothing and possibly their skins.

The pirates were very real, she understood. These were just very lazy pirates who didn't even go to sea to do their raiding. They waited for stupid foreigners to get off the boat, and grabbed them.

"I have," she said – in Pel because every word of Usmiri had gone from her head, "diplomatic credentials. I am the new aide. For the Palleseen Resident. It is very – very important I reach the Residence." The Residence had a name and she couldn't remember it. "There will be a reward." Making large with money she didn't have.

The man who had found her leaned forwards over the little round table, that was scattered with wooden cups. The woman with the jacket poured something nasty into most of them, and put one in Loret's hands.

"Drink," she said. Usmiri, but Loret knew that word.

She hadn't enjoyed being on the ship, on the ocean. She got sick, and everything smelled, and she'd been terrified that someone on board would know too much or get too curious. But she understood now that being on that ship was the zenith of her later life. Because it had been better than being on the Archipelago and waiting for the jaws to close on her, better than the camps. And it had been better than being in a cabin crowded with ferocious pirates about to kill, strip and devour her.

She knocked back the cup, all of it in one go. It was… on one level it was horrible. Unlike anything she'd ever drunk and simultaneously horrible in a way she'd never even imagined. Not taste-horrible but actually existential. On the other hand it set her brain on fire in a way that burned away all the fear and uncertainty and apparently even uncovered the rough foundations of her Usmiri because suddenly she remembered how to say, "Show me the way to the embassy if you please," and said it quite loud and without much gap in between any of the words. For a second and a half, something was lit in her, as though she was one of those fish from the deep depths, that set itself on cold fire to stave off the dark.

The pirates found this hilarious. And, she realised, quite impressive. Whatever she'd just drunk didn't normally get knocked back in such a cavalier way by visiting foreigners straight off the boat. The man grinned at her. He had a terrifying grin. Three of his teeth were made of greenstone, intricately carved and then varnished over with some kind of clear lacquer, presumably so they didn't just start to fester with ingrained bits of all the people he ate. She realised she was staring.

He put a hand on her shoulder, and all the way around her shoulder because her shoulders were slender and his hands were enormous.

"Islerwoman," he said, like it was a title of honour, "I shall take you to Slate House. If that is where you need to be."

And that was the name of the Residence, and he had spoken

in Pel. Not good Pel, and the accent was horrible, but the thing about Pel was that it had been constructed to be easy to learn, and so it tended to turn up everywhere any people of two different lands needed to make a deal. Even the Loruthi, Pallesand's great rivals across the world, had used Pel to give orders to their mercenary legions when fighting against Pallesand.

They gave her another cup of the sharp, savage stuff. It tasted of fish, but it seemed to her that they'd used better fish to make the second shot, because it wasn't as objectionable as the first. By then a small part of her wondered whether she shouldn't just stick around and see if the third cup would be squeezed from an almost passable grade of fish, and where else the pirates had tattoos. That kind of go-with-the-flow thinking was why she'd had to get off the Archipelago, though. Easily led, that was her. When the bald man was lifting her up by her elbow to lead her out, it was probably a good thing.

She remembered very little of the trek through Alkhalend. The dark kept its secrets, and she had a disjointed, fish-beer-smeared impression of a lot of boats, and then a lot of plain buildings, big and small, and then after a while she was labouring up a path far too steep. By then the fish had worn off, and the heat had begun to work on her. Even with the sun down, her shirt was clinging to her like a drowner, and her uniform jacket must be a mess of spreading stains. The idea of just swanning about with nothing but a few leather straps above the waist seemed entirely appropriate.

"There," he told her. There still weren't enough lamps, but they seemed to be in a street of tall, ornately carved buildings. Obviously fancy, yet crammed in together without gaps or gardens, speaking eloquently of some intermediate social stratum. "Slate House. Good weather, Islerwoman."

She felt she'd received rather more help than the ability to down a cup of fish should really have earned her. The fact that, straight off the boat, she looked like someone pirates should offer hospitality was alarming, and something of that must have communicated itself to him. He laughed at her and jabbed the pad of his thumb into her forehead hard enough to rock her back on her heels. "You are my niece," he said, in clear Pel. She was not under any circumstances his niece. She was a child of the orphanages, no living family and, in any event, none of them had been a huge bald pirate. For a brief, fish-tainted moment she thought it might have been nice if one of them had.

On another level she knew exactly what he meant and she'd fled here to get away from that and somehow found it waiting for her. A saying, bobbing unwelcome to the surface of her mind. *All seas are the same sea.* Meaning, as far as she was concerned, run as far as you want, you can't escape the trouble that is *you*.

Then he was gone. She barely saw him go. The night ate him, and there was just an echo of his laugh left over.

She knocked at the door, waiting for the neatly buttoned Palleseen functionary to open up and look down his nose at her. A return to normalcy. An opportunity to proffer her papers and get settled in. To sleep in a bed that wasn't slung between two walls and got rolled up every morning. Except the woman who answered, after a pause, wasn't neat or buttoned or Palleseen. Loret recognised Usmiat clothes, sure enough. A woman with a floaty shawl over her shoulders, with a tight vest fastened to the side, with baggy trousers and pointy little boots. And a hostile, foreign expression.

"Slate House," said Loret, in Pel and then Usmiri. "This is Slate House." Because she'd been trusting some random pirate to know where the Palleseen Residence was and that suddenly seemed foolish. She'd been proffering her papers and the woman snatched them from her. Loret was suddenly terrified she'd never get them back.

She got as far as "Please," when the woman hissed annoyance between her teeth and then said, "You'd better come in. Your timing's immaculate." She had vanished inside even as she spoke. Loret dithered at the threshold for a second and then followed her.

There was one lit chamber inside, the shadow of the Usmiat woman occluding the lamps briefly as she ducked inside. Loret scurried after, finding a well-appointed room. Well- and Pal-appointed, she noted. The furniture and some of the wall hangings were local, but there was the Charter of the Temporary Commission of Ends and Means up on one wall; the thing they made everyone learn by rote at the phal even before you knew what most of it meant. There was a map of the Archipelago, and a copy of that famous picture of the Liberation of Jarokir. Slate House, then, but instead of courteous and efficient Pal staff there was this woman – this woman even now buckling a *sword* about her waist, Loret noticed. And there was a man, an Usmiat man with a big cloak thrown over the back of his chair. A bearded man with a high forehead and a crystal goblet in his hand, looking at her quizzically.

"Excuse me," Loret said, "may I speak to the Resident please?" She was acutely aware that the woman still had her papers.

"Cohort-Invigilator Loret," the woman read there.

"Yes, I am. I am a Cohort-Invigilator of Correct Appreciation, Outreach department, sent here as aide to the Resident. It is very important that I present those credentials to the Resident. To Sage-Invigilator Angilly. She is a very important woman, and she will be very displeased if I am prevented from seeing her."

The Usmiat woman gave her a long, arch stare, and then settled the sword about her hip. "Do you know duelling etiquette?" she asked.

"No," Loret said. "Why would I know duelling etiquette?"

"They didn't teach you that in the phal?"

Loret blinked, but presumably this woman was on the Resident's staff somehow, and so had learned about Pal things. Certainly her Pel was very good, barely a trace of an Usmiat accent. But impudent. "They had more important subjects to teach us there," Loret said, trying for haughty but aware she was coming off more as petulant. And honestly she hadn't gone to the sort of place where duelling was on the curriculum. A bad start to life that she'd backed with a whole load of bad decisions.

"Well you'll do," the woman decided, and then turned to the man. "I suppose I have my second."

He stared at her. He hadn't really looked anywhere else, certainly not at Loret. "I am asking you, once more, not to do this."

"I don't see he's left me any choice," the woman said, with a shrug. "I don't *want* to. But… *he* wants it. Because he's got nothing left, otherwise. He's ruined. I ruined him."

"Not just you," said the man. He had more of an accent but, as appropriate for a servant here, his Pel was also very good.

The woman said nothing for a moment. Shrugged again. "Mostly me," she decided. "So he goes home with my blood on his blade, or he doesn't go home. It's not an ideal situation, but you know how they are, with personal honour and duty and all that. He's in a corner and, the way he sees it, he cuts his way out or not at all."

"Excuse me," Loret put in. "I'd really like to speak to the Resident now." *Have they killed her?* she thought suddenly. Maybe these two well-spoken Usmiats were *not* servants at all. Maybe they were villains who'd broken into Slate House. Maybe the Resident's corpse was cooling on the floor of an upstairs room. And right about now she should back away, except she didn't have anywhere she could go. A foreign city, at night. Even the pirates were somewhere back through a maze of twists and turns she could never have replicated. *Duels. Swords. What have I got myself into?*

"Come on," the woman decided, and grabbed her arm. The man stood. A moment of stillness.

"Not you," said the woman.

"I'm supposed to just return to the House of Tranquillity?

Return to my bed. Wake refreshed in the morning and wait for them to bring news of whether you live or die?"

"Yes," she said. "Because I am about to do something both spectacularly illegal, culturally offensive and diplomatically inadvisable, and of all the people who cannot possibly be there to see it, you head the list. Also, you wound me. I thought you had more confidence in my form." She flashed her teeth in something between grin and grimace. A predator's look.

"I would make an offering in your name, but all the gods hate your people," the man said, gathering his cloak about him.

"With good reason," the woman admitted.

"Gil. Live." He put a hand where her neck and shoulder met, thumb on her cheek. Loret saw the woman bite her lip, all that insouciance falling from her for a moment. The man's hand trembled. Between them was a whole skein of tugging emotions that she felt she shouldn't be a witness to. Private things only exposed because the pair were being pulled away from one another.

"Excuse me," she said, her voice dry. "I do not wish to be a second in a duel. I am a Cohort-Invigilator of the Palleseen Sway and I must speak to the Resident. Please will you take me to the Resident. It is very important."

"You can let yourself out," the woman said to her friend. "Just don't get yourself stopped within three streets of here. Whoever's blood gets shed tonight, you can't let it get on you."

The man withdrew his hand. The woman turned to Loret. "Come on, then. If you're coming."

"I'm—No, I'm not coming," Loret said. She felt as though the words she was speaking and those the woman was hearing didn't line up. "I'm—"

"Cohort-Invigilator Loret, reporting for duty," the woman agreed. "Good for you. Welcome to the staff." And something shifted in the way Loret saw her, as though the light of the lamps hit the woman's face differently. So that she saw not an Usmiat woman, but a fellow Pal with the pallor of the

Archipelago scorched off her by years in a hot land. "I'm Sage-Invigilator Angilly. Consider this your first formal duty. I need a second and you're it. Commendation for arriving in the nick of time."

Gil's Best Diplomacy

The Louse Monks had their sword rituals into which none might intrude and live, but the Usmiat took their own duelling traditions just as seriously. Two traditions, as it happened. Clavamachy was the clash of great curved falchions, full of sound and fury. Skiamachy was the poise and angle of long straight blades. Two schools of the fight, the man's duel and the woman's. By ancient tradition, they did not mix. But then, when you were a foreigner, inherently transgressive in a thousand ways, shedding blood in a forbidden manner was just one more.

As well as not knowing anything about duels, the new girl turned out not to be very good at long uphill walks. Or at least her breath was rasping before they'd ascended three turns up the cliffside path. Sage-Invigilator Angilly – Gil to her friends – didn't think she'd work out. *Pack her off on the next boat home. Ask for someone who isn't still wet from the phal.* She'd always thought there were two types who got into Outreach and ended up as a Resident's aide. The sort who were overly keen, as she'd once been; the sort who were overly embarrassing to have back home but whose family meant they couldn't just be busted down to trooper and sent to the front lines.

"New girl," she called back.

An interrogative wheeze suggested Loret was listening.

"Who're your people? Got an uncle who's a sage or something? Got an aunt who's a secretary to the Commission?"

"What?" Loret asked blankly. "No."

Which, given that she patently wasn't over-keen, suggested a third class of candidate, the all-round fuck-up who got shoved on the boat because nobody wanted the job.

"So, Usmai," Gil tried. "Plum post. Lots of candidates."

"What?" Loret said, as though comprehension of her native language was heavy baggage she'd had to leave behind on the trail. "I mean yes."

"And you angled for it because…?"

Loret slipped on the loose slab that Gil had just pointedly stepped round.

"Because…?" Gil repeated, in case that had been misdirection trying to kill off the topic.

"Plum post. Like you say. Can we stop a bit?"

Gil did in fact stop, turned on her heel and looked back at her. Looked at her properly. A somewhat gangly woman – girl, really. Hair hacked about just off the shoulder, too short to tie back in a regulation bun, too long to look soldier-neat. A proper Archipelago pallor; interesting to see whether she was the type to go brown or just boiled-ham in the Usmiat sun. A round, unhappy-looking face. No kitbag, no luggage, her entire travelling world in a single satchel slung over one shoulder. "You sure you don't have some really senior types in your immediates?" Gil asked.

Loret just looked miserable. Gil's previous aide, now invalided out, had also had a face that showed just about every thought and emotion in his head, but he'd also been very good at the rest of his job. This kid's entire recommendation was that she'd been able to find the Residence without getting knocked on the head and thrown in the harbour.

"No," the girl said. "Is that a problem?" The surliest kid in the phal talking back to teacher.

Gil smiled. She was about to go and die under the edge of someone's sword, or else kill someone, for preference. She didn't really need this. Specifically, she didn't want to become *this* person again, because it had been a while and the jacket didn't fit.

"I understand 'magister' is customary," was about the most she could cushion the blow.

The girl choked like someone had force-fed her lemons. Gil fully expected her to insist that *Magister* was earned, rather than just coming with the superior rank. Which was literally untrue. As proof of which, Gil had *magistered* a great many people who hadn't earned it, over her career.

"Magister," Loret said, apparently as an all-purpose bandage to every missed opportunity to date. It was so bald-facedly disrespectful that Gil laughed.

"Fine," she said, recommencing the climb. "Look, I appreciate you made the trip out here, but the situation in Usmai is a bit knife-edge at the moment. No pun intended. I need someone who can actually *do*, you know. Initiative, local knowledge, tradecraft."

"What?" Loret said it the same way every time, as though the world around her was a font of lunacy and only she was being reasonable. "Magister," she added, too late.

"I'm just saying I don't think you're a fit for this post," Gil told her. "Assuming I don't end up with my head and my shoulders pursuing separate careers in about an hour, I'll write you some sort of an excuse and you can go home."

"What?" Loret said again, and then, "No! No, wait, magister! I can do... Initiative. I have initiative. And for – it's hardly fair to ask for..." Losing her breath on words already so that she had to run to catch up with Gil's heels. "I mean I've only just got here. How could I have local knowledge?"

"I mean in my day we read the dossier on the boat," Gil drawled. "I understand it's still the done thing."

"I didn't – they didn't give me a dossier," the girl got out, which suggested something dreadful had happened to basic procedure back home. "Wait, what was the other one?"

"Tradecraft," said Gil patiently.

She actually heard the yawning pause behind her as its own quality of sound.

"What's that?" asked Cohort-Invigilator Loret blankly, and *seriously*?

"Next boat," Gil said. "Sorry, Cohort. Things are going to get very hot in Usmai shortly and I don't just mean the weather. I need someone who knows the business. I'll write you an excuse."

"Magister!" Loret gasped. "Please! I'll do tradecraft! I'll learn it."

Gil sighed. "Enough. We're here." They'd been crossing the fringes of the palace gardens, all those secluded glades, and now she saw the handful of people ahead, the sand, the circle.

The thing about illegal honour duels in Usmai wasn't that it was hard to find somewhere to hold one. It was that it was hard to find somewhere that someone else wasn't already holding one. They were mad for their sword-work over here, which she actually rather liked, it being the one thing she'd come out of the phal with a real aptitude for. And, yes, the local traditions were a bit weird, but you got used to some and worked your way around others.

On any given night there would be at least half a dozen assignations like this. Usmiat nobility or the more aspiring class of merchant or even palace staff, whose differences just couldn't be settled any other way. And in general it was a skill thing, first blood and a doctor on hand in case anyone got too accurate. In cases of more serious enmity it was to the surrender, and as much blood as anyone had stomach for until then. Mostly surrender and first blood happened simultaneously, though. Usmai wasn't the Archipelago, but it was a civilized barbarian nation by Pal reckoning. Very few people actually got killed on the end of a sword in peacetime.

This was going to be different. Because this was a matter of foreigners, the truly civilized, and that meant that they were going to have a very serious go at killing each other.

Tarcomir, her opponent, had brought two of his own staff

as seconds. His embassy had always been over-supplied with personnel, while she'd limped along with a single aide because all the Pal funding went over the border in Peor where the Sway had a proper foothold. And now she didn't even have a proper aide to bring. Just Loret, whatever she turned out to be.

"You're late," the man said. He had stripped away the long vest with all the medals and braid and decorations, that she thought of as his armour. Standing there in a shirt so baggy she'd be stabbing empty cloth as much as body if she even landed a strike. They had a dozen lanterns lit around the circle, tablethi-fire behind red glass to give the arena a properly hellish aspect. The light glinted on the gold beads in Tarcomir's elegantly forked beard, the bees and scarabs that were symbols of prosperity and luck where he came from.

"Magister," said Loret, "they're Loruthi."

Gil blinked at her. Made a big show of nodding sagely. "*There's* that specialist local knowledge, see?" The girl's face darkened, knowing she was being made fun of. Gil sighed massively. *I am about to probably die. I don't need this.* "Cohort-Invigilator Loret, may I introduce you to the Bashonin Tarcomir, Emissary of the Loruthi Palatine Council and my opposite number here in Alkhalend. If it isn't too inconvenient for you on your first and last day in the job, you're here to witness he and I do our level best to kill one another." And she felt the kick, then. Inside her. The one she'd been putting off. Because she was bitching at the new girl, but it was because she'd been trying not to think about this. "Unless, of course," she added, fighting a little to keep her voice steady, "there is some alternative, at this late hour?" That was what you were supposed to do, of course, with illegal duels to the death. Pal and Loruthi and Usmiat traditions all. You asked.

She waited for the haughty rebuke from him. She had, after all, ruined his career. Turned him from a man whose name had been about to deliver Usmai to his homeland on a plate, to a man who was cursed in every tea house and smoking den where the Loruthi diplomatic service met. The man who had lost Usmai to the Pals, just as his people had lost the war to the Pals. A scapegoat for how it had all gone wrong.

"You know what they demand of me," he said. His voice was quiet, sad. She'd rather he was raging. "The next boat home. All our staff here, and in a dozen other nations. As part of the treaty." The one that had ended the war, and that the Palleseen had written most of, being the winners. Loruthi global reach might never recover.

Just like Loret, Tarcomir would be on the next boat home, and when he arrived they'd burn him in effigy and he'd end up filing papers somewhere if he was lucky. Unless he arrived with some pyrrhic achievement to throw at the feet of his superiors, like a dead Pal Resident. Some tiny revenge for all his nation had lost.

Either that, or he'd be on the next boat home anyway, but in a box.

She wanted to go to him. She wanted to raise the spectre of all those times they'd just been the two foreigners in a foreign land, sharing a drink and setting this tiny corner of the world to rights because they could. Because life was easier if you just realised you had more in common with the man behind the big desk in the other embassy. They'd got on like that for years. Even after the war began, it hadn't come to Usmai.

Then he'd done some things, used his influence to tilt the scales. Then she had. And she'd done it better, really. Cheated, risked more, gotten lucky, however you shone a light on it. She'd won and here they were. Not friends any more, not even a little, save that she could absolutely have refused when he called her out. Have let him go home in disgrace, not even this last chance to stem the gushing flow of his reputation. And so, because they had been friends; because of all those shared drinks; because he had been a friend even when their nations had been enemies, she was going to give him the chance to kill her.

"Magister," said Loret, in such a tone that Gil wished she'd never stood on ceremony, "you can't *fight* the Loruthi emissary?" And it wasn't a question except she made it one.

"Well, that will make the next ten minutes absolutely hilarious," Gil told her, "because we're surely about to try."

"The war's over," Loret said, apparently assuming that Sage-Invigilator Angilly, Palleseen Resident in the great nation of Usmai, might have been overlooked when they were sending out the communiques.

"The war," said Tarcomir, in his good Pel, "was a long sentence. This, here, is the punctuation to it." Because frankly the Loruthi were better poets than the Palleseen. "Come on." He dodged between two lamps, strode out into the sand circle, and turned.

He had his falchion in his hand. Not quite an Usmiat clavar, as her own service rapier wasn't quite a skia. And you did not under any circumstances pit one against the other. Not in Usmiat tradition or law, and honestly the technicalities of it were actually a bit challenging anyway. The red light kissed the hacking edge of his sword, and it took no great imagination to picture it biting flesh. Her own long needle seemed pitifully inadequate.

"Or there's the new way the locals like, if you prefer." He'd seen the way she was looking. His smile could have been meant pleasantly, but that red light turned everything to malice.

"Baton?" She considered it. The Usmiat nobles loved their firearms. Two fools standing at range with levelled rods, gabbling out the command words to punch holes in one another without ever having to be *good* at it. Flash, bang, one or both or neither falling over. Honour, apparently, satisfied. And she supposed it was easier. One would not have to work up a sweat in order to get killed. *Very* civilized, therefore, and probably it would catch on back home soon enough. A bit *too* civilized for her, though. "I mean, I lugged this weight of steel all the way up here. Wouldn't want it to be for nothing." A grin at him, and the flash of his bright teeth back, and then they remembered they were enemies.

"All right, then." He twirled his blade, a glittering arc,

loosening his wrist. "Come on then. Hop to." The traditional duellist's invitation, that sounded so much better in Loruthi.

She walked into the circle. Loret had some other thing to say, presumably about how this couldn't possibly be happening, but right then Gil reckoned she'd spent enough time on the useless girl. *Honestly it might be easier if Tarcomir* does *kill me. At least I wouldn't have to deal with Loret. Looked at that way, he's doing me a favour.*

Because of the local prohibitions, and because nobody back home would be so gauche, she had never fought against someone with a sword like that. Tarcomir probably had, because the Pal style was more common out in the wider world. Advantage Tarcomir. And she'd been hoping that her little needle would at least be quicker, but when festivities commenced he was at her with such a blinding flurry of strikes that she lost the initiative immediately. He didn't just run onto her point either, which had been her other secret weapon. He shouted at her, something fierce in Loruthi, and basically set about carving the space within the circle into chunks too small for a whole woman to stand in. Not wildly; there was an awful measured poetry to it, a formal style honed over the generations by people who were keenly, academically interested in the absolute best way to hack the human body to pieces without exposing oneself to the same treatment from one's opponent. And she could see how, if she'd had the same sort of sword, she could have thrown herself into it and turned those cuts aside with her own wheeling, spark-striking blows. She could have tilted *his* momentum until it became *her* momentum, and then it would be *her* subdividing the air around *him* until there wasn't anywhere big enough for a whole body. And they did this with blunt blades for practise, she understood, but there must have been a lot of broken bones in training nonetheless.

Her narrow blade wasn't suitable for that kind of clash. Probably she'd just end up with a pair of stumps if she tried it, one at the quillons and one at the shoulder. Instead she fell back on footwork and on fending. Never giving him a perpendicular edge to smash down on, but always sliding him away along her sword. Trying to bind him out of line, trying to catch him with the spurs of her guard, trying to get on the inside so she could lunge. He was constantly turning the wrong way, though, or the wrong way for the style she'd learned. Her inside line was constantly ending up on the outside of him.

They broke. The night was cooling but her shirt was a reservoir of sweat already, her hair plastered to her brow. The red light caught Tarcomir's wide eyes, his bared teeth. He yelled at her again, trying to make her flinch. That was another Loruthi fighting thing, shouting. Back home that sort of thing would get you sent off with a reprimand.

She bellowed back at him, called him a son of a fucking demon whore. Said it in Loruthi, too, because if you're going to do something, do it properly. With the initiative well and truly taken back she chased him around the circle for a while, lancing at his chest from high guard, from low. Letting his sweep decapitate a lantern, stabbing him through the calf.

She fell back instantly, because that was how she'd been trained. One touch, appeal to the referee, finicky argument about technicalities, you know.

Tarcomir wasn't doing that. He just came on, and whatever damage she'd just done was washed away in a flood of desperate adrenaline. His blade cut through some of the space she'd been using to stand in, leaving her sprawled sidelong because it had been the only way of getting clear. His arc swung easily into a downward-cleaving stroke that she was just able to deflect with her own blade. He tore up the sand and she ran him through.

Clean.

At least it was clean. Right up under the ribs, and no amount of baggy shirt could foul her aim. Not a textbook perfect strike, because the textbooks assumed you'd never be running your opponent through while lying on your back, but aside from that her instructors would have politely applauded the hit.

Gil gasped as though she was the one with the sword in her. Tarcomir leaned over her, his weight forcing down against her quillons. She bitterly wanted his face to be in shadow, but the red light was all over it, the agonised clench of his features.

She wanted to apologise. To offer to go again. She'd stabbed him while she was on the ground. Obviously it had been his play and she'd done it wrong. They should sit down and talk through the technicalities of the pass and just how things had gone awry. Have a drink. Like they used to.

He groaned. Her arm trembled. He was about to collapse onto her because she couldn't hold him up any longer and it was a task he had abruptly lost interest in himself. She twisted, and when he crashed to earth it was beside her. Her sword sprang from her hand.

She sat up. Tarcomir's two seconds were staring at her. They both had swords, and probably they had batons, or if they wanted to get old fashioned there were always knives. She had just disarmed herself, and all the fight was out of her anyway. Probably they should come over and finish her off, so they could save their own careers back home. Not as though the new girl would stand in their way.

But they waited until she left the circle, as was proper, before going to retrieve the body of their employer. They even removed the rapier, left it there on the sand, blood smeared from the blade like a fallen flag.

Angilly dropped to her knees, which was when the locals arrived.

The thing about illegal duels to the death was, of course, that they were actually illegal. Against the pronouncements of the Alkhand. And there were such things as legal duels to the death, but only with explicit permission from the highest, which was not going to be extended in arrears to a mismatched pair of pugilistic foreigners intent on shredding what was left of their diplomatic relations.

The locals, in this case, were a half-dozen palace staff armed with batons, whom Gil reckoned she could have faced down if she had to, in most other circumstances. Not beaten them in a fight but stared at them and waved her credentials and made threats until they went away. There were the same number of non-combatant palace functionaries, but they were just garnish and wouldn't have tipped the scales. There were also three Louse Monks, and that was where her control over the situation ended.

She did exactly the wrong thing, as they intruded. She went back into the circle for her sword. And there, within the circle, holding a sword, she was a combatant again, and in her sight still, the dead man she'd killed without the Alkhand's permission. And, at the same time, a foreign national, a dignitary, an ambassador.

It was, therefore, a complicated situation. One of the Louse Monks stepped forwards, the red light painting his alien features like blood. They were a weird, uncomfortable lot, these monks. Their strip of tonsure, their alien provenance, their angular frames. Her eyes slid to the weapon in his hands, helpless as someone skidding down a slope. A thing the length of a spear, half of it the forwards-curving blade. A weapon that could cut a horse in half. More reach than her rapier and just as fast. Just... ridiculously fast. She'd seen the monks in action, both in display and once against some outlaws. Very briefly.

She understood, right then, that killing her would absolutely be the simplest way of dealing with this, in the eyes of the monks. Honestly, killing someone was usually their preferred problem-solving option. Right now, severing her from the world would solve so many problems.

A lot of those problems were her own. She could almost sympathise. That had been the corner Tarcomir had been backed into, after all. All that paperwork on her desk back at the Residence, and this new girl too. Easier to let the Louse Monks cut her down.

"Well," she said, and jammed the rapier in the ground. "I suppose you want to take me somewhere. Until we can sort this out."

The Louse Monk met her gaze. He didn't want to take her somewhere. He wanted to *send* her somewhere, and just where that might be was a matter of theological dispute. Unless you were a Pal and didn't believe in any of it. The fact that she didn't have a weapon in her hands any more did not prevent him from following his preferred solution. Arguably it made things a little easier, even. But that was a step too far from the Louse Monk path, apparently.

He clicked at her, annoyed, inhuman. One of the functionaries stood forward and ordered the armed guards to take her, which they did. She cast one look back at the shapeless dark thing that was Tarcomir's corpse.

The Shadow of the Throne

Slate House, because of the roof. A Palleseen material, imported by a previous Resident who'd wanted it between him and the thunderous drumming in the rainy season. Odd what people did, to bring a ghost of home to them. This whole street was given over to such transplants. The tall, narrow houses pressed in against one another were the homes of foreign merchants, emissaries and other wealthy expatriates. From this serpent's head, weighed down with its burden of unconvention, the street coiled down until it spiralled to a dead end deep within the cluttered shanties of the Sand Lanes, where the foreigners' hospital took in a constant round of fever victims, heatstroke and septic insect bites.

After the two Pal women had left Slate House to head for the duel, he waited a few minutes in the silent house. The embassy of a foreign power, the servants dismissed precisely so that he could visit without their seeing him. If Gil had any top-secret documents lying about he could suddenly become a very successful spy.

The two Pal women. The flustered newcomer who surely wasn't quite twenty years old, and his friend. He probably wasn't supposed to claim the Palleseen Resident as a friend. Cordial and arm's length only. It wasn't something he was good at.

He left through the same side door, his cloak swathed about him and his hood up. If he were stopped…

If he were stopped then nothing bad would happen to him.

The monastic order who walked the streets at night and kept the peace would know him and defer to him. Nobody would be throwing him into the House of Hard Angles to dwell amongst the ghosts and never see daylight again. They wouldn't even throw him in a cellar overnight like a fractious drunk. They'd bow and back off into the shadows. But they'd know. Word would get out, or else it would be hoarded like treasure, to be spent when there was the most advantage. Let nobody tell you that monks – even the Louse Monks who served the throne as its guardians and police – didn't play politics.

He made his way up-city. Unlike most of his people, after he'd completed the standard noble curriculum of the Moraseum he'd gone overseas for more schooling. To keep him out of the way of his brother, probably, because there's only so much infighting one family can live with. He knew full well that most cities had an up and a down, and sometimes it was a physical gradient but mostly it meant money. Money which, in defiance of all other things, was naturally drawn *upwards*, out of the hands of the lowly. In the city of Alkhalend, however, *up* was literal. The city stretched from the seafront up a cliff face that past hands had cut into tiers ascending from the modestly successful all the way to the palace of the Alkhand himself and the grand estates of the Emorandi.

He was not the Alkhand, but the palace claimed him nonetheless. Certainly the relationship felt that way. If there was any claiming being done it wasn't on his part.

He evaded any attention in the intervening streets. Another skill that someone in his position shouldn't really have acquired. He'd love to say that he was one of those storybook princes who led a daring double life as a thief or a vigilante, but in truth he'd learned his padfoot ways at the overseas school, because the masters there had been harsh if they caught you outside the dorms at night.

Even less need to evade notice once he was within the Constellar Gardens that surrounded the palace. They were at their best after nightfall, the flowers gleaming like a thousand stars and casting a lambent pallor across each path. He saw at least three couples promenading late, seeking some secluded nook or grove for a midnight assignation – men and women whose faces he was careful to forget. And the guards, of course. The monks, still as topiary, almost invisible no matter how much light the flowers cast. Only the gleam of their long blades betrayed them.

They marked him, but by then he was the prince in the palace grounds and what was remarkable about that?

He even sat for a while, listened to the fountains play, contemplated the universe in that way the gardens were designed to aid. Tried to master the rhythms of his heart, which jumped and jittered with anxiety. Tried not to think of Gil. Failed.

It could already have happened. There might even now be a runner heading for the palace, tracking blood on their feet. This stupid thing. This foreign honour. Not that dying stupidly was exclusively a foreign vice. In fact, the Palleseen themselves were strongly averse to it, he understood. A nation of the rational and the reasonable with no time for that kind of flamboyance. Which made it all the more stupid.

The gardens were wasted on him. The water clocks had sounded the midnight bell. He was sick with being unable to help. At last he retreated inside the palace walls.

In some distant wing he could hear music, high pipes and the braided voices of singers intertwined. The throne room itself was shadowed and quiet, though. Like a tomb. The dark between moons poured in from the high windows and filled the room to bursting with night. If he hadn't known every inch he'd have been rebounding from pillars like a drunkard. As it was, he constructed the space in his head. At one end, the Mirror Throne glimmered in his mind's eye, surrounded by its still pool that few might cross safely save the Alkhand himself, for fear of the blades of his guards. The unseen seat had a gravity to it. He sensed his course drawn off true until he could feel the cool of the waters at his toes.

The Mirror Throne – his eyes, adjusting, could just make out its huge, scallop-backed shape. A dreadful, hungry weight that drew all the world to it. The nail that fixed the nation of Usmai in the map. And he'd sat on it, of course. When he was child enough to know no better. All the Alkhand's children had, and been disciplined for it. Sat there with his legs out straight because he'd wanted to put his spine against the overarching back. Pretending to be a philosophical Alkhand listening to wise counsel, perhaps. When his elder brother had taken a turn, the older boy had sat on the very edge, hunched over, feet dangling, as though about to send a thousand soldiers to death or glory. And then they had been discovered there, and learned even princes could get the palms of their hands beaten with a rod.

Now, in the dark, he turned away from the barely glimpsed throne before he could repeat such a crime. And nobody would beat the palms of his full-grown hands for it now. They'd talk, and rake his character and past over the coals, but when you were the heir you could get away with a great many things.

Though not everything, as his warlike elder brother had discovered.

There was a breath. Not his. He froze.

"Kaleithi…?" A voice like a ghost. And he would have preferred a ghost. One did not have to worry or care for ghosts. The pity they evoked was momentary.

He held his breath, tried to make himself not there, but his sandals scraped the inlay of the floor as he sought to back away, and the voice called out again, "Kaleithi… I'm sorry." A lifetime of grief, two lifetimes. An old man waking, not knowing where he was, or when.

"Father, it's me," he said. "It's Dekamran."

And a moment, in which his father could not even remember who he was. An old man, left abandoned on his throne in darkness. A darkness that he couldn't even see. Dekamran braced himself for what might come next. More plaintive demands for the old man's wife, Dekamran's mother, who had walked away years before. Demands for the elder son that might see that turbulent figure recalled from exile. An old man alone and disjointed from time might call for anything.

There was a whispering. Words Dekamran couldn't catch. The Alkhand was attended by at least one advisor, though not a living one. And what did it imply, when a man needed a decades-dead ghost to tell him what the present was? Most likely the ghost took what hollow pleasure it could in the reminder, for today was only the emptied rind of all the Alkhand's better yesterdays. Yet a man who ate only yesterday must starve, as they said.

"Have they left you alone here, father?" Dekamran asked. The sorrow in his heart was looking for a way out, and anger was as good as any. That the palace staff had just gone off to their revels and assignations and abandoned the old man in the dark! And yet, when he returned to the throne, at the very moment his feet were at the pool's brink, he registered the other. A statue in the dark, still as the water of the pool, now taking one measured step.

His eyes found a tall, slender figure. Lhisamena, chief of the Louse Monks, the throne's protectors. More foreign than any Pal, for all they had lived within Usmai's bounds for centuries. He heard the click-click-click that was like a regular person clearing their throat, and then her low voice came to him. "You know us better, princeling." No respect from the Tesemer, the Louse Monks, but nothing new there. Now he knew she was present, his skin itched with the proximity, knowing somewhere in the shadows was a blade. He spoke the words that flared the tablethi in the lamps, just the handful that hung from long cords down the spine of the vaulted ceiling, and watched the muted radiance glimmer back from the mother-of-pearl walls. A phantom light, said to reveal true intentions to the eye of the Alkhand.

The Louse Monk was a stiletto shape, too thin, too angular, her head tonsured in a strip along the ridge of her skull, ash-pale hair flaring on either side. Cradled in her arms was the long-bladed, long-hafted falx, the weapon her people preferred. A brutal hacking thing, save they danced with it. None could fight like the Louse Monks and, as foreigners from beyond any cities and shores, they owed allegiance to none but the throne. So it had been for generations. And if Dekamran, the acknowledged heir, had stepped into that pool and encroached on the person of the Alkhand, she would stop him. With her blade if she must.

Her face, high-cheekboned, sharp-chinned, parchment-coloured, lacked expression. Between her slightly-parted lips, something flurried and quivered.

On the throne, the Alkhand let out a long breath of disappointment and understanding. "Dekamran," he said. "You have a petition?"

"Father, it is... late. Perhaps you should retire to your chambers. The business of the court is done." The business of the court had been enacted mostly by functionaries and counsellors and palace servants, whose work came and went with the sun. But the sun meant nothing to the Alkhand. It had set for his grey stone eyes almost thirty years ago, never to rise again.

"Do not think that I am dead," the old man said. Dekamran could hear the faint wheeze of his breath, the liquid threaded through his words. In his lap was a skull set with inscribed greenstone plates. From it, the voice of the ghost whispered poisonous truths.

"Father—" Dekamran said. He was standing before the throne and should be kneeling, overflowing with honorifics. The monk's stern gaze judged him.

"Do not think I do not know," said the Alkhand softly. He sounded wise, and yet Dekamran had no idea what it was he felt he knew, or if he was talking to Dekamran or the skull or his vanished wife.

He bit his lip. "Please help me bring the Alkhand to his bedchamber. He must rest," he told the monk. Trying to instil an authority into his voice that he had never been able to master.

She nodded, a single bird-like motion. She was permitted to step through the waters to the throne, because it was her role to stand between the Alkhand and danger. Her bare feet left no ripples in the perfect mirror of the pool. Even her reflection seemed hazy and ill-focused. An alien thing that the world resented having to reproduce.

She spoke into the ear of His Tranquillity the Alkhand Oparan, and the old man nodded wearily. He gathered up his skull and his robes and broke apart the glass of the waters with his sandalled feet.

"I know," he said, as he passed Dekamran. One lined hand reached out and touched his son's face, hooking at the chin. "But when I am here, sometimes, she comes to me." Said so that Dekamran understood the old man knew it was only memories. And even those, the skull would disabuse him of. An ageing man, a sick man, but most of all a man whose wife had donned a mask and turned away from him, in a way that meant she could never be found again.

When his father was ensconced in his own chambers, with one of Lhisamena's kin standing guard within, Dekamran knew he should retire to his own. There was a cool bed waiting for him. A solitary one, but it need not be. There were musicians or poets or courtesans he could summon.

Instead he sat with the lamp burning, a book of verse half-regarded in one hand, and waited for word of Gil.

Gil Behind Bars

Custodian Coregan, Keeper of the Fifth Key. Which was a very grand way of describing a relatively minor personality within the administrative hierarchy of the palace. A man who knew where his loyalties lay, however. To the nation, obviously. A loyal servant to the Alkhand just like everyone was. Except, of course, with the old man in such a withdrawn state these days – these years – it was very easy for a minor official to get ideas about just what was best for the Alkhand and the nation. Ideas about the desirability of Kepishi like the Palleseen getting cosy with the nominated heir to the throne. And now here he was, and here was that Pal woman who was so full of herself, locked in his cellar.

Alkhalend had a two-tier system when it came to prisoners. There were no dedicated watch houses where some locals with a badge and half a uniform could throw drunks and petty criminals, because the Louse Monks served as guardians of the city streets and nobody would trust them with a prisoner for any length of time in case they got bored. There were officials who had cellars in their townhouses where malefactors might be held until some decision could be made from on high. Lesser officials got to lock up the drunks and the brawlers, but Gil's custodian was a man she remembered seeing around court, a way back. Back in the bad days when Tarcomir's star had been high and the Pals had been on the diplomatic back foot. His name, she recalled, was Coregan or something like it, and he was of a station to lock up people who were In Trouble, but who were still Important.

The other tier of incarceration, not involving people's cellars, was for if you were really quite seriously In Trouble. For that there was the House of Hard Angles. The terrible, haunted edifice that dominated the Sand Lanes and plagued the dreams of anyone who might want to advance their lot by illicit means. Thieves, killers and corrupt officials had all vanished into that place, and Coregan's expression had strongly suggested he wanted Gil to follow suit and cease to be his problem.

Gil had tested the boundaries of her imprisonment with professional care. She'd asked for food and water. She'd got the plain rice and meal he reserved for his servants. She'd asked for light, pen and paper. The man had stood on the other side of the bars, handed over a single lit stub of candle and explained bald-facedly that there was none of the rest to be had. At the last she'd asked for a bowl of scented water and a loan of clean clothes. Coregan had said the house had nothing in her size, and the water he'd given her was stagnant, the sort hawked through the Sand Lanes with a scum of green on it.

Not an admirer of the Palleseen, then, was Coregan. She guessed he'd owed his position at court to the patronage of those who'd backed the Alkhand's eldest son in the succession. The exiled prince, currently stewing at Mantekor with a host of armed followers. There had been quite a sweep of the palace after Dekamran had been swapped in as heir, a move that coincided with the decline of fortunes of Lor and of Tarcomir. The eldest prince had pushed his luck too far, with his incitement and his raiding, and the old, blind Alkhand had suddenly turned out to be not *that* old and not *that* blind.

And now here she was, within the power of a man who had every reason not to love her.

She met Coregan's gaze as he stood at the top of his cellar steps, the light of his lamp playing over his closed, hating features. With one last hard look, he left her to her little thumb of candle, and her thoughts.

Gil stared at the dying flame, drowning in its own wax. Probably something deeply symbolic there. Dekamran would have found the poetic in it. She wasn't good at poetry. Sometimes it seemed she was only good at things that left the world in a worse state, like tradecraft and stabbing friends.

She checked inside her clothes for the little blade. Finding it still strapped under her arm didn't bring much joy, because all the fire of the fight had gone the way the candle was going, leaving her sour and shaking.

Loret would, she guessed, just have to work something out. Live rent free in Slate House until a new Resident was appointed. A little initiative and she could probably swot up to be a halfway decent aide by then. No next boat for Loret. A positive for someone out of this situation.

Oh, she was catastrophising. She was in someone's cellar. It wasn't the noose or the axe. There would be due process, and everyone would say that she should be executed or thrown into the House of Hard Angles, and probably none of that would happen because of her diplomatic position even though she probably really deserved it.

Except...

Bad things happened to prisoners all the time. Not a uniquely Usmiat thing. Being someone's prisoner was generally regarded as undesirable. Gil's bad feeling about this night had been entirely focused on the duel, but now she was beginning to appreciate she might just have opened the door to a whole other mess.

If Dekamran asks, what will he be told? Under proper circumstances there should be a trail of witnesses leading all the way to the steps of Coregan's basement, but that sort of trail had a habit of being scuffed out by too many feet. And she was a woman of violence. Dangerous. She'd killed an important man. Understandable that someone might decide precipitately to put her out of the way. Especially if they really didn't like Pals.

Sitting there in the cellar as the light died, it felt like her first time in a long opportunity to just reflect. There had been the war, there had been Tarcomir. Now there was just her, in the hands of an enemy. And, looking at the situation shorn of excuses, there was a fair amount of justice in that. Working in Pallesand's diplomatic service wasn't a job for an ideologue. You had to make too many compromises to come out of it blowing the trumpet of Palleseen perfection with a clear heart. Yes, when the Pals moved in, the result wasn't necessarily happy for the incumbents. Yes, the sort of creeping influence she was peddling led to places being incorporated into the Sway, placed under the governance of a Perfector, *civilized*, in that particular Pal way. All those traditions and gods, the festivals, the monks, the idiosyncrasies, the language, the stories, all of it done away with because they got in the way of efficient perfection. And she'd been off the leash and in foreign parts for long enough that she'd become fond of those things herself. She could see why you'd miss them.

And she wasn't just a symbolic presence here. If Coregan and his friends wanted to blame her for the way their nation was going, that was fair too. That Tarcomir had singled her out for a challenge had been entirely just. She'd schemed. She'd worked behind the scenes, pulled strings, fought tooth and claw to change the trajectory of the Usmiat body politic. And won, so that the Loruthi and their chosen prince had ended up out of favour, and she and her own candidate elevated. It had been her, as much as anyone. She had been that good at her job. Left with no escape, she'd take her death and claim it for Pallesand. But…

Back when the pro-Loruthi faction had been in the ascendant, she hadn't actually minded so much. Not an ideologue, after all.

Not a fanatic for perfection, nor yet a profiteer looking to funnel the treasure and magic of Usmai back home. She'd shared drinks with Tarcomir in his ascendancy, bartered for crumbs, done what she could to cushion the blows to Palleseen interests and individuals. And for the rest of the time there'd been... him. The second prince, the hapless one. The one who'd travelled and seen places. The one who was just... pleasant. Nice, that dreadful word. Whose company she'd settled into, one loser gravitating towards another, the lesser ambassador and the second son. And, in his company, she had taken a good long look at herself and what she wanted and understood what she had to do.

It had been the Alkhand's eyes and the skull he carried, that had decided her. The lesson there, about what happened to sons of the blood who didn't get to wear the White Petal Crown. She'd sat and drank and laughed with Dekamran, and all the time she'd known it wouldn't last because his elder brother couldn't let it. There would be a coronation and Dekamran would...

Disappear, probably, and she'd never even know what had happened to him. And so she'd acted. She'd done her job, basically. Destabilised Loruthi influence, screwed over Tarcomir, found a way to ensure that the Alkhand could not ignore the excesses of his then-heir. She'd done it all and they were absolutely right to hate her for it, and imprison her for it, even kill her for it. But her superiors back home had heaped her with plaudits she hadn't earned, because she hadn't done it for them.

Dekamran would never know. It would be her time to disappear and leave him fruitlessly asking questions. But he didn't know all the things she'd done, either. He'd just watched in amazement as the long death-sentence of his future was transformed to gold and opportunity. Because he was the man he was, she could never tell him, or come collect on behalf of Pallesand, for raising him up. She wanted him to keep thinking of her as just his friend.

Sitting there, in the dark now, she admitted to herself that she wanted more than that, in a very different and unprofessional way, and probably this whole imprisonment-maybe-death was a good thing for that reason, too. Better than just mooning over things you couldn't have, that would destroy her career and their friendship. Better to go into the dark now, at the zenith of things.

She was maudlin, it was true, but it was like that after a duel, with her. Especially when she'd just killed a friend.

While she moped, presumably Coregan was sitting up in his own chambers. Eating the good food in the light of his lamps while his servants dashed his shoulders with scented water. Perhaps writing a missive to his former patrons in Mantekor. But by the time any instructions came back to him, someone would have tracked down the missing Pal Resident. Meaning Coregan would have to make the call himself, about whether to do something rash. Which would he prefer to be damned for? Action against the current heir, or inaction against the interests of his preferred candidate, the exile?

She'd just about pegged him as the inaction type, all talk and no sword, when he turned up at the top of the stairs with a pack of servants and she knew she'd been wrong.

"I am the Palleseen Resident," she told him. "What's your play here, Custodian?" Standing with her arms folded as though she hadn't just murdered someone.

"Word has come from the palace," he told her. It was a lie, she knew with absolute certainty, but he was establishing a story that his servants could testify to. "The House of Hard Angles awaits the pleasure of your company."

She held onto her composure, but inside she felt her guts twist. Because of all the places you didn't come out of, the House was high on the list. Not even the dead could escape it, people said.

She tried to be the quintessential Pal who didn't care about the superstitions of other people. She tried to stand as though his servants, armed as they were, couldn't possibly take her anywhere she didn't want to go. They actually hesitated on the steps, until Coregan berated them. When they laid hands on her, Palleseen privilege failed to manifest in any appreciable way.

Coregan might not be up to murdering the Palleseen Resident in his own cellar, but bad things happened to people in the House all the time.

Coregan's home was, of course, a long way from the prison. The nocturnal streets were quiet, though. Not that thieves and villains did not try to take advantage of the darkness, but the Tesemer, the Louse Monks, patrolled even the Sand Lanes sometimes. The luckless rogue who met with them would find they saw in the dark far better than regular humans did. Ending up in the prison was a kinder fate than most nocturnal villains met.

Gil saw several of them watching from the shadows. She even tried to call out, the first time. That was when Coregan's people discovered that they could cuff and shove her, and twist her arms, without repercussion. And the monks just watched and did nothing. Somehow she didn't see them going hotfoot to the palace to tell Dekamran what was going on.

Coregan was playing things smart. This was his very narrow window of time when he could lose her in the buried cells of the House of Hard Angles before anyone asked questions. And, in her absence, any such questions would be easier to answer in the negative. Later, he could return to the House with a writ of his patrons in Mantekor, and a sharp edge, and the matter would be laid to rest.

With that in mind, Gil started working on her own little sharp edge.

The convoy trekked all the way down into the Sand Lanes,

where mean little houses clambered rickety one over another like beetles disturbed from under a stone. All the way to where the shadow of the House of Hard Angles fell, even though it was a moonless night. Gil saw the glimmer of the place ahead. The phantom radiance of the sigil-inscribed stone doors no ghost could pass, runes sparking with a sickly amber light that attracted only the largest and most deformed-looking moths. The place had been a tomb once, they said. Fitting enough, for somewhere so many were still buried. She'd given up trying to threaten Coregan with the wrath of Pallesand, to suborn his servants, to shout out to anyone awake in the nearby buildings. Who cared about shouting in the Sand Lanes? There was always someone being robbed or assaulted, or just the lesser kind of people falling out and screaming at one another. One more voice, no matter the language, no matter the tone, would go unnoticed. She felt as though she'd fallen into the gaps of the city, abruptly disconnected from everything she knew. And very shortly that would become literally true.

Coregan's people pressed close to her, but since they'd entered the Sand Lanes their attention had been far more *out* than in. Aware of that, Gil had been busy with her hands. They had taken her sword when they took her, but she'd talked about *tradecraft* earlier in the evening, and that translated to having the aforementioned blade hidden in her bodice. Hence she was very tense, while trying to seem very casual, by the time they reached the portal of the House of Hard Angles. There would be one chance, honestly, because once she was bundled inside, probably she'd not be getting out again.

The inscribed doors opened and there was a woman there. A young one. Gil blinked. At the girl's shoulders, of all people, were a pair of Cotto thugs, tattooed and fish-stinking, the rank weed of the docks practically dripping off them. Coregan stared. Gil stared. The Pal girl, the inexplicably-present, formerly useless Pal girl, stared.

"*Loret?*" Gil demanded. Not hopeful so much as incredulous.

In that moment of surprise, a couple of Coregan's people tried to lay firmer hands upon her and she decided this was her moment. Her wrists, that had been bound a moment before, were abruptly free, severed cord whipping away. She showed them the gleam of a knife in her hands. A razor, honestly, but still something sharp. One of them clutched for her and she left her shawl in their grip and a dart of blood on their thumb as she danced back to Loret.

Loret's face was white in the ghastly radiance of the doors. The smile she fixed there wouldn't have fooled anyone. "Ah there you are," she declared loudly, like a bad actor in a worse play. "It's all right! I've found the Resident!" When Coregan lunged forwards, trying to snag Gil's arm, Loret actually clasped his hand. "Thank you, magister, for returning her to me!" A Pal gesture, a Pal honorific, all horribly inappropriate, all too loud. Even the Sand Lanes had gone quiet to listen.

Coregan's servants milled. They all had bludgeons and knives and one woman had the steel length of a skia. The Cotto looked ferocious, but if it came to a brawl here at the doors of the House, they were only two.

Gil dropped into a fencer's stance although, given her current choice of sword was all of two inches long, not one she could really sustain in the clash. Her mistake was, though, in assuming Loret hadn't actually been talking to someone.

Behind them, behind Loret and Gil and the Cotto, something moved in the darkness of the House of Hard Angles.

There was this other tradition, to Alkhalend's prison. Its master was never local. Never even some regular foreigner like a Pal or a Loruthi. The place, unnatural as it was, could not be trusted to mundane custodianship.

Gil felt icy, knowing someone was at her back in the gloom of the place, behind the ghostlight of the sigils. Someone, something. Perhaps just one of the cadaverous monks who tended the place. Perhaps the current master of the prison, who was simultaneously its highest-profile prisoner. Like the

Tesemer in their day, one more who had come to serve the Alkhand from further afield than anyone could imagine.

She looked Coregan in the eye and saw that he didn't have the stomach for a fight here, where the Warden of the House of Hard Angles might intervene. Not if he had a hundred soldiers at his back.

He stepped away, and in that moment Gil passed like water from his notional custody to standing as a free woman beside Loret, here at the utter threshold of the prison. *Close, but you'll have to do better than that.*

With a final venomous look, Coregan and his people vanished off into the dark of the Sand Lanes. Doubtless the man would be writing a bitter letter to his friends at Mantekor soon enough, to let them know what had happened. Perhaps he'd even be packing his bags, now he'd so clearly declared himself an enemy of Pallesand and the current favourites at court. Right then Gil, exhausted and with a death on her conscience, couldn't spare him another thought.

Back at Slate House, of course, she felt so wide awake that if sleep never visited her again it wouldn't surprise her. She threw herself down behind the desk, and then remembered that the staff – the regular non-diplomatic sort – were all dismissed so Dekamran could come and go without eyes on him, meaning nobody could bring her tea. And Loret wouldn't know where any of the things are.

Speaking of whom, apparently her new aide was owed a reappraisal.

"Who are you, exactly?" she demanded. The other woman – girl? Woman? Say woman – started. Volunteered no answer, not even the prescribed *Cohort-Invigilator Loret reporting for duty, magister.*

"Where did these pirates come from, exactly?" Gil tried.

The two Cotto had sniffed out a flask of sharp ramaht she had in a drawer, and made short work of it. Now they grinned at her. The woman had sharp teeth and an illustrated cleavage. The man had an actual sea-scorpion inked onto his face, the arc of its claws tracing the rims of his eye sockets like predatory spectacles. The Cotto loved their theatre. Not that they weren't a pack of murderous pirates, but also they loved their theatre.

"I promised them money," Loret said, suddenly panicky now everything had passed. "I didn't know anyone else. Money. Magister, there... the Residence has money? I said fifty shillings."

It was a lot of money to treat two pirates to shore leave. It was arguably not a lot of money for the continuing liberty of the Palleseen Resident. An interesting meeting of philosophy and finance. "Catch." A key, that Loret fumbled and then snatched from the air second try. "The cabinet to your left."

Gil watched the girl – woman? Maybe girl – very carefully. Because you learned a lot, when someone opened the bag holding the Residence's emergency fund and saw all that good shiny stuff. *Am I going to have to find a new place to put it, I wonder?* And she decided she maybe would because Loret had a moment of utter stillness that said *I have never seen this much money in one place before*, and there wasn't even that much in the bag.

Still, she counted out fifty shillings for the Cotto and they seemed more than happy with their night's profitable loitering. Gil knew it was always worth having happy pirates. She had Loret count out another ten shillings in return for the pirates kicking about the servants' quarters like a pair of ferocious butlers until dawn, just in case of trouble.

"I met them on the docks, when I got off the boat," Loret said after they'd ambled off downstairs. "Then after you were taken, they found me—"

"They know me," Gil said. She felt incredibly tired and yet strung taut, unable to rest. It wasn't that long ago she'd been fighting. Before that she'd been working herself up to the fight.

Her body didn't know what it was doing. "So you went and got a couple of pirates, and then…?"

"They told me about the prison and said there was one of ours in there. I thought it must be you and…"

"And?"

"And something," Loret said. "I was going to… something. And it wasn't you. But then it was you. Just as we were coming out."

Gil rubbed at her forehead. "On the basis of your complete inability to properly report, I now accept that you have never heard the term 'tradecraft'."

"Please don't send me back."

Gil's eyes flicked open. "What?"

"I need this post, magister. Please. I'll do… whatever."

So, she was going to do something, and now she's promising me whatever. A very wide ranging skillset my new aide has. "I'm sure I'll find a use for you," Gil said. "I mean, you earned that much tonight." She frowned, inwardly kicked herself more awake. "Wait, what you said just now… Who's this Pal woman in the prison who isn't me?"

Mosaic: Blood Royal

The ancient tradition of the corpse-emperors of Moeriband was that the Imperial line, those preserved cadavers whose encysted ghosts held court and commanded legions, be whole and perfect. Who wanted to be governed by only eighty per cent of a corpse? Being necromancers and additive surgeons, they had a variety of solutions to any physical omission, of course. And that empire fell, or at least retreated into its tomb-palaces and sealed the doors from the inside. After which its various former tributaries set about shrugging off the mouldering old traditions. The idea of bodily wholeness in a ruler persisted, however, which combined with a crooked sense of familial loyalty to produce some truly appalling acts of mutilation when it came to succession struggles between siblings.

His Tranquillity, the Alkhand Oparan of Usmai, wakes past noon, thrashing at his silk coverlet, the sound of buzzing in his ears. A fly. A fly only, in past the screens and now quartering his chambers seeking egress. Only a fly…

He'd sat in court all morning, hearing three petitions. Two from rich Emorandi, each with some grievance against a neighbour over boundaries, trivial disputes brought by those who brook no judge below the Alkhand himself. And, though in each case one must be less satisfied than the other, everyone went away feeling their wealth and importance had been recognised. The third petitioner, the stammering voice almost strangled by its surroundings, had been an artisan whose house and livelihood had been taken by some more wealthy artisan. This is Dekamran's doing. Oparan's newly-elected heir insists that, for each session his father sits, at least one voice issues from the needy, sponsored by the prince or someone worthy looking to gain his approval. Oparan loves the boy for his sense of justice but despairs of him for the enemies he makes every time he opens his mouth. *You will be Alkhand. You have won yourself that much, after so long. Will you cast it aside?*

Was this why your mother walked away? She could not bear to see her children turn on one another. What will it be, Dekamran? You against your brothers or they against you. Will it be blade or poison or the cord. Or will you be merciful and use the wasps, like your uncle…?

After three petitions, his cough had returned, the gravel grating in his chest, the high wheeze in his throat. His strength soaked away into the substance of the throne, and he dismissed the rest and had the monks guide him to his chambers. He should have Dekamran sit before the Mirror Throne and judge in his place, display his wisdom and education, but the thought makes Oparan's hands clench about the regalia of state. He tells himself it's because Dekamran, even at thirty years, is still learning. Certainly he's still learning to be hard, the way the Alkhand must be hard. Hard like stone. But it isn't just that. What if Dekamran is *already* that hard man? What if, behind that soft voice and the tender guiding hand on his father's elbow, ambition has already crept into him, curled up and made a home? If Oparan surrenders even that much of his power, what if it only makes Dekamran hungrier? His second son, the mild one, brought up on a melange of foreign philosophies and somehow only taking away those elements that make him softer. Unless it's all a front and the face Oparan can't see is twisted with impatience, waiting for his father to die. Woe betide the parent whose children no longer need his guidance.

Servants come and wash him, give him fine tea gifted by

Palleseen merchants. A musician plays sweetly and then, at his gesture, sadly. Sadness is on him now he's woken.

It won't be long, even. Whichever child has the ambition for it, the throne will be theirs soon enough. The cough grows only worse, the grit flowering in his lungs, the residue of what Oparan's own brother did back in the day, when they fought.

He reaches about his bedside until the familiar contours of greenstone inlay meet his fingertips. His brother, Sorthist, whom they called the Serpent's Fang because every encounter with him was an ambush. Sorthist, the elder, the disinherited; Oparan, the younger, the ambitious. They came close to tearing Usmai apart in the echo of their father's death.

Sorthist caught him. Brought his hellion younger brother back to Alkhalend. Threw him in the House of Hard Angles. Brooded for long days over how to secure his future on the throne. In the end, the Serpent's Fang would not countenance outright fratricide, but instead took a leaf from the book of the old dead Empire. He would render his rival unfit to sit upon the throne. He had placed a nutshell over each of Oparan's eyes, and in each shell, a wasp.

The fly swings back across the room. He hears it, knows it for what it is, yet the fear still rises in him. A thirty-year-old fear.

The last sight life gave him: the nutshells closing over his eyes. The crawling horror within. Darkness. Agony.

Basilisk wasps, they're named. In the jungles, their nests are of clay that bakes hard as rock. Around them, the stone corpses of beasts unwise enough to come too close. Out in the villages there are many who have some patch of their skin, a finger, a whole hand gone to grey, smooth stone, unfeeling and unmoving.

The musician finishes, waiting. Oparan stares into the past with his dead stone eyes while, through his body, the tiny shards of stone dust poison his blood and inflame his lungs. Under his hands, the ornamented skull of Sorthist is smooth and reassuring. *My victory.* For, blind as he had been, he escaped the House of Hard Angles. He was reunited with his allies. He sat astride a war-beast he could not see, and his blindness lent him a mad courage, leading the charge against the darkness and inspiring furious courage in his troops. Rather than trust fickle eyes, he built pictures of battlefields from the words of scouts and generals, and won each clash because he was not subject to the distractions of the world.

He listens to his breath sound, as though it, too, is a musician. Sorthist's long revenge against him. Under his hand is his revenge against Sorthist, though.

He makes the sign that banishes his servants and the musician from his chambers. He must be alone with his final advisor.

"I fear," he tells the skull, and its hollow voice issues back to him, *I too, brother.*

"My sons," Oparan whispers, and Sorthist's ghost speaks back, *My nephews.*

History is set to repeat itself. His eldest son banished, his younger unready. And he, the Alkhand, unable to reconcile these opposites, to welcome back the first or prepare the second. And the younger two will be nothing but pawns, barely more than children.

His Tranquillity, the Alkhand Oparan of Usmai, bows his head and weeps, so that hard stone tears rattle from the skull of his brother.

This is how it goes with the Successor States that arose out of the ruin of the old Empire. They jostle and fight. One grows strong, and most often that one is Usmai. An Alkhand comes whose very word causes his neighbours to tremble, whose coffers fill with the gifts of those who would rather give than be taken from. And then come the heirs. Always it is the heirs. Either too few or too many. When Oparan's father died, even two were two many, as the ghost inside the skull could tell you. When Oparan's fingertips give up their hold on the arms of the throne, there will be not one, not two but four children watching to see what happens next. And the Pals will tell you this is exactly why you don't have a hereditary system of government, but then you haven't seen the vicious departmental infighting that goes on when there's one Professorship and a dozen ambitious Sages trying to claim it.

So whose hands will be on the knives, when it happens? Whose servants will step forwards with the nutshells? When the Alkhand finally surrenders to the fate his long-dead brother doomed him to, and the wasps come out again. There was a dossier that Gil read, on the boat to Usmai that first time. The sort of dossier Loret was supposed to have swotted up on, and hasn't. It laid it all out, the Pal take on each of the royal offspring, with especial reference to how each might be bought, coerced or manipulated into backing the Palleseen cause. But there's been a lot of water under the bridge since then, and Gil has passed some of it herself. As the Alkhand lies heavy with stone and melancholy, where are his heirs?

Enshili is fighting.

She is, from a certain point, the safe one. Whatever murderous and potentially entomological intrigues result from the death of her father, they won't consume her. She can't inherit. She lacks the biological requisites an Alkhand requires. Instead, she will be a game-piece for whichever brother does assume the throne. There will be some key ally best won over with a marriage. A royal princess, sister to the new Alkhand, is like a shackle of iron to bind some powerful man into loyalty to the throne. That the new Alkhand will need her for such a purpose is the sole reason that she, at nineteen years, has yet to be married off already at the whim of her father.

Enshili has decided she is having none of it. Initially a childish whim, the sort of rebellion fondly tolerated until it becomes relevant. Now, though, she can see exactly how the nation is sliding sideways as her father declines. And while she supposes she probably loves her father, in an abstract sense, she also barely knows him. She knew her mother, but her mother left them for the dream of the Grove monks and never came back. She knows her younger brother, but only as the boy who spent their collective childhood spoiling things for her. Her friends were the children of palace officials and Emorandi and every one of them primed by their own parents to win her over for future advancement. There was a moment, just a couple of years ago after her eldest brother was exiled, when she realised that literally nobody in the world actually cared about her, and that the lack of sentiment was firmly reciprocal.

So she fights. And, while a noblewoman of Usmai is permitted – encouraged – to learn the formal use of the long, straight blade, this is not that kind of fighting. She has a new fencing master. A forbidden one. A foreigner. Worse than a foreigner. She has spent the last two years making a bonfire of all the lessons her tutors taught her about duty and obedience and her place in the world.

Her teacher is a woman and very beautiful when she takes her mask off. The mask is of bone, carved to resemble a twisted, demonic visage, all horns and teeth and spines. Even that is borderline forbidden, because Usmai inherited the old Empire's loathing of demons, and the circumstances in which they might be represented is strictly controlled. Not in a mere duelling mask, certainly.

Enshili wants a mask just like that. She has been on at her tutor about having one made, to the woman's incredulous delight.

Her tutor would not win a formal bout against the palace sword masters, probably. She'd not fight one, though. She'd throw sand in their face and then stab them, impale them from behind, get them drunk and then poison them. The tutor is a very pragmatic person. In their bouts she teaches Enshili about the off-hand blade, the feigned stumble, the signals of weakness that hide only steel strength. She teaches the princess that rules are things you can throw before your enemy's feet so that they trip.

Enshili has learned more these two years than she did in all her formal education. Soon enough some brother is going to be wearing the White Petal Crown and telling her who she's going to marry, and any such groom is going to have a shock of a wedding night, if they can even keep hold of her long enough for that. She tells her masked tutor this and the woman crows with laughter. The foreigner, doing her bit to destabilise the state, or the world. There must be a motive there beyond mere love of chaos. Enshili doesn't care. She's starting to love chaos herself. All these things, that her brothers and her father and the court have no clue about. One more fire laid under the foundations, slow-burning but eating away the feet of the throne.

Premath does not fight. The youngest brother, the odd one, the one nobody really cares much about. He is not going to inherit either, and so nobody has spent time preparing him for the throne. Instead, left to his own devices, he has decided to be the worryingly intense scholarly one. No friends but many tutors. The Alkhanate of Usmai has many ways to be religious, to the despair of the Palleseen, and the old death cult of the Moeribandi still occupies a position of ceremonial authority. Clinging on with its bony fingernails despite its parent empire's ossification and demise.

Premath was born Premaran, but had his name changed to fit the approved suffixes of the dead Empire. He spent his childhood reading tomes of theology that defeated many grown scholars. Learning from the Moerends, the old death priests, about just what was supposed to happen after people died. Becoming the favourite of His Quietude Arkanith, the mirthless, grinning head of their order. He knows how those who please the gods of death migrate to a dusty, morbid afterlife, where everything is understood and the Favoured exist in a sterile paradise forever. And everyone else has to go back and try again, reborn as this or that, until eventually everyone will be Favoured and the world itself will be left just as sterile and cold as Heaven. And a few, a special handful, please the gods so much they stay on in the world, in their dead bodies, to teach and guide the rest. To almost every scholar since the empire collapsed, it's seemed an unappealing vision of the afterlife. To Premath it makes perfect sense. A system simultaneously complex enough to exclude the layman's comprehension, yet systematised enough that the right kind of mind can perfectly master and understand it. He sits at the feet of Grand Moerend Arkanith, that old bald man who is not, in fact, an imperfectly reanimated corpse but you wouldn't know from the look of him. A man with the public disposition of a civil servant and the hidden heart of a mad fanatic. Who has found, in Premath, exactly the promising royal student he has been searching for all his long life.

When the struggle for pre-eminence comes, Arkanith has plans for young Premath that have nothing to do with inheriting the throne and everything to do with a greater kingdom.

Which brings us to Dekamran. While his father sleeps, Dekamran does indeed sit before the Mirror Throne. On a stool brought by a servant, clear of the still water surrounding the seat of power. He has no authority to hear petitions or make judgments, but he talks to courtiers and petitioners and… anyone, really. He makes lists of what might be accomplished without the Alkhand's seal. He gets people into the same room and explores under which rock agreement might be found. And many people want the Alkhand's formal judgment, even if it might go against them, because they are important people and that is how it is done. But through words and reasoned argument and the fact that he's the elected heir now, Dekamran chips away at the long queue of court business that would otherwise come to trouble his father. And tries, in his way, to do so in a way that might satisfy the dictates of reason and perfection.

His education wasn't all Palleseen, at that foreign place his father sent him off to. Still, he learned a lot over there, and he's often in the company of the Palleseen Resident, whom he plainly thinks of as an ally. A friend. Who is, in fact, his closest friend, and a woman he greatly likes and admires. Which, as anyone can tell you, is not a tenable position for the heir to any throne, vis a vis a foreign diplomat.

So he tries to solve his nation's problems in a way that Gil would approve of, and also in a way that does not contravene Usmiat tradition, and sometimes those two circles overlap just enough that he can find room for compromise.

It's not just the frowns this draws from Usmiat traditionalists that are the problem. It's that his understanding of Palleseen perfectionism, as actually practised by the Pals, may not be as perfect as he believes.

Which leaves the eldest. Gorbudan, even now reading the words of a messenger hotfoot from Alkhalend. Gorbudan: just as the Alkhand's dead brother was the Serpent's Fang, so Gorbudan is the Tiger-Crab of Mantekor, named after Usmai's most feared predator. His seat in the fortress there is flanked by the open claws of one such beast, his own kill, each grand enough to crush a human torso.

Gorbudan is the image of a warrior prince. He has the familial high forehead and deep-set eyes. Mild and thoughtful in Dekamran, febrile and intense in Premath, sullen and closed in Enshili. In Oparan, their exemplar, they are weighted with years and sorrow and distant memories of the sun. In Gorbudan, they are transformed into a fierce fire, a commanding look that soldiers would throw themselves into the breach of a wall for, or charge the enemy batons. A look that turns cold and sharp-edged when it sees how foreign powers gnaw at the edges of his inheritance.

Over the border in neighbouring Peor, the Kepishi from Pallesand are well and truly established. His compound at Mantekor plays host to plenty of Peosts who have fled even into the bosom of their traditional rivals to escape the persecution of the Pals. In Peor, you must worship your gods behind closed doors, or only at certain hours, or not at all. You must sell things by Pal weights and for Pal coin, and the Alkhand of Peor is a child of seventeen who you can barely see for all the Pal uniforms clustered about the throne. Advisors, they call themselves, but it is the sort of advice that leaves no room for refusal. That is what they tell Gorbudan.

For years he successfully staved off the Pals, from his position as heir presumptive. The warrior son, the hero. Everyone knew he would inherit. It didn't matter how many times his father grew enraged with him. His recklessness, his assumption of small powers that should have been the crown's sole province. The way that, in the end, the court looked to him and not to the Mirror Throne, as though his father's actual death or abdication was only a formality. As it should have been. Gorbudan saw the Pals strengthen their hand across the border, and cultivated their enemies, giving preferment to Loruthi merchants and befriending their ambassador. Seeing in them the lesser of two evils, and a power that did not have the same insidious foothold. Easy enough to cast them off, when Gorbudan was on the throne and the Pals no longer a threat. And the war between the two Kepishi powers had seemed inordinately fortuitous. His father had declared that Usmai played no favourites in the conflict, of course, but Gorbudan was a man of action. He knew opportunity when it hailed him. While any hope of overseas assistance was absent, he had set about taking his followers over the border into Peor and uprooting everything the Pals had built there.

People spoke long about the discipline and might of the Palleseen army, but he was the Tiger-Crab of Mantekor. Where he struck, they could not defend against him. When their sweating, slogging infantry gave chase, they could not catch him. He was well on the way to making a continued presence in Peor too expensive for them, a tally of burned plantations, factories in rubble and dead clerks weighing down their ledgers until they drowned in their own red ink.

Until his father, who had sat mute through over a year of his son's victories and the growing murmur of adulation about the court, had suddenly found a spine between his belly and the back of the throne, and banished him.

Not just banished; hardly the first time for that. Banished *and* disinherited. Named flabby, gullible Dekamran as heir. Severed Gorbudan from the succession in favour of the man who spent half his time swilling the same cup as the Palleseen Resident.

And then, as Gorbudan had stewed over his exile in Mantekor, there had come the news that the Loruthi had lost. Had signed a humiliating peace with a Pal army at the very gates of their own capital.

And here are Coregan's words on the death of Tarcomir, the Loruthi ambassador, Gorbudan's former ally. Murdered in an illegal duel by the woman, the Pal Resident, who will not ever be punished for it because soft Dekamran will see she's not.

Gorbudan's face darkens like storm clouds. He was born for another age, really. An age when one hero with a sword might turn the tide of battles, take the enemy flagship by leaping first from rail to rail, stand in the breach and defy an army. An age fading into the pages of books when his father and his uncle clashed three decades ago. An age that the Pals have already consigned to the tomb with their reason and rules. Because he's no fool, even though he is a hero, he's well aware of it. Personal courage and inspiring words have not been entirely excised from the world, as tools of war, but they must be backed with intelligence and discipline and careful planning. But he's good at those, too, and he has the support of many. People will march to his drum when they understand it beats louder than any other.

He bears Dekamran no ill will. Some contempt, for being so easy a dupe of the Kepishi, but if Dekamran could be trusted to just become a monk then Gorbudan would let him stand on any street he liked, distributing alms. The Pals won't let that happen, though. Which brings us full circle back to what a brother does with a brother, when there are multiple brothers and only one throne.

The wasps are always an option, though that didn't work out so well for Sorthist, he of the skull. Hands, then. Feet. What is the precise minimum level of disfigurement that might render a man definitively ineligible to sit upon the Mirror Throne, without veering into fratricide. Or is it to be the skull, and the bound ghost whispering therein? The precedent his father set.

Gorbudan sits in his hall at Mantekor beneath the shadow of twin claws, fighting battles in his head.

Drathel Behind Bars

The Sand Lanes were where the poorer citizens of Alkhalend lived. Houses built on houses until the lanes themselves ran in the shadow of beetling eaves nine-tenths of the time, between dawn and dusk. People said it was because it was all built on sand, that the buildings sank an inch a day, pressed down by the weight of their own extra floors. A lie, of course, as the handful of stone buildings showed, most especially the House of Hard Angles. But what did happen was that, on the highest tides, the sea slopped over the defences and flooded the Lanes, leaving another inch of sand as its gift when it ebbed away, slowly smothering the lowest storeys. And so the lie was made true.

It was Loret's first experience of royalty. She and the Resident kneeling before a haggard-looking old Usmiat man wearing more wealth, in cloth, metal and stones, than she had ever seen. Not the grand audience chamber with the Mirror Throne; an antechamber to the Alkhand's own rooms, and the man sitting in a gilded chair with red padded cushions. It was an honour to be seen by the Alkhand. Save, of course, that the Alkhand saw nobody. The blindness upset her more than she'd expected. *Stone* eyes! In the quiet of the room, along with the old man's laboured breathing, she could hear the faint grating sound of them shifting in their abraded sockets.

"There was a time," Angilly had said, as they'd waited for admission, "when I had to burn every scrap of credit I had, to secure an audience like this. Back when it was Gorbudan in line for succession, and the Loruthi riding high."

And Loret almost said something about the man Angilly had killed, the ambassador. And didn't say it. And wondered, after, if the Resident had left that thread dangling to see if she'd be so undiplomatic as to pull on it. They were still feeling each other out, as potential colleagues. Loret felt she was failing both ways. Failing to get any kind of a handle on the Sage-Invigilator. Failing to put over the sort of impression that a competent aide should.

Then the man had joined them, the same man who'd been – in far meaner clothes – at the Residence that night when Loret arrived. Here, he'd been in his finery, as though the tatty chancer she'd seen before had walked past a magic mirror and come out as his own dream-reflection. There was a moment, a beat, between him and Angilly. A point when Loret strongly felt they wanted to touch each other, but absolutely couldn't. It was the first time they'd seen each other since before the duel. This was a meeting that might not have happened at all. Before Usmai, for Loret, had been the camps. People crammed elbow to elbow, constantly renegotiating their boundaries. It was true she lacked a lot of the skills one might expect from a diplomat's aide, but she'd become very good at reading how things stood between people. In her estimation, Angilly and this man could barely keep their hands off one another. Some ways past just being friends, or maybe just really wanting to be. And since Angilly was the Resident and this man was plainly some high palace official, the Palleseen operation in Usmai was veering away from perfection in some interesting ways. Was that something she could use as leverage, if things came to a throwdown with Angilly? If she was threatened with the boat again? She filed it away.

"He's not happy," said the man.

Angilly practised insouciance. "About me, or just in general?"

The man bit his lip. "The next courier ship from Lor is going to be carrying some sharp letters."

Angilly set a derisive tilt to her chin, to show what she thought of that. "Just as well a paper cut is all anyone will be getting from that quarter for a while, given how the war went."

"Hard woman," he noted. Judging, but not entirely shorn of admiration.

She let her callous front collapse. "Yes, well. That's the line from back home, anyway. I didn't want to do it, but it's done, and we'll just have to make the best. Speaking of...?"

He nodded. "Let's face the music, Resident."

And, just as a servant opened the door for them, Angilly leaned in to Loret and said, "Oh, Loret – His Patience Dekamran, prince-elect of Usmai."

So it was that Loret got to stand in front of the Alkhand of Usmai fighting not to choke, because the man whom her new employer was plainly very into was also the heir to the throne and that was *surely* some way beyond standard Palleseen diplomatic practice.

The old man certainly looked angry about the Loruthi situation. Sightless, that disapproval seared across everyone there present and, given Dekamran had been at the Residence right before the stabbing, that seemed fair and just.

"The death of the Loruthi emissary," said the old man, said Alkhand Oparan of Usmai. Just that, no comment, only those words and a hungry silence.

"Your Tranquillity," Angilly said, "nobody regrets it more than I." Sentiments that might even be true. "Both the fact of it, and the manner in which it was done. It is no defence to say that there was an even chance of it being he, kneeling before you, seeking to explain how it was that he had killed the Palleseen Resident. It was a matter between us, as individuals and as nations, and our own honours had no other recourse. I am sorry for it."

Loret weighed the words. This was not how diplomacy was done, she was sure. Diplomacy was an international code of honey and lies. Not this storybook stuff of honour and duels, which also happened to be true.

The Alkhand sighed, and she heard the high, sharp note in the midst of it that was his sickness singing in him. "It is my will," he said, "that this be considered a thing belonging to your war, and not a thing belonging to my nation, or within my jurisdiction. That is what I shall say to the Loruthi, and that is what I say to you. A regrettable coda to a struggle that my land has always remained neutral in." And Loret had heard enough to know *that* hadn't been entirely true but, given which way Usmai *had* previously skewed, small surprise they wanted to stress that neutrality now. "It is my pleasure, therefore, to stay my hand from the just punishment we might otherwise decree."

"The Alkhand is merciful," said Angilly.

The skull beneath the Alkhand's hands made a bitter sound, and Loret saw the man's fingers clench on it, as though trying to pry its rich furnishing away with his nails. She understood, though. The Alkhand might or might not be merciful, but he was well aware that Pallesand had won the war, and the hawks of its administration would be flicking through the atlas even now. Oparan might be old and sick, but he could feel the wind on his face and knew which way it blew.

"Pallesand esteems its good relations with the Alkhanate of Usmai," Angilly said, "and I, myself, regret any pain my transgressions have caused you, and give thanks for your kindness." Then, as though it was nothing but an afterthought, "If I might speak on another matter that touches the relations between our great nations?"

The slightest tightening about the Alkhand's face. "Speak."

"There are not so many of my compatriots within Alkhalend," Angilly said casually. "I do my best to keep track of them. I know we Palleseen can be brash, and some of us do not take the proper care to learn the ways of our hosts. However, if we transgress, it is my role as Resident to spare your servants and administer correction to my countryfolk myself. Word has reached me that one such is being held within the House of Hard Angles. I would beg your writ that I might bring her out of there for proper disciplining."

Oparan's face was hard to read, as though more than just his eyes were stone, but Loret guessed this was news to him, and that the woman she'd seen in the prison wasn't there by royal decree.

He made a dismissive gesture with the hand that wasn't on the skull. "If such a one is there, then you have my writ. If this compatriot of yours has crimes to her conscience, I trust that the justice of Pallesand will live up to its reputation." Simultaneously stern and sarcastic, quite a feat.

Loret had assumed, the previous night, that they'd just go charging back to the prison the moment Angilly understood the situation, but apparently the life of a career diplomat really wasn't all duels and derring-do. Sometimes you did things the formal way. When they stepped out of the Alkhand's presence, it was with a document written by Dekamran, and sealed by the monarch's own hand.

"I will find you an escort," the prince said.

"Not necessary," Angilly told him.

"I don't want to have to explain to your replacement how some thug stove your head in because your purse looked full," Dekamran said lightly. "Or how you got into a duel with some—"

"Don't," she said.

"Sorry."

She nodded. Clenched her hands. For a moment she was leaning into him, the prince, right there before the servants, before the door to his father's chambers. Then she drew back. Loret felt her throat dry with the tension of it.

"An escort," Dekamran repeated firmly. "And I'd go at the head of them if that was even remotely appropriate. But they won't go past the gates of the House. You know that. Once inside, you're on your own."

Loret, who had been within the gates of the House already,

and thought little of it, now understood that there had been risks she hadn't known she was running.

"Well, almost." Angilly looked at her. "This is my new aide, by the way. Possibly. If she keeps shaping up. She's proved a box of surprises so far."

The escort was a dozen of the palace servants. They weren't guards, exactly, by Loret's estimation. The men had cleavers and the women had rapiers, but they wore bright clothing, shawls and vests and flapping trousers. Going into the Sand Lanes, they seemed to be a walking invitation to robbery, but apparently the Alkhand's writ was strong enough that they served as protection instead. Seeing the district by daylight was a crooked wonder. On either side of streets that were literally just scuffed sand and the occasional sea-worn slab of rock were great stacked buildings, home built on home with a riotous lack of planning. Poles and planks leaned in at all angles to buttress a construction that had grown with almost fungal abandon. Beams were propped from one side of the street to the other overhead, to keep leaning edifices just separate enough. At Loret's back, the cliffs that formed the upper city extended in tiers that ran with waterfalls from above, so that the sun struck rainbows all across the skies of the city, quite the most breathtaking sight Loret had ever seen. Elsewhere was the great shifting maze of the docks, workshops and warehouses, trade factoras and mills. All of which meant that the lesser citizens of Alkhalend had been left a relatively small area for their dwellings, so they'd built *up*.

The House of Hard Angles was a stone building, unornamented and without windows. Nothing else in the city was anything like it. It hunched on a rock in the heart of the Sand Lanes, worked blocks set without mortar, so close together Loret couldn't have fit a piece of paper between them. Six-sided, with six towers like stubby fingers. Solid, Angilly said. Not there for a watch to be kept, or signals to be lit on. Part of the geometry of the place. Its hard angles.

Around the door, the sigils flared. They were not, Loret saw now, incised into the stone of the frame. They flickered balefully in the air, an inch clear.

"Ghosts," Angilly said, seeing where she was looking.

"These are ghosts?"

"No, they trap ghosts. The whole thing traps ghosts. Probably other things too, but the locals don't have any truck with demons or the like. The Moeribandi, back in the day – you know about them?"

Loret did not know about them. Probably another thing that would have been in the brief she hadn't seen. Angilly rolled her eyes.

"Never mind, then. This was a ghost prison first, though. Or else it was a place ghosts lived. All sorts of ghost business anyway. But these days it's a prison. The bad prison. The one you don't want to get sent to."

"Because of the ghost business," Loret said, thinking about what might happen, if you died in a place ghosts couldn't escape.

"That and other things." Angilly looked from her to their escort which was plainly happy not to be going past those doors. "This is not my favourite part of the job."

"You've done this before?"

"More than I like to recall," Angilly agreed. "Back in the day, this happened all the time. Some merchant of ours, some messenger, getting slung in here with nobody the wiser. Back before the Alkhand changed his mind about the succession. And if I wanted a writ to get them out, I'd have to go beg Tarcomir to use his influence. On account of I didn't have any of my own."

Loret remembered the man Angilly had stabbed to death the previous night. *No good deed goes unpunished.*

When she'd turned up here the previous night, her hails at the door had been met by some old bald woman she'd assumed was a guard. In daylight she discovered the prison's staff were monks of some kind. Alkhalend had a lot of monks, Angilly said. Spoken not even with the traditional Pal disdain for the topic, just as a matter of fact. This lot were the oldest: Moerends, the priesthood of the old Imperial death cult. Left stranded at the high-water mark of the state that had originated them, they'd become a kind of civil service in this part of the world. Still religious, but such a dry, pragmatic devotion it barely offended Palleseen perfection.

The middle-aged man who opened the door to them this morning was also bald, and the lead and antimony applied to his face lent it a gauntness it didn't really possess by nature. He examined Angilly's writ and then admitted the two Palleseen without comment.

"I didn't have a writ," Loret noted. "They just let me in."

"Yes," said Angilly.

"I said I wanted to see the Pal woman they had, and they took me there."

"Yes."

"And when it wasn't you, I said I wanted to go and they took me back to the door."

Angilly nodded, regarding her.

"They... didn't have to do any of that, did they? Especially the letting out part." Loret heard her own voice tremble, saying it.

"Oh they're very good at people going in," Angilly said. "But not the letting out part. Unless you've got some god watching over you?" She laughed. Loret laughed. Good Pal laughter that didn't have any truck with gods. Loret listened to how hollow the echo of it was, as it fell away into the void of the House of Hard Angles.

There were lamps inside, but not enough and not healthy ones. Not even flames, but a pale greenish-whiteness that leaped and crouched in imitation of them. Certainly not the steady radiance of a magical tableth-fuelled lantern. Loret was about to joke that maybe they burned the trapped ghosts, then killed the words in case it wouldn't be a joke at all.

The House of Hard Angles descended into the ground. It was built on a rock, and the rock went deep; so did the prison. Each long, narrow hall was lined with barred alcoves, and down the centre of each hall was a vertical slot that gave onto every hall above, and every hall below. Only a foot wide, that slot, enough to step into and break your leg, not enough to fall through unless you were very slender and very unlucky. Loret, who was slender enough, didn't feel like testing her luck and kept well clear of it. She'd peered down it once and seen the glimmer of those dead lamps all the way down, a receding constellation that seemed to pitch vertiginously far too deep into the earth. An abyss, surely far more cells than any city could need. She'd seen the mass camps her own nation threw up when enough people had been sufficiently imperfect. The House of Hard Angles felt as though you could have poured all the damned souls of such a camp in and have room for a dozen more.

"It's not that big," Angilly said, at her elbow, and Loret realised she'd stopped still, and that her breathing was ragged and harsh. The Resident touched her arm and it almost made her jump into the abyss.

"It's…?" she got out.

"Or not the part that they keep people in," Angilly told her. "A few hundred at most, at any time."

"Oh." That was better, surely.

"The rest is for ghosts."

"Oh." That was worse. And this place was *old*, so how many ghosts, exactly…? And not even a prison, originally, Angilly had speculated. Some religious place, where ghosts were… what? Cared for? Prepared for their fate? Except it had all gone wrong, like so many things had gone wrong. She could feel the air full of invisible, jostling presences, trapped, hopeless.

The monk who had been leading them, down steps, along halls, stopped abruptly. There was a corporeal presence in the cell ahead. The same woman Loret had seen, who was very much not Angilly.

The cells in the House of Hard Angles hadn't originally been designed for physical comfort. Or even occupants, given that the bars, where they existed, were plainly later additions. Possibly the open alcoves were crammed full of invisible spectres. Loret didn't intend to find out. In this cell a plank had been bracketed to the back wall, though, and the woman was lying on it. She got up hastily when Angilly and Loret arrived. She was Pal, sure enough. Dark hair cropped short with a fang of a widow's peak. Hollow cheeks, a Pal shirt and breeches but some wild, flowing scarf about her neck and shoulders. A belt full of pouches and bags.

"About time." She nodded at Loret, seeing only one woman even slightly in uniform. "I thought you'd skipped out on me, kid." She glanced at Angilly, then looked again, seeing past the clothes to the face.

"You are?" Angilly asked her.

The woman in the cell gave her a brilliant smile. "Fellow-Archivist Drathel. A humble traveller."

Angilly nodded. "Does that translate as necromancy or decanting?"

The smile cracked. "You are the…?"

"The Resident, yes. What got you thrown in here?"

"A misunderstanding."

Another nod from Angilly. Loret looked from one to the other, because there seemed to be quite a detailed conversation going on between them, only neither woman was saying most of the words.

"You're on Palinet's staff?"

"Not quite. Met her. Roving brief."

"But from…?"

"Started that side of the border, yes," Drathel confirmed. "Must have wandered."

Angilly nodded again, as if suspicions confirmed. "It's customary to drop in at the Residence, before trying anything on. Just so we can keep the paperwork straight, you know."

"Must have forgotten," Drathel said. "Know better next time." Acknowledging she was in the shit but not actually penitent about it.

"Well you should probably come visit the Residence now," Angilly told her. "We have better accommodation. More congenial. Tea."

"Tea," said Drathel, "would be good."

The Moerend monk stepped forwards with keys and unlocked a grill that turned out to just pull away entirely, without hinges. With effort he jockeyed it back from the bars, perilously close to putting a foot down the abyss. It was not, Loret decided, a system that anybody had given much thought to. As soon as sufficient gap had been created, Drathel eeled her way out and was shaking her legs on the free side.

"Any possessions?" Angilly asked her.

"Well," said Drathel. "I mean. Not that they're going to be giving back to me."

"Decanting, then."

Drathel made a noncommittal sound, as though it was too trivial a matter to be discussed in this sort of company. Loret reckoned she just about understood it then, from context. A particularly Pal sort of transgression.

"Tea, you say." Fellow-Archivist Drathel finished with the kinks in her shoulder blades and then stopped dead because a dozen figures had just advanced into the pallid light. They were dressed as locals, and as well as their hooded shawls they had scarves up to hide their faces, and knives in their hands.

Angilly's face was set. "You and I are going to have words," she told Drathel, "about just what the hell you *did*." She drew her rapier in one practised motion. Loret hadn't even realised she was wearing it. "Get into the cell."

"I've just got out of the cell," Drathel pointed out.

"Get in or they'll swarm us." Keeping the newcomers at her steel's reach, she backed away. With her off-hand she was plucking other trinkets from her belt. A baton, pressed into

Drathel's hand. A knife likewise. And Loret had her knife, of course. The uniform belt had come with one. She took it out. In her hands it seemed barely a tool or an eating utensil, let alone a weapon.

The monk had vanished away into the darkness. Possibly to get help, but Loret wouldn't put money on it. After all, there were a dozen assassins here and, while that might indicate supernatural powers of stealth on their part, a donation to monastery coffers seemed more likely.

The fact that they'd patiently waited until their target was freed, so as to skip the inconvenience of the bars, was almost impressive. Very neat-minded killers. Although they hadn't thought to bring batons of their own.

For a moment, Angilly's long needle of steel was a barrier that kept them all away. Loret caught a murmur of Usmiri words. "Who is she?" "The Denizen of Slate House." Meaning the Resident, but the word they used had connotations of demons and infestation. *So you've met us Pals before then?*

"The woman is a tomb-robber," said presumably the chief assassin. "She has earned a death. Go, and let her collect it."

Angilly nodded. The same nod she'd used with Drathel. "She's a Palleseen citizen. A Fellow of the Schools, apparently, so quite a senior one. She'll get all the rapped knuckles she's due and be on the next boat out of Usmai. Be happy with that."

The assassins indicated their general unhappiness by going for them. Loret was jostled back into the cell, where she really didn't want to be. Drathel was already there, with Angilly holding the door. Loret saw one of the killers fall back with a slashed-open arm and a curse.

Drathel levelled the baton and spoke the word. That same standard Pel word the tablethi all used, to spark a killing bolt of fire. A feat of everyday magic every Pal had seen countless times.

It didn't go that way. There was a reason the killers hadn't brought such toys. Instead of just blowing a hole in the nearest assassin's chest, a forked web of spitting power crackled from the baton, earthing into every alcove and stone around them, and for a brief instant Loret saw the ghosts. Hundreds of ghosts. Crammed into every inch of space in every nook of the place, screaming mouths, clawing hands, phantom jaws gnawing on phantom faces, fingers digging into eyes, soundlessly howling at the chains that bound them to this terrible place.

Just an instant, and Drathel dropped the baton and leaped back with a curse. The assassins, too, hadn't been ready for it. Scattered, stared, swore.

Angilly, now, *she* was ready for it. She rushed them, lunged, backstepped, lunged again, then lashed the edge of her narrow blade across the conveniently bared throat of another victim. And the power of the baton had conducted away into the stones by then, so Loret didn't see the ghosts of those three dead killers rise howling into the air, to be caught here evermore, but she knew they were there.

One of the assassins had recovered enough, by that point, and there were still half a dozen or more in the fight. There was a brief grapple and then Angilly fell back, hissing in pain and with the back of her hand to her mouth, sucking at her own bloodied knuckles. Knuckles of the hand that had held the sword, now spinning to a ringing stop on the ground.

The Resident dragged out another knife, off-handed.

"Don't take this as how the job usually goes," she told Loret out of the corner of her mouth. "Mostly it's paperwork." Facing so many knives, there was an *aliveness* to her that was like standing next to a fire.

One of the killers kicked the sword so that it fell into the gap in the floor, down through all those ghost-crammed levels to who knew what other hell was below?

"Who's that?" Drathel demanded. She was pointing. Loret thought it was just a weak attempt at distraction but there was actually a man there, stepping into the outer fringes of the light. A tall, broad-shouldered figure. Not a Pal. Not an Usmiat either. Big, foreign. Its face was inhuman abomination – no, a mask.

Glass-eyed, a coil of hose where the nose and mouth should be. A thing of weirdly mechanical horror.

"Sod me, it's the Warden," Drathel answered her own question, and the capital letter was inherent in the way she said it.

Some of the killers were hesitating then: plainly this Warden wasn't on their side. A couple fancied their chances when it was down to just knives, though, and went for it. Angilly, bloodied and off guard, skittered backwards into the cell with a man clutching at her collar, slashing at her face. She warded off the blow awkwardly, taking it across the back of her arm, and then Loret…

The other man had rammed her hard, trying to get in. He was stuck in the gap for a moment, one foot the wrong side of the bars. He had hold of her, also through the bars. Was shaking her as though somehow it was her stopping him getting in to murder them all conveniently, and she…

It was back in the camps. The hunger riots. The cart overturned, what meagre meal there was being trodden into the mud because everyone was fighting over it and she…

Had become fed up of just taking *it, the blows, the abuse. And so she…*

Her hand came away bloody. In the back of her head, like a memory, the frantic piston-arm motion of *stab and stab and stab and…* Blood all the way up her jacket. The taste of it in her mouth and she didn't know if that was real or just a memory of when…

The Warden had stepped forwards, she saw, as she sagged against the bars. He had a sword now, that shone in the dark with its own light, conjured from air. The assassins were trying to face him off but their feet kept turning coward on them and giving ground.

"The Warden," Drathel said distantly, still weirdly fascinated, "will save us."

"That's not the Warden," Angilly stated flatly, and something terrible came up from the slot in the floor. Something bristling with motion, far too many frenzied legs and fangs and segments, that couldn't possibly squeeze itself through that narrow gap, and did so, and scoured the hall of every killer who didn't run, and then went after those who had.

That was enough for Loret. That was when she decided she no longer consented to having anything to do with this horrible place or any of these horrible people, *or* their monsters. And so she slipped down to her knees, leaving a trail of red down the bars, and toppled sideways, unsure how much of it belonged to the man she killed, and how much of it was hers.

Old Friends

The capital, a major port: of course Alkhalend has foreigners like a beggar has lice. They throng the shifting Water Lanes where their boats dock, or live alongside their workplaces in that part of the city given over to industry and the creation of things. A handful, the lucky, live in the embassies and foreign-built houses at the foot of the waterfalls, where the wealth starts. And many, those who can't hold down a berth or pay decent coin, end up rubbing shoulders with the city's own in the Sand Lanes, where somehow there is always room. Whole communities, knots of expatriates, refugees, chancers, opportunists from every port, crammed in one beside the other like an atlas folded shut.

Loret was whimpering, gasping. Gil did her best to chart the width of the wound without hurting her more. The killer's blade had gone into her side. A bad place. Who knew what internal geography had felt the bite of it? Gil shrugged off her shawl – a fine one, a gift, a fortune in good thread and weavers' time – and tore it apart. Sat the girl up and wound it about her, tight as she could. She just needed to keep the blood in, just for now, just until…

Drathel, who was doing nothing to help any of this, kicked her. Not hard, not an attack, but to get her attention. Gil glanced up, the single moment she could spare from her work. The man was standing over them. That grotesque mask, like someone had taxidermied a machine.

Not the Warden. The Under-warden, the Warden's assistant, this man.

"We didn't bring this trouble to you," Gil said, around the edge of shawl she was biting down on, pulling tight so her busy hands could knot. And it wasn't true, because Drathel plainly had, but what sort of a diplomat would she be if she couldn't lie through her teeth?

Drathel, she noted, had put Gil between herself and the man. Plainly thinking the same thought.

The man knelt. Pulled the mask so that it ended up dangling under his bony chin. A hard, ugly, honest face, and Gil reckoned he was probably all of those things, but all in the shadow of the other things he was.

"It's good for her, sometimes," he said, "to have something to chase." His voice was weirdly accented, his Pel awkward. The stresses constantly on the verge of turning what he was saying into some other meaning entirely.

He held something, fished from the satchel at his belt. His clothes were some kind of uniform, darned and too-much worn. He stripped off heavy gloves. The hands beneath were big-knuckled, long-fingered, a strangler's. His device clicked and sparked like he was trying to set fire to Loret for good measure, then gave out a faltering blue radiance. It clashed with the ghostlight of the House of Hard Angles, guttered. He hissed, pressed it to the cloth pulled taut over the wound anyway.

Loret screamed and kicked. Elbowed Gil hard in the chest. The echoes of it skittered upwards and downwards, too far in either direction. Somewhere, something bristling with legs and chewing over the last of the assassins raised its dreadful head to listen.

There was a place, not far from Alkhalend. A stand of trees, no more. They'd built a monastery there, because *more monks* seemed to be the first instinct of the Usmiat, when confronted with a problem. And the monks themselves were also a problem, because people went into that order and donned the mask, and never returned. Vanished, from the least of beggars to the Alkhand's own lost wife, and no power existed that could hail them back. Special monks, for a special place. Just a stand of trees, save that sometimes things came out of it. Terrible things, useful things, lost things. Things that were monsters. Things that were people. Sometimes one of each. Around the start of the war, the Warden and its man had been two such things. They'd caused a lot of trouble, before they had been introduced to the House. Given that the man, at least, could be reasoned with, the pair had been made rulers of the place. Allowed a stipend and some concessions, if they kept it in line. The House of Hard Angles, maintaining its long tradition of unorthodox governors.

The Under-warden shook his device, applied it again, harder. A moment of utter brutality beyond any torturer. Another throat-stripping howl from Loret. He shook his head.

"They lose their power," he said, and then something moved in the darkness, making every shadow a haunt of spindly legs and the serpentine flails of antennae. His charge, his ward, his mistress, his god, who even knew? "Go." A human moment, when just the man inhabited his face, and not the monster's mate. "Or stay." Not an offer but a threat.

The monks were waiting to convey them to the warded door. Drathel and Gil, with Loret strung between them, trembling, crying out every time they jogged her. The Moerends stared, disapproving, as though the girl's ghost had already crept halfway out of the gash in her side and should by rights be the property of the prison. But if Loret was going to die then she would die on the far side of those sigils, and ideally she was going to live.

Outside it was still the clear light of morning. After all that darkness, the sight seemed almost miraculous. Gil's mind had moved on to night, giving the day up for lost.

"Right." And Drathel was abruptly not supporting that side of Loret, leaving the burden for Gil and one of the escort to hurriedly shoulder. "I'm—"

"Coming with me," Gil told her flatly. "Staying where I can see you. While I help Loret." Already starting to move, dragging the escort with her by sheer force of will. "Then back to the embassy, where you and I are going to sit in a room and work out just what the fuck you did and what's going to happen to you."

"With respect—"

"Is that clear, *Fellow*-Archivist? Or else you are not only cutting yourself off from any assistance from the Residence, you are putting yourself outside the Palleseen Sway, and I'll write to Palinet in Peor to make sure she knows to have you shot on sight as a deserter." Still moving, feeling Loret's shudders and gasps and the sticky wetness of her blood.

"Harsh," Drathel observed, still with that veneer of archness and distance, the worldly-wise adventurer rolling her eyes at all these rules. Gil had lost a good sword on her account, and maybe by the end of the day she'd have lost an aide. She wasn't going to let Drathel just scuttle off into the cracks.

"Resident," said the woman who'd taken Loret's other shoulder, "there are surgeons in the palace..."

"Too far," Gil said. And possibly Loret was beyond regular surgery. And where had *that* come from, in the girl? She'd ask, of Loret, 'Where did you learn to fight?' except learning maybe wasn't a part of it. A rage, a fury from nowhere. Loret had taken the hit, yes, but the man she'd killed had been carved up like the girl was serving him at a table, a dozen manic strikes of the knife. Not exactly how they taught it in basic training.

"Resident," said the woman, "where are we going?" Because Gil's determined course was taking them only deeper into the Sand Lanes. Through meaner streets overshadowed by their own slanting upper floors, past hungry eyes. Children ran past on skinny legs, screaming at them and plucking at the escort's fine clothing. Sullen Usmiat men and women paused in their drinking to stare. They bundled Loret through a circular space between teetering buildings where a trio of monks were teaching thin youngsters stories of gods and good behaviour. If Gil still saw things like that with Pal eyes, she'd see deprivation and the furthering of ignorance, shackling these kids with superstitions that would prevent them ever entering a rational world. With the eyes that seven years in Usmai had given her, she knew that these same monks brought food into the Sand Lanes every day, found work, sponsored art. Palleseen rule would take away the monks and their stories and charity, and expect the theoretical principle of perfection to rush in to fill the gap of its own accord. Being the good Palleseen she obviously was, she knew that eventually the doctrine of perfection would provide a better life for everyone. Being a realist she knew that, over the course of that *eventually*, a lot of children would starve.

By then, they had left the impromptu street school behind and had come into sight of the Fever Lodge.

It had set up during the war. A clutch of foreigners turning up on a boat, at least a couple of them Pals. Just like Drathel, they hadn't presented themselves at the Residence. Nor had they been delighted to come to the attention of the Resident later. She knew deserters when she saw them.

But it was like so much else, here in the shallows of the Palleseen Sway. When perfection came into its full glory, all these things would be swept away. Until then, they were useful. Especially when you had a critically injured woman's arm clenching and trembling over your shoulders, and no other hope to save her.

In the three years of the Fever Lodge's existence, it had built a reputation. Several conflicting reputations, honestly. The Sand Lanes pulled in a lot of different directions. But one such reputation was for feats of medicine beyond the usual, or the natural. That was the sort of currency that any number of criminals, cults and dissidents would let you spend. On occasion the Residence had taken it too, as payment for overlooking the place's existence.

Right now, turning up with a full armed palace escort was not going to endear anyone to the Lodge's denizens, but Gil didn't think she had much choice.

The vacant-faced man sitting on the doorstep jumped up when he saw them coming. Gil took a better hold of Loret and then told the escort to make themselves scarce, because they wouldn't help. And there was a lot of argument in their faces – they had Dekamran's orders, after all – but she just barked at them, full Sage-Invigilator Don't-You-Know-Who-I-Am, until they retreated. And then turned the same voice on Drathel to get her to stay. Because Drathel was short on useful qualities but she had a shoulder suitable for supporting a dying aide and that was the sum total of what Gil required from her.

"Help. Now," she told the man. The blankness was gone from his face. He nodded, went in and left the door open for them to follow.

Inside it was chaos, but a peculiarly familiar sort. The chaos of a phalanstery during a break in classes, or a military camp just before the fighting starts. Someone was screaming from further inside the nest of rooms and that, too, could have fit either. It was a Palleseen sort of chaos, because these were Palleseen people.

At the man's gesturing they got Loret onto a table and he started to peel away the red-soaked rags Gil had wrapped her in. Loret was out, then. Being manhandled through half the Sand Lanes had been too much for her, but at least that had stopped the cries and the whimpering. She was very pale, as though all the blood in her had already been wrung out. She was cool. She shivered.

Abruptly another of the Lodge's proprietors was there, putting them all in his shadow. A huge man, a Pal, reaching into his many-pocketed apron. Forcing a vial to Loret's bluish lips, giving the slender man a fistful of powder to sprinkle on the wound itself. Then turning a pig's small eyes on Gil.

"Resident," he said. "Magister." On his lips not a term of respect, she felt.

"Heal her," she told him. "Fix her up. As much as can be done."

His face was a fist that had beaten down more urgent demands than hers. *Deserter and worse. One letter home and doubtless I'd hear the full tally of what you did before you ran.* She'd seen his back once. More than one whipping had written a story there, the precise and regular script of a military man gone bad.

"Help me with the table," he said. "And then price."

They got the table into the next room where an old Jarokiri woman was exploring someone's innards with the glowing tip of a knife. She glanced over, rolled her eyes. *Never fucking stops, does it?* that look said. The woman she was even now stepping back from was Usmiat; the vast majority of their patients were. The Lodge's patrons didn't usually wear Pal uniforms, no matter how much blood had soaked into the cloth.

"Jack," the old Jarokiri spat. "Close up." And the slender man with the mild face took over with needle and thread.

The old woman looked at Gil with the sort of patient loathing most people reserved for intangibles like storms or plagues. "So nice to see you again, Resident."

Gil, for her part, stared right back with similar sentiments. Because she didn't like the big man, but this woman, this hard old stick from Jarokir, gave her the chills. She'd been in Jarokir, as a child and, later, in service. It had been a god-ridden place before the Pals had got hold of it. A lot of terrible things had been done there. Gil knew it better than most. Some of them had been done to her; some of them she had done. It was not a place held fondly in her memories, and this old crone had it written all over her.

"Save her," she said. Directed. Ordered. Begged. A lot of different ways to hear the same two words.

"Squeeze them," the crone said to her hulking accomplice. "Everything they've got."

"You can be sure," he rumbled, and then he was moving for the door and, because Drathel and Gil were between him and it, they were driven from the surgery, and the sight of what would get done to Loret.

The Fever Lodge went on and on, room after room delving

into the irregular, diseased heart of one of the Sand Lanes' great piled-up edifices. Past the surgery was a space that had been made by knocking out three walls of smaller rooms. There were props left, but the ceiling bowed and buckled like a reptile's hide, until to stand beneath it was to feel you were in your own grave. Drathel seemed to take it in her stride, but by Gil's estimation she was a woman who'd made a habit of creeping into buried places and filling her pockets with what she found there. All in the name of the Palleseen Sway, of course. The difference between a pirate and a privateer of the scholarly world.

At one end of the room was a rack of swords and a circle of floor spread with sand. An Usmiat fencing ring. The swords were skias, the long, straight blades that were cousins to a Pal rapier. Women's swords, because one of the Lodge's other founders taught here, styles that higher-class duellists would not approve of.

"Let's see your coin," said the big man, businesslike as a usurer. When Gil emptied her purse – that fistful of the Residence's emergency supply she'd brought – he stared at the bright money as though it was mud and ashes. And Drathel had a comment on her lips, and either it would be passing judgment on how little coin was there, or on the amount being too much for just some slip of a girl. Gil didn't want to hear it. Told the woman that very clearly with no more than a look. And surprised a more complex expression on the tomb-robber's face. Not more benevolent but certainly more thoughtful. *Watching the Resident not blink, dealing with people like this. Re-evaluating my operation here.* Drathel was seeing someone who could be of use, rather than just be in the way. Gil wasn't sure she wanted to be of use to Drathel, but that was a battle for another day.

"What else do you need?"

The big man stared at her for a moment as though trying to work out just what cuts he could take from her carcase and what wine went with the meat. Then he stomped off, shouting for his boy. "Where's the requisitions list? Where are you, you waste of space? Get in here!" Just like any quartermaster chewing out his lazy assistant. Pal sounds. Army sounds.

"This place stinks," said Drathel, but she said it like she'd been desperate for a bit of stink; like a connoisseur of stinks intrigued by the prospect. "Who even are these clowns?"

"Doctors," Gil said. "Quacks." *Miracle workers, occasionally.* Right now the old Jarokiri woman would be seeing just what the damage was, past the slit in Loret's skin. She'd patch up what she could, stitch and repair, and the big man would dispense. And then it would be down to their third, the woman they called the Reckoner, to make good on what was left. It was an uncanny piece of business, and all the worse for plainly wanting to stay here under its stone in the Sand Lanes, rather than be held up to the sun. *Cults and gods and magicians and who knows what?*

"This is in your remit, is it?" Drathel asked. "Only I thought it was all soirees and treaties and bailing reprobates like me out of trouble." She smiled, a peace offering. *Let's try it again on the other foot.*

Gil wanted to dig her heels in, then. Wanted to rake Drathel over the coals. But that was because of Loret, and it had been Gil who put Loret where the knife could find her.

"Fine," she said. Then the big man turned up again, face like slapped thunder, complaining that kids these days were never where they were supposed to be. He had a list, though. Gil looked down it.

"I can get about half of this." From Pal merchants who owed her or wanted to curry favour with her. From Usmiat grandees who saw her as the best way to getting their words into Dekamran's ear. From a handful of rather less-savoury contacts she had made, in her seven years in the city.

The man's face suggested it would be a shame if they only sewed Loret halfway back up.

"I will get all I can. All there is to be had," she told his ill-temper. "And the Residence will owe the Lodge." *You had better be worth this, Loret.* She knew that, had the slit-open kid been some Sand Lanes beggar, they'd do the work for pennies and promises. But she was the Resident and she'd turned up with an escort and so they'd squeeze. And she'd let them have every drop they wrung out of her, because they were preternaturally good at what they did. She never knew just when she might need a surgeon who wasn't shackled to either the palace or the Palleseen Sway.

Later, she sat out front, waiting for word, watching the business of the Sand Lanes in all its myriad complexities. Deals brokered, futures made or let go of, the buying and selling, the conspiracies. Ambling Usrani monks whom the worst cut-throat wouldn't threaten, shifty foreigners off the docks looking for a good time, villains, victims. Life, in all its stinks and flavours.

She knew just what scent Drathel had been talking about, though. The commodity that drove the Palleseen military and its industry. Magic. For when just a scalpel and a suture wouldn't do. There was a lot of errant magic worked into the grit of the Sand Lanes. It was where Alkhalend consigned everything that refined sensibilities didn't want to deal with. Like the ghost-haunted House of Hard Angles. Like fortune tellers and foreign cults and the woman in the Lodge who taught the sword in all the wrong ways.

Drathel, sitting beside her, hadn't said anything for a while. She was watching the slender, open-faced man, the one they called Happy Jack. He did look happy, actually. Gil had thought he was simple-minded, when she first saw him. No sane person who understood the world should have that kind of vacant, dazed smile. Right now, he was sitting nearby, scattering crumbs like he was feeding birds, beaming down at his hands. And no birds ever came to eat at the table of Happy Jack but, when you looked again, the crumbs were always gone.

When the woman arrived, the one who taught sword, she

touched him on the shoulder in passing, and he looked up with such fondness it made Gil angry. It made her hate herself. It made her think of that very small list of people she had truly, fiercely clasped to her, in her past life, and how she had managed to hold on to precisely none of them. Because of what she was, and the way the job went, and all that. And here was some foreign beggar, on the meanest street of a city foreign to both of them, and he was so fucking *happy* with the nothing he had. The nothing he had and the woman he shared it with. And the woman who taught sword glanced at Gil, saw her impotent, mean-hearted rage, and fed off it, the bitch.

A boy shambled in, after. The big man's delinquent son, a gangly teenager and already in with every bad crowd the Sand Lanes had to offer. Soon after that they heard the man's bellowing, *What time's this? Bed not even slept in, is it? Where's the money that…?* And the boy's shriller tones, lightning to the man's thunder, shouting back.

"It was the Halberandi place. The old tombs," Drathel said quietly. "Not even on your side of the border. I didn't think they'd follow me across."

Gil waited.

"There's so much there. Centuries of charged stuff, just stacked up in holes in the ground. And I tried to just make an offer, but it's *religion*. You can't argue with religion. You can't say, 'What's the point, just hoarding it all under a stone?' With what they've got there, I could charge a thousand tablethi." The little magic repositories, size of your thumb's end joint, that powered the modern world and the Palleseen Sway. Weapons, lamps, tools, engines. The infinitely interchangeable currency of the magical world. But the power had to come from somewhere. And Drathel, whatever her personal failings, was a cog in the grander machine just like Gil was.

"So I'm sorry, if I've caused you a headache. Peace?"

"You're still in my custody until I can find someone to repatriate you to," Gil warned her.

"No. Fine. Fair. And I didn't mean for your girl to get… obviously I didn't."

Gil couldn't tell, really, if this was self-serving. If the woman really was sorry, or what. She had a sense that Drathel could believe a great many things in the moment, that she could disavow a moment later. The term from Pal philosophy was *Pragmatic Flexibility* and the scholars were still out on whether it was a good thing or not. Probably good right now, but to be corrected when perfection allowed. Like most of Gil's life, honestly.

Then the big man was rapping on the shutters overhead. They'd done what they could, and it was time for Gil to see if that was enough.

There was a sword class going on at one end of the hall when they re-entered. The clash and scrape of skias made for strange accompaniment by which to talk to a physician. The teacher went by the name Caecelian, meaning *The Viper*. She moved like it, fighting with a knife in her off-hand just like people didn't around here. Which made learning it so useful if you were after handling yourself in the street rather than just the circle. Caecelian taught from behind a mask and the mask was a demon's face, and that was another transgression. But then transgressions were, Gil suspected, what the woman was made of.

The student was all scarved up, trying for the anonymity of the killers in the House of Hard Angles, but Gil had good eyes. Tradecraft, like she'd told Loret. Outreach, the Archipelago's diplomatic department, with one hand over the table to sign the documents and one under the table to hold the knife. That was how the saying went. She had learned to recognise the body language and not the face.

Is that who I think? Watching the student, a girl younger than Loret despite all the braggadocio she'd tried to don with the street clothes. Seeing her stumble and recover and bring her practise blades back into line.

The Reckoner – the last of this coterie of monsters – had set up her table in the corner. Scales, weights, just as though she was about to sell them a packet of spices. She was another foreigner, golden skin chased with a faint shimmer as though she'd been dusted with diamonds. A round face now. When Gil had first seen it, it had been hard and haunted. In three years it had filled out, become comfortable even as the woman's frame had grown to take advantage of the looser Usmiat clothing. Looser than a Pal Accessory's uniform, certainly, which was what Gil was damn sure she'd once worn.

When they brought Loret in, the Reckoner's face tightened a little. She popped a candy into her mouth, rolling it around from cheek to cheek, considering. The girl was still very pale, leaning on the big man. On his arm. On half his arm. He could have propped up a dozen of her. She was alive though. Her eyes found Gil across the room, wide, panicky but holding it in. Gil nodded at her, as reassuring as she could manage.

"Show me." The Reckoner's Pel still had a big dose of her native accent, almost like singing. They'd put a too-big shirt on Loret to replace the bloody rags she'd come in. Too big but still Pal issue and Gil wondered where they'd found it or who they'd stripped it from. Now the big man hoiked the hem up, businesslike as a merchant opening a shopfront. Gil saw the neat stitching, the old Jarokiri woman's script that said *This may yet heal.* And if she'd been just a regular, that would be it. Perhaps some tonic from the big man to aid the process but Loret would be pale and limping and fragile for months. Gil was paying for the full service, though.

"Fine." The Reckoner tongued the sweet around her mouth. "Sit her."

The big man filled his big lungs to bellow, but the boy was actually where he was supposed to be, putting a folding stool where Loret could sink down into it. Gil saw him look over at the fighters as he retreated, eyes following the pass of blades, the pass of bodies. No secret why he was suddenly so diligent.

The Reckoner placed weights on the scales, one at a time, loading down the arm and still adding more, as though she didn't understand the purpose of the tool she was playing with. Her face screwed up, the candy pushing out her cheek like a thumb.

She sighed, closed her eyes. The scales trembled.

Beside Gil, Drathel jolted and swore.

The arms of the scales tilted. Gil wondered if there was actually an invisible hand on the empty side, something Drathel could see. To her it was just one more damned thing about this place. One more fragment of foreign depravity awaiting a good perfecting. Save, of course, that it worked.

The scales balanced, swaying a little. The Reckoner sat back with a long hiss of breath, favouring one side. Loret's bared skin was clear. And if they'd pulled this little trick before the surgeon's work then probably the Reckoner would be bleeding out on the floor, but the stitches had crossed over with the wounds, so everyone would live.

Loret made a noise. Stared at the foreign woman whose brow was taut with pain now. Stared at Gil, at the two duellists. At everything in the world, as though she couldn't work out how any of it had got there and wanted to go back to first principles. And probably the big man had her on some serious drugs and some of it was that, but Gil reckoned it was still quite the blow to your worldview, being brought back from blood and shock like that.

"I think it's time the three of us strolled back to the Residence," she announced brightly. "If you're up to it."

Loret stared. Her lips moved and Gil silenced her with a gesture. You *never* thanked the Reckoner. The Reckoner had been *paid* and she didn't take tips. That was what the scales were about. A very precise and balanced transaction.

"Come on," said Gil, "I have paperwork to sign. Or, if you're my aide, maybe you do. March, soldier. Come on." And a jab under the ribs to Drathel, that made her yelp. "You too." Because

Drathel had been looking at the Reckoner like a sot at a good vintage, and Gil didn't want any of that nonsense on her patch.

The big man had a couple of items to add to the list then, and that was mostly mummery so the fencing student could leave without having to jostle elbows with the Pal Resident. Which suggested they knew exactly who they'd got under their roof, which suggested that things were flying apart rather more than Gil had realised, under the Alkhand's own. The elbows which did jostle them, as they filed out into the shadow of the Sand Lanes again, were those of the boy, shoving past them as though she wasn't the Resident and he wasn't just a skinny Pal youth still growing into his bones. He had a bulging, clinking satchel slung over his back, off on deliveries. Chasing them all out the door, the big man's voice bellowed at the kid's receding back.

Loret let out a ragged little breath. Not pain but the hollow where the pain had been. Walking without aid, but still with fragility to every step as though waiting for the Reckoner to welch on the deal and just give it all back. "What the hell," she asked, of Gil, of Drathel, of the world, "was all that?"

"And make sure you count it this time!" the big man roared over her. "Or I'll bloody cut you off, you little waster! Boy! *Are you listening, Boy?*"

Boy

His name isn't Boy. *He tells the big man, his father, his name isn't* Boy. *Quietly. Under his breath mostly. Often, like now, when he's moving away. One day he'll shout it. He's fifteen. He's not* Boy *and he's not* a *boy. But Oathan – the big man – has been calling him Boy since he was seven. He's had to hold on to his own name like a family treasure preserved from raiders. Kept at the bottom of a pack as the pair of them moved from military camp to military camp with the army. He's an army boy. Never a soldier – not quite old enough to enlist, though he could fool a recruiter. But he won't. He hates the army and the Palleseen Sway because they're what he knows from more than half his life. Because that's what Oathan is. Palleseen army. His father. The big man. The liar.*

He had jobs to do. Most kids had chores, he knew. The younger brats of the Sand Lanes got to sit with the jolly frog monks and learn stuff, but everyone had to fetch and carry, run errands, stand lookout. Some of the local kids were already a solid hand at some craft or other that small fingers could manage. Others just cleaned or fixed or cooked at home. Everyone had parents who didn't have the time to do all the adult things because of all the other adult things they had to do to put food on the table. Two parents, some. Others just one. The Boy – his name was Kilbery, not Boy – wasn't unique in that way. People died, left.

Oathan – the big man, not his real name – won't talk about

the Boy's mother. For the understandable reason that he hadn't known her. Oathan – just an Usmiat-sounding name he took on here – wasn't his real father, either. Who'd believe such a vast hulk of a man could be made entirely out of lies? But the Boy hadn't really known his mother either. She left him to go to war, like his father. The Archipelago was full of orphanages that were full of children whose parents went away fighting, because often those parents didn't come back, for obvious reasons. The Boy – Kilbery, as he constantly reminded the world, albeit sometimes under his breath – had no other family. They'd all died too, though not in the fighting. In some way that was never spoken of. He'd heard the story, since. The sorry details. Which had left him a true ward of the orphanage, until Oathan – or the man who would eventually call himself that – turned up.

Oathan the dispenser, the alchemist, the army man. Only now he wasn't an army man. Just one more expatriate in the Sand Lanes with useful skills, and no wish to ever see the inside of an army camp again. That's just about the only thing he and the – and *Kilbery* – agreed on.

He preferred the Sand Lanes. He preferred Alkhalend because, unlike many of his youthful peers, his business wasn't restricted to the district. He had business. He'd brag about it to goggling young faces, to derisive older men and women. He was important. You didn't mess with him.

Right now he had a clinking satchel of importance that needed to get to its proper owners, but he was working his own business, which meant following people. Living as a kid in an army camp made you a top grade skulker, because the place was full of petty officers who'd clip your ear or give you things to do. And while he'd shot up from a scrawny twelve-year-old to a gangling teenager over the three years the Fever Lodge crowd had been in Alkhalend, he was still a shadow when he needed.

Following two sets of people at once, though, that was a skill. That they were both going uptown helped. He could get up on the middling levels of the Sand Lanes, run over ladders and planks and make the small jumps it was safe to, when you had a heavy satchel of breakables. Picking his path, he could keep them all in sight. The three Pal women whose youngest member had been stabbed up. The girl who fights. Not that Kilbery harboured any romance about the girl who fights, obviously. And everyone who noted that he always seemed to be in evidence for the lessons reckoned he was watching the sinuous lines of Caecelian's body as she put it through its martial paces. Because the Viper was beautiful and elegant, almost impossibly so sometimes. Because it was hard not to watch her, when she willed it. The girl student was ugly. A high forehead and everything below it clenched into a frown. Of concentration, when she learned. Of utter mulishness the rest of the time, and towards everything in the world save her teacher. The Boy knew that look. He felt it clench his own face when people didn't use his proper name. She was a kindred spirit.

And she came to the Sand Lanes to learn how to fight. Not to do formal fucking about with fake swords like the rich people did, but to *fight*. The blade in and out and the blood. Kilbery had a knife. In fact he'd had a succession of knives because every so often Oathan – the man who wasn't Oathan – took them off him. He practised the passes, the footwork, when he thought nobody was watching him. All the street kids did. Half of them were already hanging around the district's thugs and gangs, running errands and petitioning for membership. Half of them would be dead before they made two decades. They joked about it. They boasted of cuts they'd made and taken, and that they'd be dead this time next year and didn't care. The Sand Life, they said. And Kilbery, underage gambler, saw their Sand Life and raised them his stories about being with an army in the big war, the Pal–Loruthi war. The thunder and the agony. The blood as you could only see it in the hospital tent where his father – not his father – worked.

The three Pal women were turning off for that odd little row of places where important foreigners lived. The rich foreigners, rather than the working foreigners who lived near the workshops, or the poor foreigners who were all over the Sand Lanes. Kilbery only knew the Resident, who'd been here long before the Fever Lodge was set up. Oathan had told him she was a dangerous woman, and not to have anything to do with her. She was Palleseen authority as far as it ran in Alkhalend, and they were all deserters. Except she'd turned up at the Lodge more than once over the time of its tenure. She did the formal fucking-about sort of swordplay – the old surgeon's disgusted phrase for it – but sometimes that turned into the killing kind, too. She'd been cut up, or she'd had someone who'd been cut up, or someone who came down with the various fevers that sometimes struck foreigners who came to Usmai. God-fevers, they were called, meaning some local deity had taken offence, but Kilbery didn't believe that. He'd grown up as a Pal, and the Pals were ridding the world of gods one by one because gods were irrational and imperfect. It would take more than a fever to stop them. Anyway, the dangerous woman that none of them should have anything to do with under any circumstances turned up at the doors of the Lodge more often than you'd think. The dread might of Palleseen authority had yet to be exercised to their detriment.

But that turning was as far as he'd follow them, because he was more interested in the fighter girl, and because he was going where she was going anyway, to do his job. She lived at the palace.

The House of Tranquillity sat at the heart of an expanse of gardens, pools and fountains, flowers they'd made shine like stars in the gloom of grottos. He'd dug, once. They put tablethi – the local octagonal oncs that looked so weird – in with the roots, so the flowers grew up magic. It seemed a great deal of waste, and he'd taken one as a souvenir, then lost it betting on taumachy. The flower had been dead the next time he'd been here, and he'd felt bad about it.

The air around the house was rainbows when the sun was out, which was about three-quarters of the year by his reckoning. The centre of Alkhalend, a stripe right down from the heights to the sea, was stepped waterfalls. Pouring down the cliff in paths shaped by rich people's architects to give the absolute grandest spectacle no matter where you stood. Running in little streams and channels and then falling again. Water dancing up from rocks and hazing the air with cooling mist. Water channelled into the covered bath houses of the upper city, where people met and gossiped and did not appreciate scruffy Pal boys peering in at them. By the time the boy reached the palace he was damp to the skin with spray, but that was how the locals liked it. It was a religious thing, with their frog of a god who lived in a big cave halfway up all these waterfalls. It was a practical thing, because Usmai was even hotter than Bracinta, which was the hottest place Kilbery had been before here.

His skulking had not sufficed to work out just where in the palace the fighting girl lived or what she did there. She entered and left through a shuttered window, up one wall where something like moss had grown hard as ivy to give her purchase. When her heels vanished in and she closed the shutter behind her, that was as far as his surveillance went.

It was wrong, this shadowing her. It made him uncomfortable and, if she'd known, it would have made her more so. He would, instead, catch up with her. Some time. Next time. Introduce himself – Kilbery, not Boy. He was a friend of her sword teacher. He was an important part of the Fever Lodge. She'd want to hear him talk about it, what they did there, what he did in the city. She'd be impressed. That universal scowl would unknot a little. She'd look at him and see someone. Someone real. Not just one more gutter urchin. Not just Boy. She'd see he was like her. Didn't live in a palace, obviously. But if she thought living in a palace was all *that*, she wouldn't be sneaking out to the Sand Lanes to learn how to kill people.

Anyway, maybe next time.

The boy – feeling very like a boy right then, not someone almost a man who had a name – sat by a pool and counted over the bottles and jars, making sure nothing had been cracked during his running and leaping. A couple of people came over to see what this nasty little piece of street shit could possibly mean, sitting here where proper people might see him. Palace servants who weren't quite guards or soldiers – fancy clothes but weapons too. He showed them the badge. The one with the fancy flower on it. They didn't like that he had it, but there was a brief note inscribed into the back of it, describing the kid he'd been just a year ago, and that was close enough to the almost-man he was now that it would stretch to fit. It didn't give his name. It just started '*This boy…*'

He sat there and knew that, in the end, he was just *this boy*. A menial courier for Oathan, his father, who wasn't either Oathan or his father. One more Sand Lanes brat running through life towards the knife or sword that would end him. Nothing to a girl who lived in a fancy house like this even if she was just the kid of the floor-polisher's assistant or something. He thought of those three Pal women, ghosting between high town and low like it didn't matter. And Pal women got stabbed too, as their visit showed, but they were free, and the fighting girl was free, and he was just *Boy*.

He was going to accomplish great things. He was nothing. He would show everyone just what he could do. Nobody would even see him. He was going to end up on a knife. He'd take the bastards with him.

All that water, falling in stages from the heights. It didn't matter how gloriously they shaped its course, or how it filled the air with rainbows. It all ended up in the sea. Some part of that flow decided it wanted to do something else with its brief time, it wouldn't matter.

Another functionary turned up and had to be shown his badge. One of the frog monks, who got everywhere and were a soft touch for a spare coin if you were short. Told him that Dolethi the poet was even now outside the baths, dressing and ready to go entertain the Alkhand with her latest verse. And not like they'd be letting Kilbery into the royal presence with his jars and glassware so he jumped to his feet, thanking the comfortable bulge of the monk's gut, even receiving a coin for his pains though he hadn't been begging. You could get all sorts from the palace, actually freely given, because people around here just had so much they didn't care.

Dolethi the poet was happy to see him, or happy to see the philtre Oathan brewed, that kept her throat sounding like silver when she declaimed her verses. And the Alkhand was blind, Kilbery had heard, so you had to have a perfect voice to keep your place amongst his favourites. After that it was the pompous man who told all the cleaning staff what to do, who prayed daily to Kakrops the frog god to cure his piles, but also paid good coin for the unguent that Oathan made; who never said thank you, and had to get somewhere nobody could see them before he took the jar and paid the money, because he was embarrassed. It was the enormous jolly monk who played a thing like a lot of metal tubes all in a row, that sounded like bells; who laughed like a whole crowd of people having a good time; who let Kilbery drink the sharp ramaht he always had a jug of, and told bawdy stories, and was dying. The stuff Oathan cooked up couldn't stop the thing that was doing it, but it took the edge away and let him laugh. It was that one guard whose leg had been broken years ago, and hurt like cold fire unless she took the potion Kilbery handed over; who had shown him a neat little twist of the wrist to get a knife out of someone's hand, and told him about when she'd fought a Louse Monk.

And then there was the Louse Monk.

Kilbery did her last. She scared him. But everyone was scared of them, so that was all right. They had some place off in the jungle, he understood, where there were even more of them and their horrible pets.

This particular Louse Monk's fighting days were done. She had one arm off at the shoulder, completely gone. Given their weapon of choice, that suggested to Kilbery she'd gone at it with another monk.

She kept the mews at the palace. It was a Louse Monk thing.

A Louse *Speaker* thing; their leaders, their elite. The horrible ones that had the horrible *thing* done to them. He'd asked around, and there were a thousand stories. Stories that didn't line up, which meant nobody really knew. The Louse Monks – Tesemer was their proper name – did things to their own, up in that place in the jungle. Their ways were not Usmiat ways. They'd come from somewhere else, from the Waygrove, like so much else that had helped make Usmai strong. Creatures from another world.

She was very tall and thin, with her head shaved down the middle. Most of the Tesemer looked at you like they'd have already killed you if you'd been worth the sweat. This one was different because she was in pain. Not the stump, which had healed over long before, but the arm. That was what Oathan had said. She still felt the arm that wasn't there, and it tormented her, because the arm, that second arm, told her she was still the woman she'd been.

She was at work when he called tentatively from the darkened entrance to the mews. Within, things rustled and skittered. They were not birds, that the Louse Monks flew.

A hiss and a click from within was the signal that he might enter safely. Her pets watched him with their great round eyes as he entered, tilting their triangle heads to follow his progress.

She had one on her single wrist, when he came in. It was just a hunched shape in the shadow at first, wings folded, head low. Two of its forelimbs were clutching some morsel that its fidgeting mouthparts chewed at. The other arms, the killing ones, folded and unfolded absently. The rest of its limbs moved it irritably from Teerasla's arm to its perch. It settled with its closed wing-cases to Kilbery, and he was glad of that.

He had seen one flown, once. Bringing her medicine out to the gardens, where she was holding a demonstration for some Luciat dignitaries. They'd released some birds, which had known exactly what was up and flurried away, desperate for freedom. Teerasla had clicked, mouth open so her tongue could speak. The creature had launched from her wrist, fast as baton-shot.

The first bird had just about exploded in the air, a detonation of feathers and torn flesh, nothing left for trophy or table. Then the creature had vaulted from the plummeting carcase, going for the other, getting above it and then diving. Impaling the desperate, fleeing bird with its killing arms. Spiralling down, preserving the kill. Windsaws, they called them, or that was how the Usmiat translated. The sight had made a powerful impression on Kilbery.

He thrust the packet of her medicine out to her. A sudden move. He hadn't meant to. She'd told him not to, when he was here.

The beast on the perch at her shoulder suddenly didn't have its back to him any more. And their eyes went all round their heads. They could always *see* you. It whirled round and its wings flashed out, the stark eye patterns screaming into his face, sparking a mad panic that had nothing rational about it. Its killing arms spread like twin knives.

Teerasla's head snapped about and she opened her mouth. He saw the tongue. Or what they'd put where her tongue had been. The segmented thing with its hook legs and button eyes. It clicked and hissed, and the windsaw subsided. Folded its wings and tried to pretend it hadn't really cared about Kilbery anyway.

He made a strained sound and held out the medicine again. She took it from him with long, sharp fingers. When she thanked him, he heard the faint scrape and click behind the words, as the thing that was her tongue made human noises.

He took the money. Nobody had shorted him. Nobody had paid in promises. Oathan would be happy. No, that wasn't true. Oathan wouldn't have that one extra excuse to shout at him and call him Boy.

Back in the Sand Lanes, his instructions were to go straight back to the Lodge. He went to a Taumachy den instead, because who was Oathan to tell him what to do? Not his father, that was for sure. Instead, he sat and watched a few fights, sitting at the edge of a loose court of street grandees: bruisers, gang enforcers, their men, their women; the kids that hung about trying to look tough and get noticed. Fortune tellers, rumourmongers, fixers and specialists. And the Boy – Kilbery, but most of them knew Oathan which made him the Boy – was an honorary in that last category, but maybe he wanted to get noticed. Maybe he didn't just want to be the Fever Lodge's errand runner.

Taumachy wasn't anything he'd seen in his army days. A local vice. The people who did it were called Beast Artists. They spent all day carving some special wood that came from up north. Making fantastical animal sculptures, setting them with cheap little gems, painting them angry colours. Then they fit a tableth in their mouths and the things came alive. Alive and as angry, so they would fight one another while everyone else cheered and drank and placed bets. Each school of Artists had its own colours and each Artist had a weird mishmash beast. Kilbery had found in himself a real love of watching briefly animated little wooden animals kick one another into splinters.

In between matches – and he'd lost some coin by then, which meant he'd have to pretend he was paid in favours, and some day Oathan was going to balance the books and things would get ugly – but in between matches he listened, and he talked. Talked about the Fever Lodge, mostly, because it was a den of dangerous and mysterious foreigners, a fixture in the Sand Lanes where half the gangs took people who got cut up within an inch of being dead. Kilbery milked its fame for all it was worth, because what other coin did he have that would actually buy anybody caring a damn about him? He told them about Oathan, the monster, the brute, who was running away from – well, the details varied whenever he told it, but he made sure it was bloody and murderous. He made up stories about how the Reckoner did what she did, and how many people Caecelian had killed in duels. They always wanted to hear about *her*, and that meant the boy was never tempted to talk about the palace girl. No room for her when the Viper loomed so large in every man's libido. Nobody wanted to talk about Happy Jack either, because he was just some simpleton who sat about feeding invisible birds. Instead, Kilbery talked about The Knife Witch of Jarokir, his own name for the old surgeon who actually ran the Fever Lodge. She, too, had a ferocious past, he was sure. She was the personal doctor to a great king, only she'd had an affair with the queen and cut the throat of her royal master, and so on and so on. And they lapped it up. He thought it was just because it was all weird and foreign and liberally coated with blood, never realising that, now he had got out from under his lying father's shadow, he was quite the inventive little liar himself.

And, when he wasn't talking or shouting on some red wooden crab as it dismantled a bright blue tiger, he listened. Heard the big men and women of the street as they talked over the concerns of the day. The expatriates, speaking in Pel to one another because it was the world's language. He spoke Pel, and had picked up Usmiri fast, so he heard it all.

The health of the Alkhand – he wasn't long for the world, people said. The end of the war – not that they had any brief for those Loruthi chisellers but the Pals were worse. Nobody even glanced at his Pal face. They talked of the exiled prince over in Mantekor; the Palleseen peacekeepers in Peor and what sort of peace *they* kept. News flowed through the Sand Lanes like the sea at high tide. The elevated denizens of the upper city wouldn't have believed how well informed their lessers were, but then to have wealth was to be insulated from the knocks of the world. Every one of these concerns was a stack of charged tablethi, and if someone spoke the word and set the business off, it would be the people of the Sand Lanes who felt it. The shortages, the hunger, the unrest. Half of them were shoring up their defences right now, and the other half were sharpening their knives and calling it opportunity.

A hand came to rest on Kilbery's shoulder, eclipsing it with at least two fingers to spare. A man sat down companionably beside him, meaning three other people had to scramble to make space. Kilbery's sidelong look caught a bared chest covered with a dense weave of tattoos, a necklace of fish teeth, a ferociously jutting chin. The rest of the man's head was too far up to see without seriously craning his neck.

"The Lodge's boy," said the man, in accent-twisted Usmiri. It was a moment before Kilbery understood, but then he nodded because if this enormous slab of muscle wanted to call him boy he wasn't going to argue.

"The woman stabbed came to you."

He wasn't sure if it was meant as a question or not, but then there was a gap, and the hand tightened on his shoulder.

"The Pal woman," he said hurriedly. And she had been stabbed, although if this man had done it, it must have been an exceedingly glancing blow. He imagined that if the big man really put a knife in someone with all his strength then his victim would just explode, like the bird caught by the windsaw.

"Lived?" Definitely a question.

"Yes." And he would have predicted that meant the Pal woman was going to have an exciting repeat appointment with a short blade, but it was good news, apparently. The man bent, showing a cheek and brow inked with intricate scenes of sharks and squid and other sea things devouring drowned corpses. A piece of work so startling in both its workmanship and subject matter that Kilbery just stared. It was terrifying. It was horrible. He wanted one of his own.

"Your master for to have," the man said and pressed three coins and something angular into Kilbery's hand. Good coins, more than he'd just lost in bets. The other thing was a scrimshawed shark curved into a ring. It would, Kilbery thought hopelessly, be a magnificent gift for, say, a girl who was a servant's child at the palace.

Behind the big tattooed man were two big tattooed friends, a man and a woman. The woman grinned at him with sharp teeth.

They were the Cotto, he knew. Coast-traders and sea-raiders and generally just a part of how the lower reaches of Usmiat trade worked out. They weren't of Usmai, didn't hold to the same customs, got murderously angry about different things.

Maybe about being questioned by lanky Pal kids, but he had to ask. "What is she to you?"

The man opened his mouth, frowned massively, then tried out a short word on his friends.

"Niece," said one, and "Cousin," said the woman with the sharp teeth.

"Niece-cousin to us," said the big man. "Very far distant but in the sea blood smells blood, you know this?"

And apparently not a question, even though it had been given the tilt of one. The man clapped him on the shoulder and stood up. At the very edge of Kilbery's hearing there was a name being whispered. *Orhuhst*. A Cotto name. *Hullseer Orhuhst*. The king of the smugglers and pirates, and of the sea in general, if you believed some stories. Not someone who just strolled into a random Taumachy den and handed out coins to kids.

After Hullseer Orhuhst and his friends had gone, obviously everyone wanted to know what the story was before the next two Artists came out with their carvings. Suddenly Kilbery – Boy? Who'd call such a grandee of the streets just 'Boy'? – was everyone's friend. And he didn't know. He had absolutely no idea what the link was, between the Lodge and the Pal woman who'd been stabbed and the Cotto, of fearsome reputation. Between those three things was just a void where rational speculation went to die.

That did not stop him making something up, of course. Just spinning the cloth of it from threads of air and embroidering it with the fool's gold of fancy. And he was very late when he finally got back to the Lodge and Oathan – not his father – shouted at him, and he didn't really care.

The Day of Milk and Flowers

The old Moeribandi Empire didn't care what other gods you had so long as you gave their death cult pre-eminence, and accepted the divinity of their cadaverous Imperial family. All those states within its bony grip held onto their local divinities: the beast gods, the weather and crop gods. Reworking their myths to explain why, despite those reverences, some old clan of necromancers held the keys to the gates of the afterlife. When the Empire's fascination with the end of things engineered its own decline and retreat into the tomb, its priesthood remained alongside all those local god cults with their holy days and rites and sacrifices, traditions as intertwined as vines.

In the dining room of the Residence, an Usmiat woman brought out breakfast. It was a kind of yellow rubbery froth with green bits in it, and white bits, and indeed red bits. Loret stared at it without appetite.

"What's this?" she asked. And then, "Magister?" She was still tender. She wasn't actually *hurt* because, between them, the old surgeon and the Reckoner at the Fever Lodge knew their business. Getting stabbed lodged a blade in the mind as well as the flesh, though. It was three days, and she still flinched from a pain she knew she'd earned but didn't carry. And that wasn't counting the other times, from before she pitched up on Usmai's shores. Loret, young, not yet twenty, had lived through what sometimes felt like a hundred years of knives in the mind.

Gil had kept her in the Residence, and to light duties. There was a room full of correspondence to read, petitions from Pal expats in Alkhalend, from merchants overseas, from other luminaries of Outreach across the Successor States.

She was improvising. She didn't really know what to do with any of it. She was sharp enough to summarise for her new employer, but she could feel a great untended void of duties beneath her feet, waiting to swallow her.

"It's eggs," Gil said, and ate some. Drathel apparently also recognised the repast and had tucked in already.

"Eggs are round," Loret said uncertainly. Round and white and small, and subtly different in flavour depending on which seabird laid them.

"Eggs and fish," Drathel added. "And spices. And… knucklebug?"

"Hatchling knucklebug," said Gil, two words that, in conjunction, Loret didn't know what to do with. She tried it. Mostly pepper on the tongue and not bad. And fish was always welcome. Grow up on the Archipelago, fish was your go-to.

"It's peasant food," Drathel noted, with an enthusiastically full mouth. "Not fit for a Sage-Invigilator, surely."

"Tradition," Gil told her. "It's the—"

"Oh." Drathel's eyes went wide. "Oh shit. It isn't, is it? Only I saw the… But today?" Delighted.

Loret looked from one to the other blankly.

"I'm going to need you to dig out my uniform," Gil said to her. The Resident was wearing a short sleeveless robe and a dampened shawl over bare shoulders. Loret, in shirtsleeves and already too hot even at breakfast, hadn't tried the local thing of flicking scented water over her clothes yet. The idea of full uniform seemed murderous. "Get one for Drathel too. She's smaller than me but not too much."

"Actually," Drathel said around the eggs, "I was going to—"

"You weren't," Gil said. The conversation tripped and fell on its face in the eggs. Drathel kept eating but her eyebrows went up.

"You don't get to swan off with a note in your pocket like you were caught playing truant from phal," Gil told her. "You are my *guest* until I can work out who to hand you back to, and then I'm going with you for the handover so I can have words. In the interim, it's festival. Enjoy Alkhalend. But skip out on me and every Inquirer from here to Moeriband will have your description on their desk."

"Festival," said Drathel. "Hooray. Just if we can get things moving after 'cos I've got business."

Gil's look was very judgy about what business Drathel might have, and the woman – the tomb-robber, honestly – didn't push it.

"Festival?" Loret asked. One more thing that would have been in that brief.

"The Day of Milk and Flowers," said Gil fondly.

"And the night," Drathel added, and the two women – they'd been in the region a while, after all – shared an almost conspiratorial look. And nobody actually explained anything to Loret.

"Lay out the clothes. Get yourself in your best," Gil told her. "We're going to see a man about a frog."

Midmorning saw them standing amidst the pools, the roar of the waterfall their backdrop, the air shimmering with spray as though all the dragonflies in the world had congregated for the festival. And the day before, Loret had gone on an errand through the better streets of the city and seen people hanging strings of flowers everywhere, real ones and cloth ones. She hadn't really registered it against the whole foreign strangeness of everything else. Not just a regular custom, apparently. Now everywhere she looked there were garlands of blooms. There was music – lyres and pipes and women singing high and wailing and wild in a way that made her heart speed without telling her brain why. And there were a whole load of richly-dressed Usmai at these pools, halfway up and halfway down the chain of waterfalls, where the big cave was. Looking back, she saw the city, the whole city and then the sea, spread out under Usmai's resplendent sun, shimmering with heat and misted water, gorgeous with flowers even on the boats at dock, even on the piled shacks of the Sand Lanes. There was more music down there, drifting on the breeze, working around the roar of the falls like gold edging on a heavy robe. The music was high and shrill, so that the sound of the water could pass underneath it.

She recognised the Alkhand, the old man with the stone eyes, when he processed down the path from the palace. The whole court was with him, a convocation of peacocks in their brightest regalia, glittering with jewels and water droplets. She saw the man, Gil's friend, the prince-elect, at his father's elbow, but the Alkhand didn't need to see to find his way. Doing this for decades, presumably. The duty had recalled a youth to him, as though he was borrowing from his memories of years gone by. There was a garden, beside the still pools, and Loret saw… a grave? A small grave, child-sized, with a couple of spade-toting palace servants standing by. Loret's innards twisted. Bad things, surely. Foreign things, like they warn you about in the phal. Sacrifices of infants to ensure…

"Is this," she whispered to Gil, "a fertility thing. Of the fields?" Picturing some poor kid dolled up and dragged out, the votive rites of terrible foreign gods.

"Yes," said Gil, and then, "No, not this bit. Later though."

They were in full uniform, and Gil's with every piece of Sage-rank tinsel she was entitled to wear. Without the constant sheeting mist it would be unbearably hot. Even with it, Loret was uncomfortably aware of the sweat pooling everywhere it could. Gil, despite dressing like a local every other day, wore the Pal clothes with a crisp formality that Loret never could. Loret looked like a trooper shorted by the quartermasters, honestly. A bit shabby, the clothes ill-tailored, too tight here, too long there. At least she didn't slouch like Drathel.

There was a play then. Or at least a little bit where some people in bright costumes came out and pretended to have a fight, and then someone else, one of the fat, jolly monks wearing a round goggling mask, came and told them to go away. There wasn't much speaking and it wasn't in Usmiri so she had no idea what it was about. Then an old bald man brought forward… skulls? Orange skulls. No, three stoppered clay jars, but shaped like skulls. With great ceremony the Alkhand's heir, Dekamran, lowered them into the hole, and the men with spades filled it in. The old bald man – he looked like the prison monks but painted up even more like a corpse – said something in that same non-Usmiri. The Alkhand said something in response, voice lifted high with a strength Loret wouldn't have credited. Something loaded with portent and significance, if she only understood a word of it. The blind man stepped forwards and ground his foot in the loose earth, spat upon it. Everyone cheered and the musicians went mad with some paean of approval.

"What is even going on?" Loret murmured.

"Demons," Drathel said, across the back of Gil's neck.

"What?"

"In the jars."

"What?" And she should have 'magister'-ed Drathel, if the woman was a Fellow, but that rebellious schoolgirl act didn't encourage it.

"Not actual demons." Leaning all the way past Gil to get the words to her. "It's about the Moeribandi Emperor defeating the Janni Despotate and banishing all the demons, you know?"

Loret had literally no idea about any of this.

"In the old days those would have been real skulls, and they'd have demons bound into them with the sort of wards we saw on the prison door, heavy duty stuff, and the skulls would have been the skulls of whoever was dumb enough to let people find out they were conjuring demons. And sometimes that still happens, but most years nobody's been going around admitting to conjuring demons – can't imagine why – so it's just some empty jars and the look of it. But this is just the first course. This is the dull bit. Now—" And then Gil dug her in the side and Drathel went back to slouching to attention, rather than slouching informatively.

The whole celebration about burying some pots in a garden – surrogate demons, apparently – was winding down. There were dancers making their way through the crowd with more garlands. Loret had one draped over her neck by a young woman who looked at her in a way that went beyond mere diplomatic relations. And she'd been feeling over-hot already.

"What?" she asked faintly.

The sour-looking bald monk with the brief against demons retreated, and now the jolly monks were out in force. Bare chested or with barely restrained breasts, sopping robes trailing in the water, they joined in the dance, they played little trumpets. To Loret, stifling in her uniform, it was starting to feel like some feverish dream, like the eggs had been spiked with something. The broadest and jolliest of all possible monks was now standing by the cave. He was shouting something, swigging from a gourd and looking three sheets gone already. Then a marginally narrower monk took it, drank and passed it along, and instead the enormous, enormously jolly monk had a little gong. Everyone loved the little gong. People cheered it like it was paying off their loans and giving out candies. Loret swayed, and Gil discreetly gripped her arm to steady her. Drathel had already undone half the buttons on her borrowed jacket and to hell with protocol.

"What?" Loret asked of the world. And then, "Oh shit, it's a frog."

The cave beside the waterfall. Its edge was carved with intricate scenes of fish and salamanders, waterweed and swimming men and women. Some of whom were doing other things while swimming. There was a lot to take in, in that carving, none of which would be permitted in any kind of Palleseen public space. The cave was also huge, more than twice the height of a tall man, but what came out of it still had to squeeze to fit.

It was, as advertised, a frog. The biggest frog in the world. A vast downturned mouth that somehow avoided any impression of ill humour; goggling golden eyes under warty, pointed brows. A hide of green and yellow and dark stripes, and she wasn't sure what was frog and what was painting. They'd hung it with garlands, although its progress through the arch dislodged most of them. A frog the size of a house. A frog that could swallow a horse with a single gulp; that could most certainly swallow Loret. She stared at it. If it had a tongue to flick, then she and everyone else were in range of its strike.

The frog regarded them sagely. One bulbous eye blinked, and then the other. The old man, the Alkhand, walked towards it, and for a moment Loret almost leaped forwards to stop him. He was blind. He couldn't know the danger.

He put a hand out. Dekamran helped him the extra step he needed, so that he could touch the poison-bright hide of the frog. Loret shuddered, but everyone around her cheered and the musicians played something enormously upbeat.

The frog opened its mouth. It did not swallow the Alkhand, but let out a booming croak that shouldered the sound of the waterfall aside. To the old man and his son it must have been deafening. In the next instant, Loret realised that everyone had really been holding back, because the croak was the signal for the serious party to get underway. Everyone was dancing. Someone, just some random Usrani monk, grabbed her away from Gil's side and spun her round, grinning into her face. Kissed the palm of her hand with lips still sticky from whatever was in that gourd and then whirled off.

"What?" Loret demanded, almost shouting over the sound of everyone else's frog-related rejoicing.

"The Day of Milk and Flowers!" Drathel shouted in her ear, linking elbows with her.

"You say that like it means something!" Loret complained.

They found somewhere quieter, the three Pal women. A set of neighbouring pools not quite conquered by the dancing. Gil's jacket was undone and slung over her shoulders so Loret shrugged her own off gratefully and tied it about her waist.

"I," said Gil, "am now going back to the Residence, because despite all this pageantry there is a lot of paperwork to do, and if everyone else is having a good time, that means I can get things done without being interrupted. Drathel—"

"Oh I've been in town for this before. Only glad I'm not seeing it from the wrong side of the bars." *Or the wrong end of a knife*, was what went unsaid but acknowledged. "You're going to trust me to come back, are you?"

Gil smiled, without the mandatory festival joy. "You're a Decanter. Go wandering all you like, you need to come back to the machinery of the Sway to offload what you scrounge up. So yes, you will, because otherwise this will become a hard country for you to do business in. Understood, Fellow-Archivist?"

"Understood, magister." And Drathel grinned, despite having just had her knuckles rapped, because apparently the Day of Milk and Flowers was consolation enough for having a leash.

Loret was one breath into asking where that left her when Gil pressed a purse into her hand.

"What you just saw," the Resident said, "is, obviously, the rankest piece of superstition and foolishness, exactly the sort of thing that perfection will do away with in the fullness of time. When Usmai is brought into the Sway and properly governed, so that things like the harvest yield can rely on rational techniques and not the blessings of basically a big frog."

"The frog," said Loret uncertainly.

"The frog is Kakrops. Patron deity of Usmai. Always has been. Built the city around his cave, the way they tell it. And obviously *we* don't approve of any gods, but Kakrops basically sleeps in his pool most of the time these days. Gets offerings, comes out on special occasions, blesses the land. You've seen his monks all over the city panhandling the rich and giving handouts to the poor. It's just the way things work around here." A brief hard look then, of a woman who'd been posted all over the Sway and seen a great many things. "There are worse gods and traditions, believe me."

And Loret, who had seen her own share of god-related malarkey, and what the Pals did when they cracked down on it, nodded.

"What do I need to get for you?" she asked, looking at the purse. "You have a list, magister?"

"Loret," said Gil. "Have fun. It's the Day of Milk and Flowers."

"People keep saying that."

"Okay, look." Gil actually looked slightly awkward, as though she was a teacher at the phal about to explain certain essential truths to a class of pubescent orphans. Which, in a way, was exactly what's going on here. "The Usmiat are really weird about some stuff. Has to be behind closed doors at all times. You even suggest that someone and someone else are having a fling, you can get called out to cross swords over it. Not that they don't *have* flings, just that the secrecy is all. You don't so much as hold hands in public. You don't name names. Or, I mean, they do all the time, but when they do it's politics and intrigue and people literally get killed over it."

Loret stared at her blankly.

"Except today," Gil said. "And tonight. When all that's off and just... go have fun, basically. With anyone you like. Or nobody. Or multiple people. So long as everyone's into it. The land is bountiful, the people rejoice."

"Wait," Loret said. "It's a sex thing?"

"It's called the Day of Milk and Flowers. Didn't you think?" Gil actually laughed at her. "Don't worry, they don't go at it in the street or anything. But it's a day when, theoretically, anyone can proposition anyone, and anyone can say no, but nobody gets to disapprove of the asking. It's... harmless enough, as these things go. Nobody getting their heart cut out. I count that as a win, where religion's concerned."

"Um." Loret wasn't sure what she thought.

"Take the money. There will be drinks and music, street theatre, that thing they do where the little statues fight, you've seen that? You should see that. And people are going to tug at your sleeve and make you offers, but they'll also go away if you say no, because Kakrops is very down on anyone not having a good time in his name. He doesn't curse much, but you do *not* want to go against the spirit of things today. So nobody's going to push you, on pain of frog. Just take in the city and enjoy yourself. I don't want to see you back at the Residence until at least nightfall. Preferably not even then."

And then, before Loret could marshal the host of objections she had – both personal and on behalf of the entire Palleseen Sway, Gil just swanned off into the crowd and she was left alone.

Mosaic: The Night of Milk and Flowers

The voice of Kakrops echoes out across the city of Alkhalend. Granting its inherent permission to transgress. To test waters otherwise forbidden; to ask, where asking would be unthinkable; to slip outside the bonds of matrimony that the Usmiat otherwise hold as sacrosanct. High city and low, and a surprising amount of interchange between the two.

There are dried-up oases of non-observance. The Moerends, the death monks, celibate by oath, and joyless by dogma, wrinkle their noses at all this frog-mandated debauchery going on behind every closed door in the city. The music and the exchange of tokens and the clasped hands in every square. It all feels a bit too much like *life* to the death monks.

And where the city's various expatriate communities have established themselves, there are those who feel it's all a bit *foreign* for them. A bit *not the way we do things*. Close the shutters and bar the doors and wait until tomorrow. Although that kind of stuffiness tends to erode away when you see the rest of the city having a good time. Plus the Day of Milk and Flowers is actually a good chance to make business contacts and friends in those parts of the city your own station usually precludes you from accessing. It's not all about sex.

★

Up near the palace, Kilbery, Oathan's boy, bites at his lip and turns the shark ring over and over in his hand. Possibly he was supposed to give it to Oathan, or maybe to Loret, but the Cotto gave it to him, which means it's his, in his book. And if it's his he could give it to someone, just like there are people all over the city coyly giving over little tokens like that, as a way of saying, *Will you…?* And the boy is fifteen. He's a man. He's absolutely entitled to go do exactly that. He even has the writ to get into the palace, although he has nothing to deliver. He could go to the servants' quarters and find the girl and give her the ring and… and maybe just that. Maybe that's all he needs to do, to make himself a pin in the map of her world. A place she might want to visit later.

It won't be this year, though. Kilbery hovers at the outskirts until his nerve finally snaps under the strain. He heads back for the riotous streets of the Sand Lanes with the ring still in his pocket.

In her chambers, Enshili, the princess, has no idea that some nobody boy from the Sand Lanes thinks she's the floor-polisher's assistant's daughter, let alone that he wants to give her a ring that was supposed to go to his father. She is nineteen – about a thousand years older than Kilbery – and has had her own string of tokens and offers and insinuations from a variety of well-placed courtiers hoping for advancement. She has taken the tokens and turned down the insinuations. Sometimes graciously but mostly so they can see her surly derision, because that's what Caecelian taught her. *If they show you an opening, put the knife in. Sometimes the only power we have is to hurt people.*

Behind closed doors, her scowl is momentarily banished. If Kilbery saw her like this, with that look on her face, his heart would break for longing.

A simple wooden box, brought to her by a servant who owes the Lodge for a wasting disease cured. Tied with a black ribbon. Within it: a mask. A hideous mask, fangs and horns and too many eyes. The work of one of the Beast Artists of the Sand Lanes, taking a day off from making miniature combatants. A demon mask. Not the same as Caecelian's, but a companion piece. A gift, teacher to student, in recognition of lessons well learned.

Enshili, whose future is absolutely to be married to someone politically convenient, does not care about Kakrops's joy or casual liaisons. She cares about freedom and that is what the mask, and the gift of the mask, mean.

Elsewhere in the palace, the Alkhand sets down the skull of Sorthist, his brother, and retires to his chamber. There, Dolethi the poet recites him a verse filled with ambiguous allusions and entendres. Speaks of all things save the union of bodies and, through that means, speaks only of that. Her own proffered token. Because he is Alkhand, and because she is his favourite but wishes to remain so, and because a great deal of what goes on during the Day of Milk and Flowers, and its night, is to do with securing future favour.

The Alkhand Oparan mourns his wife, who left him for the monks of the Waygrove and their masks. The weight of her absence destroys him, day to day. But not today. Today a god has given him permission to set that misery aside. As the land rejoices, so should its ruler. Today the skull and the sadness confine themselves to a further chamber and he listens to the verses, the honey tones of a professional speaker of beauty, and lets himself know joy.

⋆

Loret, then. A stranger in the city, only here a few days and she's already been stabbed and then unstabbed, seen a chaos of tormented ghosts and a ghastly centipede monster and a frog the size of a house. It's all been a bit much.

She drinks. She wonders if she should go find the Cotto, the pirates, but she's sensibly wary of them. They're not local. She doesn't know if they're part of this whole frog thing or if their devotions are of a very different character. And she doesn't know how their course intersects her own. She's wary of what they see, looking at her. Why they helped her out. What they *know*. Instead she watches acrobats, listens to music, sits out in the sun and swelters, her uniform cap shading her eyes, until a random passing monk upends a jug of perfumed water over her shirt. She leaps up and squawks at him, but she's cooler for it.

Then there's a woman. An Usmiat woman. Sitting there next to her, a bit drunk, talking as though they're acquainted. A look, under the eyelashes, around the curve of the cheek, assaying, flirty.

She can, Loret realises. It's not permitted, obviously, by the Palleseen ordinances. Not merely fraternising with the locals, which is simultaneously banned and goes on everywhere Pal troops are stationed. But fraternising with the locals as part of a religious rite is obviously right out. It's exactly the sort of thing the Palleseen Sway is erasing from the world.

But the frog god, and the drinks, and all of it, they're weights on the other arm of the scales. And it will mean nothing. No cords binding her, no complications. She and the Usmiat woman watch the dancers whirl, and who knows what might happen next?

Whatever might or might not happen, some of the blades lodged in her mind are gone by morning. Just a few of the many. A little pain eased, the little healings that can be achieved via the blessings of frogs.

*

In the Palleseen Residence, Gil is indeed attending to the paperwork. She's changed out of the straitjacket of her uniform, but the pen and the paper and the words are all Palleseen. Tedious but necessary stuff. Loret should be doing it, really, but what sort of a cruel employer would she be, to keep her aide slaving over a desk today?

Amongst other reasons for wanting the girl out of the Residence.

When he arrives, it's later than she expects. She was beginning to think he might not. He's an important man now, no longer in the shadow of his brother. He'll have had plenty of offers.

But here he is, after all. Wearing the simple clothes of a simple man. Dekamran, heir to the Mirror Throne. Even though this is a day where all bets are off, for liaisons, this is surely forbidden. To her, if not to him. The Palleseen Sway is not bound by the edicts of the frog god, and does *not* approve. There are diplomatic boundaries that must not under any circumstances be crossed.

That have never, before now, been crossed.

Fastidiously, she closes her inkwell and blows a little on the paper to dry it. She stands, her mouth full of objections.

They never did. Seven years in her post here. They never did. This day came and went and there was always a reason. Because, tradition bedamned, people talk. Because it would be ammunition for the adherents of Gorbudan to use, to sully Dekamran's name. Or because the war was on and it would let Tarcomir and the Loruthi undermine her position. Some reason or other, why they never did. Reasons that time has washed away into the sea.

"Really, Kam?" she asks him. "All the beauties of the palace. All those musicians and dancers and contortionists showing off for you, and you end up here. It's a bit miserable, isn't it?"

He produces a bottle of sharp ramaht, the good stuff, and pours two libations into bone cups. All very deftly done without taking his eyes off her. He doesn't have the classic Usmiat good looks, that are rakish and dashing. That was Gorbudan, the elder, the hero. Dekamran is soft around the edges, his beard not quite hiding that he has at least one and a half chins; the nose, that on his brother is fierce and raptorial, maybe just a little too big on him. But he smiles like the sun, and Gorbudan never really smiled at all. Bared his teeth, but not smiling.

"I am a great disappointment to my people and my family," he says, and they both raise a cup and sample the vintage, which is very sharp indeed. "I have seen the beauties of the palace, Gil. Every day I see them."

"And if I have all this paperwork to do, and can't possibly tear myself away from it?"

"Then I will go sit somewhere and compose mournful verses about how forlorn are they who pine. And the verses will be very bad, for you know I am no poet."

"You make it sound like a positive duty to the world, to stop that happening." And she feels… breathless. As though that Pal uniform was still clenched about her chest, holding her in. Seven years. Seven years of knowing this man and becoming aware of his qualities. Dekamran crossing swords with her, in the woman's style no less, when nobody else would. Drinking with her while Gorbudan and Tarcomir rode high in fortune's favour and divided the world between them. Being her ally, when the Palleseen cause in Usmai was lost, and no other in the palace would so much as spare her a look that wasn't a scowl. Coming incognito to the Residence on the evening when she was to fight and kill Tarcomir, her enemy, her friend. She feels, abruptly, as though she's a girl in senior phal, sneaking out with a boy for the first time. Ridiculous.

She drinks, rattles the cup on the desk until he refills it, just as though they're old comrades in the mess tent. And why go to such lengths to banish Loret from her presence, if she isn't going to say *Yes* at last?

She meets Dekamran's gaze, the prince, the heir, the man who could do so much better, and says it.

★

The night is passing, the city no quieter. Over in the Sand Lanes, Happy Jack has finished feeding the non-existent birds and gone inside. Elsewhere, the other luminaries of the Fever Lodge are reacting to the Day of Milk and Flowers each to their own. Oathan has gone to a brothel, he knows, because the man will *not* consent to any kind of communion that doesn't come with a price tag. The old surgeon, the Jarokiri woman, has retreated to her rooms with a bottle and her memories of an old man who died. The Reckoner has gone out into the streets, drink and sweet honeycakes and a man or a woman or both. Because she was someone who never permitted herself anything, once. They broke that, in her, and now she is rediscovering how to enjoy herself.

Jack cooks. There's precious little that Oathan, the alchemist, can't teach you about preparing a meal. Jack cooks, and waits to see if he'll be eating alone.

She turns up at last. Just as the food's almost too cool to eat. Not that she eats, but it's the show of it. His own token. The Viper, Caecelian – as with all of them, not her real name, but he's never known her real name.

"I'd thought you might, you know..." he says. It's been known. It would have hurt him, taken a lot of the Happy out of Jack. But it's part of their deal. That hurt he felt would have been a love token too. She's broken, that way. It's how she was made, the small print of her.

"I had offers." She sits down across the table, smooth as temptation, grinning at him. "I have a bag stuffed with rings and pendants, love poems and perfumes."

"And?" Jack asks her.

"And they will await me in vain, and I will feast on their tears," she tells him. And it's a horrible thing to say, really. Especially as it's true. But he knew what she was, from the start. And because of that, because he alone sees her for what she is, she has come back to him.

In the early hours of morning, before the sun can stir, Gil sees Dekamran out of that same side door. Because tomorrow is just a regular day, and he must be gone before there are complications.

She has done something bad, she knows. Local customs don't carry much weight with the Commission of Ends and Means that governs Pallesand. Probably she can twist the wording of a report to make it sound like some masterplan to extend Palleseen influence across Usmai, to control the man who will be Alkhand. It's not a report she wants to write. To commit such thoughts to words would go some way towards making them true, and that's not how she wants it to be, between her and him. She wants an Alkhand who is a friend to Pallesand, obviously, and in that she's doing her job. She wants Dekamran as *her* friend, though, and keeping both of those ambitions intact is a very fine needle to thread indeed.

When she returns to Slate House's dining room, Drathel is there at the table. Not actually with her boots up on it, although her manner very definitely admits to the possibility.

The Decanter just raises her eyebrows, smiles amiably. And who knows what licensed depravities Drathel has been up to, yesterday and last night? No end of trouble she might have gotten herself into and probably some of the local temples need to count the spoons. And the tomb-robber walked boldly in through the front while the heir to the throne was creeping through the side door like a thief. Probably she knows nothing, and that smile is mere greeting and not leverage.

The Louse Speakers

Much of Usmai is forested. Much of Usmiri, the language, references this in etymology and figures of speech. Such as the Alborandi, those who belong to the trees, the monks who tend the Grove. But their word for the Grove itself is something apart. It is long, awkward to say, as though giving speakers a chance to reconsider talking about the topic at all. It is a word from elsewhere, just like everything else from that quarter. Those Pals who know of it have named it the Waygrove in Pel. Just a stand of trees, unless and until it becomes a gateway to everywhere and forever.

"Monsters," Loret said, "riding monsters."

She probably thought that she was saying it too quietly for their mahout to hear, or else that the creature did not speak Pel. Neither were guaranteed, and an Ibaleth had no readily interpretable body language to human eyes. They were very still until they moved, when they could be very quick.

The three of them – Gil, Loret and Drathel – were in the same howdah, the fourth of five in the procession. On either side, past the swaying walls, the dense jungles of Usmai reached up, closed in, overhung, mottling the sunlight with green. Pal eyes saw an impenetrable waste of land-use, but the local villagers would be through those trees every day, picking what was in season, cultivating, tending. To the right eyes, it was not a natural landscape. There were wilder places, further north. Two days out from Alkhalend, though, this was all cupped within human hands.

Behind them, the end beast of the caravan was carrying supplies and guards in relatively equal quantities, as was the lead monster. The Alkhand and Dekamran rode in the second with courtiers – Gil could hear the faint murmur of strings and song from there, one of the old man's favourites entertaining them. The third was full of functionaries and servants. The three Pals rattled about in the fourth like peas in a whistle.

Each howdah was borne by a monstrous beast, scale-hided, shield-headed, moving with a ponderous inevitability along paths that their passage alone kept clear. Ogrodons, the Usmiat called them, and their handlers were the Ibaleth, who had come from the Grove. And while the blades of the Tesemer monks were swift and sharp, it was surely these ponderous behemoths that were the armoured fist of Usmai, when it came to keeping its place amongst the states of the coast. Gil had heard that more than a few of the creatures ended up on the Loruthi side during the war. The Pal reports of their battlefield presence made for quite some reading.

Perhaps they'll lend them to us, next time round. A howdah swaying along at roof height, on the back of an invincible armoured monster with a trio of enormous ramming horns, bristling with disciplined Pal batons. Definitely something to chalk up on the 'tactical advantages' side of the slate.

Of course, that would mean coming to terms with the Ibaleth as well, and it wasn't as though you could fit them into an Accessory's uniform.

They were lizards. And when she'd read the brief, seven years back on the boat to Usmai, she'd pictured people with scaly skins. Or else people with reptile heads, the way some cults drew their gods. But the Ibaleth were lizards. Their mahout was perhaps four feet, nose to haunches, and another six feet of whip-like tail. She – apparently they were mostly *she* unless they turned into *he* – had enormous golden eyes, and was draped up the front wall of the howdah like a mascot, sunning herself, almost entirely motionless. Her hide was green-brown, with red and bronze designs painted down her flanks and on the flat top of her snout. Nothing like Usmiat iconography, some unique alphabet or art of their own. The one non-lizard thing about her was her hands, double-thumbed and dextrous, with which she held a goad. There was a baton hung beside her, too, one of the long and ornate pieces the Usmiat made, that were such beautiful examples of the craft. Apparently the Ibaleth were not just expert monster-handlers but also crack shots when they needed to be. Those eyes never blinked, the Usmiat said.

They lived all along the river above the city, in a warren of mounds and holes that was their own place, no humans welcome. They had their eggs there, and a very big lizard queen the Usmiat called Kass, their best approximation of the sound the Ibaleth named her with. The lizard-language was a lot of hissing and some throaty gobbling noises, none of which was really available to a human vocal repertoire. Having been resident for centuries, they understood Usmiri and probably other languages, and they could write replies in deft, elegant characters.

Loret, the newcomer, had been given a good chance to see the Ibaleth the day before, because it was time for the Alkhand to renew Usmai's treaties. The days after the Festival of Milk and Flowers were given over to that, a ceremonial shaking of hands with the nation's strangest allies. The *things* that had come from the Waygrove, over the years, and been incorporated into the Usmiat world. Yesterday the Alkhand had sat on a rug by the riverbank and the Ibaleth Queen Kass had slithered out of the water to pay homage and gift him pearls and a carved ogrodon horn: wealth and the promise of military service. In return he had offered fish and a handful of muddy earth: food and land. Then the Ibaleth had brought up five massive stomping ogrodons, and shot off a lot of batons into the air, to Loret's alarm, displaying bright-coloured bellies and whipping their tails around. The Alkhand and his retinue had embarked on the beasts for the next leg of the journey, leaving the Ibaleth to get busy.

"To get what?" Loret had asked. The Day of Milk and Flowers hadn't taken the edges off her Pal prudishness, Gil noted.

"Eggs, kid," Drathel explained. "They don't lay eggs this year until the Alkhand has confirmed they're good to stay."

"But you said they'd been here for centuries..." Loret frowned. And then seemed to come to some understanding, because maybe she'd lived somewhere you could never be quite sure of the neighbours. Gil had been trying to get a sense of Loret, who she really was, the contradictions of her. A while since she'd had to cold read someone to quite that extent, but the tradecraft never quite left you.

"So, Loret," she gestured for the girl to join her at the rail, looking out at the trees, then had to scrabble to stop going over because the ogrodon chose that moment to lurch sideways.

"It's like being on a ship in a storm, isn't it?" Drathel was at the back, looking past the rearmost beast back the way they'd come.

"No," said Loret. In fact she seemed to have the rock and sway of the beast mastered. One more odd little quirk.

Gil had tried to quiz Loret already, of course. Received precisely as much information as there was in the assignment papers the girl had handed over. And she didn't want to end up in that awkward 'So why do you want to be in Outreach?' territory, as though she was visiting a phal and trying to get the students interested in a career in the diplomatic service. And yet the girl really *didn't* seem to be keen, and surely the department wasn't so short of volunteers.

And the stabbing. Not exactly that Loret had been *good* at the stabbing, but with enough vim and speed, you didn't actually need to be good. Stab someone a dozen times, one of them would take. And Loret had got a good dozen in, within the space of about three seconds.

They had a long journey, just the three of them and the mahout, and it wasn't as though the lizard would be telling anyone her life story. Time to pin down Loret.

She opened her mouth, questions mustering in her throat like ill-trained soldiers, getting in one another's way. Because her mind hadn't been on it. She hadn't done the prep expected of her, unforgivable at her rank. Other things had been demanding her attention.

"Why'd you pick this dull lot, anyway, kid?" Drathel did the job instead. "Paperwork and dancing around foreigners in big hats. I mean, I guess it's a *career*." Spoken as though a good post in the Palleseen Sway was very much what you did if you couldn't get anything better.

"Don't poach my aide, please," Gil said mildly.

Drathel grinned at her. "I'm just saying, if you don't want her I'm sure we can use her over the border. A good knife hand and a bit of initiative."

Loret winced, obviously wanting to disavow either. And Drathel visibly saw the wince and began salivating at the chance to torment the kid all the way to where they were going. Gil put aside the personal knot that had been occupying her and decided she was going to be professional after all.

"I found the brief I got sent by Palinet, in Peor," she said, apropos of nothing.

"Good for you," Drathel told her sunnily.

"The Halberandi monks, the ones you... got into trouble with?"

"Oh, the magic-hoarders. Yes. Due another visit. I mean that's out of your jurisdiction, right? So no objections." Drathel turned from her scrutiny of the trees and leaned back on the rail, flicking away a fly the size of her thumb.

"They are known for sending killers out after those who wrong them," Gil noted.

"I noticed. I'll be more careful this time."

"And they use the cord. It's a big thing. Not shedding blood. Goes back to the old Moeribandi wholeness-of-body doctrine. But you're the scholar. You'd know that."

Drathel lounged, watched, waited.

"Perhaps you can explain how Loret ended up stabbed, in that case." Gil adopted a matching position of ease beside her at the back rail, while Loret looked uncertainly between them. "Whose knives, Fellow-Archivist? And from whose side of the border?"

Drathel was abruptly not so full of herself. "I see," she said, "that sometimes it helps to be the class swot. Magister."

"If only just one in ten people across the whole Palleseen Sway would read the brief properly, how much easier all our lives would be," agreed Gil pleasantly.

"I might have gone to poke Mantekor a bit."

"I thought so." Mantekor, where Gorbudan was brooding and gathering followers. Dekamran's unruly brother.

"Just in the interests of seeing what they might have, magic-wise. Decanting's a hungry business," Drathel said.

"I have paper and pen. By morning I want your report on everything you saw there before they chased you out."

"You're giving me *homework*?" the woman complained.

"In return for which you can omit from that report whatever it was you actually made away with, that had them chasing you. You see? Meeting people halfway. It's what Outreach is all about." Gil gave the woman a brilliant smile.

Loret, who'd been staring at the trees, trying to pretend that none of this was anything to do with her, let out a shocked cry and recoiled as though she'd been shot. Their mahout had the baton in its scaled hands instantly, writhing up to jut the weapon over the rail, vast eyes wide.

"A… *thing*," Loret got out, white as a sheet. "Bloody reason, there was a…" She wanted to say *monster* but they were currently *on* a monster that was being controlled by a different monster, as if the word had lost all meaning.

"Ah," Drathel said sagely. "I guess that means we're almost there."

The Ibaleth and their thunderous beasts weren't the only things to venture from the Waygrove's *elsewhere* to find a home in Usmai. Past Alkhands had been canny in welcoming the strange and making use of it. So it was with the Tesemer.

The place they lived in had been a temple once, some sect that had earned royal disfavour. The Tesemer had been given permission to claim it, and they had done so with blood and steel and the claws of their beasts.

They were assembled, waiting for the Alkhand. Not so many of them, really. They had never been numerous, because the life was hard. They weren't exactly beating off applicants with a stick. Two hundred, perhaps three, assembled in the compound they'd claimed as their monastery. They made a fascinating cultural study, to an Outreach eye. All the same, at first. The robes, that weird bisecting tonsure. Gaunt, hard people. Angular, stick-insect people. Then you looked beyond the surface, that unified front they tried to show. You saw the gradations of otherness in them. The way that the original alien strain of people who'd come through the Grove had taken in Usmiat men, taken on Usmiat students. How they were a people now striving towards an otherworldly ideal they could not quite achieve. Still swift, though, through ruthless training as much as heredity. Still eminently deadly with blade and beast, and loyal enough to the Alkhand that he trusted them to stand with bared steel beside the throne. The royal guard, divorced from factions and families. Or that was the theory.

There was a core to them, those in whom the old otherness ran strongest. Or perhaps those into whom it had been grafted, given the ghastly practices they kept up. They spoke out of narrow mouths, kept their lips almost shut, and for that Gil was grateful.

Some had their hunting beasts, the windsaws, to hand. They would give a demonstration later, butcher some poor local fauna in the name of showing how dangerous everything about the Louse Monks was. Others were riding their mounts, the things that had so alarmed Loret as they paced the ogrodon convoy through the trees.

Hooklopers. Like 'windsaws', like 'Waygrove', a word whose original you might as well translate into Pel because it surely didn't originate in this world. They were horse-sized, and their six walking limbs went straight down from their segmented carapace, like a horse's, not sprawling like a bug. But they were, nonetheless, bugs. Tall, flat-sided things, land-shrimps with a shocking turn of speed to them. The front four limbs were hooked and vicious, mantis-like and mantis-nasty, more than capable of carving up armour or ripping down a barricade. They were fleet as horses, better on rough ground. The Louse Monks fought from the saddle with their long falxes or man-tall bows. Between them and the ogrodons, the Usmai military was a holy terror.

The Tesemer loved their ceremony. To Gil's eyes, they clung to it. As the Alkhand sat, waited on by his servants and his son, they clashed in dazzling bouts of bladework. They galloped their segmented beasts up and down the field before the monastery, piercing the hearts of targets without even seeming to aim. They flew their ugly little hunting monsters at a variety of luckless game. They painted their faces with jagged markings and wore bracers with jutting spines. *Look how terrifying we are*, was the general theme of the festivities. To Gil, the Palleseen cosmopolitan, it was all a little aimless. A people who had come from some other place – lost, fleeing, searching, who knew? – and could never go back. Children wearing their ancestors' old clothes, performing plays in a language they barely spoke any more. The *True Speech*, they called the Tesemer tongue, desperately larding their fading memories of it with significance.

The Grove led everywhere save the place you wanted to get to, they said. The Louse Monks had been washed up on this foreign shore, their ways slowly eroded by a thousand little compromises. From would-be conquerors to raiders and brigands, from that – when the Usmiat had finally brought them to heel – to just one more part of a polity wise enough to know an asset when they saw it. Tamed beasts, were the Tesemer, just as much as the monsters they rode or hunted with. And they knew it and hated it, but had grown used to the kennel.

Drathel had been horrifying Loret with whispered stories of all the grotesque traditions the Louse Monks indulged. Most of which were probably true, maybe even the human sacrifice and the rotting tree stump gods. Just because they were semi-domesticated these days didn't mean the Tesemer were *nice*. Just because they put on a show didn't mean they wouldn't kill you for real. Gil blocked the murmuring and the horrified gasps out, watching the back of Dekamran's neck instead.

It wasn't usual for the heir to come on this little jaunt. He had no function in the ceremonies. It was his father that all these oddnesses were swearing their fealty to. It wasn't usual for the Palleseen Resident to be here either, of course – the Tesemer had given her more than a few hard looks to show just how not-usual it was, because they were not fond of the Palleseen. She'd come because this was on the way to getting Drathel off her hands. And Dekamran *said* he'd come because his father was sick and frail, and travelling was hard. And Gil didn't believe him.

He didn't so much as turn to look at her throughout all the displays of barbaric martial prowess though. Not the slightest crack through which she might spy out his real intentions. And so she just sat and sweated into her formal uniform and tried to read his mind through the back of his head.

*

That night, it was the three of them again, Pals together. They'd been given what was presumably a very mean cell in the monastery, no beds, just three straw mattresses. And obviously the Tesemer lived hard monastic lives without luxuries, but at the same time there were rooms down the corridor where the Alkhand's *servants* were enjoying a decidedly higher standard of living.

"There are some things," Drathel said, "which are well overdue a dose of perfection." She looked down at the mattress. "I think sleeping outside on the ground would be easier on the back."

"Except they give the hooklopers the run of the place after nightfall," Gil told her.

Drathel contemplated the pros and cons of that, and opted to stay inside. "You ever see them in action?" she asked. "They as good as people say?"

"There was a rebel Emorandi clan, about four years ago, just before the war," Gil said soberly. "I went with..." With Tarcomir, he of the duel. "I went with the punitive force, to bring them to heel." Gorbudan the warrior prince had led it. He'd given the Louse Monks their head and they'd loved him for it. "I don't know how they'd do on the flat, in the open, against batons, but out in the trees they were... sincerely terrifying, honestly. And you know standard drill against cavalry – shoot the mounts first, big fleshy target? Only the shells on those things will scatter anything other than a direct hit. I saw it with my own eyes. And don't let those bows kid you that the Tesemer won't pick up a baton." And the hooklopers ran straight, with those six legs flurrying smooth below them, none of the up-and-down of a horse. A very stable saddle for shooting from.

Drathel was left with her eyebrows up, her mouth open, and probably something disparaging to say that didn't seem quite as appropriate now. "Huh," she acknowledged at last. "Right." And then a shift, a pointedly casual tilt to her lounging, "So they're visiting the Alborandi next, I'd guess. Another sect to go shake hands and make promises with?"

"They are. We're not," Gil agreed.

"But—"

"I thought you were desperate to get back to your people, Fellow-Archivist?"

"I mean the Waygrove, though, now we're here..." A decidedly mutinous caste to the woman's face; a Decanter's acquisitive instincts. "I hear they have magic masks."

"You have no idea what they would do to you, if you got hold of one of their masks," Gil decided. "No, we three are crossing the border into Peor tomorrow, and you can take me to your commanding officer, and then they and I can have a chat about rogue Decanters stirring up trouble on my patch, frankly."

Drathel rolled her eyes. "You see," she said to Loret, "Outreach is no fun. Come over to our side."

Loret looked between them. She'd tucked herself into a corner of the cell, shoulder blades trying to dig into the stone. Culture shock, Gil reckoned. A good Pal girl straight out of the phalanstery, confronted with a succession of foreign abominations that couldn't just be corrected at the point of a baton. Except she didn't reckon Loret was that kind of kid. Loret had dirt under her nails before ever coming to Usmai; blood too, probably. Didn't mean she could just face up to the Tesemer's circus of nightmares with equanimity, but still...

"Talk to me, Loret," Gil invited, and the girl plastered her own magic mask on, a brittle smile with nothing behind it at all. She was fine, that smile said. She was the dutiful aide. *Please don't send me back.*

Later that night, with Drathel off bothering the royal servants, she tried one more time, sitting down beside Loret, just two Pal women in shirtsleeves, all badges of rank removed.

"If you can tell me, tell me," she said. "Outreach isn't the army. Nobody in our department turns up with clean hands. Or if they do, they get them dirty soon enough. You think I've no regrets? You watched me kill the Loruthi ambassador. Not exactly textbook, right? So if there's something you want to tell me, I have the ears for it." And it was true. She'd been dragging along plenty of regrets before ever coming to Usmai, and her record hadn't improved since. But Outreach was that part of the Pal machine that had to fit within the imperfection of the rest of the world. There was a lot of room for the unconventional.

Loret's eyes were huge, in the evening gloom. "You get the dispatches from home, magister? What's in them?"

Gil frowned, because that wasn't where the conversation had been going. "About a million tedious reshuffles and interdepartmental spats, honestly. And whatever it is that the Commission has removed from accepted conduct this month." Trying to be dismissive, but there was something in Loret's face that undermined her.

For a moment it was there, in the girl's face, on her lips. The truth of her, the thing that was Loret. That accounted for the sneaking and the stabbing and the utter cluelessness and the fear. And then the girl just swallowed it down again, like bitter medicine. That bright glass smile came back and she explained that it was fine and she would learn and – unspoken but clearly heard – *Please don't send me back.*

Later still. Loret sleeping, fidgeting, whimpering to herself, just about the worst person to share a room with. Drathel returned, quite drunk and having won a handful of maybe-enchanted tat from the Alkhand's servants. Now snoring on her back; also the worst person to share a room with. Gil, lying awake, staring at the ceiling. Awake, and it wasn't either of the others responsible for that. Her own mind was quite equal to the task of fending off sleep and neither of her fellow Pals were responsible for that.

In her mind, the garlands of cloth flowers, the music, the release of taking the uniform off. Not the physical uniform, that tight jacket with all the buttons, because she wore it as little as possible. The uniform of the mind. The strictures expected of the Palleseen Resident of Slate House.

She couldn't have gone to him, after all. Milk and Flowers wasn't a Pal thing. She couldn't just have turned up at the palace gates with a jug of ramaht and a raised eyebrow. But he had come to her. And if she was ever up before a superior, she'd just say that it would have been profoundly undiplomatic to turn him down. Sometimes Outreach had to bend to local customs. Yes, magister, even in *that*. One must occasionally suffer for one's service. All for the greater good of the Palleseen Sway.

He was not strong, but he was kind. And it had been permitted. That one night. The custom.

She sat up, drank some water, splashed some on her face and shoulders and hair. Listened to the breathing of the other two. Asleep, genuinely, both of them.

No.

She stood, went out into the corridor, found an unoccupied cell. She could read over Drathel's scribbled report and try to spot the omissions. Or draft her own dispatch, because she should have one ready for the next ship home. She could dangle some hooks about her new aide, for example. *Who is this green kid you've sent me?* That would be the professionally responsible thing to do.

She even got her notebook out, her pens. Her little reading lamp with the tableth fit into the slot. Stared at the blank page. Put it all away again.

No. Absolutely not.

What had gone on, up until now, was explicable. Was, at least, capable of being shown in a light that maintained her professional decorum. Worthy of a rap across the knuckles, no more. *Don't let it happen again, Sage-Invigilator…*

Thinking through the tortuous twists of it. Not realising she was hugging her knees just like she had when she was a child in the phal. Not a woman just a year shy of forty with a dynamic career in the service. Another decade, deliver Usmai to the Sway, they'd make her a professor and everyone could forget all the equivocation a career in Outreach was built on. She'd be safe. She'd have that big house on the Archipelago and what foreigners did would become something she just read about in the reports.

You get the dispatches from home, magister? And she did, but she was suddenly worried about what wasn't written in them, that Loret knew.

She had the terrible sense of things coming to an end. Doors closing. Opportunities receding.

In which case.

No.

And it was *No.* Under no circumstances. Absolutely positively not. On the one arm of the scales, the Palleseen Sway and proper conduct and just basically professionalism. And on the other side…

Him. And her.

She went out into the corridor again. Stones cold against her bare feet, slightly fuzzy with moss. And it had been a while since tradecraft had required her to really padfoot it around somewhere, but these were skills she had acquired, and never lost.

She knew where he was quartered. In truth, it had been burning a hole in her mind since they'd retired for the night. And she was the Palleseen Resident, and there were diplomatic matters to discuss, and if he looked at her in *that* way, then that could be what this was about. Just business. Just two public faces speaking formal words at each other.

When she found him, he was still awake, dressed in a loose robe, sitting by the window. Dekamran.

No, said her career and her professionalism, even as she gave him her best professional career smile. *Just one small bureaucratic detail, your highness. Sorry to trouble you.*

The festival flowers had been taken down. The frog god's

writ had been revoked. That night of license had been and gone. What happened now was for closed doors, a secret that could ruin either of them. Not by the ways of Usmai, nor under the ordinances of the Palleseen Sway, was this permitted.

His eyes, on her. Knowing all these things, as true for him as for her. His smile.

Shocking, liberating, to discover that *I want this for me* somehow outweighed all those weights in the other pan of the scale, and that he wanted it too.

Monstrous Regiment

Successor States are no stranger to the baton, as an instrument of hunting or war. The noble cavalry of nations like Usmai are crack shots from horseback or the howdahs of the ogrodons. The local artisans produce remarkable artefacts, long and elegant, spiralling with serpents, inscribed with sigils of accuracy and efficiency, each one a work of art to grace the hands of an Alkhand. They do not produce them in bulk, though. The price of a battlefield dominated by the hereditary cavalry class is an infantry that makes do with less.

It was surprisingly like coming home. If you discounted the heat, the flies, the stagnant water stink of the place, just like home. For Loret, not necessarily a good thing, but there had been a lot of strangeness in the last few days, and monsters. A little home at least meant familiar terrors.

A Palleseen military camp. She'd never been a trooper, never trailed the baton with the army, but she knew the drill. The other camp, the camp she'd been in, had been run and disciplined and ground under the boots of the soldiers. When they came into sight of the tents here, and she heard the shout of drill statloi and saw that nest of uniforms then, yes. Home. Almost.

She shivered. Not like she was desperate to be repatriated to the Archipelago – anything but! – but for just a moment she wanted to be… Not a place but a time. A kid – even more of a kid. When the uniforms hadn't meant what they came to mean.

She tugged at her own shirt collar, fidgeted with the jacket tied about her waist. That same uniform, ill-fitting as it was.

A lot of the uniforms up ahead were pale, not the charcoal of regular troopers. Accessories, then. Some company who had decided to take up all the advantages of serving the Pal military a thousand miles from wherever they called home. Either because home was dirt poor and the pressure of a Pal boot was squeezing the money even from that dirt, or because a squad of Pals had turned up and conscripted them at the point of a baton. Or the recruiting statlos had been persuasive, who knew? Even Accessories didn't regret joining up sometimes. Except, as the three of them reached the perimeter sentries and got a better look, the Accessories all looked a lot like locals. Usmiat. Or, given they'd crossed the border not long before, presumably these were Peosts. The uniforms erased any markers of precise nationality.

She'd thought maybe it was just the fact she hadn't travelled much. Maybe people looked like this all over. Except Gil was glancing about and frowning. They had a watch statlos escorting them by then, and *she* was Pal, certainly. All the statloi and officers, and some of the rankers, they were in charcoal-grey off the Archipelago, just as you'd expect. But a big chunk of people under arms were just... people from around here. Locals. Just like you never did, in the army. Even Loret knew that.

"I'll go fetch him myself, if you still want someone to shout at," Drathel offered. Her eyes glittered with mischief. Drathel was one of those people. Loret had known plenty in the camps. People to whom the rules didn't apply, and who would absolutely try and talk you into the shit that they were so assiduously courting. And somehow they'd walk out clean as a whistle and the stink would just be on you. On the other hand, those were also the people who could get you food, medicine, whatever you needed, if you could pay. Mixed blessings, people like Drathel.

"You go do that," Gil told her. "I'll wait here and think up some interesting questions. We can have a little quiz, like in the phal."

"Oh, he'll love that," Drathel grinned back. "Regular bookworm type, is Flint."

The two women smiled. Loret could almost see the sparks of clashing personality in the air between them. Gil had maintained a tenuous upper hand so far but, here, Drathel was apparently amongst her own people. This was the company she was nominally attached to, within the Palleseen in Peor.

Gil commandeered a couple of camp stools and sat down, every bit the lord of all she surveyed. A Sage-Invigilator, no small woman even in a big world. Loret, the nobody, sat in her shadow and had that one moment to change her mind.

She hadn't said, before. She almost said it now. *Shall I say, about back home?* Because Gil seemed straight, and they were a long way from the Archipelago, and there had been all that talk about Outreach and flexibility. Just maybe, if Loret told her the truth, Gil would be able to handle it. Not just give her subordinate over to the uniforms and send home for a new aide.

Loret moistened her lips, watching the stern caste the woman's face fell into, when Gil was thinking. Because it was either say something now, or never, surely. The time that had passed since she got off the boat was a door slowly closing.

Gil glanced at her. Those sharp, suspicious eyes. Tradecraft. A woman whose business had more than a touch of the sneak about it, for all the diplomatic formalities. Anything she said and anything her face said could be a trap and a lie.

Loret made her own face host a vague smile, vacant even. Just the useless aide who didn't know anything. And Gil had plenty of other things on her mind, and the moment passed.

Then Drathel was back and, with her, a big Pal man, uniform jacket open down the front and flapping, his shirt greyish. His hair was ash-blond, receding a little. His stubble glittered in the sunlight.

"Well stab me," he declared. "*Sage*-Invigilator, no less. I'd've put up bunting." One of his Accessories ran up with another stool and the man dumped himself into it with a groan of wood and canvas. He was somewhere between thirty and forty, a bruiser gone slightly to seed now he had all these people to fight battles for him, but still not someone Loret would want to get into a scrap with. His knuckles were scarred, speaking of merits earned the hard way. Around his neck there was a pendant of ivory, jade and jet, rods and wheels and carved beads. Magic, maybe. Of ritual significance to some cult who probably wanted it back.

The same Accessory came back with a clay jug in the shape of a skull – like the ones she'd seen buried in that weird demon-stomping ritual in Alkhalend. Cups were laid out on a folding table and distributed without much thought for precedence, so that Loret was holding hers before Gil's was even poured. Not, she judged, a calculated insult, just the sort of informality you got after enough time outside formal supervision.

"Sage-Invigilator Angilly, Fellow-Monitor Postry," Drathel supplied. "The boss. Mine, anyway."

"Flint," said Postry. He knocked back the contents of his cup and his attendant refilled it. Loret sniffed her own. It smelled as though you'd mostly use it for cleaning spoons.

"Flint," Gil echoed. "Fine. Flint, then. What the hell is this? You're Outreach under Palinet?" Meaning the Peost Resident.

"We're our own. Ventures," Flint said.

"Fine. So what the hell is *that*?" Gil's face didn't seem to know whether to laugh at the man or chew him out for insubordination.

"Highly dangerous experimental logistics. New way of operating; could explode at any time." The man fished out some exceedingly dog-eared papers and waved them until Gil snipped them from his fingers. While she read, Flint saluted Loret with his cup.

"You're the new kid," he said, and Drathel supplied the name for him.

Loret nodded warily. She'd known people like Flint in the

camps, too. He and Drathel seemed a good match for each other. The sort of people who were your friends until they weren't.

"Basically," he said, to Loret, but really to Gil, "Ventures means we're here to push the boundaries of how things are done a bit. I mean, you're both Outreach. You should know. Right now, Peor's panicking because Usmai could come over the border in force any day, or else Goshumai comes down from the hills to slap them about for all the slappery that went on last time. And the Resident is... limited. Not like she has *that* many troopers in the actual garrison and she needs those to defend our stuff. Lots of unrest in Peor, on account of how our Alkhand keeps squeezing everyone, and everyone's dirt poor. Shoddy way to run a country, honestly."

"The Alkhand we're here to support..." Loret said uncertainly.

It seemed very unfair that all *three* of them just looked at her as though she had said something extremely naïve.

"So some bright spark on the Archipelago sent you over here with basically a blank piece of paper stamped with the Commission's seal," Gil said. "Since when you've just..."

"Done," Postry – Flint – agreed. "You don't like my Seraphi?"

Loret didn't know the word. Drathel murmured, "Like the monks and the lizards and all that menagerie they've got in Usmai. Foreign forces sworn to provide military service."

"Accessories," Loret supplied uncertainly. But it was plainly not that, because you never let Accessories serve in their own homeland's army. That was just asking for trouble.

Gil's expression said the same thing. Flint laughed at it. A Fellow, laughing at a Sage, but it was his camp and his command and also, plainly, his general disregard for regulations.

"Look at it from their point of view. Those Peosts, they're crap out of luck. Every neighbour they ever had gave them a kicking, and when that wasn't going on, their own rulers were pulling the boots on to do it themselves. Every generation they get given spears and marched off without kit or training to get killed over which prince gets his arse on the gold chair. Their current ruler's some kid who doesn't care about anything except concubines, magic brain candy and spending all the money. And then along comes Uncle Ventures, village to village, offering them uniforms and batons and hope. Giving 'em a chance to feel what the inside of the kicking boot feels like, not just the toe-leather."

"Batons," said Gil thoughtfully.

"Bloody straight," Flint agreed. "You should see them, at the start. The three faces, we call it. The shock, when you put a baton into their hands and not just a pointy stick. The bloody disgust, when they see how plain our kit is, compared to those fancy toys the nobility swan around with. Then they work out our military issues can shoot at least half as straight as some noble's fancy piece of battle-scrimshaw, and we just handed out fifty of 'em and a bandolier of tablethi apiece. You should see that third face, Resident. Real fucking nasty grin they get, when they realise how one visit to the quartermasters brought 'em halfway from serfs to soldiers."

Gil cocked her head on one side. Loret waited for the explosion, the outraged superior decrying the risk. There were ten armed locals for every officer or statlos in dark grey. It was a mutiny waiting to happen.

Gil handed the tatty wad of papers back. "They've not shot you yet," she admitted, with perhaps the quantity of grudging respect one might have fit on her smallest fingernail.

"They know who their favourite uncle is," Flint said. "And they know Uncle Flint will feed 'em better than they'd get in their villages after the Alkhand's tax collectors've been. And more. Opportunity, in this man's army. Plenty of monasteries and noble clans and rebel villages around these parts don't like the Alkhand. Makes 'em fair game. Good pickings, and they see soon enough that our writ and our reason are better than any curses the local priests might be throwing. They're learning that just because a thing's a thousand years old doesn't mean it won't fall over if you kick it hard enough. Whether it's a temple or a way of life."

"And the Alkhand?"

"There are a lot of sweet little birds at court in our uniforms," said Flint. "Singing in the Alkhand's ears about how good it is to have candy and concubines and money, and if we just upped and left, maybe it would all dry up." Abruptly the chumminess was gone. Flint, the hard man, the breaker, the looter. "This is what the Commission wants, magister. The old ways are slow ways. And what do you think brings folk to perfection soonest? All these Peost lads and lasses in my company are seeing they can fill a pair of uniform boots faster than they could those little pointy things the locals wear. Or sandals. I mean you can't even *fill* a pair of sandals. The coins just run straight out the gaps." And Uncle Flint was back again, as though he'd just turned away to signal for the jug again. The skull-jug, the demon-vessel.

He caught Loret looking at it, as his aide topped everyone up. Everyone save Loret, who hadn't dared try the acrid stuff. "You know this?" he asked.

"You're drinking out of a demon jar?"

"I mean, we emptied it first," Flint pointed out. "Use your elbow, Cohort-Invigilator. Drink. It's good for you."

She'd heard that one before, but then Drathel said that actually it *was* good for her, because the sharp smell was a tonic that kept the swamp fevers away, and serving it from a demon's prison helped too. Peor wasn't the healthiest posting for a Pal straight off the islands. You took your medicine as part of every meal.

Gil had been about to say something, but now visibly went back over what Flint had said. "Emptied?"

There was a look, then, between Flint and Drathel. As she knew them by type, Loret knew that look. *Do we try the big con?* basically. How much could they get away with, in front of this authority figure? Or how much could they keep hidden?

"You should meet my staff," Flint said, playing vague and watching Gil's face from the corner of his eye. "Polite thing to do, don'tcherknow. Drathel, go find Croskin would you?"

Drathel's face said she wasn't entirely sure that was a good idea, but she went.

Gil took the opportunity, intended or not. "Your subordinate almost got her throat cut in Alkhalend."

Flint shrugged, as if to say that *almost* was the only important word there. "It's going to happen," he told Gil. "You think she listens to me? Decanting trumps everything back home. So long as she can dump her magic gabble on every boat out of Peor, she's got the Commission's heartfelt thanks. That spat we had with the Loruthi got expensive, right?" Because magic powered everything that Pallesand did, but war most of all. Loret remembered. A lot of people had to do without, as the cost of the conflict started to bite. The tide of Palleseen affluence had receded, and things that might have remained hidden had been exposed. And now the war had gone away, but so had a great deal of the magic. Places like Peor or Usmai, brimming with gods and relics, looked very tempting. All that ritual tat, those artefacts, that *gabble* as the soldier's cant went, which could be decanted down into the tablethi that powered every weapon and toy in the Pal arsenal.

Gil looked like she had something sharp to say about all of that, possibly that Flint should keep Drathel on a literal leash. Then the Decanter was back. With Croskin.

It had to be Croskin. Not a Pal name. Not, as Loret had thought, a local name. Not a human name.

Gil stood abruptly, her hand on her sword hilt. Flint just snickered into his cup, his back to the *thing* and somehow not worried at all. Croskin smiled. By default: its mouth just stretched that way. A snaggle-toothed upwards curve that spoke of imbecilic murder.

It was, Loret, decided, the cap that was the worst. Croskin's head was big, chalk-white, puffy like a fungus. A bulging brow, a heavy jaw, almost no nose. The Pal uniform cap balanced on it, off-centre, constantly about to fall off. It should have been funny. Nothing about Croskin was funny.

Croskin was hunchbacked, apishly long-armed. Tattered wings projected through split seams in its jacket, stunted and useless. Its skin was dotted with barbs. Its thick fingers, the hooked toes of its bare feet, sported yellowed talons. Shorter than Flint but more massive about the chest and shoulders, a beast you wouldn't want to get within reach of, save it was right there at Flint's shoulder like the worst butler in the world. And in uniform.

Loret had been treated to more than her fair share of monsters in the last few days, but they had been foreign monsters, unknown quantities. This, she knew. She'd seen the like driving the machines of factories or called up by army conjurers. Flint had a demonist on his staff and they'd called up a demon, fair enough. Against the local preferences, but it happened. Except for the uniform.

Most demons didn't bother with clothes. When they did, the clothes were just *them*, the way they looked. Except someone had stuffed Croskin into a Pal uniform. Almost literally. They'd had to unpick the seams then re-sew it once the demon was wearing it. The thorns of its skin tore the fabric in a hundred places. It looked powerfully uncomfortable, but then just being a demon looked uncomfortable. Perhaps the uniform wasn't much of an added indignity.

"Are you mad?" Gil asked.

Flint shrugged. "They sent us over with a demonist. What was I supposed to do?"

"Where is this demonist? I'd like a sharp word about local customs," Gil said. And Loret thought of all the stomping and spitting and the jars shaped like skulls, and that was without there even *being* a demon. Just the general thought of them had bred a whole dedicated ceremony. And here was Croskin.

"Companion-Invigilator Galversty," Flint said grandly, "cannot be here with us at the moment. On account of how he didn't drink up his tonic and succumbed to the swamp fever. Which was when we discovered some very loose seams in his contracts, because Croskin didn't go anywhere. Sort of got donated to the department."

"Postry. Flint. I have nothing against demons. They're a useful tool like a knife or a shovel. But having one *here* is too much of a risk. Shoving the wretched thing into a uniform isn't fooling anyone."

"Cohort-Monitor Croskin," Flint said.

"Magister," Croskin croaked.

It didn't just have a uniform. It had a rank.

"I think we need to show the Sage-Invigilator your command."

It had a command.

"Magister," Croskin said. It had the intonation down perfectly, just like any soldier.

Croskin's physiology meant what it *didn't* do was march. It hopped and lurched, and occasionally helped itself along with its knuckles. Those little wings quivered and flapped as though they thought they were helping. Croskin loped through the camp, and the local conscripts, the Seraphi, made space for it, but didn't spit or curse or make religious gestures. A wary détente, between fellow wearers of the uniform.

She saw Gil noting all of that. The veteran diplomat learning something new for once.

They crossed through the entire camp that way – enough pageantry that it was plain Flint was showing off – and then moved on through a screen of trees into the *other* camp. Which brought Gil up short again, and Loret too, because here was Croskin's command.

They weren't all in uniform. Several of them couldn't possibly have fit, but even they had armbands or caps or a jacket tied about their necks like a cravat.

No two were the same, but there was a certain common aesthetic to most of them. Elements of eagle, serpent, crab, tiger, the traditional predators of the region. Bright feathers and beaks, pincers, fangs and scales, striped hides and amber eyes in differing combinations and arrangements. At least thirty of them, and when Croskin gave out a bellow they were on their feet and shambling into some kind of order. Loret had seen worse in uniform, honestly. The ones with hands even had batons.

Demons. A squad of demons mumming as Pal soldiers like some dreadful play.

"It's Drathel's fault, of course," Flint said from over Gil's shoulder. "You dig for magic anywhere in this part of world, eventually you turn up these weird little skulls all stoppered up with seals and sigils."

Gil's face was absolutely unreadable. "So, while you were recruiting the locals..."

"We were recruiting the *locals*," Flint agreed. Very casual, hands on his hips, undone jacket flapping. Very tense, braced for the slap.

"You said your demonist was dead," Gil pointed out reasonably.

"Very sad. We all miss him," agreed Flint.

"So who... are these *recruits* contracted to?"

Loret suddenly understood what sat behind all that utter horror that her superior wasn't showing, everything locked behind her still, calm face. She was no conjurer herself, but everyone knew that the one solitary thing keeping a demon in the upper world – and the one thing keeping it from running absolutely amok – was its contract.

"I mean, I'm no book-learning academic," Flint said, unconcerned about the thirty fiends from the Realms Below that were *right there*.

"Croskin signed them up," Drathel said simply. "When we unearthed them and unstoppered them, there they were. And about to go right back Below because when we freed them, there wasn't anything keeping them on this side of the borders. But Croskin's contract really is very... loose. He gave them a choice. One chance to stay in the world, where they'd all rather be. Because I'm no expert, but I understand the Realms Below aren't terribly pleasant, even for demons."

"They're serving… Croskin?" Gil said through tight lips.

"Cohort-Monitor Croskin?" Flint asked.

"No, magister," the demon rumbled. "We are contracted to Pallesand."

Loret thought about that, about just how many different voices comprised even the Commission that governed Pallesand, let alone the entire nation and its global Sway. It could not work, obviously. From any human perspective it was nonsense.

But not from a demon's eyes. And it struck her that Croskin was the only one here using the proper Palleseen military address, as alien in its mouth as the hat on its head.

"Troopers, three steps forward!" Croskin bellowed, its voice filling with uncomfortable resonance, late echoes from nowhere tripping over one another after the shout. The host of demons, the bird-things, the crustacean things, born from the nightmares of antique yesterdays, lurched and skittered and scrabbled until they'd formed a new line. Batons sloped over shoulders, where there were shoulders. Spines straight, where there were spines. It was… it should have been horrible. It should have been ridiculous, like Croskin's hat. And yet there was a desperate earnestness bleeding from the sockets and joints of that monstrous host. And Loret made a sound, a squeak really. It probably sounded like fear or laughter, but it was empathy. She read, in those horrors, a single unified plea, and it was one she knew. *Don't send me back.* They had been prisoners. They had been locked in skulls and jars, buried for centuries. They had known cruelty, these things that had been shaped for cruel deeds by cruel masters. The uniform wasn't freedom but it was better than the alternative.

She had no idea what Gil thought of it all. What she *said* was, "Well it's Palinet's problem, not mine. Don't bring them across the border into Usmai."

"Wouldn't dream of it," Flint promised. "You're staying the night? You want my tent? I'll get my aide to clear my shit out of it." Probably meaning all the incriminating loot he'd taken from those temples.

They did stay the night, in the end, because while Gil might have wanted to just swan off towards the Usmiat border, the night was coming on and they'd just seen enough demons to people every shadow between here and Alkhalend. And Drathel made her move, as Loret had known she would. Found a moment when Gil was out of earshot and made her offer. And Loret did her usual thing: nodded, smiled, committed to nothing, hoped the problem would go away. They so seldom did.

The next day, Flint decided he had only been playing at the interdepartmental pissing contest previously and gave them a full honour guard of demons back to the border.

The Mask Wearers

Dekamran, the second son. The spare. Permitted to broaden his horizons, because the eldest son was so robust it seemed as though even gods could not overcome him. Dekamran, educated by Pal and Loruthi tutors overseas, yet somehow coming home with the vices of neither. Not the destruction of icons nor the acquisition of gold. If he were to become Alkhand, what age of reason might result? A time of international treaty and public wealth, enlightenment and reason that might polish Usmai to a shine, rather than scour it all away like the sandpaper ideology of the Palleseen.

The heart of Usmai's strength and strangeness was the Waygrove. The heart of the Waygrove were the Alborandi. The monks of the mask.

Dekamran had travelled, learned, read. The Killinbraan Nautical Institute, where he'd been educated, had a whole library of atlases and travelogues. There he had learned that the mystery at the core of his homeland was not even unique. Some five or six places, where the wood within the Grove intruded. Where things might enter or leave this world. At certain times. With the proper observations. There were other phenomena, he'd read. Some claimed there was a desert, as well as a wood. Some claimed certain regions of the sea were doorways, though it seemed to Dekamran that a ship lost to storms and a ship transported to another ocean were indistinguishable to those not on board.

Yet no other nation in the world had so adjusted to the ragged, tree-edged hole within its borders as the Usmiat. These days, only the Alkhands of Usmai made formal treaty with the Grove, welcomed those lost souls who ventured from it, and gifted the Grove with an order of monks to tend and propitiate it.

The Alborandi, they were called. And each year, after the Day of Milk and Flowers, the Alkhand's path must take him to the Grove, to renew those bonds between man and monks. Just one more duty, like going to the riverbank homes of the Ibaleth, like watching the Tesemer charge back and forth in martial splendour. Save that there was more. Baggage. Personal burdens the Alkhand brought here. Dekamran, too.

The man's wife, the son's mother. Kaleithi, who had left.

Sightless though he was, Dekamran felt his father tremble when they came in sight of the monastery. *Monastery* was a grand word for it. They had some gardens and fields, to feed their bodies. They had a palisaded compound with a few simple huts inside. There was no gate. The front of the compound, where the path led to, was just a gap in the stakes. Any enemy, sneak thief or wild beast might have wandered in. The back of the compound was also just a gap in the stakes. And any enemy, thief or beast that wandered out that way might never be seen in this world again, if the stars were ordered just so. And what wandered *in* through that gap might be something never seen in this world before.

This was the Alborandi all over. The simplicity, to the eye. The vast undertow of complex things unseen and all around.

The monks themselves were much in evidence. Figures in simple robes, tending plants, carving wood, setting little offerings in tree-cut niches, passing back and forth about unknowable errands. The robes themselves were not so different to other monastic orders about Usmai and beyond. A wanderer of some minor order without even a monastery to their name might wear just such a thing. It was the masks, though. Faceless wooden masks. Eyeless, painted with bright colours as though a child's fingers had daubed them, yet in a way that spoke pattern and meaning. Each mask different, yet they blurred one into another in the mind. And they all walked the same way.

The Tesemer had provided an escort. Not that the Alkhand and his convoy of ogrodons should need protection, passing from one monastic holdout to another within a few days of Alkhalend, but the Louse Monks never passed up an opportunity to remind people of how fierce they were. Hooklopers had skittered alongside the huge scaled beasts, weaving in and out of the trees, displaying their preternatural agility. The monks astride them had sat, angular robed puppets, some with hoods, some with broad hats; long blades slanted over their shoulders or holstered on the saddle. A brooding presence always at the edge of the eye, like storm clouds coming in. But loyal. Loyal to the Alkhand and the Mirror Throne, which had tamed them and let them call Usmai home.

There was a moment, when the convoy came to the Alborandi compound. Dekamran missed Gil, then, because she'd have joked to him that it was a monk-off. That Palleseen irreverence which always made him laugh. And with his father clenched tense as a fist beside him, he could have used an excuse to laugh. The Louse Monks had ridden their hooklopers back and forth before the lead ogrodon, their steel flashing in the sun. They had their beasts rear up on their back four legs, severing the air with bladed forelimbs, shaking segmented flanks so that their carapaces rattled like baton-fire. And the Tree Monks, the Alborandi... didn't really seem to notice. A few of them stopped what they were doing and stood there, but those masks had no focus to them. And the Tesemer were fierce and warlike and incomparably skilled in the ways of the blade, but they would forever be subordinate to these placid, vacant masks. Because they were just creatures who had come from the Grove, and these masks, these men and women, *were* the Grove.

Dekamran helped his father down from the howdah. The

Ibaleth, the Tesemer, the other little orders and dens they'd visited, these guests of Usmai had come to give gifts and make displays and otherwise honour their Alkhand. Here, it was Oparan who made the first move. Dekamran passed him the offerings one by one, pressing each into the old man's open hands so that nothing might be dropped or forgotten. Carvings. The work of the Beast Artists, but not intended for the seedy practice of taumachy. Certain mandated and sacred forms, resembling no beast or thing ever seen, only created for this solitary purpose, painted in prescribed ways. And, after those, the masks. Three; it was always three. Blank curved shields with a simple loop of leather at the back. The monks had seemed absent and distracted, taking the other things, as though it was all some child's game and they were just too polite to tell the old man they didn't really want such nonsense. But the masks, they wanted. Carved from sacred woods, infused with magic. Alborandi-in-waiting, ready to be painted and consecrated and given… whatever it was the monks put into their masks. Whatever it was that, when such a mask was donned, made them all the same behind it. Men, women, old, young, fat, thin. Even now, Dekamran could note the differences. But look away, look back, he could not have said for sure which monks had been there before, which had changed places with each other. The masks stood between him and their wearers. That was the problem.

His father handed the final mask over. The hands of the receiving monk were calloused with work, but slender. A woman's, Dekamran thought. For a moment his own heart clenched, like his father's must surely be doing with every beat. *Is it…?* Waiting for the moment when those hands lifted to take the mask from the monk, to reveal a face. Any face. Her face.

It didn't happen. It never happened, not here.

The servants were pitching the Alkhand's grand tent, for the Alborandi had no accommodation fit for a ruler. Barely any fit for a human being. Oparan, the blind master of all he surveyed, leaned suddenly on Dekamran, lurched into him. A murmur of concern passed through the courtiers. The monks paid no mind.

"I had thought..." Just a whisper, from the old man. Just for him. One arm clutching at Dekamran's own for support, the other crooked around the ornamented skull, his constant companion.

The servants at the tent redoubled their efforts, the rich furnishings materialising around Oparan as his son guided him in. The bed, the couch, the screens, the fabulously ornate tapestries woven so thick with texture that the old man could see them with his fingers.

"I dreamed," said Oparan, and Dekamran shooed the servants out with a look. The Alkhand's dreams were not common currency. Not oracular, not sacred, just a window into the man's mind that should not become wider gossip.

"Father." Settling the old man onto the couch, pouring ramaht for them both, pressing the cup into Oparan's hand. And by tradition the Alkhand drank from a jewelled horn that must be replaced precisely in its stand if it was not to spill, but Dekamran had made steady inroads against those customs which caused his father indignity.

"She came back," Oparan said. "At the pools. I saw them take the masks away. And it was her." His voice shaking, recounting events he would not have seen even if they had happened, but Sorthist's wasps had not been able to touch the inner eye. "I believed it. I woke, this morning, and it was true for me. Then I remembered." Voice shaking, backed by the faint rattle of stone.

In Usmai, marriage was sacred, not to be walked away from, and none more so than the union of Alkhand and Alkhani. Yet marriage was imperfect. Matches were ill-made. A spouse brutal, bitter, faithless or just wrong. You did not walk away from a marriage, but monastic vows dissolved all bonds. A year, two years, spent outside the world as a novice in some order, and when you returned you were cleansed of those parts of your past you wished to be free of. That was how it was done, from the least beggar to the Alkhand. Not that the spouse of the Alkhand would *ever*... until she had.

And perhaps Kaleithi, Dekamran's mother, had felt that simply distributing alms on the street, proffering the begging bowl, even learning the sword with the Tesemer, these would not have sufficed to remove such weighty chains from her, as had bound her to the throne. So she had taken on the mask. And there were always those who never did rejoin the world and made the monastic life their own. And, two years after taking the mask, Kaleithi had not been amongst the mask wearers to reach up and bare their faces to the spray and the sun in Alkhalend. Nor the year after that, nor after that. Seven years now, she had been gone. The mask had taken her and not given her back.

His father slept, then. Worn out from travel, from illness, from grief most of all. Dekamran ventured outside.

He had not been there, when his mother had taken the mask. He had not come with his father to the Alborandi each year, to renew whatever fealty actually existed, between the Mirror Throne and the masks. He was the son who had gone overseas. The son who spent too much time at Slate House with the Palleseen Resident. The spare son nobody needed because there was Gorbudan, the warrior. Needless to say, Gorbudan had been there when their mother had walked away, while hapless Dekamran had still been on the boat, trying to get home. That was the thing about Gorbudan, he was always where he needed to be. Like here.

He was waiting, when Dekamran exited the tent. A handful of retainers standing at a respectful distance, but since when had Gorbudan, warrior prince, needed others to defend him? He wore green and gold and black, that had been Sorthist's colours once when their uncle and their father had fought for the throne. War colours against Dekamran's blue and white and gold of peace. He had a clavar at his belt. And what was Gorbudan's status, anyway? Not quite a renegade, but banished from court. Was he permitted to be here, in full view of the Alkhand's courtiers? Yes, but also no. A tacit understanding that he not be where his father might be, not come under those blind eyes. The permeable edges of exile.

Gorbudan, the hawk, the fighter. That commanding eye, that strategist's brow. When he had been heir, the court had looked on him and known just what Alkhand they were getting. A man who would find some pretext to muster the armies and take them over the borders into Peor or Goshumai. A man who would trouble the dreams of his fellow monarchs, so that they sent gifts and sweet words and treaties with favourable terms. A strong man, to the benefit of the histories, but not necessarily to the individual nobles and courtiers who might have their own ambitions. Not a man for compromise, Gorbudan. His vision or none.

Standing there, and between him and his younger brother – the heir, the man placed above him by their father's decree – just such a space as an energetic swordsman might cover, in a step and a cleaving stroke, to simplify the succession.

Dekamran, who wore no sword, halved that distance. Why make the man exert himself? Gorbudan's face was a mask as unreadable as the Alborandi.

Dekamran halved the distance again. Every eye was on him. The servants, the court. The ornamented orbs of the Ibaleth mahouts. The narrow gaze of the Tesemer, tense as wires.

Gorbudan's eyes catalogued the spectators, finding one omission. No Angilly here with her quick rapier. No Palleseen presence to threaten diplomatic reprisals against the whole nation of Usmai. Not that Gorbudan, the warrior, feared the Kepishi and their armies. Or anything.

Dekamran spread his arms, as though inviting the strike. And Gorbudan's speed with a clavar was legendary. Out of the scabbard and through an enemy in an eyeblink. Cleaned and back in its sheath in another. Usmai held its breath.

The lunge came, a heartbeat later than everyone was ready for, catching every watcher wrong-footed. Leaving the two brothers embracing each other. When they broke apart, there was the same look in both faces, the hawkish, the soft.

Dekamran hadn't thought the man would come, but if the two of them were ever going to settle their differences, what neutral ground was better than here, before the Waygrove? When he'd dispatched his messengers to Mantekor, he'd told nobody his plan. Not even Angilly, because she'd have tried to talk him out of it. And, failing that, she'd have insisted on being here. And that would have ensured failure, because Gorbudan hated the Palleseen. Had fiercely disliked the Palleseen even back in the days when his star had been in the ascendant. Loathed them with a passion now, because he saw their hand in his fall from grace.

Dekamran didn't believe it. Or, if the Pals were involved, it was that Gorbudan had been burning their holdings in Peor against their father's injunction, during the war. Taking his own place as heir for granted. Dictating his own foreign policy until their father had been forced to cast him down. But, to Gorbudan's eyes, it was the Pals that had him exiled, somehow.

Now they sat within a hut, just one of the plain shacks the Alborandi used, for when the rains came fierce enough that even the masks took shelter. And Alborandi were still coming and going, storing sacks and boxes up in the eaves or sitting at their cryptic meditation, but masks had no ears. The brothers might as well have been alone.

"He's taking it hard," Dekamran said. "Being here."

Gorbudan nodded. They'd had a rug laid down, in the absence of even a stick of furniture, and were sitting on it like children.

"Just being," Dekamran added. "Just... He has good days and bad. Mornings when he hears a half-dozen petitions, a couple of emissaries. Makes wise judgments and everyone nods along. And then there are days he's just... not there. Sits with the skull on his knee and talks to it about... before. Loses himself in other days."

Gorbudan nodded. Dekamran was waiting for the curl of the lip, the hard elder brother telling him what he should have done, that he couldn't have done. The things Gorbudan would do, in his place. That would make the nation function, whether or not the Alkhand came to court. And Dekamran was the man who'd gone away and had the Usmiat-ness rubbed off him at a foreign school, but Gorbudan's sword could cut through all the ties of tradition when they got in his way.

"And the sickness is worse. In his lungs. And elsewhere, the doctors say. It spreads, the stone. Little shards, here and there. It will be in his blood some day, they tell me. And then his heart." Their father's heart, turned to stone. That would be the poetic outcome, the fitting end for a grieving man. But Dekamran knew enough to understand they meant some sharp-edged flake of petrified blood would tear its way through the flesh of the organ. A dreadful, painful death of invisible bleeding. No fit fate for an Alkhand. Or anyone.

"And the despair," he added. "The despair most of all. And while there is no cure for any of these things, I know a medicine for that last. To have you back at court."

Gorbudan made a noise, not a word exactly, just a surprised grunt. Dekamran had ambushed the master strategist.

"You would stand down...?"

"No." Dekamran shook his head. "But I would welcome you back, and have you at my right hand, my most beloved and valued advisor."

Advisor was a Pal word. Those men and women clustering about the Peost throne with their hand about that nation's throat, they were *advisors*. A mis-speaking on Dekamran's part then? No. Just a tearing down of any misunderstandings. *I am not as soft as you remember.*

"What use is an advisor not listened to?" Gorbudan said flatly.

"But I would. Precisely because you would say the things I never would."

"And at your other ear, the Kepishi woman."

"Even so. Because the Palleseen are a great power in the world, and it would be foolish to just pretend it were not so. And they have much to offer us."

"I have seen what they have to offer, in Peor," Gorbudan said. "Brother, you are a fool. To even make this offer to me shows me you are still a fool. I love you. You are my blood. But you are still a fool, and living amongst the Kepishi has only sharpened your folly. Honed it until you would cut the throat of our nation if they asked you."

"You think very poorly of me."

"I love you, as my brother," Gorbudan said fiercely. "I would there was a world where a man like you was right. A man who could look out from his balcony and see only peace to the horizon. A sky without clouds, a sea without storms, a land without troubles. Perhaps somewhere through the Waygrove there *is* such a world, and all men there are content and know no fear. But that is not our world. Our world is a sword-world, a baton-world. A place of struggle where the strong use the weak. And yes, Pallesand is strong. But that means they must be *fought*, or they will use us just as they use the Peosts."

"Our father leaned on my arm today, and I bore him up. Am I using him, then? Am I a cruel despot, for lending him my strength?"

Gorbudan scowled, rolled his eyes at the sophistry. "You have made your offer. A place at your feet as your dog, and you will perhaps take heed when I growl. Shall I make mine?"

Dekamran, who had known this was coming, just nodded.

"Step down. Now, or when the time comes that our father can no longer govern. Step down, with my blessing." Gorbudan stared at him for a moment, not speaking but plainly with more to say, then came to some inner decision. "I was going to say, join some order, become a monk. Step aside from the court entirely. Even that would not be wholly safe for me. There would always be someone who felt they would profit more with you on the throne, not I. They would seek to draw you back. But I could live with you as a monk. Good works and philosophy. Teaching. You would be a good teacher, brother." Holding up a hand against Dekamran's rejection. "But I have heard you. You have already offered me more than is wise. Having me at court, at your right hand, think how many would rally to me every time you made a decision that displeased them. Think how much incentive I would have, to give you poisoned advice. You would have the throne a year, at most two, before my supporters rose up against your mildness and begged me to save them from the kindness of the Alkhand. Instead of just standing aside for me, you offer me the throne in a way that would only harm our family and our nation." Gorbudan pressed his thumbs into his palms, first one hand then the other, a duellist's habit. "If you, the fool, can go so far in your offers, then I, the wise man, will meet you halfway. Step down from the succession and sit at *my* right hand. You would be a better *advisor* than you ever would be Alkhand. Your mildness to temper my steel. And I will have you speak to the Kepishi on my behalf, to blunt my words until they go away mollified, if not satisfied."

"And when you march across the border to drive them from Peor, how should I mollify them then?" Dekamran asked him.

Gorbudan laughed – not the disdainful crowing Dekamran had expected, but softly. "You would find a way," said the warrior prince. "That is your gift. I could speak only stones to them. You would find a way to paint them as cakes, and the Kepishi would eat them and declare how delicious they were."

Dekamran closed his eyes for a moment. No great risk. If violence was to happen here, seeing it coming wouldn't help. To Gorbudan everything was a fight with only one winner. Peor and their neighbours, or the great overseas power of Pallesand. The

Alkhand Gorbudan would rule over a generation of war, driven by the sincere belief that he could not be defeated. Because, in the pit of his heart, he believed the rest of the world saw things exactly the same way, most especially Pallesand.

From Gorbudan's perspective, the Alkhand Dekamran would destroy the nation just as effectively, not in fire and war, but in gifts and concessions until there was nothing left in the palace but empty rooms stripped of their finery.

A middle road, surely. Dekamran with his warlike brother's advice to restrain his generosity and willingness to compromise; Gorbudan with his peaceable sibling telling him to keep his sword sheathed just this once. Usmai both strong and at peace.

I know I would listen to him, Dekamran thought sadly. *I do not think he would listen to me. Even if he believes it now. Even if he swears it before Kakrops and the Grove and the death of the Moeribandi. Not once the crown was on his head.*

And yet...

There was rattle and clink of metal and he opened his eyes. Gorbudan had unbuckled his sword from his belt and placed it between them. He met his brother's eyes, face still guarded.

"Speak to our father," said the warrior prince. "Tell him that I would return to court, with his permission. Tell him I swear to cause no trouble, that I will kneel before the throne as a son should. I make no promises to you, about whose throne it will be later. I cannot. You are my brother; I will not lie to your face. But for now, I will be meek in our father's presence. If it would help him. If it would lift his sorrow even a little."

Dekamran swallowed. Not all he'd asked, but more than he'd hoped for. Of the two of them, who would have thought it was Gorbudan, in the end, who had the compromise in him.

He opened his mouth to agree, to exclaim with joy, to say so many things, and then the wailing started from outside.

What the Skull Said

Tempting to see Dekamran and Gorbudan as echoes of those other, older brothers. But neither Sorthist nor Oparan were the scholar-diplomat in their youth, nor yet the warrior prince. The old blind man had been a great hedonist, while his own father lived: women, song and sharp ramaht and a host of sycophants like the tail of a kite. The Serpent's Fang had been difficult, cruel, clever, binding followers to him by bribe and threat and compromising knowledge. They had mocked and belittled each other long before they found themselves at the heads of armies.

The Moerends who bound him into his own skull had known what they were about. And a ghost is not the living. Something is always lost in translation. But a skilled necromancer, divinely-inspired or not, can preserve what there is, binding something that feels, to itself, as though it still exists, and remembers who it was.

That was why Oparan chose the skull, in the end. Not just a death, for the brother who had blinded him. And really, despite the theological hairs the priests split, it was a versatile ritual. A very close cousin to the one that they had used on demons, when demons had come to trouble Usmai. Exactly the same as the ritual used, with great respect and ceremony, on the ghosts of poets and scholars who were preserved to teach an increasingly moribund curriculum to the monied young of later generations. So that the old Empire word for a sage implied 'one fit to be preserved'. And yet Oparan had meant no respect when he gave the order, his brother in his power and his backside newly on the throne. Sorthist, the Serpent's Fang, would suffer. He would be bound, and made the plaything of his victorious sibling. A toy, to be shaken like a rattle, to be talked down to. To sit on the arm of the throne like a monkey in a cage.

The ghost had raged, at first, which had delighted Oparan. Sorthist had schemed and plotted. He had sought to poison the mind of the one man who even listened to him. To no avail. Oparan had been riding high, and the venom of the Serpent's Fang had been a heady vintage to him.

Whether ghosts can change over the years remained a matter of debate, to Moerendi priests and Palleseen necromancers both. Sorthist had changed, but perhaps it was simply that there was an inner man always there awaiting discovery, and Oparan's own decline that brought it out.

A decade, that decline. The last failing years of his marriage, his wife drifting from him, not content with her place at court, her children, most certainly not her husband. The woman who he had come to lean on, a vine to a trellis, who had grown sick of the clutching, creeping prison her life had become. Her exit, to the pools, to the mask. Then each successive year, with her not returning. And, at last, the understanding that she never would. She had chosen the Grove and the mask. Or else the Grove and the mask had chosen her.

Long, bitter years, and who could the Alkhand speak to of it? The philosophy of the priests brought no relief. What use the Moerends speaking of death and reward and return when she had not died, just taken herself away to where he could never find her. Pry every mask from every Alborandi in the kingdom, he would never uncover the face of his wife.

In the end it had been just him and Sorthist. The dead brother, the skull.

Sorthist, almost thirty years dead. The cruel and the crooked. The ghost of him had listened as his brother, his killer, had poured out his heart. Lamented, grieved, beat at his breast, all the ways the master of the House of Tranquillity was not permitted to behave. In such a way, Sorthist came to know his brother for the first time.

Oparan sat in the lavish tent his servants had assembled for him. The heavy fabrics, the ornate furnishings, even a fountain, endlessly churning through the same waters through the power of a pair of tablethi. All brought on one of the great ogrodons, the monstrous beasts from another world that are his to command. Brought here to a hole in the world where anything might step forth and offer itself into his service. All these things he might have, for only a word. To be Alkhand of Usmai was no small matter.

He wanted none of them. Nor yet the poets and the musicians, the clever disputers, the priests, the gossip of the courtiers. He sent them all away. Just him and Sorthist, the ghost in the skull.

It spoke misery into his mind, they said, that ghost. The dead brother poisoned the living with words. There were reasons the wise did not surround themselves solely with the dead. Why else did the old Empire wither?

What the skull said was this: *Tell me, brother.*

Oparan, the Alkhand, the victorious, the blind, said, "I saw them."

Brother, alas, came the distant whisper that was Sorthist. Audible only in these moments of quiet retreat.

"In my mind, their masks," Oparan said. "Like candles. Each one bright in my mind. They were mocking me."

They do not mock, Sorthist said.

"She was there, amongst them."

That is not how they are. Sorthist, living, had known many things and magic not the least. Now he experienced the world with a ghost's senses, to which certain mysteries were plain and clear. Sorthist knew that Kaleithi was not behind any of the masks out there, that Oparan could not possibly have seen. That Kaleithi, the thing that was to *her* as the ghost was to him, sprang out of existence beneath the mask, and could not exist so long as the mask claimed her. In other lands where the wood of the Grove intruded, Sorthist had read, the bodies of the masks of the monks were lost to the world forever. It was the singular genius of Usmai that meant sometimes, when the mask came off, the man, the woman, sprang back into being. Cleansed, severed, free.

And sometimes not. Not ever.

"Brother," said Oparan, the ruler, the great man, winner of battles, he who imprisoned his brother's ghost as a jest, and now had nobody else to talk to. "I can't."

Do nothing foolish, counselled the Serpent's Fang.

"The drink is stagnant water in my mouth," Oparan quoted softly, the lament of another bereft Alkhand from centuries gone. "I am accompanied only by an absence. Fire does not warm me. The finest words of the finest speakers are... stones, brother. They are stones." Stones like his eyes. Like the sickness slowly eating its way through his body. Cold and joyless. "Brother, I would put off these raiments." Speaking in the formal mode of the elder verses, because they had known the human heart in those days. Not like the busy, living people around him, his children, his court, who demand that he sit in judgment or hear petitions or *do*.

He had come to the Alborandi once more, as they insisted. The constant round of ritual like coral building over the sunken ship of state, generation after generation, until what had once plied the waves with bold vigour was just an encrusted mass, entombed by its own ornament.

Brother, no, said the ghost, but Sorthist had been dead for decades. What did he know, in the end? What could he even remember of the human heart?

Oparan put the skull of his brother down on the cushion they always placed by his seat for the purpose. By his other hand was the sceptre of his office. One more grotesque weight, one more glittering symbol of wealth and power wasted on his stone eyes.

Brother, said the ghost. Not for fear. It would be a release, that was all. The end of a long nothing, trapped within the confines of his own bones. Yet the ghost begged, *Brother, no.* For, in the long years after his death, and most especially in the long years since Kaleithi left, Sorthist had discovered that he loved his brother, his killer. The man he had never really known in life, but knew in death more intimately than anyone.

Oparan took his time, placing in his head where the skull was, feeling the ridiculous, unbalanced heft of the sceptre. No tool for a man who had won battles, who had ridden in the howdah of an ogrodon, brandishing a sightless sword and heedless of the enemy he could not see. The inspiration to his troops, the father of sons and a daughter, the husband to a woman who he had loved and driven away and never been able to cut away from him.

Here, now, in this place, he understood what was truly important. Not the victories, not the battles. Only her. And if she would not come back to the world, that left him just the one alternative.

He brought the sceptre down. Struck true. Beneath the gilded weight, old bone shattered. A moment's howling grief and then the ghost of Sorthist dissipated into air, nothing to hold it in the shape of the man it had once been. Going to its judgment, reward or rebirth, if you believed the Moerends. Going back to the fabric of the world, if you believed the Pals.

The Alkhand Oparan walked until he found the boundaries of the tent they had raised for him. Felt until he found the gap through which he might escape it. Walked towards the masks like candles, bright in his mind. Extended his hands, ignoring the sudden cries of alarm coming to him as in a bad dream from many years ago. Felt the worn grain of wood beneath his fingers.

The Warrior

Enough has been said about the dynamism and the destiny, as though in the hour of Usmai's need, prophecy had ordained a hero of myth be reborn to save the nation. Strip it all away and what is Gorbudan? A sincere man. A clear-eyed man. A man who believes. And there are demons and necromancers and monsters from beyond the Grove in the world, but none of them more dangerous than a man who believes.

The pair of them spilled from the hut, still with that fragile unity binding them. Dekamran; Gorbudan. The princes, the eldest sons of the Alkhand.

And where was the Alkhand?

Panic, they saw. The bright courtiers rushing back and forth as though a colony of parrots had been disturbed. Men and women calling for each other, for their Alkhand. Lamenting, shouting at one another. No knives or swords bared. No attack. The Tesemer standing very still in the midst of all that charging about, blades over their shoulders but nothing to strike at. The ogrodons stomping and snorting, horned heads tossing back and forth like unsecured ballast in a storm, upset by the noise. And in the midst of all these things, no clue as to the cause of it. Only the expanding cloud of effect, the spreading wave but the dropped stone already sunk out of sight.

Gorbudan recovered first, seized the nearest man by the

shoulder, scowled and snarled and stared until he, and not what had happened, was the courtier's master, the prince to whom the world must account. "Tell me!" he snapped.

"The Alkhand!" the man cried, and then understood who was before him. "Your father!"

"Where is our father?" Dekamran demanded. The man, the courtier, stared from one face to the other, sibling-close and never more so than now.

"The mask," the man breathed. "He took the mask."

Gorbudan felt the world tilt beneath him. "No," he said, or perhaps he just thought it. Or it was Dekamran who said it? "Show me. Show me the mask. The monk. Show me."

The courtier, wide-eyed, sweat-shiny, shaking his head so that his jowls quivered.

"Show me!" Gorbudan demanded, and Dekamran rushed past him, staring past all the riot of colour that was the Alkhand's travelling court disintegrating into its component pieces. At the monks. The Alborandi, just going about their business. And one of them must be wearing finery. One of them must be a stocky old man weighed down with sorrow. One of those blind masks must hide blind eyes. Their father was sinking away from them into the dark oblivion of the Grove's mystery, but they could surely plunge a hand into those waters, grasp his wrist, haul him back to the light.

Dekamran ran from one monk to the next, staring at them, trying to recognise them. They had been people once, from all walks of life, rich or poor. They had accumulated such a weight of debt in life, physical, emotional, existential, that they had chosen this last resort of those who needed to be free. The mask. The Grove. The mystery. Each one of them had been someone, once, and where were those someones now? Where does the knot go, when the string is pulled loose? Where the song, when the singer falls silent? Not even the ghost of it remains.

Gorbudan watched his brother, little Kama, the kind one, the soft one, rushing from mask to mask. Moments ago there was a man, the Alkhand, their father. A minute ago. Two minutes. He couldn't just be gone. It was a trick. A lie. The Alborandi mystery could not swallow the ruler of a nation and leave nothing at all.

"Brother," he said. His voice croaked, barely ventured from his lips, certainly couldn't carry the vast distance between him and Dekamran.

Alkhand Dekamran, the kind, the just. Worse men had sat on the Mirror Throne. In another age, a kinder age, he would be the perfect lord of a prosperous nation. A man to whom brother regents would look up. A man who would usher in a time of plenty and enlightenment and be praised by the poets for a thousand years.

But not this age. This was an age of wolves and tigers and crushing claws.

He signalled his retainers, that handful he had brought in case his kind, just brother had learned treachery from his Palleseen allies. Gave his orders and saw their expressions. Fear, yes but, behind it, their faces said, *At last. At last, my prince!*

Dekamran had given up on the masks and the monks, now. He was shouting at the courtiers, who were still rushing back and forth and shouting at each other. Demanding to know where his father was. Who had seen him? Surely someone had…?

When the first of Gorbudan's retainers laid hands on him, he did not understand. He thought the man was trying to help. Seeing only someone who was *not* just blindly panicking. Dekamran seized the man right back, gave him orders. *My father, he's here somewhere. We can find him. Help me.* Then the second had his other arm, and a long straight sword in her hand, and he understood. His gaze was dragged sideways across all of that wasted movement, that meaningless stir that was the court, until it came to rest on Gorbudan.

One by one, people slowed. Stopped. Gorbudan strode to his brother, his clavar in his hand, that familiar weight. There was none at the court who could defeat him, one on one, but formal duel and chaotic skirmish were games with very different rules.

I may die now, he understood, but he had never been a man to shrink from opportunity. Which made him the man that Usmai needed right now.

By the time he stood beside Dekamran, all eyes were on him. Bitter irony, that his brother had invited him to stand there only moments ago. He had agreed to it. They were to have been united. A middle way.

"The Alkhand Oparan has retired from the world." A sudden stab of grief even as he shouted out the words, making them hoarse and harsh. "I am his son. He named me heir, before the Kepishi twisted him from true." Watching the Tesemer start to move, the Louse Monks with their long, curved blades and hard faces. Seeing who amongst the court looked to him with hope, and who with fear. "I claim the throne, by right, and for the good of Usmai," he told them. "For the strength of the land. For the independence of the throne." And, speaking straight into the face of the leading Louse Monk, the Preceptor Lhisamena, who had led his father's guard for decades: "Will you bare your neck for the Palleseen blade now?"

"My father named me heir," Dekamran called. The retainers shook him, put a blade to his throat, but he would not be silenced. "My brother wants only war. He will build only ruins!"

Lhisamena, Louse Speaker, clicked and rattled in her mouth, the thing that was her tongue twisting and fidgeting behind her lips. She spoke in her own language, the True Speech of the Tesemer. Her people closed in, a loose semicircle before Gorbudan and his retainers, blades at the ready. Some of the courtiers had steel out, too, clustering into cliques, some for him, some for Dekamran, the wise ones declaring for nobody but just watching and waiting.

"Will you lift your wrists for their shackles, Lhisamena?" Gorbudan said. And the Louse Monks were loyal, none more so. Trusted to stand by the throne, above all the factional politics of the court. Everyone knew. But the Alkhand was gone. Unmade by a mask. So where did all that loyalty go?

I will make you warriors again, Gorbudan made his face say. And he was the warrior prince, everyone knew. The fighting hope of Usmai. The captain of the border raiders. The man who would defy the might of Pallesand.

Lhisamena whirled from him and let out a shrill, inhuman sound. Her hookloper burst through the crowd, scattering the bright colours of courtiers left and right, and an instant later she was in the saddle, her falx held high overhead to catch the sun.

"The Alkhand Gorbudan!" she cried out, or at least the thing that was her tongue made the words. "The Tiger-Crab of Mantekor! The Alkhand of Usmai!"

The ground before the Alborandi palisade exploded into violence. Gorbudan didn't see who fired the first shot, but the man to his left, one of the retainers holding Dekamran, was abruptly down with the char of a baton-shot through his chest. In the next eyeblink one of the Tesemer had lashed out with her falx, clipping the head off a woman who had been drawing a skia. Whose side had she been on? Gorbudan had no idea. The Louse Monks had reversed their semicircle – not facing towards him now, but defending him. Some of the courtiers were fleeing into the trees. Others were already clashing, blade to blade, and he felt that it was personal rivalry and old grudge that drove them, not loyalty to one brother or another. It was as though they had all been wearing masks a moment before, that bound them to civilized and reasonable behaviour. And now the masks were off and the swords were out.

I have done this, he understood, but also, *I had no choice.*

A scatter of baton-fire crackled around him. He saw Lhisamena striking to either side with her long falx, even as her steed reared and plunged amidst the crowd. Its bladed arms came away bloody and people scattered every way to get out of its reach. Then she was skittering aside as an ogrodon thundered up and tried to grind her and her beast beneath its stomping feet. The swing of the monster's horns came so close past her that she had to lean flat against the back of her mount to duck under them. In the howdah above, Gorbudan saw a woman, some doyenne of the court, brandishing a sword, shouting for Dekamran and the rule of law. Beside her, the Ibaleth mahout had its long body coiled along the length of a baton, sighting up.

Gorbudan made himself move. Led his people, grabbed Dekamran by the collar and hauled him through the melee. A man challenged him and then a woman. He cut them both down, knowing that they were bold and he could have used them, and now they were dead when more craven courtiers hid and cowered and lived. Another of his retainers fell back, shot dead by the Ibaleth sniper. He saw a Tesemer leap onto the ogrodon's flank, climbing its harness like a pirate storming the high castle of a ship.

"Stop this!" Dekamran was shouting. "Brother, please!" And probably he had some deal, a concession, a compromise. He always did. He never understood that sometimes to stop or to concede was to know defeat. The kind man, the just. The wrong man for the days to come.

Two of the ogrodons had just charged off into the trees, smashing the trunks down, either gone wild, or their mahouts deciding that the fight wasn't for them. Another seemed to follow, then wheeled massively. Teetered back on its hind legs. Brought its front feet down so that Gorbudan felt the shock of it. The horns projecting at him, at Dekamran, at everything. Past the painted shield of its head he saw the Ibaleth mahout slotting a tableth into its baton with two-thumbed hands.

The monstrous beast began its charge. The last argument of Alkhands, that would not stop for spearpoints or arrows or the walls of forts. It would trample him, trample Dekamran. The pair of them crushed dead in its shadow and who became Alkhand then? In that moment Gorbudan had no understanding of what side the thing and its mahout were on, and perhaps neither did they.

He was the warrior, the hero. He waited until the last moment, knowing that, once the ogrodon had committed to the charge, turning it was nigh impossible. He threw himself aside, and his hand was twisted about Dekamran's collar so he brought his brother, his enemy, with him. Saved a life that might have profitably been left to the horns and pounding feet. Landed with Dekamran atop him, and had the man been hard, been a warrior, he could have had a knife in and out of Gorbudan there and then, and cut his way to the throne with ease.

He was not. Gorbudan slung him aside, hauled him away, mastering the moment yet again. He saw the Ibaleth loose its weapon, one of the Louse Monks plucked from the saddle by the shot. Then Lhisamena herself was atop the howdah, driving her blade into the lizard creature, carving it up with three swift passes that were no less graceful for their brutality.

Gorbudan saw the palisade of the Alborandi staved in where one of the ogrodon had smashed it down. He saw masked bodies lying like loose puppets, caught by stray shot. The bright silks of courtiers ground into the mud, and who knew which side they were on, or any side at all. Dead Tesemer, dead Ibaleth. *I have done this.* And, again, *I had no choice.* The words he would keep saying to himself until they became true.

He stood and waited, sword in hand, while the last of it played out. The final clutches who fought for Dekamran and would not surrender, cut down by the Louse Monks or Gorbudan's own loyalists. And some who did surrender, too, because the Tesemer bloodlust was up, and throwing down a sword was sometimes just an invitation to strike. But it ended. Gorbudan's voice ended it. The blood already shed ended it. The ear-shaking scream of an ogrodon collapsing to its knees, its sides pierced by a dozen falxes, its tail splintering trees and bodies in its death agonies.

"What have you done?" Dekamran hissed. For just one moment, Gorbudan felt the same shock, the same horror at what had happened here. But then he remembered who he was, and the rightness of his cause. He held his head high, as they knelt to him, the Tesemer, the surviving court, a couple of the wisest Ibaleth who understood the sudden turn that history had taken.

"Alkhand Gorbudan!" they cried. Those who still could.

He let out a breath. It felt as though he had been holding it forever.

"We ride for Alkhalend," he said. Because it was imperative that, when news of his accession reached the palace, it was he and his followers who brought it. He would need a messenger to speed to Mantekor, too, where the bulk of his followers were. And one other thing.

"Where are the Kepishi?" he asked Dekamran. "I know they left the city with you. They are not here. Where have they gone?"

Dekamran would not tell him, of course. Still desperate to defend the foreigners who were gnawing into the heart of Usmai. But this was the Alkhand's court and there was always someone who knew. Someone who had overheard what arrangements the heir presumptive had made, with the Palleseen Resident, about where they would meet again.

The Blade

Sage-Invigilator Angilly. Sage being an elevated rank just short of that class of supreme academics who sit on the Temporary Commission of Ends and Means and direct the Palleseen Sway. Invigilator, locating her within the School of Correct Appreciation, responsible for the arts, law and, more recently, less conventional departments like conjuration and diplomacy. A member of that peculiar stratum of Pal society where family got her just so far, then abandoned her to her own talents and ambition. An orphan; a product of the Pal phalansteries that teach superiority, discipline and inventive evasions of infallible rules in equal measure. Neither an ideologue nor a rebel, with an intellectual flexibility not encouraged most places in the Sway, but positively welcomed in Outreach. And very, very good with a sword.

"You keep looking at me," Gil noted. "When you think I'm not looking at you."

"I never," her aide spat. "I mean. Magister. I wasn't."

"What did Drathel offer you?"

"I – magister – nothing – just – no, nothing."

Gil could see the village up ahead, through the trees. The road here from the border post was well-travelled, mostly by the smaller sort of merchant. Peost and Usmiat traders with their carts and mules and families just… getting on with life, really. And if Peor was straining under the Pal yoke or the war was over or all of that, they were more bothered about the taxes and the bribes crossing the bridge over the Osio. Perspective, really, that what she thought was so important didn't actually have to touch these people.

"I was thinking about snails," Loret said defiantly. Which would have been a non sequitur if Gil hadn't told her about the place they were meeting up with the convoy. And was a lie, too. Or at least snails had been lagging way behind in the girl's thoughts, if Gil was any judge.

Gil thought about just stopping right there and telling Loret that if she was going to start keeping secrets alongside all those other qualities undesirable in an aide, then there really would be a boat in her near future. She didn't have the heart, right then.

Although Loret wasn't the squib of a girl who'd come fresh off the boat to watch a duel. Knives and monsters had gone some way towards toughening her up.

Flint hadn't raised an eyebrow, when he'd been introduced to a Palleseen Resident with barely a whiff of the uniform about her, but then he'd been on the coast long enough to find out how damn uncomfortable Pal dress was in the heat. Loret, in her shirtsleeves, had tanned like a sailor, and the ill-cut hair worn loose made her look like an itinerant who'd lucked into Palleseen hand-me-downs. Gil's last aide had been all stiff spine and propriety and there were times when that just wasn't useful. There was still just a little too much flinch in Loret to trust her with anything covert, though. She was frightened of her own shadow.

Or of something. *I will write home. Someone has saddled me with a bad crate of tea here, and thinks I won't notice.* Loret was some high-ranker's hellion bastard, maybe. Some Professor-Inquirer's by-blow too important to bury but too embarrassing to keep on the Archipelago. Something. Yet there wasn't the cockiness Gil would have expected from any of that. And there *was* the stabbing. The stabbing wasn't usual, for maverick brats with a protector to hide behind.

The village ahead had grown up around yet another monastery, because historically the Usmiat tried to solve all manner of problems with *more monks*. These particular monks worshipped a snail.

Or not a snail. Not like the Usrani in the capital venerated sleepy old Kakrops the frog. Snails, maybe, in aggregate? As a concept. The ideologically pure concept of snailness? She'd had it explained to her, and none of it had made a blind bit of sense. And you'd think that would make for some spectacularly lazy monks. There were plenty of them on the road, though. Heading towards Peor and other points, taking their teachings and holy books and good works. Or at least works somehow related to snails. The Spiribandi sect encouraged the life of a wandering mendicant, which also didn't fit with Gil's perception of snails. Save that they always walked, and shouldered great bulging sacks and packs, so maybe what they got out of snails was that you had to carry your life with you.

They were one more group that had come to Usmai from elsewhere, and with whom the Alkhand must renew the bonds between church and state, though. They'd come from over the Garmoers rather than from some other world, but the diplomatic model was the same. And as a career diplomat, Gil could appreciate a tradition that could take something like the monsters from the Grove in its stride.

Loret yawned, and not for the first time. Honestly, when she wasn't stealing weird looks at her superior, she'd been shambling along like a necromancer's prentice piece. The previous night the two of them had holed up in one corner of a lodging house, one of the network of hostelries kept at the Alkhand's orders and tended to by yet another sect of monks. Loret hadn't had a good night of it, kicking and muttering and fighting with her clothes until Gil had to swat her awake to make her stop. Nobody had got much sleep that night. Loret looked so bleary this morning that, if Gil had been a superstitious foreigner, she'd be thinking about curses and soul-stealing and dream-demons. All of which were absolutely real, but the Pals had countermeasures and weren't supposed to lose sleep over them.

"We're early," she observed.

Loret's new yawn had an interrogative quality, but not exactly high-level calculus to come to the conclusion. The little village and the monastery together weren't exactly a bustling metropolis. You couldn't have hidden five ogrodons anywhere, let alone the bright colours of the court. There were just the locals sitting outside their houses and workshops, working at leather and cloth, pickling and preserving food, shaping wood. Beyond, waterlogged rice fields were already halfway into the new crop, children swarming the edges with slings to keep away scavenging birds. The smell of agriculture, that melange of growth and decay, mounted a determined assault on the nose. Heady odours of rot rose from the knucklebug pens where the all-purpose waste-devourers and table protein grubbed and scrabbled. Gil was about to point them out to Loret, because the girl had *not* taken well to discovering where that nice pink meat she liked came from. But Loret was obviously quite capable of making herself miserable this morning.

"Let's impose on some monks," Gil said.

Loret looked at her blankly.

"We're going to be waiting around. Maybe an hour, maybe a day. The Alkhand won't be hurried along. May as well get someplace with a roof where they'll feed us. Not snails, by the way. That's right out under doctrine, apparently. Caused a major faux pas in my predecessor's day when they found out we had recipes for them." She was forcing the levity a bit, because honestly the girl's manner – *doomridden* was the only way she could describe it – was getting to her. "Loret. Girl. Cohort-Invigilator Loret, do I have to order you to tell me what the hell is eating you?"

"What?" Loret stared at her. "You can do that?"

Gil could just about remember when she had a military-issue stick up her arse enough to have asked that kind of question, but with Loret it wasn't a stick. It wasn't the girl having been brought up to have faith in the infallibility of the system she was a part of. It was more that she *wasn't* quite a part of it. "Loret, you do understand that's how the chain of command and orders and the whole rank business works? I can give you orders and you have to do what I say. We haven't just been playing some weird game all this time."

And there was a distance between them, with those words. Not physical, but as though the space between them – just past arm's reach, really, so they could have grabbed one another's forearms easily enough if it hadn't been weird to do it – that gap was suddenly a border that Gil would have been violating treaties to cross.

"I won't. I don't have to. Nothing. It's nothing. I'm fine." As though Gil, at thirty-nine, had inherited a sulky almost-grown daughter from first principles. And that distance. It was not for a junior, a *Cohort*, to start throwing up walls and closing doors.

"Loret," said Gil, and stopped. The girl had her hand to her knife. Actually to her knife. Not that Gil had never been like that, with a superior. When she'd been young and stupid. But she'd been wise enough to keep it below a table or turned away, not right out in the open like a challenge.

"Loret," she said again, a subtle change of tone. *What is it you want? Think carefully before you commit to it.*

"I—" Loret said. Her knuckles whitened on the hilt – useless if she wanted to draw it quickly. It was as though the arm just wasn't obeying her. "Just had a dream. A bad dream. It's still…" The other hand, making claws at her straggling, sweat-lank hair. "Of home."

Gil made the mistake of trying to set rank aside then, just an older Pal woman to a younger, stepping into that distance, trespassing over the border. And Loret shouted "No!" Almost a scream. The knife was out – very quick indeed and to hell with what her grip had been doing a moment before. Gil's own instincts came out of the sheath then, and she backstepped and had her sword drawn, putting the girl at the point of it, making distance so she could use her reach.

Loret stared at her. Off-hand forwards, presenting the back of her hand and arm, absolutely about to go for the sword so she could get past it to the flesh. Every part of her terrified except for her hands, which she'd apparently rented from some stone-cold murderer.

"Loret," said Gil again. Her heart was beating like it had before she'd fought Tarcomir.

A sob came out of the girl as violently as if she was vomiting it up and she turned away, almost wrestling with the knife, almost ramming it into her own gut as she fought to re-sheath it. Gil had a moment where the simplest solution to the suddenly-more-pressing issue of her problem aide would be to stab the girl in the conveniently-presented back, and she did at least spare it a thought. And then, because she was a civilized woman, slid her sword back into its scabbard again. Because the paperwork would have been a nightmare, honestly.

Loret had her face on again, when she turned. Knife away and expression blank, as though it had all just been her dream, and now she was awake again.

"Well, that happened," Gil remarked, as if to herself. Very cool, very collected. Heart still yelling *fight, fight!* "So, we are going to have a talk now. Superior to subordinate, employer to employee. You and me, just women together. But a talk."

Loret stared at her, mutinous eyes, bland face. Her right hand, the knife hand, held well away from her belt as though to spare it temptation.

"But we'll get under cover at least, because it's going to rain, and because it's time to eat, and because if we're both sitting with some food and a few snail jokes to break the ice maybe things will be easier."

"Magister," said Loret. A plea, really. *Don't ask me*, but there was not asking about a bad dream, and then there was not asking about a bared knife blade, and Gil was old-fashioned enough to feel there was a material difference between those two things. Her rather rocky relationship with her new aide was, she felt, about to plunge off the cliff and into the sea.

The doors of the monastery were closed against them.

Gil almost walked into them, because a significant part of her attention was definitely on the shifting and disputed territory between herself and Loret. She turned to the door monk, ready to reel off titles and maybe throw Dekamran's name around a bit, if they were being awkward.

There wasn't a door monk. Not a snail-follower was to be seen, not the least shard of a shell of one.

The monastery was on a mound – not grand enough to call a hill really, just a lump of land that some monks had been ceded by the crown and found acceptable. The village had grown up around it, and without leaving a respectful distance, so that wood-and-adobe houses abutted right up against the monks' stone walls. In rural Usmai, peasants didn't tend to have big doors. Rolling wicker screens were the local custom, that could be covered over with wax-cloth when the rains came. The screens came down with the dusk, came up with the dawn. It was noon. They were down. With the distinct impression that they had been up just moments before two Pal women had taken the slope to the monastery door.

Gil rapped briskly, trying to pretend this was all within tolerance, just a little local eccentricity. Her shoulders itched where she'd even halfway turned her back on Loret. *She is not going to stab me. She's… afraid. Something spooked her, and it wasn't Croskin's demons. I just need to find what.* What wasn't in Gil's reports from home, perhaps, given what Loret had said before. *Nobody is getting stabbed today.*

Loret made a sound, one of those annoying squeaks she did

when some trivial peculiarity of Usmiat custom wrong-footed her. Gil turned, though. Cued by some subtlety of tone. Saw who was standing behind them on the path, halfway down the slope.

Stabbing had just been put back on the departmental agenda. Moved to the top, in fact, as though the meeting chair was in a hurry to get away.

A Louse Monk. A Tesemer. A tall, long-limbed woman with a broad hat and simple robes, but there was no mistaking the alien-ness, the Grove-ness of her. A woman whose ancestors had come from elsewhere, and rigidly taught their traditions to each foundling and child. Her falx was tucked into the crook of her arm, haft down along her leg, the blade jutting past her shoulder like a scorpion's sting.

Gil took two steps away from Loret. Because, if this was her trouble, she didn't want Loret catching it. Because if this was *really* her trouble she didn't want Loret in knife-reach of her.

There was not a single local to be seen. Monks and peasants both had more sense than to be out in this kind of weather.

"You have a message?" Gil called down. "From the Alkhand, perhaps?"

The Louse Monk opened her mouth and the thing rooted there clicked and shivered. "I have a message," she said, "from the Alkhand." She began walking towards them. Taking the slope with the ease of flat ground, her weapon still held back and behind, as though it wasn't any kind of threat, just some awkward piece of ceremonial tat the woman was obliged to carry; that she'd trip over, otherwise.

Loret, bless her, was doing her blank act again. Gil wasn't sure whether she'd prefer the girl stabby or not, honestly. No guarantees about who would get the wrong end of her knife, if so. Could be any or all of those present.

"Get clear," she told her aide. "This is serious. Get clear." No idea why one of the Louse Monks had decided to lodge a formal complaint with the Resident but there weren't any good possibilities really.

Loret didn't get clear. She just stood there doing fish impressions, looking from Gil to the monk, until the distance between them had shortened to the precise balance point.

Gil was ready for it. It was, after all, her private study, this sort of thing. A keen amateur, at the very least. She knew the falxes of the Tesemer had as much reach on her as she'd have had on Loret's little knife. When the monk's casual advance turned seamlessly into a whirling attack, she was moving.

Not back, because once they'd started throwing those things through their paces they could just keep pushing you. Forwards, because probably the Tesemer, in their arrogance, hadn't studied Pal duelling like Gil had studied their sword displays. That surprise was her one and only chance to end the fight a happy way.

She came damned close. That was how she'd remember it. A moment of pride even though it hadn't quite come off. And she cheated, because Pal duelling etiquette started the fight with sword in hand, but in Farasland she'd learned a really nice little quick-draw that had let her take the unasked-for gift of an ambush and return it to the giver with interest. She saw the cleaving upwards line the falx had to take and let her lunge carry her underneath it, the line of her blade grating against the back of the weapon, fending it away with high guard and drilling her point down towards the Tesemer's gut. Caught a fold of robe, tore a tiny hole. The monk slid sideways, so fluid a motion that there seemed nothing of footwork or human anatomy in it. The falx, like a third combatant with its own agenda, cut back at her. The monk was momentarily off-balance, though. Gil punched at her face with the pommel, took a circling step, tried to wedge her blade in the woman's ribs, then actually drew the shallowest of lines up the monk's cheek as she disengaged.

Louse Monk blood ran red, it turned out. Probably not many people found that out. It wasn't going to be information she'd be sending home to the intelligencers any time soon, by the look of things.

The Tesemer made distance between them, which Gil turned into more distance because her opponent had that dreadful reach on her. Probably she should say something diplomatic now. Disarm the situation with a joke and a canape.

The Louse Monk swept her straw hat off and spun it away, revealing that strip of tonsure, the wild hair either side, so fair it was almost white. That was her concession, her admission of Gil's sword skills. That the hat was in the way.

Then she attacked in earnest and Gil's world was chopped into increasingly smaller slices. She gave up any attempt at trying to counterattack very swiftly because the monk wasn't leaving her enough space to slip even the slender blade of a rapier into. Where the blade wasn't cleaving, the haft swept about to knock her sword out of line, and neither of them ever still. The two halves of the monk's weapon, despite being physically part of the same straight line, seemed to spin and dance independently, and always the hungry inward curve of the blade was like jaws trying to bite down on her. Gil fell back on her footwork, immaculate and oft-practised from her days in the phal. No piste or fighting circle, no rules and no quarter, but her feet were very interested in remaining attached to the rest of her, and for a couple of fraught minutes they kept her out of trouble.

She made the mistake, then – finding herself still whole and breathing – of trying to reverse the way things were going. If your strategy was just running away, you couldn't win. Pal doctrine and good duellist's sense. Kidding herself that she'd seen an opportunity she took it. Caught the falx-head with her guard, bound it away, pivoting the angle of her sword against it to take the butt of the monk's weapon straight to the face.

It hit hard. Enough that for a moment she lost track of things. Somehow her sword was still in the game. The shock of the next blow against her guard brought her back to current affairs.

The monk went for her, then spun away so suddenly Gil thought she'd been shot. It would have been convenient, the monk getting shot right then. A benefit for Gil's ongoing health given the sorry state of her guard.

She almost stabbed Loret. Because the monk had been falling back from Gil's aide, and that resulted in Gil's aide passing through the volume of space notionally covered by Gil's sword. Somehow Gil had enough control over her jumpy reflexes to not murder her ally, but that probably wasn't extending Loret's lifespan by much because she was going up against a falx with a pen-knife.

The monk had been spooked, Gil guessed. Had already written Loret off, and the girl's immobility for the fight to date hadn't altered that assessment. Except Loret's teeth were bared to the gums, her eyes white all the way round and she screeched like a mad falcon as she ran herself right onto the monk's blade.

Or would have done. Seriously. From a girl scared of everyone to one with not one thought of self-preservation. But Gil, wrong-footed, off-balance, threw herself into a desperate lunge. Made her rapier the key threat, so that the monk had to fend it away. Gil closed and closed. Got a hand snagging the robe, the sleeve, the haft of the falx, just for a moment. The monk had iron claws jutting down from leather bracers, a nasty little piece of costume jewellery. She raked them across Gil's shoulder, shredding her vest and shawl and skin. Then Loret was carving in, still screaming. Something inhuman, as though the sound came from a part of her unconnected with breath. Hacking with the knife, gripping the collar of the monk's robe. And yes, they bled red, and kept on doing so until Gil couldn't believe there was so much blood in the world. Until – from a distance well out of knife-reach – she was just shouting the girl's name over and over because the monk was already dead.

Loret let out one last, long scream. A different one. A horror at herself, at the knife, at the bloody three-course banquet she'd just carved out of the monk. She dropped the weapon, hands clutching at each other. Her eyes, turned to Gil, were agonised. Her mouth, open, trying to speak, but just screaming for a moment, as though the fighting thing in her hadn't finished, had one more thing to say.

Loret sat down, gasping for breath. Frantically wiping her hands on the earth and simply getting them filthy with blood-greasy dirt. Her lips moved, words there that Gil couldn't disentangle, that didn't seem like Pel at all.

She was frightened, just for a moment. Of the girl. Not even of the monk but of the girl who had saved Gil's life.

Then the rest of her mind caught up and she was frightened of the monk. Of what the monk represented. Of why a Tesemer might be here, trying to kill her.

The monastery door was solid, but she kicked in a few screens until she found an old man who looked like he could be in charge, and then she threatened him with her sword and with her nation until he gabbled out answers. Although, she thought, maybe it was Loret, the simple fact of Loret in the world, that actually got him talking. And Gil could understand that, honestly. Loret being in the world was giving her some serious concerns.

From the terrorised local she heard the news from the Alborandi compound. The Alkhand, the brothers, all of it. Understanding that, while her back was turned, a new age of Usmiat history had begun.

City of the Alkhand

There were wars. There were guilds and monopolies that emerged from the woodwork and took issue with how you did business. Outside the Palleseen Sway there were cults and temples who decided that the way you lived or worshipped or didn't worship was a problem and maybe you shouldn't live here any more. Inside the Sway there were a thousand rules and regulations that all came down to 'Do literally every smallest thing exactly the way we say or it's fines or confiscations or Correct Speech for you.' And sometimes an oasis of calm, a brief span of years in a tolerant place where a foreign face could find some welcome. But history always got you in the end.

The boy, Kilbery, shadowed Happy Jack across half the Sand Lanes. All the way to the prison, the House of Hard Angles, in fact. Not a place people tended to visit of their own free will, though right now it was busy nonetheless. The Alkhand was cleaning house.

Jack was not being marched there by the Louse Monks or palace functionaries, neither of whom likely knew he existed. Jack just visited sometimes. It was what Oathan called 'the Difficult Wives Club'. And Kilbery was just old enough to think he knew what that meant, and not in fact old enough – or possessed of sufficient occult understanding – to actually know.

Jack got to the door and the Moerends, the death monks who served at the prison, let him in without demurring. Just about everyone in the Sand Lanes knew Jack. The simpleton Kepishi. Not a Pal or Loruthi, just some random foreigner with barely a thought in his head. Kilbery understood that the man wasn't actually a fool, he just had no hard edges to him. He'd been through a lot; they'd all been knocked away. The boy had heard the fringes of the story. In the army, in an occupied city, Jack hadn't had much to be happy about back in the day. Now he was, and somehow that ray of sunshine that had touched him made people like him. Because he'd got what he wanted and just said *This is enough.* Jack would never stab you or sell you for another per cent of the take. People had learned that – and that he had dangerous protectors if you tried to push the other way – making Jack the Lodge's de facto ambassador who could go anywhere. Even to the House of Hard Angles. Even to the man who ran it. They were, Kilbery understood, just friends.

To Kilbery, the kid, living in the shadow of Oathan's hand, scrabbling at the shape of the world as he sought his place in it, all this made Jack very simple-minded indeed. But Oathan said *Wear your own boots. Nobody else's will fit you*, and that was the end of any discussion on the subject.

Anyway, Jack reached the prison without anyone deciding to pick a fight, and Kilbery was glad for that. Despite looking down his young nose at the man's complacency, he also didn't want to see anything happen to him. And it wasn't so very safe to be a lone foreigner at large in Alkhalend right now.

The Alkhand was dead, long live the Alkhand! Except even that wasn't quite true. There were a dozen competing stories about just what had happened to the old Alkhand, the blind man in rich clothes Kilbery had only ever seen at a distance. He had been killed by this son; he had been killed by that. He had been taken by the Pals or some other foreign power. He had been vanished away by a god. He had become a monk. He had walked into the mouth of the Waygrove.

He was gone. That was the inarguable upshot. He was gone, and his nominated heir, the second son, was gone. Instead,

Gorbudan the firebrand had arrived at the gates of Alkhalend and declared himself Alkhand. They'd held a ceremony at the pools. That precise point halfway up the waterfall cliffs where you could see it from just about anywhere in the city. Kilbery had climbed on the rickety leaning roof of the place above the place above the Fever Lodge. He'd stolen the little folding glass that Oathan had stolen from someone else, fit a pilfered tableth into the slot and seen a great deal of juddery, too-close detail his hands weren't steady enough to make best use of. The Tiger-Crab of Mantekor, the warrior son, had looked fierce and impressive, Kilbery had to admit. Done up in all the finery and with armour on as well, the four-panelled corselet that Usmiat noble cavalry wore. He'd stood in the pool, his silks trailing in the water, and the Usrani priests had coaxed Kakrops out from the cave. The big frog had been painted with jagged, warlike shapes. Little scenes of stick-men battles down his bulging, warty flanks. His protuberant eyes, big as a torso each, had goggled at everything with the same vacancy as Happy Jack. Then the cadaverous bald man who was Grand Moerend had turned up with a lot of skull-looking regalia and rushed through the formalities and, lo and behold, Gorbudan was Alkhand. Nobody had really got into the festive spirit of it, Kilbery felt. Everybody very on edge throughout.

That had been seven days ago, and Alkhalend had not seen seven such days in living memory. Or not, at least, since the old Alkhand and his brother had thrown down. That was what the street sages said.

Kilbery had not gone to the palace. Even though he had dearly wanted to. Those royal retainers who needed their pile cream or the pills that drove away dreams of possession, they sent servants to the Lodge to collect. Kilbery wasn't scared, obviously, but right now nobody wanted to see a Pal face anywhere near the House of Tranquillity, not even a boy's. Because if there was one thing Gorbudan was specifically known for it was not liking Pals. Not liking any foreigner who had been using the old Alkhand's light touch to worm their way into the city. There were plans being made at the Fever Lodge, Kilbery knew. Fallback plans of the kind a group of fugitive deserters always had half-formed in the back of their minds. Happy Jack's plans, in fact. Because that was the other thing the man did. While everyone else spent their brain-space on the knots they'd made of their lives, Jack was just a loose piece of string you could tie up any way you liked. His visit to the Difficult Wives Club this morning was not just a social call but him tentatively exploring their options for getting clear of the trouble, like a surgeon with a wound.

Kilbery hadn't been to the palace, and *she* hadn't come to the Lodge. Fencing lessons were off, or at least Caecelian was just teaching a handful of street bravos. The girl, the sullen one, had not been seen near the Lodge since Gorbudan entered the city. Not that Kilbery was worried, obviously. Not that she meant so much to him that he was practically gnawing his fingers off for want of news. Being the brash streetwise youth he was, that would obviously be beneath him.

He did chew on his knuckles a bit, when he worried, and there were certainly tooth-marks there now.

With Jack vanished into the shadows of the House of Hard Angles, Kilbery returned to the Lodge. Oathan would already be stomping and storming about him being late, and the man's temper was due to take another knock because there were a handful of deliveries the boy hadn't even been able to make.

He found the big man, the Reckoner and Tally, the old surgeon; the three of them sitting around a table that, in other days, saw a lot of blood. They had the serious tea out. Not the regular kind for everyday or for guests. The last of the little bag of Oloumanni blend Oathan had been saving. Kilbery knew from the heady smell.

Defiantly, he dumped the satchel on the table, making the jars rattle. Leading with the knowledge he hadn't been able to do his job and waiting for the man to make something of it, by word or deed. Cuff him, shout at him, call him *Useless child*. All the usual. Instead, all three of them just stared at the bag like it was full of snakes and tax collectors.

"Go on, then," Oathan invited him. Still a bit pugnacious. Still a potential overture to a bawling out, maybe just giving the boy enough rope before kicking out the conversational stool. But it didn't feel like that. Kilbery looked into his father's eyes – not his father, but all the father he had right now – and saw fear. You had to look hard for it, it was buried deep and Oathan's eyes were small and narrow, but it was there.

"The *Tarsier*'s left dock," Kilbery said. "Just took off last night, they said. Cut and run. This morning there was a mess of the Alkhand's people come to talk to the captain, real angry they couldn't."

Oathan took that jar out of the satchel, placed it to one side. A thorough accounting then.

"And Magister Fallery's gone." The Pal who had the import-export warehouse in the working district beyond the Water Lanes. "Gone with his family and all their servants, and everything they could carry. Gone down the Peor road, they said," Kilbery reported. And still no hard word from Oathan or any of them. An attentive audience, in fact. It didn't make him feel important. It was unnerving, the way they were actually listening to him.

Oathan took the little wooden caddy from the satchel, six wax-sealed vials rattling. His blunt fingers touched the last failed delivery, the big jar with all the yellow pills. Chewing at his lip.

"Sier Lioban," he rumbled. Meaning the patriarch of a big Emorandi clan with a mansion up on the cliffs, within easy stroll of the palace. A man high in the graces of the old Alkhand.

Kilbery swallowed. "Exiled," he said. "The house is all shut up. A monk told me, though. They said he was saying, about the second son, you know. About how it was meant to be before… before it happened. Exiled yesterday."

Oathan picked up the big jar, turned it round in his hands. A moment's tension, when Kilbery thought he'd throw it across the room, but then he put it down. Temper tantrums with breakable goods weren't something an alchemist could allow themselves.

"What about on the Lanes?" Tally asked.

Kilbery tried to look virtuous but there was no pulling one over on the old woman. "You've been to some drinking den or one of those ridiculous puppet fights or something on your way back. I know you," she told him. Not angry, not even unkind, just saying. "What's the word?" And she shifted over. Kilbery stared. Nobody actually went and got him a seat or anything, but abruptly there was a seat-sized gap between Tally and Oathan, and when he went and fetched a camp stool, it fit there perfectly and so did he.

"Half of them saying it's all rich men fighting and won't come here," he told them. "But there's seven more full cells in the House overnight. And they say it's Pals. Pal merchants who were holding out on their dues." Customs, taxes, and with the old Alkhand so distant, and his heir being a friend of the Resident, small wonder the Palleseen doing business in the city had tried to push it. Except nothing made Gorbudan happier than an excuse to give the ghosts more company. "And two of 'em not even Pals, they say. That woman who did the magic fish thing, they took her." And then he had to explain what he meant, because the priestess of some Faraslandi sea cult probably wouldn't have appreciated the way the boy described her. "And Doctor Grau. They took him too." The Allorwen spice trader who'd run here years ago when the Pals added Allor to the Sway, and had now been taken up for one of them.

Kilbery looked around the table. Tally was a Jarokiri, patently not a Pal but no Usmiat either. The Reckoner was from the Divine City, an isolationist little place of strong magic that didn't even appear on Usmiat maps. And Oathan was a Pal, and if Pals were a target then he was the biggest in the city by weight.

"I don't want to have to move," the Reckoner said quietly. "I like it here."

"I don't want to have to move into the House of Hard Angles," said Tally sourly. "That is most certainly something I don't want to do."

"We can just lie low," the Reckoner said. "The city will find its equilibrium again. This is just the new man telling us all he's in charge." She scowled, briefly as sulky as a small child. "I don't want to move."

"Fine," Oathan told her. "So you get *her* to lie low, will you?"

Awkward looks around the table. The Reckoner said, "Maybe Jack could..."

"Jack has no control over *her*. That's literally their deal," Oathan pointed out. Meaning the Viper. Meaning Caecelian. Who was not here, hiding behind doors and talking about leaving. Who, if anything, was even more out and about since the troubles. Walking the city with her sword and her attitude and the sheer fact of her being. Because she *was* trouble. That was literally what she was. And Kilbery reckoned she missed her favourite student, and he could understand that.

"She's going to get us all fucking hung. Or shot. Or fed to the frog," Oathan spat.

Then someone was banging at the door and shouting, and all four of them leaped up from the table, each a different way, giving themselves space. In the next moment Kilbery recontextualised the noise from *They're coming to arrest us*, to *Someone's in trouble*, and so long as that someone wasn't one of them, that was just fine.

Oathan gave Kilbery a look. Normally those looks, those *shouldn't you be doing something* looks, were just one more thing for him to buck against. Right then, though, it was a look that included rather than dismissed him. He was one of them. He went to the door and opened it, standing back and behind it in case of trouble, hand on knife.

What came through was a patient, though. A man with a black and blue face, arm in a sling that had been a scarf not long before. Another man supporting him, his own baggy clothes red-smeared and his scalp cut open.

Kilbery closed the door, and by that time Tally had the tea things off the table and the Reckoner had slung a sheet down, from conference to surgery with the ease of long practise.

They got the man with the carved-up arm onto the table, and the two women set to work, each in their own way. Kilbery had placed the pair, by then. The badly injured man was a Pal, a pimp actually, here in the Sand Lanes. Not well-liked, but a local business like any other. His friend with the superficial scalp wound that Oathan was even now looking at was his bodyguard, a punchy Maric sellsword who'd obviously been earning his keep. Their story came out between winces and oaths. Not even some delegation from the palace come to kick over one more Pal getting fat as a tick off the back of Usmai. A husband, in fact, whose unhappy wife had been making visits to the establishment. He and a bunch of his friends had turned the place over. And not like those resentments hadn't been simmering for a while, Kilbery reckoned, but suddenly a place owned by a Pal – or just by a foreigner maybe – was fair game. Not by the order of the new Alkhand, not even some blanket decree, but because someone looked at the tilt of the scales and reckoned that certain transgressions would go unpunished now, that might have been slapped down just a few days before.

The Fever Lodge had a lot of friends in the Sand Lanes. They'd worked hard to build that trust, because they'd been spectacularly friendless on arrival. If you were all Pals and their Accessories, but also fleeing Pal justice, that left you precious few places to turn. So maybe nobody would be turning up with sticks and torches to the door of the Fever Lodge just yet. Until, that was, someone turned up who they couldn't save. Or who didn't want to pay whatever price they demanded. Or who wanted to get fresh with the Viper. Or who felt the Reckoner's tricks offended some religious edict of their particular sect. Or something else.

The boy didn't want to leave either. For a variety of reasons, and though the girl was in there, so was the fact that this was the first place he'd called home in living memory that wasn't an army camp or an orphanage. But he had a sense of great weights on the move, that didn't care what they crushed. And honestly, if the new Alkhand wanted to sharpen a knife for Pallesand, the state, then Kilbery didn't grudge him. Not like anyone at the Fever Lodge had fond memories or they'd still be with the army. But right now, someone was stacking up a real big bonfire of everyone Gorbudan considered an enemy, and you'd get scorched if you were standing anywhere near. Plus a whole load of people in the city really *were* the man's enemies, on account of how they'd been cosy with the other brother, or done business with the Pals when doing business with the Pals was just the way things were done. Or some other reason. Everyone had cheered when they'd put the White Petal Crown on his head, but there had been a lot of doubt in the echo.

They patched up the pimp, squeezed him for all he could pay. Just because he was the injured party didn't mean anyone there liked him. He'd earned his bad reputation with plenty of bad deeds and the Reckoner added a few weights to the scale for that, sure enough. His bodyguard, scalp stitched, gave a nod to the medicos as they left. Someone anticipating repeat business.

Kilbery helped Tally clear away the bloody sheet, dumping it in the acrid disinfecting tub with the others. Oathan scrubbed the tabletop almost absently, scowling at his own hands. The Reckoner sat and nursed her arm.

"Those monks with the monkeys," Tally said. "Maybe. They'd take us in. They owe us."

Oathan grunted. "Until the Alkhand's people turned up with a writ. They don't owe us *that* much."

"The Cotto," Tally suggested.

"Will sell us," Oathan decided. "To literally anyone. Don't trust pirates."

"Well then it's Jack's plan, then," said the Reckoner softly. Kilbery felt a chill go through him.

"That," said the big man hoarsely, "is an *extreme* option. Less safe than staying here."

The Reckoner shrugged, one shoulder only. "Jack doesn't think so."

"Jack's an idiot."

"He knows the place," she said. "And he knows the man. If we can—"

Another rap at the door. Another moment of tension. "Not a moment's bloody peace," Oathan growled, lurching to his feet again. Kilbery was at the door without needing to be told.

A woman, her shawl up. A local. Not a local. A Pal. Oathan's face set hard. Of all the people none of them wanted to see right now, of all the lightning rods to call down trouble on them, here was the very acme and exemplar.

"What do you want?" the big man growled, as though daring the woman to go on fire so he could refuse to piss on her to put her out. They only let her inside because having her on the doorstep where everyone could see would be worse.

And the woman stood there, before their united and hostile gaze, and told them exactly what she wanted. The help that she was begging, because right then she lacked any of the usual currency of influence she'd have to spend. And impossible, anyway. Nothing that any of them could help her with. *Go away, woman. Go bother someone else so that when the Alkhand finally notices you creeping about underfoot, it doesn't track mud to the door of the Fever Lodge.* That was very much everyone's attitude, Kilbery could tell, and he stood right there alongside Oathan and Tally and the Reckoner and fit that exact same expression on his face. A united front. Not wanting anything to do with any of it.

Except Jack came back, just as the Pal woman was explaining what she needed and why it was somehow in their benefit. This desperate gambit, because they were apparently the only people in the city she felt she could call on for help. And Jack just said, "Oh aye, I know that. I can do that. That fits the plan perfectly," without reading the room at all.

Alkhand of the City

A man who hears the whisper of sand. Not that he would have wished evil on his father but, had this happened when he was in favour, how much better things would have been. Now he has had two years away from the throne, and sees all those who have crept into positions of power. Time-servers, bag-fillers, the pouches strung from their belts are full of Palleseen coin. A mix of those who seek to sell their nation, and sycophants who simply seek to buy favour by any means. The old man had been blind, and his new favourite son went through life with his eyes closed. Gorbudan hears the whisper, time rushing away, and knows he cannot be delicate in his first months, even days, of rule.

Half the court changed in those first few days. A handful of the powerful and influential cordially announcing that they were retiring from this or that role, after Gorbudan met with them and promised this or that degree of favour, or withholding of consequence, if they stepped down. A further handful, similarly powerful, telling the world that, entirely of their own notion, they were retreating to this or that monastic order, abandoning the trappings of their secular and worldly life. After rather more pointed conversations with the new Alkhand on the general tenor of: *I know just where your loyalties lie, but you are important enough that this dignified lacuna to your public life is permissible. Or else the throne is at war with your family, and nobody wants that.* A rather larger spate of lower-grade functionaries being dismissed, minor courtiers informed they were not welcome at court, key-holding individuals across the city relieved of their positions, losing stipends and titles and houses that went with the honour and not the individual. Gorbudan would have preferred to sow and reap with more care, but right now word of his accession would already be all over Peor, would be on a boat heading to Pallesand, would be burning through the neighbouring Successor States. There would be a sword-time in the future, and when it came he could have no knives at his back. Hence some had been cast down who probably did not deserve it, but rather that than the alternative.

And there had been the others. Three Emorandi clans who had tried to stand up to him. Not united, because those weighty families were all feuds and rivalries, and so he'd dealt with each in turn. Exiled them from the capital, sent them to sulk on their estates. Held their grand houses, mills and nearby farms, in the name of the crown, to be returned on evidence of good behaviour. And they weren't even fanatical converts to Pal perfection, or standing on a belief in patricide. They weren't even tight friends with Dekamran decrying the man's death in the scrum at the Grove. He'd have respected any of those a little. They were powerful civic families who thought the new Alkhand too unsteady on his feet to push against them. They came to him, their fingers still stained with the letters they'd doubtless dispatched to Pallesand, mentioning that if a sudden power vacuum occurred at the highest reaches of the Usmiat government then they were, of course, available. They came and demanded this or that honour, made veiled threats about this or that alternative to the man who hadn't been supposed to inherit. Always other options, they suggested, unless the fool they took for their new Alkhand gifted them this or that sinecure or estate.

Understandable, from their point of view. Oparan had been a man of the court. When he'd ruled actively it had been through political games, rivals against rivals, the balance of factions and interests. That was the stagnant pond these people had grown fat in. And Usmiat succession was tricky. The election of the previous Alkhand was everything, and Gorbudan being oldest didn't count for much. And if the elected heir was dead in a skirmish outside the gates of the Alborandi, didn't that mean Gorbudan was next in line? But Gorbudan had been in exile at the time, and so... Uncertainty. Cracks enough for greedy thieves to force a dagger in to pry open the succession. All of this, implicit in the disrespectful way they spoke to him, only days after they'd cheered his coronation.

He'd called for the Louse Monks. Shown them, in that Tesemer steel, that the old royal bodyguard were in no doubt who'd inherited. Gorbudan was not just a politician. He was the warrior prince. In the two years of his exile they'd all forgotten it. It seemed so recently that they'd been gathered around him, his father an unheeded appendix on the Mirror Throne. Men and women like this had hummed with approval as he'd told them about how Usmai must draw the sword it had left unheeded in the scabbard for a generation. How, unless the fighting spirit of Usmai awoke, the Kepishi would creep in and poison every well. Look at how it was in Peor.

Two years and they'd all forgotten, leaving him with the bitter understanding that they'd never really believed. Just nodded and smiled because he was the heir. So now they were all on notice, and the worst of them were gone. Those who had written to him, served him in exile, done favours for him when he had no means to repay then, they found themselves with new honours and places at court, new estates, new houses with another clan's livery and furnishings still inside them. And some of them were chancers who'd been playing all sides, but he could only hope he was putting no-one at his back who was an enemy. He simply had to keep winning, because nobody has friends like a victor.

The Mirror Throne was a hard seat. He had cast aside the cushions his father preferred. Gorbudan, sitting hunched forwards with the great scalloped back looming behind him like the very shadow of history. Sitting with a scabbarded clavar across his knees as though he might strike the head from the next petitioner in a fit of martial rage. His face – and he knew it very well, because a statesman and a general both must understand how others see them – was a soldier's scowl, the eyes like steel, the beard a dagger, the brows crooked like the spread wings of a predatory bird. His father had managed perhaps three petitioners before retreating to poets and melancholy. Gorbudan sat on that hard seat for hours. Had food and drink brought to him, so he might not interrupt his counsels. Burned through a hundred years of Alkhalend's business, great and small, in six days of intense governing. Aided, from the third day, by the spreading knowledge that the Alkhand did not dance like the court had danced. He spoke straight, tore through veiled threats, kicked down false modesties and spat in the eye of flattery. Blunt, plain talk and the minimum of negotiation, and so a hundred appointments were unmade and made, honours stripped and given, monopolies and concessions redistributed. Firstly the great clans of the city, the Emorandi with grand manors overlooking the waterfalls. Then the native merchants and factors. Then those foreigners he would meet with, who had made themselves a part of Alkhalend's fabric and yet remained of good repute. A handful of Loruthi, a Bracite cloth merchant, a veiled Sansovaalli with a serpent's voice who had nonetheless been a friend to Gorbudan's father and grandfather. Kepishi who had no reason to love the Pals.

And he hadn't given orders to simply throw every Pal out of the city. He had been tempted. Perhaps later he would. Right now he didn't have the sheer numbers a citywide purge would take, and also he wasn't a mad tyrant. No matter what they were doubtless saying about him, in quarters high and low. He would not trust or advance the fortunes of a single one of them, but that was a long step from throwing them all in the House of Hard Angles.

Where accusations came to him, though – corruption, greed,

cruelty, disloyalty – he didn't hesitate. Let that serve as a warning to the others. And where word came to him of those same foreigners cheated, attacked, insulted, robbed, well, the Alkhand would attend all matters in the fullness of time. Eventually. In their due season.

Before him now was the broad figure of Follo, Preceptor of the Usrani. The monks of Kakrops were a faction no Alkhand could afford to offend, because they were beloved by all. They contributed a thousand minor servants of the public good to Alkhalend, from the palace down to the Sand Lanes. And here was Follo, jolly, bare chest and belly a liquid fall of flesh as though the city's own waterfalls had been made into a man. And the Usrani were often fleshy, but their boast was *Where we are, we eat last*. The man took his prodigious gut about the mansions of the wealthy, peddling blessings of fertility and fortune from the frog god, but the donations he took away went straight down the cliff paths to the poor.

The changes the new Alkhand had been making had interrupted the man's careful network of charity and redistribution. In the long term, Gorbudan knew, the graft and corruption he'd banished from the city would make everyone richer. Eating was a short-term need, though. Various of the officials and families and even foreign merchants he'd displaced had been regular targets for Usrani panhandling. And here was jolly Follo, smiling, jesting, reminiscing about events from Gorbudan's childhood that he'd almost forgotten. Not mentioning Dekamran, not even slightly. And, by not so mentioning, absolutely drawing his attention to it. Kakrops, as part of his remit for abundance, was a god of the family too. And nobody had levelled the finger at Gorbudan and screamed *fratricide*. There had been a fight, spontaneous, erupting out of the shock of the former Alkhand's unexpected retirement. People died in fights. Obviously Gorbudan hadn't *meant* it. Obviously he was very sorry.

Obviously he would pledge from the throne's own coffers, so

that the Usrani begging bowls wouldn't be less full tomorrow than they had been yesterday. Even though the throne's coffers were already pledged in multiple directions. Some of those merchants he'd met with had been talking about loans, barely able to keep the glee out of their voices as they thought about the Mirror Throne owing them, with interest. Gorbudan clenched his fists, nodding. Yes, of course, everything you ask for, Follo. And, as Gorbudan the man, of course he supported the Usrani. What was Usmai, without its patron god and his favourite monks? As Gorbudan the Alkhand he counted the coins and felt his treasury like a hungry man feels his belly.

After Follo it was more priest business. Specifically His Quietude the High Moerend Arkanith. The man who had crowned him, because while Kakrops was the religion of Usmai's people, the traditions of kingship were those of the old dead Empire. Arkanith, an emaciated stick to Follo's quivering bladder, a man whose faith required him to look as dead as possible. The skull that sat so patently beneath his parchment skin, brought out with black lead and white antimony just in case there was any doubt about just what awaited all men and women in time, even the Alkhand.

And Arkanith had his own agenda, ambitious in a way Follo wasn't. The Moru faith had clung on for centuries. Every child of the Emorandi was schooled in stories and histories and languages that had no presence in the world beyond that curriculum. Every high ceremony and holy day needed a skull-faced priest in evidence, funerals especially. Every death carried a tithe to the old dead temple. But Arkanith wanted more. Money, mostly, because that was what you measured religious respect in. Sinecures and public positions for more of his cadaverous followers. And right now, he had Gorbudan over a barrel and he knew it. So yes, more preferment for the monks of death, why not? And like the treasury, Gorbudan was aware that some of what he was promising had been handed out twice or thrice. Which meant his only solution would be to expand the reach and wealth of Usmai until all those claimants and creditors could be satisfied.

Peor, the weak, the Pal-ridden, was just over the border. And it wasn't as though he wouldn't have to march across the Osio anyway, because if it wasn't him going to whip the Peosts into line, exact tribute and throw out the Kepishi, then it would be some manner of Pal-funded expedition coming to him.

Lhisamena had reported that the monk she'd sent to make an end of the Pal Resident had failed. Simple as that. A dead Tesemer – their unbeatable gods-damned duellists! – and the Kepishi woman vanished. Across the border to Peor, doubtless, to plot with her kin. And that worried Gorbudan because Sage-Invigilator Angilly was no fool, nobody to be dismissed. The news of Dekamran's death would have reached her. Her own chosen candidate for the throne, excised from the succession. Neither she nor the Palleseen as a whole would take it lying down. Hence his plans for an invasion of Peor, and yet more of the treasury promised towards modernising the sea wall defences.

The Pals had flying islands now, he'd heard. But there were ways to deal with them. Tarcomir had told him, before the Loruthi emissary's idiot death. Magically challenging ways. More expense.

And then there was the matter of the family. His dear family. What was left of it.

He kicked himself off from the throne, clearing the still waters around it with a single stride, not even getting his feet wet. And he was allowed, of course. The Alkhand and his personal guard could disturb that pool. And yet a little barb of the boy he'd been remained, who had been disciplined for daring to sit on his father's seat, dabbling his toes in the still mirror that surrounded the Mirror Throne.

*

Premath, his brother, was confined to his quarters. To Premath – formerly Premaran before he had undergone a particular level of Moerend initiation, and changed his name – that was no hardship. Gorbudan's youngest brother had always been divorced from the regular business of the palace, finding only one interest in life. When Gorbudan arrived at his chambers, the boy – man, young man – turned on him a face still showing the faded skull painting of the death cult. His rooms gave the impression of being sparsely furnished while actually being cluttered with *stuff*. Traditional Moeribandi ornament was very samey and dull, grey and sombre. Tapestries showed the dead figures of the great and the lowly alike being judged by death-gods, sent to their rewards or rebirths. Paintings were of skull-faced Almuers, sages worthy of having their ghosts bound to the physical world so they might better instruct the living in how to die. And actual bones. Gorbudan didn't even think that the Moerends themselves collected bones but Premath did. Jars and pots and bowls of them, as though he'd held some cannibal feast a decade ago and nobody had ever cleaned up.

Premath wished to join the priesthood, Gorbudan knew. It wasn't technically permitted, for a prince. Their father had refused, when the boy had first petitioned for it at age twelve, and every time since. Gorbudan could say yes. Could just stand on the authority of the Alkhand until the dissenting voices were silenced. It would even win him much-needed credit with the Grand Moerend. Except.

Except a brother gone to the death monks was still a living brother. Except, three years down the line when Gorbudan had been forced to offend some major family, some faction, or the Pals were looking for options, that living brother would still be there. And he wasn't fool enough to think that all the monastic vows in the world would mean they couldn't stick Premath on the throne if they really wanted. Custom and tradition were strong, but so were coin and steel and the enchanted wood of batons.

"Is it time, then?" Premath asked. His eyes, lined with the

faded lead of last week's face paint, flicked to the Louse Monks standing at Gorbudan's back. But they were there as bodyguards, not executioners. It was not time to send Premath to the reward the death-gods doubtless had ready for him. Gorbudan did not ever want it to be that time. Not for his little brother. Not weird, creepy Premaran, whom he and Dekamran had teased growing up. The last person in the world who'd want to be Alkhand, surely.

Except old corpse-faced Arkanith whispered into the boy-man's ear constantly. Did the Grand Moerend dream of a second death-empire, with a skull-painted Alkhand on the throne of Usmai? Absurd. Ridiculous. Possible. The city that Gorbudan had returned to in triumph had gained a great many shadows in the years of his exile.

"I was thinking," Gorbudan said softly, "of a meal. A meal for the family." Renew bonds, recall childhoods, just the – just the three of them.

Premath looked at him with wide eyes. "Oh no," he said. "Oh no, I don't think so. I don't think that would be appropriate. Not in our period of mourning." And technically they were mourning, but there were traditions for that. Even mourners had to eat.

Gorbudan opened his mouth to point this out, and Premath added, "*Double* mourning. Our poor brother." Mild words. Casual words. Accusing words. And there were arcane and convoluted Moru traditions for the deaths of multiple family members. Of course there were. But that wasn't what Premath meant. Premath meant *I would not trust what you fed me.*

Gorbudan wanted to stand there, with the Louse Monks as his witness, and swear that he would never harm his little brother. Not Premaran. Not odd little Premath. But the Alkhand's word was an argent cloth, as the saying went. Lies did not become it.

*

He looked in on Enshili too. His sister. Barely grown and already an orphan. Premath's half-painted face had, at least, maintained a veneer of polite familial relations. Enshili scowled at him as though she'd cut his throat if she could get within reach. But she'd been like that before his exile, to him and to Dekamran and their father, all. And she, at least, he would not have to kill. She would never sit on the throne. Instead, he would consign her to the hell of some foreign court, some unwanted match. As soon as the maps were clear enough of hasty annotations for him to know where best this greatest of all diplomatic gifts might be bestowed. No sentiment. He couldn't afford it. And, honestly, woe betide whatever prince or potentate ended up with her.

He turned and let his feet lead him back to the throne room, and all the backed-up demands of his new rule, feeling Enshili's eyes throwing daggers at his back.

Open Windows

There had been a time when she'd been merely difficult. Sharp enough to see the hole they were going to try and bury her in. Observant enough to understand how her mother wasn't happy with where she'd ended up – Alkhani of all Usmai, but sometimes that's not enough or not what's important. Educated enough to understand that in Lucibi – where they had a prince her age – they didn't even let someone go join some monks to get out of a marriage. In Lucibi, the Divine Light Priesthood said it was a lifelong commitment. No matter what. Finding that out, she'd started to play with knives. Just difficult, though. Never actually stabbed anyone. Or not seriously.

More difficult still, when Gorbudan was exiled. He'd been her favourite brother when she'd been younger, because he took no nonsense from anyone. By the time of his exile, she'd worked out that he was, from the perspective of a marriageable sister, a potent nonsense-exporter instead. She'd get no repeal of sentence from him. And Dekamran would have served her the same way, just with more hand-wringing. And probably still to Lucibi because you couldn't exactly marry someone off to the entire Temporary Commission of Ends and Means.

Probably there were worse places than Lucibi. Probably there were worse lives than a princess's. She rejected it, though. Inside her head she rejected all of it. And then had come her teacher.

The meeting, that should never have happened. The offer, that had followed. Caecelian, the Viper, seeing in Enshili the Princess something nobody else ever had. Not potential, not value, not goodness. The first two were inherent in her by birth and the last was something she didn't care to pursue. Chaos. Trouble. Caecelian had looked into Enshili's face and the expression on the foreign woman's face had been an arsonist seeing a stock of oil barrels, a poisoner confronted with the city's water supply.

Enshili had looked on her and seen freedom.

Escaping the palace hadn't been easy, but dodging her attendants had been her pastime since she was eight. She'd never gone far. They knew she'd turn up for mealtimes. Finding the right window to break out from had been the test, really. When she half-dropped, half-fell to the ground below, Caecelian had been waiting. Had adjusted the girl's stolen servant's clothes to hang better. Shown her how to walk the Sand Lanes like you were born there. And now Enshili came and went and nobody saw her. Like the worm that carves its trails in the fruit without blemishing the skin.

Two years of that. Of learning the street, of learning the sword. The real sword, not that prancing they did in the circle. Feeling the *real* of it, the way nothing in the palace was. The life you only got at the very edge of death. And Caecelian, the beautiful, the wicked, the monstrous. Enshili loved her, and loved her all the more because of how monstrous and forbidden she was. And Caecelian loved her back, if the Viper could love.

Enshili thought that the Viper could not love, not as people loved. But whatever poisonous heart-fluid she had in her, surely she bestowed it on her student, and maybe even on the odd little Maric she lived with.

And now this.

Her father had gone to do the rounds of fealty. Dekamran had gone with him, which wasn't normal, but then Dekamran had been overseas for schooling, so a lot of what he did wasn't normal. It should just have meant fewer eyes on her in the interim. And now this.

The Alkhand Oparan was… gone. Not dead. Perhaps never dead, now. Gone to follow their mother. Of course he had. Obvious, now, that he would; all those years of mourning. Except nobody had seen it coming. And somehow, it hadn't just been Dekamran witness to the fact. Gorbudan had been there, too. Swords had been drawn over the succession. And if you drew a sword on Gorbudan, well, there was only one way that was going to go. So the news that came to the city had been of a lost Alkhand and a dead heir, and it had been brought by Gorbudan himself, backed by armed followers and the Tesemer.

He'd been to see her, two or three times. Looked at her like a farmer with market day looming. A prize piece of livestock he wanted to get a good price for. And she hadn't given him the full glower of her surly act, because he'd come back with Dekamran's blood as sure as on his hands. She hadn't recognised him. Oh, the face, yes. But not the man who wore it, not really.

It was time, therefore. Honestly, she'd been putting it off. It shouldn't have taken shed blood in the family to prompt her. Caecelian's wisdom: trouble came fastest from a clear sky; the unseen blade is hardest to parry. Misery and wickedness in all things. And she'd smile, that sun-bright flash of teeth, and Enshili would smile back. And she hadn't made the move, and she knew Caecelian had been a bit disappointed. That her student's old life, the pomp and the strictures of it, still had that much hold.

No longer.

One last thing, really. One last tie to sever. Misery and wickedness. She went to see Premath.

There was a guard, a Louse Monk, on her brother's door. There was a secret space that ran between their rooms, though. A narrow shaft, an ornate gilded grill at either end. Ventilation for the most stultifying days of the year. She could lever her end off and wriggle her way in, hiss at him until he came to talk to her. Nobody else knew.

"I'm going," she told him.

Premath made a noise. She imagined the look of him. Hair cropped down, just a fuzz growing out now they wouldn't let the servants shave his scalp any more; the face with just the echo of his Moru painting. The shadow of the skull.

"I can't stay here. He's a murderer. I hate him." And she didn't hate Gorbudan. She was trying to. Saying the words helped. She didn't even know if he was a murderer. Like the official story said, people died in fights. Especially Dekamran, the hapless, the man of peace. But she said it and, each time she said the words, it became more true for her.

"I want to leave too," Premath whispered. For a moment she thought he meant go with her. Her heart leaped for joy, plunged with irritation. What use was he in the Sand Lanes? Not like anyone would need the more arcane points of death-cult theology explained to them. But he didn't mean that, of course.

"What can I give you?" she asked, knowing that this was one of those open-ended agreements the Viper always cautioned her against. Whatever he said next, that would be on her. Misery and wickedness in all things.

"Just my paints." Premath sounded near tears. "They won't let me paint." Their brother, trying to dismiss all suggestion that the third of Oparan's sons would be allowed to just sit somewhere in a priest's robes. And Enshili understood. There was no temple or monastery so remote that they'd not follow Premath there. The ambitious, seeking a figurehead, sniffing the trail of the blood royal after Gorbudan had made enough enemies to look vulnerable.

"I can get them." Enshili sealed the contract. Felt something move, in her, in the world. That was how it was, Caecelian said. When you agreed to do a thing, you did it. Did it the worst way, sometimes, but still.

She left her own chambers. There were multiple ways and she was mistress of all of them. She had a guard, too, but that needn't matter. And Premath's paints were easy enough. A small wing of the palace was given over to Arkanith and his Moerends, dull functionaries that they were. Plenty of the little stone pots they used, marked up with the ornate, dead alphabet of the Moeribandi Empire. The antimony, the lead; the white, the black. Greasy unguents marked with the scooping of priestly fingers. She stole a jar of each. A small wickedness, but all added to her tally. One more small way to ruin the world for someone. A spark of satisfaction in her, like Caecelian had taught her. *In this only do we have our hand at the throat of the world.*

Back in her rooms, back in the narrow vent, working at the corner of Premath's grill until she had it loose and could push the pots through.

"Thank you." His voice was hollow with the only emotion a death cultist could permit himself. "Sister."

"I'm going now," she said. "Forever."

"As am I," he whispered. She thought she'd been wrong, before. Now she knew she was right. The contract, fulfilled in the worst way. Misery and wickedness. The white, the black.

"I wish…" she said, and her own voice trembled. Tears attacked the corners of her eyes like stinging insects. She suddenly missed Dekamran more than anything in the world. He was always kind, when he wasn't teasing her. He always had something to say that made her feel better. Except, as she'd grown older, she'd realised that they were building a prison around her, brick by brick, and *making her feel better* just meant *making her stay put* while the walls went up. Maybe, in the end, it had been Dekamran doing her the worst service, and Gorbudan, the honest, the ruthless, who had been her friend.

"Goodbye," she said, and touched his fingers, through the pried-loose corner of the vent.

She was clever, leaving her own chambers again. Clever, leaving the palace through that one window nobody else thought you could get out of. Had her stolen clothes about her, the scarf, the shawl. A bag of food, money taken from the rooms of those haughty servants she hated most. A knife. No sword, because that was more than she could have hidden in her rooms, but her teacher would have one for her in the Sand Lanes. All very clever, dodging her way out of the prison just as they came to bolt the door.

Except, as it turned out, not so clever. She was just skulking her way through the Constellar Gardens around the palace when the voices hailed her. At first she just thought they'd seen a scruffy Sand Lanes girl and were going to chase her off the way she'd been going anyway. Then her name was on their lips, and "Princess!" and she understood that Gorbudan had been keeping a closer watch on her than she'd realised. Or else she'd been unlucky. Either way here were four of the palace staff. A snooty woman she'd stolen coin from, three servants. Fine clothes, and the lead woman had a skia at her hip that was more for show than for use. Enshili gripped her knife.

They didn't even really note it. Didn't consent to the fact that the royal princess had pulled a knife on them. They were just here to take her back to the palace. She was being a very troublesome child. Her poor brother would despair. And she wanted to shout at them, *Which one?* The dead one, or the one even now turning his face into a skull. Or the murderer? Gorbudan Kinslayer; Gorbudan Exile. He would despair, would he?

No words came from her. Their sheer refusal to see her as anything other than a disobedient little girl who should be in bed, it disarmed her. Robbed her of the ability to fight them. This was it, her grand rebellion. Put down as easily as the Pals did their troublesome subjects in the Sway.

The woman frowned, just like any senior palace official, always glad of a chance to bring the surly little brat down. She opened her mouth and it exploded in blood.

Enshili made a sound.

The woman dropped to her knees. Her face was fixed in that outraged expression, as though to get a sword through the small of the back was simply *not done*.

The three servants scattered. One scattered downwards into

a fist of bushes, his throat already weeping red. The other two froze, then, not even seeing their attacker.

Enshili saw her. Saw the beauty of her, the strike of the Viper. Caecelian lunging from the dark to drive her sword up under the second servant's ear; spinning to put her knife, that constant off-hand, up under the ribs of the last. Bringing her blades up to her lips one after another, blowing on them so that the blood evaporated in a mist and left the steel shiny and clean.

She looked at Enshili and smiled. Murder, in that smile. Murder and forbidden things. Only the lead official had even been armed, and the Viper had stabbed her from behind. But they'd have taken Enshili back, and made sure she had no other chance. And if Gorbudan could murder for the sake of statecraft, then he had no cause to complain when his own people were served the way he'd served his brother.

Murder, in that smile, but also that toxic thing Caecelian had instead of love.

"Misery," whispered her teacher.

"Wickedness," Enshili said. Then the pair of them were fleeing the gardens and the bloodshed for the doubtful safety of the Sand Lanes.

The Warden Behind Bars

No more feared place in Alkhalend than the House of Hard Angles. The terror of serious criminals, traitors and misbehaving children. Especially in the Sand Lanes, where its windowless walls loom large over all. The dead place, administered by the death monks, where the ghosts are. And other things, from time to time, that might be constrained by the same sigils as bind a ghost. Fear of the prison looms so large in Usmiat minds that almost nobody stops to ask why.

There were cells and cells, in the House of Hard Angles. The prison fell into earth, level after level. Damp, running with briny condensation. Lit only by the corpselight lamps that fed off the ghosts themselves to produce a wan radiance. The lower reaches murmured with tides, the wash of the sea. From deep below rose the background murmur of waters descending into chasms, as though the underworld of Alkhalend had its mirror to the bright waterfalls above. Prisoners were not taken all the way to such deeply buried levels, of course. Why would the monks wear out their sandal leather on so many stairs?

Only, say, if they had a prisoner whose existence none must guess at.

Dekamran, the second son, in durance.

He had been in here, by his best reckoning, seven days. Thinking back on it, the betrayal of the Tesemer should not have surprised him. They were warrior monks. They pined for mythical days when they were the final cutting argument of some other world. In their eyes, playing bodyguard to an old man had been their duty, but not their destiny. Give them a choice of two Alkhands and they would choose the man who promised them bloodshed. But the Moerends, that was a surprise.

The death priests. Law and custom and the intricate, dusty ceremonies of their brittle corpse of a religion. When Dekamran's continued existence was revealed to them, they should have stood on doctrine and tradition, threatened Gorbudan with post-mortem punishment for usurping the elected heir. Except some deals had been done, some concessions made, and they had taken Dekamran down to this tomb of a cell and buried him alive in the House of Hard Angles.

Dekamran had never been a vengeful man. Not a part of his nature, he'd have said. Concessions and agreements and putting grudges behind him. That was the Alkhand he would have been. Those who had been his opponents would have found an open hand extended to them, if they would mend their ways. He would have found a way to win over each sect and faction and foreign interest. Build a golden age for Usmai out of mutual benefits for all.

If he woke tomorrow and found himself on the Mirror Throne, he would do such things… He would have that dried stick Arkanith and his best death-cultists up before the throne and show them their own deaths in the mirror of the waters. He would show the Tesemer that skill with a sword wasn't the final word to win a war, and have them thrown into the Grove to go try their treasons in some other world. He would fill every damned cell in the House of Hard Angles with those who had kissed Gorbudan's feet when the usurper took the throne.

He would not do any of these things, obviously. If he had the chance, then doubtless his better nature would return with better fortunes. And he wouldn't have the chance.

He was buried deep in Alkhalend's most feared prison, but that was only a temporary state of affairs. A man who feared him enough to consign him to this place would grow to fear him more than that. Dekamran living represented an open wound in the new reign of Alkhand Gorbudan. A wound that only Dekamran dead could heal.

The Moru death cult, the writ of Kakrops, plus half a dozen other traditions and religions with some hold on Usmai, they were none of them positive about kinslaying. Brother slaying brother invited a variety of curses. Why else had their uncle, Sorthist, chosen the basilisk wasps instead of just a headsman's clavar? An Alkhand, a ruler, must be whole. That was the Imperial tradition all the Successor States had inherited. Save that history was peppered with counter-examples. That Alkhand of Peor with a wooden foot, the Eunuch of Goshumai, the Dusarch of Lucibi two generations ago whose body had been slowly devoured by a curse. He'd ruled wisely and well, Dekamran recalled, and surprisingly long. And there was their own father, of course, who hadn't let the wasps rob him of his birthright. Like so many traditions, these things held up until someone of sufficient power needed them not to.

The prohibition on kinslaying would, Dekamran suspected, go the same way.

Today he had a visitor. He'd had the monks, of course, bringing him food, taking away his waste, always polite and deferential save that, after each visit, it was they who were permitted to leave while he stayed behind bars. The monks performed the quiet tasks and observations the prison demanded, but they were not the Warden.

The man who came to see Dekamran was not the Warden either, though most people forgot that, and promoted him to the title. The Warden's assistant only. The foreigner. Just the latest thing to come through the Grove and find service with the Alkhanate of Usmai.

"What is it?" Dekamran asked him. "Is there news? Is it my time?" Trying to sound very brave. And wasted. The man's face, plain, blunt, didn't even register the attempt.

"I thought you might know." His voice was clipped, an accent not strong but unique. Speaking Pel, in fact, and Dekamran couldn't really account for that. Had the Pals extended their Sway to other worlds and just never mentioned it?

"Know?" The man plainly didn't mean Dekamran should have some prescient foresight of his own execution. It seemed a sentence drawn from the middle of an inner conversation the man was having.

"About this place," the Under-warden said. Ill at ease. "You're important, they say."

"I am the Alkhand!" Dekamran shouted. The echoes battered about the walls like moths, before falling through the long slot in the floor, down and down to all those further levels. "I have been robbed of a throne! Release me, and you shall have whatever reward you desire. Wealth, promotion, luxury. I will make a palace of this place for you!" A moment before speaking, he'd known he would face this man with dignity and reserve. Now he gripped the bars and begged. "I am the Alkhand, not my brother! I should not be here."

"Nobody should be here," said the Under-warden. Just a man in a strange uniform, a mask to scare children slung about his neck. Just a man from no place anybody had ever heard of, from the wrong side of the Grove. Just a man who was not the Warden, but inextricably bound to it.

Dekamran rested his forehead against the bars. "What," he asked, fighting back tears, "do you *want*?"

"This is a prison for ghosts," the Under-warden said. "Why is it?"

"What?"

"Those who built this place followed a death god," the Under-warden noted. "In my home we had a death god, too. We would have built a place like this for our god, had we thought of it." A broken little hitch in his voice, which Dekamran realised was a laugh. "You have something terrible here we never thought of. You can't know what an achievement that is, Your Tranquillity."

The address due an Alkhand. It should have been mockery, but instead was just a foreigner thinking he was being polite. "But your death god, your death religion, is not like ours. You honour death and ghosts. So why this place? Please?"

"Ah." And Dekamran, the reader, the idle scholar, did actually know. A useless piece of trivia, really. Who knew he'd be able to expound on the topic one last time before he died? "An Emperor, in the old days. When he was dying he wanted to take his court with him to his reward. He built a house for them to retire to. He made sure none of their ghosts had second thoughts." Dekamran shivered. "I think… he had this place all ready for his death, but they buried him elsewhere. For fear of what he might become maybe. So this place was just… here. And then…" And then the palace of death had become the prison from which even ghosts couldn't escape. As his ghost would not escape, when the end came for him.

"Am I a ghost?" the Under-warden asked him.

"What?" Dekamran said hollowly.

"Are we ghosts, to be trapped here?" Then something was coming. A rustling, a skittering, as of many feet. The shadows thronged with a rushing mass of spindly legs. The Warden was coming. Dekamran fell back from the bars, as though they'd save him. The Under-warden turned his long face aside, and the sickened light surprised an expression of wan joy there.

The Warden emerged from the gap in the floor and scrabbled its segmented length up into the ceiling. The lamps of the House barely seemed to alight on it, making it a thing of shadows and glints. The Under-warden extended an arm to caress its seething flank as it passed and his face was happy.

In the wake of that, a voice: "Oi oi! Hello?" More Pel, accented. A small man, just wandering about in the lower halls of the House of Hard Angles as though it was any taverna of the Sand Lanes. He drew closer: a skinny creature with a wooden box on his back. In one hand he had a jug. In the other a couple of tin cups, Pal army surplus.

"You about?" he asked the Under-warden. "Important club business." He waved the jug, which sloshed.

"Hello, Jack." The Under-warden looked down from the bristling darkness the ceiling had become. "Yes. I'm about. Let's go." Just a man, talking to a friend. About to share a drink. Not in any way the familiar of that monstrous *thing* hanging overhead. A thing that, Dekamran realised, had *led* the little visitor down here to them. The Warden, on a guided tour of its domain.

"Not been this far in before." The little man, Jack, looked about him. "May as well...?" Receiving a nod to the half-spoken sentence, he shrugged the box off his back and shoved it against the bars on the far side. It had a few holes piercing its sides, like a trap for knucklebugs or rats.

Dekamran watched this pantomime blankly. The man, Jack, nodded to him mildly, as though they were meeting in the street and there weren't bars between them. Then the pair of them were strolling off, leaving the box behind. Soon after, and to Dekamran's great relief, the brooding presence of the Warden had seethed off into the upper reaches of the prison.

Later – an hour perhaps, he had no way to be sure – the little man ambled back and reclaimed his box. When he hefted it onto his shoulders, he made a big thing of it, as though it was heavier than when he'd brought it in. As though the expected vermin had indeed been tempted inside and trapped, though Dekamran had seen not one living thing come near it.

Two days after came the other visitor, the one he'd been expecting. Gorbudan.

The Moerends escorted his brother down. Perhaps the new Alkhand didn't want to see the Warden and its human aide, the final reminder of what a terrible place it was he'd consigned his brother to. And then the Moerends left, so that it was just the two of them. Brothers together, save one of them was on the wrong side of the bars.

"Brother." Dekamran was fighting really very hard to be casual, unconcerned. To be the calm man, the philosopher-Alkhand ready for death. He was not ready for death. Even seeing that face spiked a terrible fear in him.

"I..." Gorbudan looked away, scowled at the darkness, looked back. Not a man for hesitation, but the pause between them stretched out until, at last, he said, "I don't want you dead, Kama."

Dekamran said nothing. It was a moment for fine rhetoric. The imprisoned prince raises the spectres of kinslaying, rightful inheritance, the frown of the gods, the castigation of history. The usurper is chastened. The heir-elect is restored. All's put right in the third act. He said nothing. Nothing would help. Gorbudan had already tried out the fit of the throne and found it suited him. There were a lot of creditable things in the man's face. Guilt and shame and fraternal affection. But not the tide of them it would have taken, to float Dekamran out of this place as a free man.

"What can I do with you?" Gorbudan asked. It seemed unfair, to place the burden on his younger brother. Surely one of the few benefits of being the prisoner, of the two of them, was that Dekamran didn't have to make the hard decisions any more. Besides, any suggestions he might have wouldn't be acceptable to his brother.

Even so: "I will go," Dekamran said.

"Go?"

"Away. Exile me. A monastery, if you will. Or – overseas. Just, on a ship. Away."

"To your Kepishi friends?"

"No. An island somewhere. Just... live out my days." A ludicrous fiction. They both knew it. A children's story they could tell each other. *And the exiled prince lived happily ever after and never troubled his brother's reign again.* How long before the exiled prince started receiving Usmiat visitors dissatisfied with the way things were going at home? Or Palleseen visitors with an interesting range of offers around the topic of regime change. A year at most, Dekamran reckoned.

"The Tesemer found me wasps," Gorbudan said. "I didn't even ask them."

Dekamran closed his eyes. "Well," he said. "Precedent, I suppose."

"He broke the skull, you know, before he... left." A sudden shift in the conversation, but the unspoken logic wasn't hard to follow. "You're a learned man, brother. An Almuer." A sage, more credit than Dekamran's education really merited. A wise man. Literally: one whose ghost is worthy of preserving.

I will speak such poison to you, thought Dekamran. And he could not understand how their father kept their uncle's spirit by his side for so long. To torment and mock the spirit at first, perhaps. But the spectre had become his most prized advisor in the end, the pair of them settling their differences. *Is that my fate?* He looked Gorbudan in the eye and knew it would not be. What happened, what would happen shortly here in this prison, the man would not wish to be reminded of.

"The wasps," Gorbudan said, almost helplessly. And the wasps hadn't saved Sorthist from having his ghost bound into his own decapitated skull. "Or... they would not accept an Alkhand who could sire no children, surely? Or who could not hold a sword. Sit upon a horse. Sit, physically sit, upon the throne. Tell me, brother, how much of you would I have to cut away, so that what was left could never be acclaimed Alkhand, yet would still be my brother. I don't want you dead. I *don't*." An argument that Dekamran himself had no agency in. Its object only.

"How much of Usmai will you cut?" he said softly. "And will what is left still be our nation? You will kill me. You will mutilate me. You will lock up my ghost. All these things you can do. You are the Alkhand now, brother. What might the Alkhand not do? Except save Usmai."

He expected Gorbudan to shout him down, but the man just

stared at him. Words were all he'd ever get from his brother now, before the end. He didn't want to waste them.

"You loved those stories," Dekamran told him. "Heroes, wars, magic swords. The prince with the flying horse and the bow that shot lightning. Maybe that world exists beyond the Grove but we don't live in it. It's not even that these days are less than those that came before. The days are greater, more full of thoughts and ideas, so that just having a magic sword and a bow that shoots lightning isn't how problems are solved. You'll start wars, brother, and then you'll understand that we live in a world where you can't just shout a battle cry and lead a charge and expect it to bring you victory."

"Kama, you would have been the best of Alkhands," Gorbudan told him, "in any other age. But right now, right *now* we have the very last chance for Usmai to remain Usmai. To save itself from becoming just a shadow of Pallesand or Lor or any other place. Since the Moeribandi fell, we have been Usmai, the pride of the world, cleaving to our own ways, knowing only our own laws. When the Louse Monks or the Ibaleth or the others came to us, we did not bow the knee to them and become their creatures. We made them ours. And you're right, the world has changed. The Kepishi do not come with their Kepi in hand to beg our blessings, but with demands and armies and lies. If we do not fight them now, they will devour us. Hold out your hand of friendship and they will bite off your fingers. How will you hold a sword against them then, when their armies come? I'm sorry, brother. I don't want you dead." A passive thing. Already gone from *I don't want to kill you*. Because, when it came, it would be just news delivered to Gorbudan, a sad incident already being carried down the river and out to sea by the passage of time. Receding past the horizon to where it need not be thought of. Not as though Gorbudan would hold the knife himself.

"You are right in so many things," Gorbudan said sadly. "But in this one thing the wrongness of you eclipses all else. I'm sorry, brother. I couldn't let you scoop out the guts of our country, offer them up on a silver plate and call it diplomacy."

He drew a knife. For a second Dekamran thought he'd been mistaken. That his brother would indeed do him the honour of a personal death, and he'd do it right then and there. But Dekamran just used the pommel to ring against the bars, and the Moerends padded out of the darkness to lead him away. Back to the sun, and life.

Gorbudan was obviously slow to come to a decision. Another two days dragged on with nobody but the unspeaking death monks for company, before his next visitors.

Not the Tesemer. They would be the ones to do it, he'd decided. The Louse Monks with their long swords and lack of sentiment. When he heard the scuff of multiple feet and saw three shadows pass the further lamps, he took it for his time. And probably there was proper form, for an Alkhand in durance to meet the assassins. A certain poise befitting the Mirror Throne he would never occupy. But his knees turned to water and he wanted to weep.

Save it was not the lean killers from the Grove. His breath caught, wrenched even. As though some hand had reached into him and twisted his ghost.

The Under-warden was in the lead; no great relief or revelation there. Behind him, though, two women. A Pal with short dark hair and a Peost scarf, carrying a sack over her shoulder. A Pal dressed as an Usmiat, who was Gil.

Dekamran made a sound, just a sound. Shock, joy, wonder. Such a sound, in its happiness, as the House of Hard Angles had probably not heard in five hundred years.

Gil gripped the bars, as though it was her trapped by them. Dekamran closed his own fingers over hers, feeling his chest overfull, emotion like a hand about his lungs. "It's you," he got out. Faint, almost, in the extremity of it. "It's actually you."

"I'm sorry it's been so long," she said. "I've... I've been making deals like you wouldn't *believe*. Plus dodging everyone who might want to sell the Pal Resident to the new Alkhand, because you can believe he's very keen to renew diplomatic relations the sharp way." Light, joking, the way she did when she was serious.

Can you help me? Please help me. But he couldn't beg. It would shame him to beg, before her. Not because of any difference in station, but because he wanted her to think he was brave. "What now?" he asked, voice trembling only a little.

Angilly actually rolled her eyes. "Well, that really depends on just how bloody *reasonable* everyone's going to be." And she jabbed the other woman in the ribs, none too gently. "*Fellow*-Archivist Drathel."

"Yes, *Sage*-Invigilator Angilly," said this Drathel, surly to the point of insubordination.

"Spill it," Gil told her.

Drathel sighed and then – rather more carefully than 'spilling it' would imply – emptied out her sack. A cornucopia of jars, tablets, statuettes, religious symbols and oddments of jewellery slewed out onto the slick stone of the floor.

"Well?" Gil demanded. Not of Drathel, this time. Looking at the Under-warden.

It was well known that the Warden could not be bribed. It was an abomination after all, some denizen of the worlds beyond the Grove. And the Under-warden was just its human servant. The weird, lost soldier who'd stumbled into Usmai and plainly hadn't found himself where he or his monster had wanted to be. You couldn't *bribe* them.

The man pulled his mask up, round glass eyes, unpleasantly organic hoses and tubes. He knelt, sifting through the treasure. Dekamran saw the regalia of every Peost temple there, plus a fair amount that had probably come from inside the Usmiat borders. A trove of arcana from all along the coast. Probably not obtained by free trade and ready coin, but right then he found he didn't care.

"It's all potent," Drathel said, sounding insulted. "You're not the only one with fancy spectacles. It's most of my departmental surplus, is what it is. It's *supposed* to be on the next ship home along with my request for a raise. So it's good enough for you, friend."

"Jack said..." From within the mask the Under-warden's voice was hollow, inhuman. "Is this... *all*?" When he looked up, all Drathel's pugnacity didn't stop her taking a step back.

"Yes it is fucking *all*," she told his mask. "I don't know what inefficient bloody ways you've got to squeeze power out of this stuff, but this is—" And she stopped, because the man had clenched his fists, the chain of an amulet coming apart between his fingers.

"Will it do?" Gil asked urgently. "It's what we've got. It's what's on the table. Jack said – said he could..." Her voice broke. She was left without it, biting at her lip, staring down at the man. Just like Dekamran, unwilling to be seen to beg.

The Warden's presence came from above. More sound than anything else. The rustle and scrape of it shifting its long bulk from level to level until it filled the darkness overhead. The Under-warden's mask tilted up, staring glassily at nothing.

"I'm sorry," he said. To whom, for what, Dekamran couldn't quite work out. "It's so little. I don't know. What if...?"

"We don't have long before the priests get twitchy," Gil said. "You think this is a lot, you should have seen the coin I gave *them*. And making temple donations is *not* what I'm supposed to be doing with Residency funds. So make your call, man." A little shake to her voice, but playing the hard woman as best she could.

Something passed then, between the unseen monster seething in the darkness overhead, and the kneeling man in the glass-eyed mask.

"Yes," he said, and hurriedly scooped up all the trinkets,

pouring them back into the sack. "Yes. She says yes. And tell Jack, yes. We have our deal. Yes." He stood, fumbled at his belt for keys.

The Warden intervened. A head lunged from the dark above. A head like a clutching hand, whipping with antennae, punctuated by glittering black eyes. It seized the section of the bars that was a door, and made of it a hole. Hideously eager, desperate to rend. Retreating into the shadows with nothing but a mangled twist of metal clutched in its grip.

A moment of contemplative silence, after that. Only the Under-warden in motion, standing up, pulling his mask down off his chin. Revealing his human face that Dekamran felt should fool nobody.

And then the gap, the hole, that had been bars. The lack of anything standing between him and Gil.

She held him. Probably she shouldn't, with Drathel looking on – the Warden and Under-warden being a thing apart, a thing uncaring about the bounds of diplomatic propriety. She held him anyway, hugging him hard enough to make his ribs creak. Then they were moving, because the priests would come soon enough, and they needed to get Dekamran out while they could.

Stone Tools

'Flint' Postry, Fellow-Monitor. Rank obtained through action, not family. Veteran of several campaigns. Action in Telmark, the Torne Islands, the brutal fighting in the Third Goupa Uprising, and then leading a company of marines in the naval element of the Pal–Loruthi War. A man who, after all that, *had no intention of just dying in unfilled boots in the regular army. Not the inventor of the new Ventures department but an enthusiastic early adopter. See enough battlefield errors and you start to value a position outside the regular chain of command. Plus there were those boots. Flint isn't Gil, who always had skin in a certain stratum of Pals' emphatically classless society. He wasn't going to retire to anywhere but an old soldier's home by normal means.*

'Flint' is a nickname given to him by his Seraphi, his local troops given arms and uniforms and a kind of watery Pal identity. Flint is a hard man, sure enough. Maybe that's what he thinks they mean. The thing about flint, though, is it's crude. Effective in a pinch, but steel is better. When it comes to the most popular drink down the Successor Coast, blunt ramaht is safe for children, sharp ramaht will get you drunk in short order, and flint *ramaht is very sharp indeed and will strip the skin from your throat and the paint from your walls.*

Gil hadn't been sure what they'd be confronted with. Postry hadn't struck her as the diplomatic type, or happy to stand on ceremony. Nor, necessarily, entirely under her command.

She outranked him – outranked everyone until you got as far as Sage-Invigilator Palinet, the Peost Resident, and even they were peers. But Ventures was new, and she didn't know if it fit comfortably under the thumb of Outreach, or whether it was some mad squib of its own.

She'd done her best with Dekamran, anyway. Found him clothes that were, if not quite fit for an Alkhand, then more than enough to dazzle the eyes of a man like Flint Postry. Loret had found her a dress uniform in Peor, as hers was currently under hostile surveillance at Slate House. Which meant she could at least stand beside Dekamran and give official weight to the entire business. A retinue of loyal Usmiat would have been nice, but who precisely could they trust?

Marching into Flint's camp over the Peost border – her, Dekamran, Loret and Drathel – she'd braced herself for something very rough and ready indeed.

But Flint had put in his hours on the drill square and remembered how it was done. They'd shifted all the tents so the heart of the camp was open and empty, and he had his Seraphi lined up in proper order. As smart as any army that was actively campaigning, and honestly the pale uniforms of Accessories flashed bright in the sun, very impressive. In amongst them, the companies of Pals in their charcoal looked dowdy and over-hot. And everyone had a baton across their shoulder, and the officers wore what braid they owned. Not bad at all.

And Flint himself, when he marched up to them, had shaved and buttoned his jacket properly, a swagger stick under his arm as though he was one of those old-fashioned HQ Sage-Monitors, back when hitting your soldiers was something you didn't necessarily delegate to the provosts. Probably Flint had served under just such an officer at the start of his career.

"Fellow-Monitor Postry," Gil identified him, "may I present the Alkhand Dekamran of Usmai."

"Your Tranquillity," Flint drawled – marvel of marvels, he knew the proper address. "Obviously we're honoured." Nothing in his expression to suggest that the Alkhand of Usmai might normally be expected to travel with a little more baggage. "I'm afraid we're a rough and ready outfit, but I've had my people set out something to eat in my tent, and we'd be delighted to play host."

They'd made a virtue out of the roughness and the readiness, rather than trying to mask it. Peasant food, but dolled up on the plate so that it was like when the Emorandi sometimes ate how they fondly imagined their lessers did. Although it *was* actual peasant food, sauced with rather better ramaht and a spicy Pal cruet. Throughout the meal, Gil watched Dekamran for signs of breaking. Because she needed Flint to behave himself and not start scratching his arse or talking money, but she also needed the Alkhand to hold himself together. Most especially because he wasn't the Alkhand yet, as everyone knew. The rightful Alkhand, surely, but the practicalities of the situation suggested the ownership of the chair and the crown, the city and the army, trumped the technicalities of inheritance.

Flint entertained, as they ate. He had a hundred war stories and told them surprisingly well, without getting into the gory details or going too heavy on the inevitable triumph of Palleseen ideology. Although the Pals always won, in his stories. Against great odds, in most cases. Gil wasn't sure if this was Flint the politician laying the ground or if he always talked like this.

Beside her, Loret ate sparingly. They hadn't had that talk. The knife talk. Events had rather overtaken them, and she'd been left having to rely on the girl as another pair of hands. Drawing a knife on a superior officer had become an almost endearing foible in retrospect.

Just like every major piece of diplomacy, nobody quite said *it*. Dekamran didn't quite ask. Just nodded and made observations on Flint's stories, deployed a bit of wit, raised a laugh around the table amongst the company's officers. Made a good impression, because he was that kind of person, and because he'd been to plenty of these things while he was overseas. Didn't insist everyone deferred to him. Simultaneously the august Usmiat dignitary and someone you could tell a slightly off-colour joke to. Perfect. And Flint didn't offer, though the fact that all his stories ended up with the flag of perfection flying over some place or other started to become notable after a while.

The man caught Gil's eye every so often. A grin, a twinkle. *This isn't me, as you well know.* Flint, who wanted her to think he was a soldier's soldier, because that was more honest than what he actually was. But sometimes a capable rogue was what you needed. *Look at my good behaviour*, that look said, practically presenting a statement of account that Outreach would have to settle sooner or later.

By the end of the meal, enough ramaht had been sloshed into the cups that Flint's jacket was undone, and Drathel had told a story about some temple complex she'd been cataloguing, over in Jarokir, only there was a whole sect of priests in there nobody had even suspected. "Worm priests of the worm god," she said, and Flint grinned, shaking his head. "I mean," Drathel added, "there *was* a worm god."

"And?" Flint prompted.

"Seen better gods. Seen better worms. Amazing what people'll build a sanctum to." And then glancing under her lids at Dekamran, seeing how much offence she'd just caused. But the Alkhand shook his head and laughed.

"It's a gap we'll never cross, I fear. When I was at Killinbraan, there was a sea ceremony. A Loruthi thing. Marrying the port to the sea, a ten-yearly thing. Your compatriots all arrived, buttoned to the chin, determined to disapprove." And the mood at the table teetered and Gil clenched her jaw, but Dekamran went on, "And then they found it was basically an excuse to break out the good rum. Your Sage-Archivist, the head of the faculty, just stood up and said, 'I hope that it is clear we are drinking this holy offering in an appropriately *secular* fashion.'"

Flint hooted, slapped the table and knocked back his own glass. Gil glanced at Dekamran and saw the strain behind the anecdote. He was a man who didn't even own the clothes he stood up in. Everything that was to have been his had been stolen from him. And he smiled and toasted and made small talk and she could see it killing him. But he was good at it, nonetheless. Could Gorbudan have done the same, had their positions been reversed? She didn't think so.

Afterwards, Flint led them on an inspection, still spinning his tales of heroic derring-do in siege and on the field. The companies of Pal regulars, veterans out of the Loruthi war and a dozen prior campaigns, hard men and women for whom the higher risk and reward of Ventures was a good career move. The Seraphi – those Peost faces, plus a few Gosht and some Usmiat who'd gone across the border for whatever reason. Those pale, Pal-pattern uniforms. The batons. She saw Dekamran note the batons, in the hands of the rank and file. The way it wasn't done.

Flint had some artillery too. Some Cyclers – Palleseen Hands, as they were called by most of the nations that had been on the wrong end of them, and by Flint as well when he introduced them. Not siege weapons, but they were good against massed formations at close range. A little line of squat bombards for wall-and-gate work. All of it wheeled and man- or mule-portable. And she'd seen the pieces on the clifftops and sea wall at Alkhalend. Bigger and punchier than anything Flint's people could haul around, but fixed in place and with limited arcs of fire. And not used in living memory, not a shot fired even in the previous succession struggle when Dekamran's father had taken the throne. Flint's crews had seen plenty of fire and fury in the war with the Loruthi. Military experience was one of the Pal Archipelago's greatest exports.

Dekamran nodded, listened to reloading times and effective ranges. As though he was just being given the tour because everyone got it, and the details were of purely academic interest, to fall from his head a moment later.

Flint had someone bring up another drink and a tray of candied ginger, in case the brief span since dinner had left anyone too famished to carry on. Leaving Drathel to talk, he dropped back to Gil.

"Well?"

"Show him," she said.

"I never knew Outreach was full of such bad ideas." A grin, his real grin, the shark's one.

"It was a bad idea to have them in the first place, Postry. But now you have them…" Dekamran had to know, basically. She would not hide this from him. His decision would be as informed as she could make it.

So it was that Flint, still with his stick under his arm, as though he was a normal officer and these were normal troops, led them through to the other camp.

She didn't know how Dekamran would take it. The prohibition ran deep in all the Successor States, but at the same time it existed as ceremony and theory. It had been historically successful enough that nobody actually *saw* demons around the place.

Dekamran certainly knew what they were. He'd have seen the odd conjurer on Killinbraan when he was there. He'd know that the Pals and Loruthi and many other foreign nations used demons these days.

"I see," he said.

Flint outlined the history of it, with a politic caution that Gil had thought more soluble in alcohol. The dead conjurer, the loose contracts. Croskin. And it was the hat, in the end. That was what Gil thought. Dekamran's eyes, straying to that stupid little hat, the Kepi of the Kepishi, sitting on the demon's misshapen head.

There were more demons present than before, Gil noted. They'd dug up more skulls since her first visit. And she still didn't quite get how it worked, save that there would absolutely be a very specific way it worked, set out in words. Croskin's contract with the entire Palleseen Sway – apparently – somehow allowing Croskin to embody new contracts, swear in new demons. Not as conjured minions but actual soldiers. Infernal Accessories, save that *their* uniforms were the dark charcoal of the regulars.

Dekamran nodded, listened. Even stood before Croskin when the creature presented itself. Received the thing's salute and stared into its barbed snaggle of teeth and its round black eyes without flinching. Then they all retired back to the tent and Gil braced herself for the questions. Possibly the accusations.

"Tell me this one thing." Dekamran's face was unreadable, a bland mask behind which anything could be stewing. Gil wanted to catch his eye, read his heart there. She wanted to grasp his hand, his arm, impart strength to him. Lend him just that extra amount of Pallishness he'd need to accept this abomination.

Flint's smile indicated he was at the Alkhand's disposal. As was the significant military force surrounding them.

"How," Dekamran asked, "do you get the Peosts to bear it?" And then, because that could cover a multitude of sins, "Your demon troopers. Peor has Moerends just the same as Usmai. It has the same traditions. The only reason you're digging up these skulls is that someone buried them."

Gil almost gasped. She'd expected so many responses. Deal-breaking responses. The outraged foreigner decrying Pal excesses. Except this was Dekamran, and he was reasonable. In the Pal definition, as well as the vernacular. And besides, if this *had* been Gorbudan, offered a company of demons to retake his inheritance, did she think he'd have hesitated?

"Well, Your Tranquillity." It was Drathel who took up the question. "Half of how the Seraphi squared it with themselves was by saying the demons were working out their crimes. Being shoved into a uniform and getting to be first into the baton-fire, on account of how they're demons and wicked and all that. Bit of a squeaky point of theology I know, but nobody says no when there's a demon offering to take the hit for you."

"And the other half?" Dekamran asked her.

"Your Tranquillity, can I speak indelicately?"

"I'm sure you can, Fellow-Archivist," Dekamran said.

"Demons scare people around here shitless," Drathel said, and Gil choked on her drink. "More than normal. Because you don't know them, except in all those stories where they're the worst thing in the world. Which is only because, when the old Empire first rose, it was up against the Despotate which had demons up the wazoo. Hence demons are the Enemy in the earliest Moru scripture. Hence all this burying skulls business. But the thing about really scary things out of the stories you tell to get kids to crap themselves and not go to sleep, the thing about those things *is*, Your Tranquillity, that it's a real different deal when they're on *your* side."

Later, Flint tactfully abandoned the tent to Dekamran, the whole and complete dominion of the Alkhand. And his own dedicated Palleseen Resident to dance attendance, backed by Loret and her knife for... Well honestly Gil didn't even want to imagine what they might need Loret's knife for.

"It's a lot," Dekamran said. They'd left him the ramaht and he toyed with the glass – fancy crystal from some part of Peor that had objected to Pal peacekeeping and then regretted it.

"It's your call," Gil told him. "Obviously, it's your call. Without your word, we do nothing."

"Really?" He cocked a sardonic eyebrow. "Not going over the border for the greater security of Peor? Not a spontaneous demonstration of the Palleseen love of international justice?"

"No," she said flatly. "And I can say that because I am absolutely where the chain of command ends right here. You understand what's going on. That Flint isn't showing you all these soldiers and engines and – and *demons* – just because he's really proud of how shiny their buttons are. But it happens for *you*. The rightful Alkhand. Or not at all."

"Sit with me." Because she'd been standing, almost literally dancing attendance. Gil let herself down into Flint's own folding chair, and then Dekamran was gesturing at her aide, too. "Loret, sit. Just… I'm taking the crown off, see? Putting it aside." Miming the actions with empty air. The crown he pointedly didn't have.

Loret looked at him as though he had gone utterly irreconcilably mad. As though Loret didn't want to sit down at any gathering that would have someone like Loret as a guest. But she did, after a moment. Hunched her shoulders in; looked very young.

"If I asked you to tell me what to do…?" Dekamran stared into his glass, the milky white ramaht swilling there.

"I'd say no. Ask me details, ask me particulars, but I can't make that decision. Because you're the Alkhand." And, when he opened his mouth for a sour joke at his own expense, she put in, "Or you're not. You're the Alkhand who will reclaim his inheritance, or you're a spare prince who's managed to escape the death sentence his brother was about to pronounce. But you get to choose. And you *have* to choose."

He opened his mouth a couple of times, as though trying to find what shape it needed to be, to let the right words come out of it. "What if I just went away?" he asked, eventually.

She'd thought of that, of course. No small thing, for the rightful heir of a nation to *just go away*, or not in a manner that didn't involve assassins. "The Archipelago," she said, eventually. "There will always be people trying to get you back into Usmai at the head of a liberation force. Especially given the way Gorbudan's foreign policy is likely to go. But I have contacts. I can pull strings. I can find… maybe something, some post where you could… teach, perhaps? In Killinbraan even, where you studied. Not live as you've been accustomed. Not the

Alkhand-in-exile in all his finery. But something. And there are other places. Within the Sway or outside it. I've served in a lot of places and a lot of people owe me." Spinning stories just like Flint and Drathel, and no idea if they were true. "If you want to walk away, you can." She'd be seriously in hock to Decanting, given the bribe the Under-warden had demanded, but there were ways of dealing with that. She wouldn't be presenting Dekamran with the bill.

"And you?" he asked her.

Gil blinked at him. "And me?"

"What happens to you?"

"Technically I'm still Resident in Usmai. I'll report. I may be redeployed." She wasn't quite sure how the whole sequence would play, and there was patently going to be a throwdown between Usmai and Pallesand, especially if Gorbudan started raiding Peor again. She would probably not catch heat for the usurpation, but she might for not putting the screws on Dekamran here and now. Binding him to Palleseen interests with a ruthless will. But she wouldn't.

"I mean… if I was off teaching I-don't-know-what in Killinbraan or living as a guest of Outreach in Farasland or something, you wouldn't be there, would you?"

Gil froze. Some part of her hurt so badly it was as if Loret had just shivved her in the kidneys while her guard was down. Some part of her actively wanted Loret to put the blade in, because it would take her mind off how she felt. *No*, she said. Or didn't actually say. Formed the word, fully intended to voice it, but in the echo of it, realised that it hadn't come out. *No, not for me. Do not make this decision one way or another, just for me.* She was a career diplomat. She could be sent to the far end of the world tomorrow, for no reason. That was how it worked. And she'd go. She was ambitious. A Sage at not-quite forty. There was a professorship and a seat on the Commission in her future. She needed to make that absolutely plain to this absurd

Usmiat creature in front of her. How *that* would never be a consideration.

She couldn't get the words out. Not even one of them. He looked at her, and her hand had crept, like some treacherous vermin, until she touched his fingers. *No*. But even that one word refused to venture forth. She just looked at him.

Dekamran took a huge breath. The grandest she'd ever known. Gods had created worlds with breaths like that. Whole myth-cycles had been spawned. To later be stamped down by the marching boots of the Palleseen Sway.

"Loret," said Dekamran. Said His Tranquillity the Alkhand Dekamran to Cohort-Invigilator Loret, Aide to the Resident, "would you ask Fellow-Monitor Postry to step into the tent please. I have something to ask him."

Mosaic: The Back of the Monster

Seraphi. The term, in various iterations down the Successor Coast, for foreign troops sworn into the service of the crown. Not mercenaries nor yet true locals. The Ibaleth and the Tesemer, refugees from other worlds, are Seraphi, along with a handful of special cases. Outsiders beholden to the good graces of one Alkhand or another.

To 'Flint' Postry, his Peosts are Seraphi, even though they are locals fighting in their own country. Seraphi serving the greater power of the Palleseen Sway, their fealty neatly abstracted from the hedonistic young sot on the throne of Peor. He can offer them more than their feudal leaders ever would.

To Dekamran, True Alkhand of Usmai, Flint is a Seraphi. All right, a mercenary also, because no small sum has been pledged for the benefit of Postry's troops and, indeed, their commander, but Flint has sworn to uphold the true rule of the rightful Alkhand. He is a Seraphi, a foreigner sworn into service.

In Flint's own eyes, he remains a servant of the Palleseen Sway and the cause of perfection, although the state of his purse is the thing he's most concerned to perfect. Explain to him that he's a Seraphi serving Usmai and he'd laugh. If Dekamran weren't in earshot, anyway.

Gil, being in Outreach and trained in twisted thinking, can hold all these things together, like the hostile ends of a magnet. Knowing as she does that they must spring apart eventually and only hoping she'll be there to manage the fallout.

The Alkhand of Usmai goes into battle on the back of an ogrodon. High in the howdah, shielded by its wood and iron walls, but present for the fight. Not a privilege Dekamran had thought he'd be enjoying today, but in the seven days he spent over the Peost border, the landscape has changed. Flint's camp had some visitors.

First there had been Palinet, the Palleseen resident in Peor. A thin woman older than Gil, with a tableth-powered wooden hand. She'd arrived, probably, because she didn't believe Flint's messengers when they said they had the Alkhand-presumptive as their guest. However, just in case, she'd arrived with another couple of hundred Pal regulars. There had been a hastily-convened diplomatic function. Dekamran had put his best smile on. The confident one that said, *Of course I am the true Alkhand.* Now he'd made the decision to do this, it all came distressingly easily. And Gil was on his side, someone Palinet would plainly listen to. And Flint was invested in the expedition by then, and that also helped. Dekamran privately felt that having Flint over the border in Usmai was possibly also a win for Palinet. The man from Ventures was probably a rather unruly subordinate to have on your doorstep.

Palinet had left her troops on loan with Flint, when she returned to her Residence. Their presence beefed up the expeditionary force but had to be incorporated into Flint's rather ad hoc command structure, found supplies and tents and ammunition. Hence the balance of the seven days. In which gap, the others arrived.

Seven ogrodons, fully kitted out for war. The howdahs reinforced with spiked metal, the beasts' horns capped with sharp steel, plated leather barding rolled up under the edge of the howdah like awnings, to be unfurled when the enemy was in sight. Each howdah boasting two or three Ibaleth in jerkins and skull-plates, with spear and goad and baton. Flint's people thought it was an attack, at first: these enormous creatures and their alien handlers just stomping towards the camp. Dekamran had thought so too, honestly, because what else could it possibly be?

A pledge of allegiance, was what it had been. And the Ibaleth couldn't speak Usmiri or Pel, so he'd had to play an unsatisfactory game of yes-and-no from their half-humanised body language to work out the details. Honestly he still isn't sure. They wouldn't commit anything to writing. Either this band of intrepid reptiles was a pack of renegades hoping to be installed in place of Great Mother Kass, down the riverbank north of Alkhalend – just because the Ibaleth were inhuman and hard to understand didn't mean they were a single unified body. Alternatively, Great Mother Kass was hedging her bets, and had sent this force to the exiled Alkhand in case she won, because being lizards didn't mean they didn't do politics.

What this means right now, though, is that His Tranquillity the Alkhand Dekamran gets to ride into battle as his father did, swaying on the back of the monster that has symbolised Usmiat power for generations. One Ibaleth is at the front with the goad, another coils about a baton at one corner of the howdah. Beside Dekamran is Gil, theoretically as his liaison with the Pal forces under his banner. His subordinate because, as far as the history books are concerned, he is in charge, and all these armed men and women are marching purely to restore him to his rightful place. An interesting piece of policy, the philosophical equivalent of a wound that maybe isn't so bad if you don't look at it. And if you can leave it unexamined long enough, it'll heal, probably, and you'll never need to know how serious the damage was.

They crossed the Peor border already. He'd half expected Gorbudan, the warrior so skilled at rushing hither and thither and always being in the right place, to contest the river. Instead there had just been a little post of border guards, good for making merchants pay their dues, not so much at preventing full-scale invasion. Flint had a couple of squads ford the river upstream and turn up on the far side of the border post, to avoid anyone telling inconvenient tales off towards Alkhalend. The border guards had the situation explained to them and unanimously declared that of course Dekamran was the rightful Alkhand and they were appalled, just appalled, at what had been going on in the capital. He'd taken their pledge of fealty personally, because they were the first of the actual campaign. Flint had wanted to send them off to Peor on the basis that their loyalty to the true heir maybe wouldn't outlive their proximity to him. Dekamran had overruled the man, though. As much to see if he could, as because he had become madly attached to twenty part-timers and near-retirees who spent their time calculating rice taxes. Those border guards are marching behind the royal ogrodon even now, not entirely sure what's going on but doing their best to seem keen about it.

The next force that had met them after the border had also been allies, but then government-by-warrior-prince wasn't to everyone's tastes. Gil had sent word to those names he'd given her, families who held estates close enough to arrive in time. Men and woman of station and power who were of his mind. Who believed Gorbudan, in his drive to cleanse Usmai of foreign influence, would scour it into a wasteland. That the world beyond their borders could not be wished away, and would not meekly stay there just because the Alkhand waved a sword.

A headache for Flint, really. Hundreds of Usmiat levy, sworn to this family or that. A small but fleet force of cavalry that the Pal commander had probably been leery of trusting much weight to. And yet a lot of living bodies to add to the cause, foolishness to turn them away. Flint gave them the rear right of the overall advance, behind Dekamran's lumbering escort. Now, Dekamran can only hope that all those oaths and protestations of loyalty were heartfelt.

They have been moving along tracks through the forest so far. Flint's better pioneers are ranging ahead for ambush, but thus far no enemy has been contacted. Ahead, though, the quality of the light suggests the terrain is opening out. Even as it does, there are whistles. Pal signals. Dekamran glances at Gil and she nods. The flags of the usurper have been sighted. Soon after, the distant crackle of baton-fire is heard.

The first squads of Flint's forces meet the enemy. They have the momentum, regulars and Seraphi in open order, pushing around the fringes of the trees, while the more solid blocks and some advance artillery move out into the open. The first Usmiat troops they meet are no more than a peasant levy. Archers and spearmen who find themselves facing soldiers dressed and armed like Pals, even though the faces over most of the collars are Peosts. And the Peosts have always been the sack the Usmiat kick around. The poor neighbour with all the swampy ground, less people. Less money, less power. A rare day in the history books when the Peosts get one over on any of their neighbours. Even the mountain-goat people of hardscrabble Goshumai had been about to trounce them before Peor went bowl in hand to the Palleseen.

The Peosts just about wait for the order to fire, but their Pal officers are also keen to get stuck in so the order just about outpaces the local keenness to redress historical grievances. The Usmiat levy are doing what the Usmiat levy traditionally does, which is form into a block of bristling spears as densely packed as possible. Wouldn't stop a determined ogrodon but it would ward off a horse charge. A tactic that the Pals, lacking a single horse between them, aren't intending to deploy. Instead, the first tentative salvo of Pal shot wreaks disproportionate havoc through the Usmiat formations. The answering arrow-shot is weak and piecemeal, a couple of minor injuries dealt, no more, and then the Usmiat break.

The usurper's cavalry is just arriving, at that point. Ready to take advantage of an enemy that's already stuck in, spear to spear. It almost tramples its own fleeing infantry, whose spears are left littering the field like a child's game of jack straws. The Pals take a game try at pot-shotting the cavalry too, but the range is too far, the targets too fleet as they wheel and flee.

That is the first engagement of the Brothers' War. Word is hustled back to Flint, who does his best to manage an ordered advance. Flint, on foot like everyone else, lacks both a general's horseback mobility and a genuine history of battlefield command. He's led squads and detachments, but proper Pal Higher Orders lead from a tent safely back from the field. Flint isn't exactly the man to head up the charge, but he's on the field with a big squad of Seraphi, towards the back of the advance and with a standard flying so his messengers can find him. He does his best, with the information that reaches him, and the orders he feels appropriate. He doesn't actually tell his vanguard *Just get stuck in, chase them down all the way to the cliffs over Alkhalend*, but that's the general sense of things some of his officers come away with.

On, then, to the second wave of clashes.

Gorbudan isn't leading his troops from the back of an ogrodon, tradition bedamned. Gorbudan is the warrior. He rides with the cavalry, the noble spearpoint that wins wars down the Successor Coast. Usmai's levy are farmers and artisans drafted from their lives and given simple weapons and simple orders. Usmai's cavalry, the sons and daughters of the Emorandi, train in the saddle, with the sword and lance and, most especially, the baton. The noble firearms of Usmai are long, carved into spirals, inlaid with precious and magically-charged materials. Works of art and deadly, no mere showpieces. Gorbudan rides in the heart of a hundred of horses, and Usmiat horses are swift and elegant, their long legs scaled and taloned like those of snake-killing birds. There was a horse god once, north of the mountains. The god is long dead but the war-happy beasts it bred persist and don't care about the theology so long as they are fed and cared for. And get to fight, for that horse god was a war god too.

There is other cavalry too. To Gorbudan's left the Louse Monks flurry along the ground on their hooklopers. Unarmoured, without reins, just the clicking of their tongues to guide their beasts, and both hands for their long, scything blades. Lhisamena herself leads them, the Preceptor of all the Tesemer. If they'd declared for Dekamran, he knows, none of this would be possible. But once they choose a side, that choice is iron. They're his, now. They will win this war for him. Send the Pals howling back across the Peost border and bring him Dekamran, alive or dead.

His own ogrodons – he has two score against Dekamran's seven – are the thundering centre of his advance, because they're very good at going straight and not stopping, not so much at complex flanking manoeuvres. His advance is a crescent, and the Pals haven't found the sharp tips yet. The dust of the ogrodons is holding their attention.

On the left flank his levy is fleeing in disarray. Hundreds of holiday soldiers deciding they want no part of the festivities. The Pals pursue, running and shooting because the back of a fleeing enemy is always their preferred target. His cavalry are fleeing too, the horses making great leaps and bounds, drawing the eye with their bright livery.

The Pal commander isn't a total fool. He has pickets wide on either side, in the trees. Gorbudan's front is wider, though, and the enemy's right has already outstripped his scouts on that side, in their eagerness to pursue. All that Pal discipline parting at the seams.

He gives the signal. Flags wave, a ripple of intelligence from detachment to detachment. The cavalry wheel and stop their feigned flight.

The Louse Monks hit the Pal pioneers at full tilt, because their hooklopers can pass through dense forest at the charge, narrow shrimp bodies between the close boles of trees, the riders hunched down in the saddle with their long blades held out behind them ready to reap. It's the arms of the hooklopers that do the worst damage, though. Four chitin sickles, some of them capped with steel, they tear into the scouts and barely slow, trailing ragged human pieces as they pass through and turn and come back for more.

Gorbudan gives the next signal and his own riders are moving, bursting out onto the field at the back of the enemy right flank – so eagerly pressing what they had taken to be their advantage. His followers spread out into an arrowhead, a wedge directed straight at the foe. Gorbudan takes up his baton, five feet of carved and enchanted wood with an octagonal tableth gleaming in the slot. He speaks the word of Usmiri that wakes the magic in it, and a shot lances through two of the pale-clad enemies, killing both, scorching the woman beyond them. His companion cavalry follow suit, and the Pal formation disintegrates before most of them even understand what's happening. Gorbudan is already gesturing at their next target, a solid block of soldiers now frantically trying to shift their facing towards this threat on their flank. As they pass, his people send another round of shot into the collapsing Pal block, so that it ceases to trouble the battlefield as anything other than a source of casualties.

The next block holds firm. Shot begins to dance about Gorbudan's riders. They race past the face of the enemy – losing a couple, but war is hungry. Their own shot lances straight back, impossible to miss so dense a slab of human flesh. The Usmiat batons take two, three as their shots lance through bodies.

Ahead, Gorbudan sees the artillery, knows the danger. One benefit of cultivating the Loruthi ambassador during the war was to learn the tricks of the enemy. This is a Palleseen Hand, a weapon like twenty rapid-firing batons all together, a killer of whole detachments. The enemy artillerists, the dark-clad Pals amongst their pale Peost conscripts, are trying to pivot it round to lead the cavalry. A moment later the sheer volume of space ahead is a butcher's block of shot, strings of tablethi rattling and dulling as the weapon chatters death at them. Gorbudan has already veered aside, though, his formation collapsing from a wedge to a serpent as it twists to come at the enemy from the side again. He holsters his baton, unships his lance and orders the charge.

The artillerists and their death-engine go down under the talons of the horses. Ahead, the next block of Pals has formed into a square, already shooting. The shockwave of collapse Gorbudan had hoped for isn't happening. He pulls at the reins and leads his surviving riders back towards the advancing line of the ogrodons.

The third clash. Flint is closer to the front now, both because he needs to be to see what's going on, and because the actual front of his force has been knocked back by the enemy cavalry on both sides. And now the beasts are coming.

Flint doesn't panic, never has. His actual suite of command-suitable traits is a bit patchwork, by Pal standards, but he can grin into the face of death when he needs to, and he does so now. His orders go out, the shrill whistles that his troops have been drilled over and over into obeying until they hear them in dreams. Ahead, the front of his advance bends and shifts, digging in here, taking ground there. On his right flank are his own monsters, that turned up just a few days ago and that he doesn't really trust. He sends a messenger over with a very polite request that the Alkhand maybe do something appropriate with them. If Dekamran can hold that flank with his lumbering brutes, honestly, that would be a real help.

The enemy monsters are stomping forwards. Are accelerating, actually. Because they're big, but they've got a turn of speed to them when their mahouts apply the goad. This will, Flint knows, be the test of him. Of him, of his forces, of Ventures as a department.

Ogrodons are the last word in war, in this part of the world. You can't outrun them. You can't stop them – often not with actual walls, let alone fragile human bodies. They'll go full tilt at a fence of spearpoints in a way horses absolutely won't. Plus you've got bloody *lizards* up top. Lizards with batons shooting down at you. Not civilized war at all.

Flint watches his front formations dig in. Two ranks bristling with batons. Just soldiers with cheap, plain firearms. The thing the locals don't do because over here war is a game for the rich, and the peasantry gets invited like the ball gets invited to the game.

The very front formation just breaks, and for a moment he thinks that's it. The sight of the monsters thundering down on them like living mountains is too much. The metal-shod horns, the armoured shields of their heads, the sheer *mass* of them. Morale shatters and the focal point of the ogrodon charge just scatters in all directions, each soldier desperately hoping to end up in some small piece of untrampled ground. But the others, to either side, hold their nerve and fire.

One of the ogrodons on the left sways. Flint holds his breath. Actually grips the arm of his nearest aide so hard she hisses with pain. The beast stumbles, shaking its head. Stopped, suddenly, when it had been charging. The monster behind it detours clumsily, bellowing, its momentum broken. On the right, one monster has its howdah slanting drunkenly, straps severed, lizards clinging on like failed sailors.

From behind Flint, the big artillery speaks. They've got the engines to the tree-edge and set up, double-time. The crack and boom of it sends a whiplash of shock through his own troops, more than the enemy. They are the heaviest mule-portable pieces he could bring, great weights of inscribed metal that eat a dozen tablethi every time they loose. Because of arcane equations of focus and power loss, they don't just throw raw magic fire like a baton, but use their explosive might to hurl an enchanted metal ball that shatters on impact.

What also shatters on impact is one of the howdahs. The whole monster beneath reels with the blow – not hurt so much, but just the physical shock of it. Dead lizards, dead human marksmen, shattered wood. And the ogrodon turning. Shaking its head, rearing up to shed the last scraps of its armour and furniture. Plunging sideways so that three more of the beasts are changing course. Another beast is just down on its knees and Flint sees a raw red hole punched into its side that he could have crawled into.

Only then, as the unstoppable tide of the ogrodon turns and blunders away from his front lines in bestial confusion, does he acknowledge that he hadn't believed they'd do it.

On his right, his own monsters press on, and nothing stops them.

Lhisamena watches the enemy flank near. Concealed in the trees, the Tesemer can be still as stones. Their predatory mounts freeze, not a twitch of mandible to give them away, until deer feed about their many legs and birds roost on the blades of their killing arms. She has a sense of how the battle is going. Losses given and taken, nothing decided. Gorbudan a flexible enough commander to adapt to the Pal way of doing things, the Pals retaining their momentum.

Let them all shed blood until one side alone still stands. A glorious abattoir. The Tesemer way. Or it is in the old stories, from before they came here. The song of the warriors they were, that lacks only the final verse to explain why they had to leave that place and end up *here*.

Gorbudan laid out his plan, last night in his tent. The part of his plan that was only for her and her people. Perhaps half her people under arms are in Alkhalend still, in case of insurgents, tricks or a force under sail coming up the coast. The other half, and most of their hooklopers, are spread in fragments across the battlefield. A dozen Louse Monks in the saddle here, a score on foot there, who needs more at any given time or place? There's only so much blood one can shed.

Her people have been dying, she knows. Where the Pals catch them still enough, that massed baton-fire is resistant to traditional counterargument. But sometimes the blood you have to shed is your own, and there's glory in that, even. They've killed far more than they've lost.

She lifts her falx, so slow and gentle that the tiny bird hopping along the facets of her mount's compound eyes does not even flutter away. The gaze of her followers is on her.

Seven ogrodons. Formidable. A wing of cavalry, traitors in bright silks, the laughing sons and daughters of the Emorandi. A ragged trail of Usmiat commoners with spears, plucked from the fields and factories for this feudal service.

In the middle of the ogrodons, a howdah with livery trailing from its rails. The flag they're all following. Lilies and frogs and skulls, the symbols of the Alkhand; blue and gold, the colours of Dekamran.

The blade comes down. They erupt into motion, into visibility. The sweep of steel that signalled her charge becomes a circling strike to behead the nearest cavalryman.

At the front, the ogrodons turn and mill and lumber back towards their own lines, scattering a company's worth of troops. The Pal centre presses forwards determinedly, the Peost Accessories feeling each foot of Usmiat soil beneath their uniform boots as revenge for the insults of history.

Baton-fire and arrow-shot greet them from the trees where Gorbudan has set a mass of his infantry. In cover, dismounted nobles and a company of peasant archers send the Pal left flank shrinking back. They're dug in there, the word gets back to Flint. Need to stop to winkle them out, and that means Gorbudan will have time to reform his centre and think up a counter to the infantry squares.

Two, three charges the Pals try against them. Peasants and rabble, after all. No match for Pal discipline. But maybe they hate the Kepishi and maybe they just hate the more familiar enemy of the Peosts, but Gorbudan's people hold, making their enemies walk through arrows all the way until they get a faceful of spears. If the faces behind the spears are terrified amateurs rather than remorseless professionals, it doesn't make the spears any less sharp or the arrows fly slower.

In the interim, a band of Louse Monks have gone all the way around the back and exploded out to attack the artillery, scattering the engineers and silencing the weapons. Flint ends up diverting more people he really needed to go *forwards* into going *backwards*, because apparently that's where the enemy is now. And those fucking monks do not mess around. And Gil warned him, and Dekamran warned him, and he didn't honestly believe it until now.

And while the artillery is silent, the enemy ogrodons are being goaded and hissed into behaving by their lizard mahouts, and turning their murderous horns back towards the Pals.

He has a secret weapon, of course. He was keeping it secret because it's the sort of thing that could really backfire, with his allies as well as the enemy. But that left flank is pinning his entire force, keeping his people conveniently stationary so the monsters can stomp all over them.

He turns and gives the order. The hideous smile he receives suggests that someone, at least, is going to have a good time of it today.

The Emorandi in command of Gorbudan's valiant flank is named Hakoran, scion of a family that has always been loyal to the Alkhands of Usmai. To Gorbudan, the Alkhand. By virtue of Gorbudan being the crowned man sitting on the throne. Hakoran is no fool, but he doesn't overthink things either.

He has a handful of his cousins here. Each one with a baton and a pouch of tablethi, each one with a skia or a clavar if things get to that. He's been ordered to hold. He doesn't particularly understand the big picture, or what a nail he's being, driven solidly into Flint's foot. He's just holding, and his people – his peons, his neighbours'; solid sons and daughters of Usmai who are also loyal to the Alkhand – are holding too. The Pals keep trying to get them to go away, but Hakoran doesn't think that he will unless Gorbudan tells him to. He's quite comfortable here. He's shot three Pals, at least one of them fatally. Other than that, his people have plenty of arrows. There's even a rather festival mood about the spearmen now, because everyone was a bit scared of facing the Kepishi. You hear all sorts of stories about that big war they had with those other foreigners. Very good at fighting, the Kepishi. Except right now they keep coming and going, and most of them seem to be Peosts anyway.

Something lands in the middle of his people. Not that he can know, but it didn't actually mean to. Flight in this air is never an exact science, if your wings are meant for other skies.

The thing – it has enormous, long arms, squat legs. Its skin is red and black scales and its face is a nightmare of tusks and horns and seven searing eyes. It has, awkwardly about its bull neck, a jacket. A Pal uniform jacket. Its wings seem to overshadow everyone there. A hole in the canopy above, the edges of branches smouldering from the heat of it.

And even that wouldn't have done it. Hakoran has his baton about, despite what he finds himself aiming at. A thing from the Realms Below. An offence to the order of the world. His duty to send it to oblivion. The spears, that had gone in all directions, are coming about. The arrows to the string. The demon roars, but it is just a demon. It's just roaring. The stalwart of Usmai are not so easily routed. He fires and it reels, the baton-shot slicing between neck and shoulder.

Then one of Hakoran's cousins calls out the alarm, because there are more of them coming through the woods. He sees Pal uniforms at first, thinks it's just that: the enemy have this one forbidden thing, little more than a distraction.

He sees what's wearing the uniforms. How many of them there are. A host. Hopping, flapping, hissing. Fanged maws agape, talons, thorned skin, tattered wings and whipping tails. Pal uniforms, where they fit. Boots over hooved feet, shirtsleeves split about finned or spined forearms. Batons in clawed hands. They advance and shoot, advance and shoot, like soldiers. But they're not soldiers.

Hakoran's people hold until the demons get close enough to charge. Hold and even send some of the things back to the Realms Below. But when Croskin and his monstrous regiment rush them through the trees, some on two feet, some on four or more, they break.

From atop the ogrodon's howdah, watching the Louse Monk charge is like watching a breach in a sea wall. The Tesemer explode from the trees on their crustacean mounts and just carve through everything closest. Dekamran's little detachment of cavalry scatters every which way, even through their own infantry. The ogrodon closest to the attack shudders, and then something hideous and many-legged appears over the crest of its side, a hookloper not climbing so much as running straight up the behemoth's barding to get to the howdah.

The Ibaleth in the howdah shoot the Tesemer at such close range that she's hurled from the saddle and her mount drops away. A windsaw clips that howdah's lip and carves bloodily into the Ibaleth sniper, tearing at her muzzle and throat. The monks are scything between all the great beasts now, though, and more than one of them heading straight for Dekamran's own. Gorbudan has understood well that all this sound and fury is meaningless if the head you want to crown has parted company with its body.

Gil is at the rail, aiming a baton, firing, scowling at the miss. She presses a short rod into the hands of her aide but the girl fumbles it, looking terrified.

"Your knife, at least!" Gil bellows into her face. "Use your fucking knife!" But Loret drops into a corner of the howdah and holds herself, shaking.

Dekamran draws his clavar, with which he was never very skilled.

The peasant infantry have nowhere to go that isn't onto their own spears. Somehow that means they hold, bunched together with their points sticking out all ways. A Tesemer scythes past them, striking beyond the spearheads with his long blade, but they push at him – eyes closed, half of them – and the scrape of steel against the carapace of his mount wards him off. Then one of Dekamran's Emorandi followers gallops by, horse mad-eyed and foaming because the hooklopers terrify regular cavalry. The horsewoman lunges, gets the Tesemer in the shoulder with her slender blade. He turns and tries to take her head off but she ducks under and lets her horse carry her away so that the man gives chase.

Gil shoots again, speaking Pel words to the baton, then throws it at Loret demanding the useless girl at least slot in a new tableth.

Their ogrodon shudders, a monk slashing across the beast's flank as she rides past. Dekamran clutches the rail, feeling useless. Feeling that this moment has been engineered by his brother to show, of the two of them, just which is truly worthy of the title. Then one of his other ogrodons brings its great blunt feet down right on the fleeing monk, a moment of such appalling and instant destruction that it seems the work of a god: woman and her segmented mount become a wreck of flesh and chitin and a shattered falx.

Then there's a monk right up there on their howdah.

Clambering over the rail, slashing at the mahout, which falls to the floor, writhing and whipping, a gash down the length of her body. The Tesemer's eyes are on Dekamran. All other things are irrelevant. A windsaw hangs in the air past the monk's shoulder, then darts forwards.

Gil rushes her, rapier drawn. The monk barely glances as she fends the Pal away. Gil won't go, though. Won't give the assassin that one clear instant in which she could cut through the succession crisis with a single blow. The windsaw flurries at her. The spread of its open wings screams panic into her face. Instead of giving, she punches the thing with her quillons, feels an empty husk of connection and the beast whirls away. In that moment she takes the butt of the falx to her temple and a taloned bracer across the face. She seizes on the contact, grapples and slaps and kicks. When she forces the monk to take one step back, up against the rail, she tries to get her rapier stuck in again. It's a cramped arena, not suitable for either combatant's weapon of choice.

Dekamran, clavar in hand, just holds back. If he went in, the monk would kill him. If he struck, probably he'd kill Angilly.

Gil is shouting at Loret to do something but Loret won't. Loret, the aide, has her knife out but doesn't seem to know what it is. The monk grabs Gil by the ear and headbutts her savagely. The Palleseen Resident drops to her knees, stunned. But she'd earned one thing. In that clear moment, the monk is going to kill her and not Dekamran.

He and Loret move at the same time. She's faster, though, the knife a better weapon in cramped quarters. The windsaw comes back to her and she shreds it out of the air. Loret screams, and the scream turns into a surprised yelp when the monk kicks her so hard in the chest that she goes right over the rail and vanishes.

The one fucking time, Gil thinks numbly.

That leaves Dekamran. And the Tesemer was going to kill Gil, who has lost hold of her sword and is still having difficulty remembering what she was doing. But Dekamran has reminded the monk of business she had to take care of.

It's the Ibaleth that saves him. Not the cut-open mahout but the other one, that has been shooting over the side of the rail. Their batons are too long for this sort of work, but the creature snatches up the goad and lashes it across the monk's face, gouging her down to the skull. She strikes back, swift and instinctive, and somehow Dekamran gets his sword in the way. The impact spins it out of his hands and now there's nothing between him and the enemy's blade.

Now it's Gil's turn. Head together, sword reclaimed, she rams it up under the monk's ribs, out past the monk's shoulder blade. Stands with a convulsive strength that sends the Tesemer off her feet and following Loret over the rail. Gil's sword, too, because it's lodged between a lot of bones. She considers it a fair price to pay.

On the ground, Loret lurches unsteadily to her feet. She rolled when she hit, and she doesn't know how she knew to, but no broken bones. In her head the thunder sounds. All around her the ogrodons stomp and bellow, batons spit, the injured cry. The thunder's louder than all of it. A Louse Monk sees her, turns his hookloper to face her. Cocks his blade over his shoulder until the forward-curving point juts at the sky. Loret has her knife. She has the thunder in her head. The lash of the storm that's in her.

She screams at the monk. Shrieks into his face and the assemblage of parts that the hookloper has. From her mouth, the tempest roars.

The monk sees it in her. Knows it, not by name but as a thing beyond all the mysteries of the Louse Monks. She sees a strange delight on his face. At a click from his tongue the hookloper flurries into sudden motion, from still to charge with no intervening gaits.

Loret keens and bursts into her own run: towards, with knife. With madness.

Three riders get in the way. Emorandi, the remainder of Dekamran's little band of followers. Behind them the spears, that never broke, are pushing forwards. The Louse Monk veers away. They're all on the move, breaking off and rushing into the trees. Dekamran lives. Loret lives. They failed. Another battle, another day.

Loret opens her mouth. Can't understand why she was going to do any of it. The tide ebbs from her. Gil is calling her name.

Gorbudan receives his messengers. The enemy are still advancing, despite everything. Taking losses, but advancing. His own side report the toll: losses, but not devastating. He could keep bleeding and bloodletting from here to the city, but right now Dekamran's people have the momentum and he'd lose more than he'd gain. By the time the fight came into sight of Alkhalend he might not have the numbers to hold the city.

He could regroup to Mantekor, his fortress. Enough walls and supplies there to hold them off, reinforcements too. But the Alkhand does not rule from Mantekor. They could not take him, perhaps, but they could put Dekamran on the throne and Palleseen soldiers in the streets.

Through gritted teeth he gives the order to fall back to Alkhalend.

Before the Walls

Usmai has lost battles. Alkhands have fallen on the field or been dethroned soon after. Other Successor States, or combinations of them, have brought their big brother to heel one way or another. Dynasties have traded the throne. Wedding alliances have been forced at the point of a sword. But Alkhalend has never fallen. Somehow things have never gone that far.

"I've sent a rider back across the border," said Flint. "Boats, y'know. I reckon we can do it with boats."

Dekamran made a noise. Flint looked sidelong at him. This was their council of war – Flint, Drathel, a handful of officers and Gil, and all of them theoretically deferring to Dekamran. Except Flint had plainly assumed the Alkhand was just going to stamp any plan with his seal of approval.

Dekamran had kept any such seal clear of the ink so far. "The sea wall has emplacements," he said. "And there is a tower here, and also here." Pointing out clifftop positions overlooking the whole city. "The engines have the reach to strike boats trying to enter the harbour. In my father's day, when his reign was young, the Cotto thought that Alkhalend was weak. It took a month to clear the wreckage of their ships from the harbour mouth."

Flint absorbed this. "Not boats. Let me guess, there's some towers get a good eye landwards as well?"

"You saw their ranging shots, when you came close to Gorbudan's camp," Dekamran confirmed.

Alkhalend, the city of the cliff, was not your standard prospect to besiege. The bulk of the city itself was in the bay below, most readily accessible by sea, but with a gate and wall at either end, the Emor to the west, protecting the factoras, workshops and warehouses of the working district. *Emor* being just 'the Gate' in Usmiri. The famous gate, the enormous arch of carved stone flanked by fortified towers that was as old as the city. Across the far side of the bay the Sand Gate was newer, less fancy, still fortified. Gun emplacements that faced inwards as well as outwards in case the thronging people of the Sand Lanes decided to take to the streets in a spirit of something other than festival. And both these approaches to the city were overlooked by the cliff, and the forts that past Alkhands had raised there to remind everyone who was in charge.

Which left, logically, an approach from the north, across the rich farmland and the noble estates of the Emorandi – the nobles, gatekeepers by literal translation. That was plainly the approach Gorbudan reckoned made the most military sense, because his forces were now encamped by section up above the city. Not pressed to the cliff edge, but in a well-ordered sequence of connected camps that made use of the Emorandi's walled compounds to build what seemed almost like a whole defensible city above Alkhalend proper. Scouts reported there were siege engines on many of the flat roofs of the mansions, even, as well as the huge old pieces in the cliff forts. The Usmiat forces lacked mobile field artillery, but their fixed emplacements were formidable.

Which was why Flint had been thinking boats and the harbour, because he and Dekamran agreed that Gorbudan would shy away from actually bombarding the roofs of his own city once the enemy was on the streets.

"We take the city," Dekamran had said. "We take the palace. The palace, specifically." Halfway up the cliffs, the jewel set into the gleam of the Constellar Gardens. At first Flint had thought the heir was just fixated on his own coronation, but Dekamran knew what he was about.

"There are a great many, within and without my brother's army, who are waiting to see how strong *we* are. How strong *I* am. You've seen already, how they are trickling to us. Why do they cling to Gorbudan? Because they see in him the great war leader? Perhaps. A few. But because he holds the city and the palace. The Alkhand rules from Alkhalend – the Place of the Alkhand, and from the House of Tranquillity, from the Mirror Throne. If that is me, not Gorbudan, he is an exile, just a man of the blood with a bodyguard of raiders. If the city is ours he must decide to either become the invader and bring fire and ruin to his own people, or retreat to Mantekor. Where we can bring our own troops. Or send our envoys."

"You think he'll be ready to talk things over, then?" Drathel put in. She'd been nibbing over Flint's shoulder at the map. "Just take a few retainers and go off into well-deserved retirement. Only he didn't think he could afford for *you* to do that. But maybe you know different."

Dekamran shot her a resentful look. He could have shot her an *I-am-the-Alkhand* look to shut her down, but that wasn't the man he was, not even here with everyone ostensibly deferring to him.

"And you'd risk him deciding that he *will* bring fire and ruin to his own people?" Flint added. "Who are also your people?" Not goading, just feeling out the parameters of the logic problem.

"He won't," said Dekamran, and Gil just stared at him helplessly. Her own assessment of his brother wasn't so charitable, but which of them knew Gorbudan best? "And neither can we," he added, looking Flint right in the face. "Whoever burns Alkhalend to win it, cannot win. Not the people, not ever. Your troops must understand this."

"They do," Flint said easily.

"The Peosts have wanted to burn Alkhalend on more than one occasion," Dekamran said flatly. "And your own troops are not here because they are deeply invested in who sits on the Mirror Throne, save that the incumbent be a friend to Pallesand."

Flint's gaze flicked to Gil. *I thought you had him on a leash*, said that expression. Gil raised her eyebrows. *Answer.*

"Your Tranquillity," said Flint easily. "I will give all the right orders. My troops will do their best. If we fight in the city, some things will get knocked over."

"There must be no looting," Dekamran settled back at the table, utterly calm, the Alkhand making a proclamation that even the gods would fear to breach.

"Your Tranquillity, my troops—"

"Will be well rewarded from the coffers of the Alkhand. As we have agreed. And the temples, the monasteries, these shall also go untroubled." Looking at Drathel, now.

Gil remembered the negotiations at the start, when she'd brought Dekamran to Flint's camp as little more than a well-dressed beggar. What Flint had demanded, for himself, for his people. What Drathel had wanted. And Gil herself. Not as Angilly, the woman, but as the Palleseen Resident who had Palleseen people and interests to look out for. An opening up of trade, unlocking the strictures under which Pals operated within Usmai. All in the name of strengthening international relations. And she'd held back. Her reports would make Dekamran out to be the hard bargainer when really he wasn't. But still, her superiors in Outreach would be happy, and surely that was a good thing.

Dekamran, no fool he, had seen the possible extras that an army might have in mind, once they got within the walls of the city of their enemies. Except their enemies must also then become their friends, his subjects, the people who consented to the new order of things.

"Listen to me." He stood, and abruptly they *were* all there at his pleasure, foreign allies come to the aid of the true Alkhand. "This can work. When the dust settles, when my brother is driven from Alkhalend, a new dawn for both Usmai and

Pallesand can break. A time of clasped hands and open gates. But it will be in the manner of our victory that we decide whether or not the people of Usmai will accept you. The word in your history books is *liberation.* The Palleseen Sway does not conquer or pillage or invade. It always *liberates.*" A pause, in which everyone was welcome to consider just what excesses of history could hide under the skirts of that one word. "Liberate my city from my usurping brother," said Dekamran. "No more. And we can forge something of value, that will last the ages."

Flint looked down at the rough map of the terrain, where his scouts had marked out all the engines and the troops. "So… boats, then?"

As Dekamran had said, there had been a trickle of supporters since they had arrived and made their own camp, north and east of the city where the ground humped up into something defensible. More Emorandi not enamoured of Gorbudan's leadership style or passed over for recognition. A few Usmiat merchants come with wagons of supplies for Flint, and for the individual soldiers of his force. A few Pal merchants who'd got out of the city with their goods, seeking sanctuary.

At dusk, though, just as their council was breaking up, there came the big delegation, the point where Gil started to think that Dekamran was right, and that the city was ripe for turning. The Ibaleth switched allegiance en masse.

A veritable tide of sinuous, scaled bodies converged on Flint's camp, to the alarm of the sentries. Not an attack, though. Several hundred of the lizard creatures, many of them clad in metal and leather gear that was a wrangling of Usmiat styles to Ibaleth physiology. They had spears and batons. Great Mother Kass herself – twice the size of any of the rest – was at their head. They crawled on their bellies before Dekamran and hissed and croaked their allegiance. In one moment, the entire river north of the city had abandoned Gorbudan.

"This changes things," Flint said. "With those big stomping lads, we can take them up top."

"The engines," Drathel said. "Our field pieces turned them. You reckon their emplacements won't?"

"Gives them something that means they're not pounding *us*," Flint decided, although some of his enthusiasm had ebbed away. The ogrodons weren't a part of his usual military toolkit. He wasn't sure how best to use them. "I'd still have liked the boats," he added sadly. And, as Dekamran opened his mouth, "I know, I know. You're a port city, you thought of boats already. But if we could get boots in the lower city… Like you said, take the city, take the palace, what's he going to do? Especially if we're putting him under pressure up top."

"Helsa Broda," said Drathel.

Gil frowned at her. "That's in… Porcyr? What about it?"

"Place I won my Fellowship," said Flint, though he didn't seem as delighted about it as he might. "Two years back. Loruthi had the place. Almost the opposite of this, really. We were down the bottom, they were up top. But there was a pass. Basically a side door. And they knew about it. Set guards and barricades. But they were waiting for us to come with the morning and we just… went. Bloody midnight rangers, we were. Night attacks, terrible idea, all the manuals say so. But the Loruthi manuals said just the same thing and they stuck to theirs more than we stuck to ours. We got into the gates before they could shut them. Held them against every damn thing until the rest of our boots could get up. Took the place. Sod me but that was a bloody night. They gave me the rank badge but I felt like I was washing the blood out of it for a month." He was, in that moment, utterly unguarded. None of the boyish cheer, the matey up-from-the-ranks soldier. A man with regrets, but also a man who had stood on a mound of dead comrades to get that badge pinned on him, and not really looked back. "So, Helsa Broda. Night attack by the side door. Tell me more about this Sand Gate of yours, Your Tranquillity."

"On one condition." And Gil felt as though a door had closed, with her on the wrong side. Flint and Dekamran making terrible bad plans, and her shut out of them.

"No," she said, and then "*No*!" when she'd heard the condition. "This is mad. You won't even get past the gate. There are siege emplacements there, you said. Looking both ways. They'd destroy you coming in, and keep at it once you're through. Listen, this can't work!"

Flint's grin was suddenly back, and she didn't like it one bit. That Dekamran and Flint were friends suddenly, like they'd been to school together. That they were feeding off one another's bad qualities: Dekamran's idealistic recklessness, his headlong rush to do the right thing without seeing all the spikes and pits between him and his goal. Flint's ambition, the self-made soldier who'd got where he was by taking risks and making bad calls that somehow turned out good. Either of them alone was bad enough. Put them together and suddenly it was trouble every which way.

And they had an answer to everything. "As to the gates," Flint told her easily, "I've got just the thing."

Misery and Wickedness

They fed on torment. Everyone knew. The substance of them was suffering. It was their meat and drink. No redeeming features, by definition. Nothing good could come of them. Which did not stop demonists contracting for their services. Did not stop the mage lords of Allor entering into symbolic marriages with the Scotolaries of Below. Did not stop, in more recent times, factory hellieurs calling up a hundred fiends to power the manufacturing engines, or a Pal company conjurer summoning a squad of monsters to throw at the enemy batons. Because they were vile and inimical to human good, that meant you could do what you wanted with them and not feel an iota of guilt.

Caecelian had noticed the boy mooning about. Wanting to come speak to her new charge, the Fever Lodge's latest inmate. And not daring to. Suddenly finding something else to do the moment Enshili looked his way. And that, too, was good. A little extra misery. A particular vintage of frustration and self-loathing.

Enshili herself had presumably noticed, given the boy wasn't subtle about it. She was four years older than the kid, though. Nothing there for her. If the Viper whispered in her ear, she'd lead the boy on, probably. But that would escalate matters to the point where Oathan – the big man who called himself Oathan now – got involved. Caecelian would have a proper throwdown with Oathan some time. She would with all of them. It was a point of faith with her. She was wickedness incarnate. She would eat them from the inside. The old woman, the Divinati healer, the big man with his pots and potions. Destroy them as a punishment for forgetting what she was.

Some day. Tomorrow. Eventually.

And Jack. Some day. Tomorrow. Eventually. Jack.

Jack was sleeping now. In the windowless room they had, in the heart of the dense pile of sticks that was the Fever Lodge and its several neighbours. The brothel, the gambling den, ten or twelve families scrabbling for space. She could see in the dark and the sun was no friend to her kind, hence she'd insisted they burrow down in here. And Jack, of course, had agreed. Jack agreed to almost everything. Except hurting people. Except misery and wickedness. He was like a sieve for those. You poured the vicious thoughts into him and they ran right out. He didn't even notice you'd done it half the time.

She looked down at him as he slept. Tried to picture her hands at his throat. A cord. A knife. Knowing it wouldn't hurt him as much as just walking away. Leaving him a letter telling him all the things she hated about him, that it had all been a game at his expense, that none of it had been true. She'd destroy him utterly, instantly, with no more than a pen and her exit.

There was a peculiar excitement, knowing that she had that power over him. There was a peculiar bitterness. Play the scene in her head all she wanted, taste the savour of it. Like drinking delicious poison. Like the sting of the scorpion that brought delirious visions before it killed.

"But why?" Enshili had wanted to know. "What is he, to you? He looks useless."

Caecelian agreed. Jack was the most useless man in the world. The meekest, the most inoffensive, not a sharp edge to him. Even his god had gotten shot of him in disgust at how weak he was. A man of infinite flaws.

One flaw in particular. The crack that ran through him all the way to his heart.

I will destroy you, she told his sleeping face. *There is no part of you I do not hold in my hand. To crush or cast aside.* Knowing the surge of emotion that was all good things, and weakness, and sex. Let nobody tell you demons feel nothing.

Enshili still wanted her to explain, but Caecelian was only interested in spreading knowledge where it would breed misery in others. Not merely in herself.

The other thing Enshili truly wanted brought her much more joy, because it promised a much greater wickedness. Enshili had wanted the mask, yes. But she'd wanted the mask because she wanted what it symbolised. What notionally lay beneath it.

The Viper had mocked her for it, as she did. "Why would anyone wish it? Don't you know how many of my kin have sought the opposite transformation? We take your forms, your speech, your quarrels, your orders."

Enshili had just looked her up and down. "I want to be free like you," she'd said. "I want to be able to do everything I want, like you." And Caecelian's heart had sung with it. That the daughter of an Alkhand, the sister of an Alkhand, would have become a demon if she could. The betrayal of a thousand years of tradition.

"Make me like you," Enshili had insisted. "Have your man brew the potion. Have your woman balance my humanity from me. Have your surgeon drip your blood into my veins. I don't want to be weak, like this. When my brother comes to claim me I want to laugh in his face, show him my fangs." All the things the princess had always wanted to say, and never had anyone to speak them to.

"Get your mask," Caecelian told her. "We hunt." And, silently and to the girl's back, *I love you. You would crack the world open. You would break the sacred tablets on the floor, piss in the font, put their writings to the flame. You would push over the Mirror Throne and pour blood into the waters. All because they told you that you couldn't. Because of all the things they told you that you couldn't. My child. My wild one.*

Tonight, she and her apprentice in wickedness were taking to the streets. Something was different. She could smell it.

To her senses, the intrusion was like lurid, diseased lamps and the sound of screaming. That was how she found him, lurking in the shadows by the Sand Gate. One of her kind.

He was waiting for her, too. That communion went both ways. In a land like this, where her only kin were entombed in bones and jars and brass flasks deep beneath the earth, the presence of another free demon was like a knife-point to the eye, impossible to ignore. And perhaps just as much of a threat.

And not *free*. Certainly not as free as she was. But not locked forever in some sigil-inscribed skull, so as free as any demon could be, under contract.

He unlurked a little, shifted slightly towards the fringes of the moon shadows he hid in. She could see him clearly enough, and she had taught Enshili some little incantations, to pierce the darkness.

Caecelian herself had been conjured up in the shape of a woman. A woman who was each voyeur's dream, hence the hideous mask she wore right now. She could walk amongst humans, though, certainly those whose prohibitions meant they'd never seen a demon. Not so this creature, her sibling monster. His monstrousness was fully on display.

"Sister," he murmured, or perhaps it was more of a gurgle. "I'd not expected such as you here. Are there those of the contracting craft in the city, hidden from these prigs who trap and bury us?"

"There are not," she told him. "Not one." And made no explanation because his ignorance was meat too.

"Is that… a uniform?" Enshili asked.

The demon moved, swifter than his ungainly shape should have allowed. Caecelian only knew to stand in the way because she'd been with the Pal army for years under her former master, and recognised certain movements. Like a baton levelled in threat.

"She is mine," she said to her brother. "You shall not harm her."

His barbed grin spread a bit, like a fungus. "What's this, Sister?"

"She is mine. My wickedness."

Enshili came to stand beside her, staring down the levelled baton. "And that is a Kepishi uniform. A Pal's."

Caecelian herself had not really noticed. The fact of his demon-ness spoke to senses that knew nothing of the mundane world. But yes, her apprentice was right and her brother had been stuffed into the garb of a Palleseen soldier. Not even his seeming, but true clothes, even with a badge of rank.

"What are you, Brother?"

That grin, inching its way to where his ears should have been. "Cohort-Monitor Croskin, Ventures Department of the army of Pallesand." The human words of him, and behind them, the demon meaning, the precise web of tensions that existed for him to hold his form and place here in the upper world. The mess, frankly. The ridiculous, poorly thought-through piece of contracting that had left Croskin stranded, clinging to the plank of it, when his summoner had died.

She laughed. Not at him. She was even a little impressed with Croskin, that he'd parlayed his tenuous existence into *this*. And the Palleseen Sway's flavour of misery and wickedness had never been one that overly fed demons, given that the Pals liked to monopolise it for their own gain, but *here* was just a little drip of nourishment.

"Come now, Sister," Croskin growled. "I've shown you mine."

"I was a demonist's pet once," she said. The human words of her, and behind them, the truth.

Croskin croaked, choked, as though the fact of her was stuck in his throat and he'd die of it. His yellow eyes bulged.

"I would worship you," he said. "Or tear you down for envy. The fact of you is like a fire." And to demons, fire was good, the more destructive the better. "I would have offered you a uniform and a badge, but I see I have nothing." His voice shook. "Sister, you are the marvel of all the hells. How the Kings must hate you!" Because, though the misery of humans was sweet, the rage of the Kings Below was pure nectar.

"You are come to bedevil the city in your uniform?" she asked him. She saw Croskin making mischief, starting fires, poisoning wells. Because she hadn't entirely understood what the uniform meant on him.

"Not quite," he said, and then the others started arriving. Some she felt crawling up the walls like lizards, like Croskin must have done. Others flew, circling in the night overhead, shapes to swallow the stars with the spread of their wings. She looked from Croskin to the Sand Gate, its garrison, its weapons. The east way into the city, but from the Sand Lanes the roads ran straight past the embassies to the cliffs.

"Get your chit off the streets," Croskin told her. A winged demon with a hide of bristling quills landed nearby, a Pal jacket tied about its neck like a napkin before dinner. A skittering, chitinous thing with six limbs pattered up to Croskin's heels. It had two sets of uniform breeches on, and a baton sloped across its armoured back.

Enshili stared at them. Almost flinching, Caecelian reached out to her, like a wine taster scenting the bouquet. Disgust? Horror? A sudden recanting of all her vows?

The girl was leaping, inside. Grinning, behind her mask. Her physical pose was all duellist's stillness, hand to her hilt ready to draw, but the sight of these monsters on the streets of her city sang in her. That all those walls would be pulled down, even to the oldest foundations. Caecelian felt a stab of love for her that was painful, agony. And that, too, was good.

The Hand of a Brother

The royal families of the Mirror Palace were seldom close. Even the least child of an Alkhand grew up mired in ritual. The happy celebrations over which Kakrops the frog god passed his vacant regard. The dour and often interminable demands of the Moerends and their leftover death cult. The countless little folk traditions and secular demands that still required a full count of progeny in attendance. Walls, fencing each off from the world and from each other. And, of course, the operation of the succession itself, when any amount of sibling affection might prove soluble in blood.

Small wonder the history of Usmai saw a parade of eccentrics, the estranged children of royalty finding diversion in obsession or excess. Sex, art, cruelty, charity, the duelling circle, the hunt. Permitted outlets for royal ennui.

So it was for those with the spectre of the crown hovering about them. Gorbudan's warrior nature, Dekamran's insistence on getting his hands dirty with diplomacy; obsessions no less than their great-grandfather's harem or his *grandfather founding a dozen monasteries. So it was, all the more, for those distant enough from inheritance that it seemed their lives would never mean anything. Merely an inconvenience for an elder sibling to attend to eventually, like a crack in the ceiling in one wing of the palace. Small wonder they sought significance elsewhere. Such as in religion.*

Gorbudan should have been up at the clifftop with his officers and his army. The morning would see them sally forth to strike at Dekamran's motley followers, because the longer he left it, the more faint hearts would start weighing up the balance of where their support should lie. Gorbudan was the warrior, that was his great advantage over slow, soft Dekamran. But a warrior cannot sit idle. Wars are won through momentum, and fighting a defensive battle would put the burden of apparent weakness onto the true Alkhand, the one who actually held the throne.

Despite that possession, therefore, he should not be here in the palace. But then the news had come.

Like one of those tales, where the protagonist states an incautious wish, and a demon hears it and makes it true the worst way. Had he not been waiting for days for the news of a brother's death?

Now he stood in a room decorated with morbid curiosities and cadaverous icons, and it was a brother's corpse he looked on, just not the right one.

Premaran – Premath, the name he'd taken in his idiot devotions – was shockingly thin. He'd worn the loose robes of a Moru acolyte most of the time and it had hidden just how his ribs stood out from his chest, the knobs of his spine down his back. The painting of his face, that Gorbudan had denied him, had plastered a false skull over the real one that had been emerging behind his parchment skin. He had been starving himself, it seemed. In protest or in religious ecstasy. It was something the Moerends did sometimes. A sacred thing. A stupid thing, it seemed to Gorbudan.

It was not starvation that had killed Premath, third son of the lost Alkhand Oparan, youngest brother of the new Alkhand Gorbudan. At dusk, after the palace had quietened, he had taken the sacramental make-up someone had smuggled to him, and daubed his face into that skull the Moerends so loved. Sat before the mirror and carefully covered over the features of Gorbudan's little brother until only death remained. And then, probably just as carefully, he had eaten the rest. The lead, the antimony, the other toxic ingredients that gave such verisimilitude to the darkness and the pallor of it all.

His thin frame lay twisted on its bed. A painful death, excruciating, yet he had not cried out even once. It was a wonder anyone had looked in on him before morning. But they had, and word had gone racing up the cliffs to the camp above, where it had found Gorbudan.

He was aware that a great deal of what he was feeling was guilt. Because *What Happens to Premath* had been in his mind a great deal. Once more pressing fraternal business had been dealt with. A monastery. Somewhere fantastically isolated, up a mountain, in the heart of the forest. Or send the boy over the mountains, to that other swathe of Successor States that had survived the encryption of the Empire. To the very gates of the Dead City. Somewhere the truly faithful were expected to travel to at least once. The House at the Brink of Death, or something like that. And Premath would never go, of course. And Gorbudan could never have allowed him to go, or to retire, or any of it. Would have had to keep his kid brother locked in a wing of the palace at the very least, with no visitors. And even then, what when Gorbudan had feuding sons of his own? What if some faction of the city would rather have Mad Uncle Premath as a convenient body on the throne, in whose shadow they could rule?

He had already accepted the guilt of fratricide, sooner or later, but here was Premath, the thoughtful brother, removing the necessity from him. Gorbudan stared down at the pitiful, contorted body, and felt a savage rage rising.

"Get me the Grand Moerend," he spat. "Get me Arkanith. Haul him from his bed. From his tomb if you have to."

The old man, His Quietude, was duly hauled. Standing in a thin robe before his Alkhand, before the corpse of his follower, the late prince.

Arkanith's face was made for melancholy anyway. Hard to say what he actually *felt*. Gorbudan waited for him to speak, to comment on the surely noteworthy dead prince in the room with them, but His Quietude remained quiet, not lamenting, not perturbed. Regarding his Alkhand with a reptilian air of patience.

"You have brought this about," Gorbudan told him flatly.

Arkanith raised an eyebrow, disturbing the papery skin of his forehead so much Gorbudan was amazed it didn't split. "I, Your Tranquillity?"

"This is one of your thousand rites of death." And Gorbudan was no scholar of theology, least of all of the dusty Moru texts that were vast and had almost nothing to say about important things like living. "You filled his head with your necrotic creed. You taught him the joy of endings. He worshipped you."

"No," Arkanith said, sharply enough to silence him. "He worshipped those things it is proper to worship. The world beyond, and the narrow road that lies along the border between there and here. Matters of true faith, Alkhand."

"And he killed himself. For your faith. Do you deny it?"

And Arkanith would deny it, and Gorbudan would be left with the choice of either simply shouting him down with *I am Alkhand!* or getting into a legalistic dispute over causes and effects. Except the old man simply said, "It is the right of the faithful to walk the path to death at their own pace. Your brother has elected to progress to the next stage of his existence according to prescribed means approved of by the judging gods, for one who is a scion of a royal house. His ledger in the next world shall be credited appropriately."

Gorbudan stared, because never in his wildest days had he imagined anything quite as barefaced as that. "You deny nothing."

"Your brother chose his end and went about it the proper way. It is to be celebrated," said the Grand Moerend, and Gorbudan's hand closed about his sword hilt. Utter sacrilege, to hack down the highest official of the state death cult here in the palace.

And yet only the greatest self-control spared the old man's life right then.

What saved Arkanith in the *next* moment was the shouting. Men calling for the Alkhand, battlefield panic in their voice. Gorbudan hailed them, and two or three burst in at once. The sword leaped to his hand, a residual thought that he'd just identified himself to Dekamran's assassins. But soft Dekamran would never, and these were just messengers.

"The assault!" he made out. "It's begun!"

"It can't be midnight yet," Gorbudan said.

"They're moving, Your Tranquillity," one confirmed. "Ogrodons and cavalry and soldiers."

"We have twice their number and a defensive position," Gorbudan spat out, as though Dekamran's Pal commander could be sent for and shown the appropriate tactical manuals, and would embarrassedly call off the attack. Nobody commenced a grand assault at *night*, surely?

Of course, it being night, Gorbudan's forces had only a skeleton picket along that defensive position. Everyone else would be jolting awake even now, scrabbling for armour, trying to get mounts saddled, fumbling fistfuls of tablethi.

"I'm on my way. We'll smash them." The moment he arrived at the clifftop, he'd bring the tide of victory with him. The true Alkhand, riding through the camp like a flag in his soldiers' hearts. The enemy had just written their own doom in the history books.

"Take this old traitor," he spat, jabbing a finger at the Grand Moerend. "Throw him in the—" Not the House of Hard Angles, that the death priests ran – and *now* Dekamran's escape from it seemed less mysterious but more suspicious. "Lock him in his rooms, under guard." He scowled into Arkanith's serene face. "Perhaps he will also present himself to a final judgment, and save me the trouble. I hope the judging gods spit on him and send him back as a beetle."

Would his people truly lay hands on the highest official of the death cult? Yes, because he was Gorbudan, and when he ordered, people obeyed. Arkanith was bustled off, and Gorbudan strode out from the palace, where his personal retinue had already assembled ready to ride back up the cliff paths to the camp.

What made him look back, he could not say. His instincts, honestly. His sense as a general, the gifts that had made him so admired. Even as the battle massed up above, he turned his horse and looked down at the quiet city below. There was enough of a moon to permit a night attack by a massed and varied force. There was enough for him to see his birthright, his capital.

Enough to see the movement of troops down there, emerging from the Sand Lanes, marching double-time for the paths that led up the cliffs to here, to the palace, to the rear of the camp. To everything.

A jolt of shock went through Gorbudan. That his enemies, Dekamran, the Pals, *someone*, had outmanoeuvred him.

"Send for my commanders!" he barked out. His retinue frowned, calmed their mounts, stared at him. He had been about to go *to* his commanders, as fast as any messenger. But now this. They hadn't seen, yet. And Gorbudan opened his mouth, feeling the vice on him from above and below, and for the first time paused, trying to work out what to do.

Mosaic: The Moral Victory

Once, there was a people called the Islermen, who lived by fishing and by trading, but most notoriously by raiding. A fierce, unsociable people with a fierce, unsociable sea god, who demanded a great deal of sacrifice and deprivation, making scarcity into sanctity. The Islermen were more a plague on others than a success in themselves, and eventually they saw this, as their god roared for more blood and treasure every high tide. The blood of those who would otherwise work for the Islermen, as well as the blood of the Islermen themselves. The gold that they ripped from the throats and vaults of those coastal settlements they descended on. All the things that the Islermen would rather have kept. And so a new philosophical concept arose that said, 'Why do we keep you around, exactly?' to their god. And, with the benefit of a great many books and, indeed, the writers of those books, who had been brought by force to the Archipelago, the Islermen reinvented themselves. It wasn't easy. The first battles the new culture won were against their own recalcitrant kin. But they brought a new way of life to their islands, based on exacting definitions of what was correct, that had no room for gods in them anywhere, *and they set a temporary commission in place, to oversee the expansion of this perfection to the rest of the world, who would, of course, be grateful. This was how the Palleseen came about. And their god? The howling, hungry fish-and-blood god? Lost to history along with everything else of the Islermen. Explicitly eradicated, and the penalty for even admitting that god ever existed was death. Vanished into history's depths, along with their original language and all the other imperfect things they'd been. They killed their god. This was the Palleseen victory.*

In the Fever Lodge, they huddle behind locked doors. All of them, for once. No stragglers out late at night, nobody thinks they know better. Even Caecelian is here, her sword across her knees, Jack leaning into her from one side and Enshili the other. Across the inner room of the Lodge they've retreated to, Oathan boils tea and makes soup, for something to do. His boy brings a bowl to Enshili – of his own notion, because Oathan has no intention of extending a welcome to *that* one – and gets a rind of a smile in response.

Tally and the Reckoner, who between them constitute the hand on the tiller of the Fever Lodge, try to work out what to do.

"A ship," Tally says. "The morning." Aware of the conflicting currents in the room. Oathan would embark the moment the tide let him. The rest, not so much.

"I like it here," the Reckoner says. She pops another sweet into her mouth. She's been sucking and crunching at them ever since the trouble started outside. And passed by, outside, and is still passing by, not stopping at their door. They know trouble in the Fever Lodge, though. None better.

"They have that spice I like here," the Reckoner says. "And they know us."

"They know us," Tally echoes. "That's the problem. You think, once there are Pal boots on the street for regular, nobody's going to ask questions about a bunch of offcomers who turned up in uniform shirtsleeves during the war?"

"A lot goes on in the Sand Lanes. Who listens to talk?" the Reckoner says. And she spent her whole life abstaining from anything that she might actually like, yielding always to the needs of others, until she came here. Here she's learned she can be selfish, and so she digs her heels in.

"Who says they'll win?" demands the boy. Everyone stares

at him as if to say, *Who said you get a say, exactly?* And yet the question hangs there.

Oathan rumbles an answer eventually. "If they win it's a bad place to be a Pal in. If they lose it's a bad place to be any foreigner in. Fucked either way."

"You don't know that." The boy wouldn't have talked back if it had been Tally or the Reckoner saying it, but right now he'll pick a fight with his surrogate father over everything.

Oathan inflates, about to bring the thunder, then sags. Stares at the kettle. Pours the tea. His sad, shrunken silence is worse than bellowing.

Outside, past the Fever Lodge's barred door, Pal uniforms hustle through the Sand Lanes. Dark and light, the regulars and the Accessories from Peost, led by a remarkable band of luminaries. Flanked by demons. Pushing through the meanest, poorest district of Alkhalend, aiming for the brightest and the highest.

Flint leads them. Not the best idea. As overall commander of the forces supporting Dekamran, he should be up top masterminding the night attack on Gorbudan's lines. Except, between the two halves of their clamshell, this is the tricky one. He's delegated the main assault to one Companion-Monitor Steggers, a former statlos with a battlefield promotion and a lot of bloody fighting under his belt from the war. Steggers is reliable, if unimaginative. Left to his own devices he'd do the right thing all the way until Gorbudan, the dashing, the dynamic, made sure that doing the right thing was the wrong thing to do, tactically speaking. Flint is hoping that he can start closing his half of the clam before the situation up above exceeds Steggers's ability to react.

They've met no resistance so far. Once Croskin's detachment of Unnaturals took the gatehouse and the engines there without a warning or a shot, his people entered the city double-time.

Him at their head, and a good mix of Pal and Peost troops, squads who have a few night actions under their belts and who he reckons are good for a bit of street-to-street. Leave this part to Steggers and they'd still be bogged down two blocks from the gate, but Flint is just *going*, no attempt to secure his backside because moving forwards is the one thing that can keep this venture alive.

Beside him, sword drawn, is Sage-Invigilator Angilly, and that is also a terrible idea. Because she outranks him, but she's also a civilian. Not a battlefield officer. The only thing that marches to her order is paperwork. She's basically just someone who can simultaneously get under his feet and look over his shoulder, which is quite the contortion. And probably she's handy with the pig sticker but Flint feels that if things get to the valiant clash of steel against steel then they're already screwed.

Beside *her* is His Tranquillity the Alkhand Dekamran. The actual point of this whole thing, who belongs a thousand miles away as far as Flint is concerned. Belongs, certainly, in a fancy tent some way behind the assault Steggers is currently leading, being fed grapes and awaiting news from his brave Palleseen allies. *Not* bustling along at the head of this clandestine invasion force as though he's actually leading the army.

But Dekamran wouldn't take Flint's *No*, and Angilly wouldn't put the potentate in his place, and so it's come to this. The three of them, the three most senior figures on the side of the usurpation party, here on the streets of Alkhalend where any fool with a baton could pip the whole business.

And yes, Flint absolutely thinks of the action as a usurpation, because Gorbudan has the fancy chair and the big hat and, as far as Flint cares, the acquiescence of the majority of the Usmai, while Dekamran has the Palleseen Resident. And the Palleseen Resident has the writ of the Temporary Commission of Ends and Means, meaning soldiers and a global reach and the pair of Palleseen Hands they're dragging along towards the back. Thus far Flint hasn't been so impolitic as to describe Dekamran's ambitions as usurping to the prince's face, but it's probably only a matter of time.

And yet they've got remarkably far. And, honestly, without Gil or Dekamran he'd probably still be fucking about and finding out deep in the Sand Lanes. There are straight paths that lead from the Sand Gate uphill to more respectable parts of the city, and thence to the cliffs and the palace. If you just go straight, though, you'd miss them. Local knowledge is definitely an asset right now. So they've led the assault force – basically three hundred uniforms and six hundred boots, plus two artillery pieces – stomping through all manner of narrow streets, under leaned-together bunch-of-sticks tenements, and past the shadow of the most sinister tomb-or-something Flint ever saw, and now the way ahead is definitely rising, and they're about to clear the shanty town and get to the good stuff.

That's where the Alkhand – the real one, he of chair and hat – that's where his response finds them.

"Ah piss on it," Flint says, seeing what's ahead. "It's them." And if they're ahead, they're on both sides too, because during the advance he had a real in-depth lesson on just how this particular part of his enemy's army do things. But of course it was them, because who else did the Alkhand trust, to patrol and police the streets of his city? None but the incorruptible Tesemer, the Louse Monks.

"Move up the Hands," he sends back down the column. "'Ware flanks."

"Let me talk to them," says Dekamran. Ahead, there is a line of robed figures with very long swords, closing off the street. And bows, Flint sees, but also batons, the long and sleek pieces that his hands itch for. Non-regulation, yes, but such works of lethal art!

"To *them?*" Even Angilly thinks this is a terrible idea.

"They serve the Alkhand," Dekamran says. "I am the Alkhand." A man who thinks saying it enough will make it true.

"No," says Angilly, and "No," says Flint, but Dekamran breaks from the head of the column, and they can't exactly jump the True Alkhand of Usmai and bundle the man to the ground. So they end up just sort of going with, and so do a bunch of Flint's people who he'd already picked for close work, cudgels and short rods, and sabres for the statloi.

Ahead, the Tesemer regard their advance blankly, as though momentarily stunned into paralysis by the sheer idiocy of the usurper. Flint licks dry lips, tries to swallow, can't.

Up at the palace, Gorbudan is going mad. He is the swift, the dashing, the warrior prince who's always where he's meant to be. Where he's meant to be is down in the streets of Alkhalend, plainly. Leading his personal bodyguard in a charge against the Pals that will halt their encroach through his city. That will give his people time to muster forces and get down the cliffs, while still holding off the night attack apparently underway up there, all without his personal intervention. So perhaps where he's meant to be is up top, seeing off the enemy, trusting that the Pals below will just knot themselves in the streets of Alkhalend until Gorbudan comes with the morning and a knife to cut them down. It's one or the other, though. He only has one self. Otherwise it's just the wind of his words, that he can feel losing force the moment a messenger carries them away from him.

He's sent a fast rider down to the city to muster the Tesemer and have them fall on the invaders. Well and good, and Lhisamena would tell him that the Louse Monks are worth any number of Pals in the close streets of the Sand Lanes. Except Lhisamena has been telling him all manner of things the Louse Monks can accomplish, up to and including providing him with the head of Dekamran, and it hasn't happened. The only situation in which Dekamran's face is before Gorbudan these days is in the crowned Alkhand's dreams, where it's looking down on him. The failure to turn back the usurper in the field has proved a serious knock to Gorbudan's confidence. The suicide of his youngest brother and the simple vanishing of his sister likewise. It feels as though the world around him is flying out of his control just when he needs to hold onto it the tightest.

He's sent up the cliffs too, but the camp up there must be in chaos. Nobody expected the Pals to just come at night. It isn't how things are done. Although Gorbudan, when he was raiding the Pals and the Peosts across the border during the war, did just that of course. He hadn't thought he'd been teaching his enemies valuable lessons, though. He hadn't thought the Pals were constitutionally able to learn from those they saw as lesser people.

And so he isn't up top, and he isn't such a fool as to descend into the streets where any stray shot could empty the crown of its current notional head and win the war instantly for his enemy. He's here, at the gates of his palace, in the saddle but riding nowhere.

The first soldiers trickle in from above. And it is a trickle, and they're nothing. A handful of Emorandi cavalry and a mess of levy, some of them without their spears, some still in their nightclothes. Wild, wide eyes. Fear. Fear of the unexpected. In simply making this move under cover of darkness, the Pals have won a psychological victory they can't even guess at. Because to the Usmiat they are the foreigners, the Kepishi with their terrible ways and cruelties and who knows what they'll do?

That's without even considering the stories of demons.

What forces come down to him – negligible, inadequate, panicky – he sends down the cliffs because surely even a rabble can hold a path from higher ground against any number of attackers. It's the perfect tactical situation. There are whole books about how nobody should ever try attacking a bottleneck uphill. Surely.

*

Lhisamena feels very still, very leaden, watching Dekamran approach. Her monks have mustered along the street behind her, falxes ready. She has others, working to flank, but she can see – far better in the dark than any Pal – that the enemy are ready for that. There are Pal soldiers stealing away into the buildings. Forcing the weak doors of Sand Lanes tenements. Putting heads and batons out onto rickety balconies, through the small windows, lying on the uneven roofs so they can aim down. The Sand Lanes are permeable. You can't just bottle people up there. Plenty of Alkhands have discovered just that, when they pushed their subjects too far.

The honour of the Tesemer took a bloody wound during the advance. *We rust*, she thought. *Where is our strength?* When the old Alkhand defeated his brother, back in the day, where the Louse Monks walked, the battlefield fell still, and they left bodies behind them like leaves out of season. But the Pals aren't from that world. The Pals have been fighting a different war these last three years and they do things differently. They have no respect.

Dekamran hails her; names her. The boy she watched grow, though always in the shadow of his more able brother. Ask her, in their childhood, which of them was fit for the throne, she'd not have hesitated. Not that anyone would have asked her. Not the Tesemer's place to have an opinion, though she always had.

Dekamran tells her – as if she didn't know – of how he was his father's choice. He quotes legalities at her. A man of words and paper, just as the Pals come from a world of words and paper. Because if you have sufficient control over the words, you can start to change and erase them. Unmake things. Delete them from the world. Until you come to someone's country and just unstitch their whole way of being. Take the garment of them and run a razor down all the seams until it's just loose pieces of fabric with no shape left. Lhisamena feels the edge of that razor at her front. Her people were already ripped ragged coming out of the Grove centuries before. The Usmiat had allowed them to keep some scraps of what they had been, back where they'd come from. Now the Pals would rob them of even that. Would turn them into a parade of jugglers performing sword tricks for the empty applause of a crowd, and nothing more.

"No," she says. It's midway into some impassioned speech the idiot boy's giving, about being right and just and all those other things. She feels the words fitting together so neatly there's no space left between them in which to *be*.

She moves, swift. She will kill Dekamran. That's the only way. He's stopped outside a falx's reach but she's swift even though she's old. She'll kill him and then she'll die but he will be dead.

A leap, her blade gone from resting against her shoulder to a downwards-cleaving strike of steel lightning. Dekamran's face, just entering into the first negotiations with shock.

The clash of steel. The woman, the Resident, her blade angled to turn Lhisamena's strike aside, just enough. An inch past the usurper's shoulder, slicing a rent in his shawl but not his skin.

She leaped without warning, which means her own people are as unready as her enemies. A moment later they come, but the Pals ahead and the Pals overhead are shooting, too.

I should have talked, she thinks. *I should have let his words just pour out and out until my Alkhand came with his army. That was my duty*. But it isn't her way. This is her way. The old way. When the shot takes her, even as she drives hatefully at the Pal woman, she dies the death of the Louse Monks.

Gil has no sense of what's going on, save that she is getting Dekamran back out of danger. Around her, Flint's people are firing, moving forwards, firing again. She hears the crackle of batons from overhead and either side. Then a hookloper comes bursting out of a side-street, tearing into the Pals with its steel-sheathed forelegs. The monk astride it swings their falx left and right, sending soldiers spinning away. All close enough that a lash of blood slaps across Gil's side and face. That she can look up and see the monk's weird, angular face beneath the wide brim of their hat.

She brings up a rod and spat the word, but her shot goes wide. A moment later the rider sees her – sees Dekamran – and wheels their mount round, the flattened body twisting to arrest its forward momentum. Gil gives the rod its command a second time, then a third. The flash of energy chars a line down the armoured segments of the hookloper's flank and puts out one of its glittering eyes. Then her tableth is dry and she flicks it from its socket, fumbling for another and knowing she doesn't have time.

That last shot at least rattled the beast, but it's still coming for her when the demon arrives. It had probably been hoping to snatch the monk from the saddle, but Gil has never known a demon that is nimble in the air. It crashes into mount and rider both, four hundredweight of hell-borne monster colliding with the scions of some otherworld's bestiary. She sees one long scaled arm catch the monk with hooked talons, ripping them from their seat. The hookloper's killing arms seize on the demon and begin busily carving it up. She drags Dekamran away before he can decide this is the time for more diplomacy.

And she loves him for it. Plainly she does. It was the noble thing to do. But he came so close to being killed!

Ahead, the Tesemer line is disintegrating. Their lethal falxes are poised, but nobody wants to try them. Instead it's batons, and though the Louse Monks are skilled shots, they lack the sheer volume of fire the Pals can throw back at them. And then the engine crews finally get one of the Hands wheeled up and levelled and she hears the extraordinary chatter of a half-dozen batons in rapid fire, the released-portcullis rattle of a whole string of tablethi discharging in sequence at a single word.

When that's done, the street is clear ahead. There are still loose monks left and right, but the steel of them has broken and Flint pushes forwards. The column gets clear of the Sand

Lanes, passing up the street where her own Residence stands. As though she might just nip in to grab all the correspondence she's missed and read through it on the march. And she wants to grab Dekamran and tell him to go hide there until all this is over. But she knows he wouldn't, and what if they lost?

The path up to the palace – and eventually to the clifftops where Gorbudan's main force is currently facing off Steggers's best shot at a night attack – winds back and forth across the face of the cliff. Where it meets the waterfall there are the elegant arches of bridges, across a carefully architected landscape of pools and rills. There are pleasure gardens and shrines and the grand baths. A path up a cliff, then, but not a goat track. The plan concocted by Flint and Dekamran, such as it is, isn't quite as mad as it sounds. And the Pals hit the ascent at a double march. They've come without packs, because either they'll camp victorious under the stars in the palace grounds or things will go badly for them. They can run, and they do. They'll be tired when they reach the palace, but Flint knows soldiers and he knows battles. Tired and in the right place wins more than refreshed and nowhere near.

They meet the first scatter of defenders after the second turn. Gorbudan's vanguard try to form up and bar their way but Flint doesn't give them the chance. Doesn't give Dekamran the chance to orate to them either, honestly, because surely there was never a usurper who believed his own rhetoric more than he. He'll talk every ear off from here to the palace and never quite understand that a deaf man can still say the word to shoot a baton.

So Flint has his front-runners start shooting the moment they're in range, and he has Croskin's Unnaturals take point. From the air, from the side, clambering up the sheer cliff that should have been an impregnable flank. The initial attack disrupts the enemy as they get into position. The realisation of what they're fighting half-breaks them and then the Pals are running at them and they go. Go, and when you're running from this sort of stupid uphill advance then you, too, are running uphill. A lot of them don't get to warn anyone of what's coming.

By then, there are other detachments of enemy who are taking up station on higher levels. They throw stones down, and then – because they couldn't exactly hotfoot it over with barrows of ready stones – they start throwing statues down. Gods and past Alkhands and figures symbolising philosophical concepts shatter around the Pal advance and catch more than a few of them. The Pals shoot back, though, keeping anyone from being too keen to peer over the edge of the path above, and they just keep taking the turns, trampling the flowers, crossing each bridge as they come to it. They don't let the defenders slow them, and the defenders don't have time to put together the sort of force that could. The one time some can-do Emorandi gets a serious blockade of spears up there, archers ready to drop their shafts down on the shoulders and heads of the advancing Pals, Flint's engine crews get a decent line on them and drain thirty tablethi in ten seconds to remove the obstruction.

And on, and between him and the level with the actual palace is just a broad expanse of ornamental pools. Flint barely marks the other major feature as he marches up to it, because there's no enemy in sight and the object is just to get across the open as quickly as possible and then take the next ascent.

Gorbudan hears the reports with horror and disbelief. The enemy below – however few of them there actually are – aren't stopping. And if their intent is to slog all the way to the clifftop and try to attack the main force in the rear, that's plainly suicide. But if their intent is to take control of the actual *palace*, place Dekamran on the Mirror Throne, strongarm some priest into saying the words and then declare him Alkhand, well, that's eminently doable. And then Gorbudan would have to decide if he wants to ruinously assault his own palace. And Gorbudan's followers would, each and individually, have to decide if they wanted to go to all that trouble and property damage, when there was a perfectly good Alkhand already sitting there who would – Dekamran being who he is – doubtless forgive any little foibles of loyalty. Gorbudan was their man because he was the winner, the fighter. Warrior princes did not lose their palace and their throne to their feckless younger brother. Tactically, it was ridiculous, meaningless. Let Dekamran have the overblown building and the needlessly ornate chair. But the considerations of being Alkhand were not those of a general.

Right then, for a moment but very intensely, he hates the Loruthi. There aren't even any Loruthi anywhere near, but if they'd only whipped the Pals in their big war, like it had seemed they were going to, then none of this need happen and probably he could even have kept his siblings by his side. And now this.

More troops are coming down, still piecemeal, still ill-prepared. Bleary just-woken conscripts, Emorandi half-drunk from the previous evening's revelry. A single Louse Monk on her hookloper, whose expression suggests that Gorbudan has bitterly disappointed her people. He wants to shout at her, *Where is my brother's head, that you promised? Where is the invincible Tesemer blade that knows no equal?*

Below, he sees the rapid flash; a moment later hears the rattle of it, as the Palleseen Hand tears into his followers and the Pals barely slow to let it happen. Any faster and they'd walk into their own shot. They will shortly cross into the grand open field of pools that forms the very heart of the waterfall chain and the paths. The point that all eyes in Alkhalend can see, the place of ritual and celebration, and coronation. Another symbolic loss, and right now enough fighting has been happening up the cliff that surely everyone in the city is looking up. Seeing the boots of the invaders trampling all over Usmai's sacred history. Because Gorbudan has let them.

"With me," he tells his retinue. "With me!" he calls to every soldier who has made it this far down the cliffs. Spears, bows, cavalry, the monk. Enough. It will have to be enough. It will not be. He knows it.

He is not without allies. He is Usmai, after all. Not brother against brother, but the spirit of his homeland against the Kepishi invader. There is one more place he can go for aid in this extremity. In his mind, it's justified. The very future of his nation is at stake and his brother cannot be trusted with it.

Flint's advance has made it to the sacred level, the pools laid out in patterns of ritual significance to the Usrani and the Moerends and a handful of other monastic traditions that are or once were influential in Usmai. The enemy – Gorbudan's people – are just coming down to the same level. Flint sees cavalry there, the Usmiat sort, horses with clawed bird legs that are just as fast as the regular kind only nastier. He sees a single Louse Monk his people somehow haven't shot yet, and makes a mental note to rectify that. He sees an expanding mass of footsoldiers spreading out as they hit the pools like someone spilled something.

Open ground is good for cavalry, but also for a good double line of massed batons, so the battlefield is considerately trying to play to everyone's strengths. Normally he'd think all that landscaping would trip up a horse charge, but he's seen the Emorandi riders gallop through root-strewn forests without missing a footfall so he's not counting on it. He feels very tired, honestly. Forty and a soldier and that was a lot of uphill he just took at a hustle.

Dekamran has that look on him again. And these are his people, damn it. Maybe it's about time he started turning some hearts and minds. Only this time he's not offering to do the open hands routine. He's almost within a sharp sprint of the palace doors. You'd think he'd be getting more and more the Alkhand with each level they ascended, like a candle burning backwards, but he's gone all cold and serious now. Eyes fixed on one man.

"Oh shit," says Flint. "That him?"

The Alkhand – the other one, the one whose possession of things really is nine-tenths of inheritance law – is at the back, just hoisting himself up into a saddle after some pedestrian excursion. Caught short, maybe, Flint considers. Happens to the best of us, and we're none of us as young as we were. Except when Gorbudan waves his clavar in the air, it's coated with blood. He's been off murdering, then. Sparing a moment from preparing the defences to settle a score or put down some rowdy underling. Certainly nobody around him looks like they're about to argue.

"We got a sharpshooter who can knock his hat off?" Flint asks. "Or maybe something a bit lower?" But it's dark still – the night seems like it's gone on forever – and Gorbudan is riding back and forth now, shouting at his troops, firing them up, getting them into place.

"Well, it's a fight then," Flint decides, given Dekamran has apparently learned wisdom. The Alkhand – their one, the usurping one with nothing but a few hard lads and lasses in Pal uniform to his name – nods. He has his own sword out but doesn't wave it around, and probably he'd be a menace if he did.

Flint gives the orders. Form up. Firing line centre, with angled wings to complicate any flanking move from the cavalry. Right flank a loose cloud of regulars who saw skirmish action back in the war. Left flank the Unnaturals, because even Usmiat horses won't charge those. Behind the lines: Dekamran, most definitively, plus Flint and Angilly and a handful of his less-winded people to relay his orders. Also at the back, because they're still manhandling the damn things, the two artillery pieces. If Gorbudan just keeps charging about saying inspirational things then maybe the Pals can set up a nice cogent answer to his rhetoric, but… No, he's done his thing and his people are arranged. His cavalry start to move, and to Flint's surprise they're avoiding the inviting flank where all the people are, carving towards Croskin's lot instead.

We'll find out just how much demons freak them, I guess.

Gorbudan's infantry form a loose order – not what the locals have done before, and they're not very good at it. When they advance some get left behind and some are too keen, and some just bunch up despite orders. It does mean that when the batons fire, they kill only about a third of the expected take. And then the orders are being shouted out, and horns sounded, and they're coming on at a run, tripping over ornamental fountains and falling in pools, but getting up and running again nonetheless.

The cavalry get up to speed, leaping over the ponds and rivulets and the mounded stones of shrines like they're riding cats, not horses. They have lances, and batons too, and the crackle of them spits out at the demons. Not a great massed salvo that would scythe the monsters down, but a few of the demons reel back and their order – never really the best – goes all to pieces because they're all different shapes and sizes despite their best efforts at wearing the uniform. Flint hears Croskin's raspy voice bellowing at them, and now the demons are shooting back. Terrible shots, most of them. The baton hadn't even been dreamed up when they'd been stuffed into skulls and pots and buried with spite and ceremony. If you have two hands and can speak Pel you can fire a baton, though, and that means around two-thirds of the Unnaturals get some shots off. A horse goes down, screaming. A woman goes down, likewise. A man falls over the back of his horse's arse and jolts about there with his dead arms spread. The riders cleave into the demons. It doesn't really work the way anyone wanted. The horses don't veer off, but they won't hit the Unnaturals head on either, so only a couple of lances find their mark. Only a couple of riders are dragged from horseback by demon claws. The two mismatched units mostly pass through one another almost peaceably.

Flint is already shouting for his floating wing on the right to turn and give fire as the cavalry cross through to his back, even as the statlos commanding that wing gives exactly the same order because he's not an idiot. The central double row of his troops fire and fire forwards, one line over the heads of the other, speaking that single word of Pel over and over until their tablethi leach from gold to lead, then slotting another in.

The enemy infantry, order themselves as loose as they like, have taken enough punishment to have second thoughts, which are terrible thoughts to have when you're three-quarters of the way into a charge. They start to go sideways, meaning they get in the way of their keener friends and don't really make themselves less of a target. The cavalry is trying to circle around back, but the side of a horse is a good target for a stationary batoneer and Flint's people are playing target practice with them. All in all it's going pretty well.

That's when the frog turns up.

Frog, singular. Frog, capitalised. Kakrops the god emerges from the cave with the inscribed arch and lets out a belching cry like thunder.

Gil is momentarily speechless. She knows Kakrops. The sleepy old, rather harmless thing. A god, yes, and Pals are technically somewhat down on those, but honestly little more than an animal infused with divinity, sleeping save when ceremony requires its presence.

This Kakrops is different. Raging, flushed black and red as though it's traded in agricultural fertility for fury in its divine portfolio. Mouth agape like a yawning void. Shaking its head and body, ten tons of sagging bulk lurching out into the open at human running speed.

"What has he done?" Dekamran – the native – cries out. Seeing what even seven years in Usmai haven't let her spot. That the red on Kakrops's flanks is the great toad's own blood. That the roaring, furious beast has been slashed and goaded until it woke. And, waking, mustering its divine power, has issued forth to deal out an amphibian smiting.

That loose-knit right flank that Flint had laid out as a tempting picnic for the cavalry is what Kakrops's bulging eye alights on, and the frog leaps. Lands in their very midst, and if that had been the usual tight Pal order they'd have half of them been crushed. Several die beneath the frog god's shadow anyway, and then the god lunges forwards. A tongue the size of a man lashes out, and the cavernous mouth just gapes around its victims, inhaling them. A handful more of Flint's people, devoured by wounded theology. No way for Pal soldiers to go.

Flint has fought across the Palleseen Sway, in the war and before it. It's not his first god. He's giving orders, sending messengers running off, getting his wing on the right to sight up. And they're Pals, who don't give a piss for sacrilege. They're Peosts, who have plenty of gods, but none that really do much, and this god is an Usmiat thing, jealously guarded against the neighbours.

Dekamran shouts out, demands they stop, shakes Flint by the arm until Flint shakes *him* off. Gil adds her voice, because they can't, they can't. All the way through the Sand Lanes and nothing on fire, barely a local roughed up who wasn't under arms, a mere handful of doors, the bare minimum of looting. Hearts and minds, the future rule of the true Alkhand – their one, the usurper – secured by the admirable restraint of the Palleseen and their cohorts. Until this.

The loose-knit formation is well set up to scatter. Some of them scatter right into the Usmiat infantry, and they have a full-on close-quarters scrap neither side was expecting until Kakrops barrels in, roaring, stomping, not caring about uniform or nationality, just mad with pain and fury. *I am your god and this is how you treat me?*

Gil turns Flint round, shouts in his face not to, but he's already got his troops in a firing line facing the frog. It's coming their way, weaving like a murderous drunk down an alley, its god-blood slicking over the top of the pools. Its eyes are mad moons, its maw the devouring horror of the night sky. Flint would have to actively give the countermand to stop his troops firing and, wide eyes fixed on the frog god, there's no way he's going to.

The massed crackle of batons sounds, so neatly in time that it's like a clap of hands. Kakrops, the benign, the ill-used, shudders back roaring. Surges forwards. They shoot again, and then the front rank are reloading and the back rank still shooting because they began offset and this way there's always a mass of them sending shot at the enemy. At god. The god of Alkhalend since time immemorial. The joke of a god. Gil can still remember Loret's astonishment. *Oh shit, it's a frog!* Those Usmiat, ho ho ho. What a funny thing to hold sacred.

It's not funny. It's tragic and terrifying. Kakrops bellows and shunts its appalling weight towards the batons. They speak and it falls back, two score blackened holes punctuating its warty hide alongside the sword-scars. The cavalry, at Flint's back now, are still taking a little shot, but they've stopped, aghast at what is being done to, and by, their deity. Not in all their days, not in all their histories or tales, has this side of Kakrops been hinted at.

The Pals speak and speak their death word, slot new tablethi, talk the god to death with their sentences. By then the Hands have been hauled and reset, loaded with strings of tablethi like jewellery about the neck of a sweetheart. The Pal artillerymen, presented with a monster, a god, ancient superstitions made manifest, need no orders and their own monsters hammer away in a vast expenditure of raw magic. Kakrops reels and staggers, his flanks and throat exploding as the baton-shot lances through him. Lifts his all-consuming maw towards the sky as though appealing to some greater divinity still, and then collapses. A vast mound, a corpse like a hill. The death of the frog god.

The reaction of the defending forces is split. The infantry, already broken, flee. The cavalry charge. Charge into the shot that the Pals were preparing for them. Charge, even though Croskin's demons hit them in the flank midway and savage riders and mounts both. Charge, and Gil grabs Dekamran and pulls him down, holds her sword up in mute defence. It springs from her hand, caught by the talons of a beast as it vaults them. Clavars and skias flash left and right, and the claws of the horses lash. Flint has his sword out, driving it into the neck of an animal as he wrenches at the rider's wrist. The demons, flying, running, loping on four or six limbs, catch up and tear into the back of them, but for just a moment the cavalry are the faithful punishing the defilers and they hold and hack and stab and shoot. Then enough horses are cut from under them, enough riders are hauled from their seats, that they, too, break and flee, trampling another handful of Pals as they do.

Flint hauls Dekamran to his feet. The Alkhand – the fake one, the one that did not just contribute to the killing of god – has tears running down his face, like a child. Like the child who learned folk stories in that very cave, who played games about the feet of the frog. Flint shouts into the grief of that face. Points his bloodied sword at the path that leads upwards. That leads to the palace. *Go, we have to go!* Gorbudan's people are running, but they can regain their nerve if their enemies aren't right on their heels, and then what will it all have been for? There's only one side getting reinforcements in *this* fight.

If Gorbudan could outrace word of what happened at the pools, then perhaps. If Gorbudan abandoned the palace and rode to his main force up above, then perhaps. At this point in time, the Usmiat loyalists are holding off Companion-Monitor Steggers's best efforts. The arrival of Gorbudan to take command would surely tilt the balance. If; perhaps. The territory of military historians to come.

But Gorbudan has seen his god die. Gorbudan has played

his part, in the death of that god, as much as the Pals have. And the Pals are meant to kill gods. If you know anything about Pals, that's what you know. Gorbudan is not a deicide by nature. But he chose to bring Kakrops into the battle, and now the old frog is just a great sack of flesh and sundered tradition.

He is not in his right mind, when he reaches the doors of the palace. It is his palace. He won't abandon it to the enemy. Not the coffers to Flint, not the throne to Dekamran, not the polished floors to the boots of the invader. He rallies all he has left, newcomers from above and retreating soldiers from below. With tears in his eyes he shouts them into some sort of order, even as the Pals come up the incline. There is no bottleneck here, no good defensive point, but the thought, the sheer *thought* of ceding the palace to these creatures is more than Gorbudan can bear.

No histories will record whose shot it is that finds him. Later, Flint will try to take the credit, but honestly he had nothing more than a short rod without the range. Some anonymous Pal trooper or Peost Accessory, loosing into the mass of the enemy, just happened to kill the Alkhand. The true Alkhand, the crowned one. The losing one, in this battle of brothers. The news isn't even apparent, until some Emorandi looks down at the body his horse is about to trample, and sees the death of all their hopes.

They flee, then. Considerately, they carry the news all the way up the cliffs and let all the soldiers up top know that there's no point, really, in holding out. The surrender comes soon after. And, beyond that, the dawn, in which a lot of painful things can be seen.

City in Mourning

The Schools of Correct Thought, the five fingers of the Palleseen hand. The notional one that grasps the throat of the imperfect, not the artillery piece, though the results are often the same. Correct Erudition for education and magic, Correct Exchange for trade, Correct Conduct for enforcement and conquest, Correct Appreciation for the arts, law and of course diplomacy. And Correct Speech, for the suppression of religion and the rooting out of imperfection, both within and without wider Palleseen society.

The docks of Alkhalend were busy. Busier than they had been since before the war, if only the visitors had any basis for comparison. And while, before, the bulk of ships flying Pal flags had been coasters come east from Peor, now they were bigger ocean-goers. Merchantmen from the Archipelago or across the Sway. Stepping out onto the shifting jetties of the Water Lanes, three out of four voices were arguing in Pel, and those who spoke Pel better tended to win.

This vessel, the *Naturae*, was not one of the big traders. A slender ship that had been, in its time, a packet vessel bringing the word of the Commission and a blockade runner taking spies and orders past the Loruthi navy. And a smuggler, independently or alongside of either of those, because its master was something of an opportunist. A man Flint could have shaken hands with, honestly.

Right now the *Naturae* was at least pretending to wear the

uniform, carrying word for the Resident in Usmai, but old habits died hard. A couple of passengers, at least, weren't quite on the manifests.

They stepped down, the two of them, and it was like they'd slipped on the gangplank and gone into the water. The babble of a living, trading, bickering city closed over them. A melange of voices, accents and all the little languages nibbling at the edge of Pel, trying to make a living. They'd travelled a great deal, in their work. The littoral societies of docks were an environment they'd adapted to.

Beyond that squabble and shout, though, the city of Alkhalend rose up, first its shoreside buildings, the warehouses and factoras and mills, then the cliffs. A wonder of the world, they'd often heard from others who'd been posted here. Nobody had mentioned the flags, though.

Yellow flags, striped with black, unrolled piecemeal down practically the entire height of the cliffs. Every tier was festooned with them, sodden in the spray, hanging like drapes at a funeral. Nothing either of them had ever seen before, but the colour choice spoke volumes.

Yellow, the age-old Usmiat colour of mourning. Black, of the Moeribandi shade precisely denoting death at the highest station.

The two visitors exchanged glances as a couple of sailors put their shared trunk down at their feet.

The younger of them was Annet. Unusually for a ranking Pal officer, she had some Jarokiri in her heritage, but in the uniform she looked acceptably Palleseen. Hence, when she caught the attention of an Usmiat dock worker and wanted to know who'd died, she received only a venomous glower and the cold shoulder.

She tried one of the Pals trying to arrange for his goods to be unloaded. The man stared blankly at her, noted her rank badges, and then said he had no idea but it was some stupid Usmiat thing and it meant everyone was on a go-slow. He'd been promised bearers and it had been the best part of an hour and who was going to do something about that, eh? Apparently in the hope that the *who* was Annet, which it most decidedly wasn't.

Her companion, Dalry, had been watching what was going on with his customary dry regard. He was a very tall old man, with a very long face. The sort of face people told things to. When he bent low to ask a diminutive local woman, speaking careful Usmiri, she answered him.

"Oh, I see." He straightened carefully up. "I fear that's going to complicate matters."

"What is it?" Annet asked him. The general hostility of the crowd was getting to her. This was supposed to be a soft landing for them.

"Well apparently, around twenty days ago, we killed god."

"We the…?"

"The uniform."

"And god the…?"

"They must mean the local toad religion."

"Killed god," Annet echoed, and blew out some air.

"I think a lot's happened while we were on the ship," Dalry said sombrely. Their path here from the Archipelago hadn't been a direct one. He bent down and gave the woman a coin, asking something else, receiving an angry response. Not angry at him, just at the world. Dalry was an old Palleseen, high ranking, good family, exquisitely educated and, frankly, very posh. Not that Annet was exactly out of the gutter, but he had an ancestor on the original Commission, and there was barely a major twist of Palleseen history that hadn't seen some kin of his involved. And despite that, he had a way of talking to just about anyone so that all that simply faded into invisibility. Cultists and votaries of banned religions would end up enthusiastically explaining their doctrine to him, so he could write it all down.

Dalry was causes, Annet was effects. That was how they partnered up and wrote their tracts. When he reported,

"Apparently they had three Alkhands in as many weeks, not long ago," he'd be thinking about the complex web of Usmiat customs and traditions that had led to such a mess. Annet wondered about how it had hit the city. What levers it pulled, which fires it lit. Who got crushed by the wheels.

It was, all in all, an interesting combined skillset. It could have suited a variety of trades. And Dalry and Annet both did their best to assure people they were just seekers after truth. Nobody who just wanted to *know* something could be sinister, surely.

"I wonder if our old acquaintance is even in place any more, given all that," he mused, and tugged at the sleeve of the Palleseen merchant. The man rounded on him, saw *his* rank badge, and went pale. "Magister!" he barked, suddenly back in his youth and on the drill square of the phal, playing soldier.

"Might I ask who is the current Resident, do you think?" Dalry murmured. And the thing about someone with those insignia on their uniform being very, very polite was that it scared the pips out of people. The implication of a decorum usually deployed over a rack of thumbscrews and a chair with straps and buckles.

"I don't know, magister!" the merchant squeaked, and then, because the man's previous ire had momentum, "but they'd better do something about these slack porters!" As though he hoped Dalry would take up his cause and carry it to the highest office in the land.

"Well, somebody must know," Dalry said. A couple of the *Naturae*'s crew had presented themselves now, ready to lug the chest. And a pair of high-fliers like Dalry and Annet should surely come with a retinue and a whole hold full of luggage, but sometimes you wanted to travel light and not have word of your coming outstrip you.

"Let's get onto dry land, Dally," Annet decided. "Let's find somewhere that serves a decent blend of tea. Or just hot water and I've got the last of the Oloumanni-Alta in the box."

"I thought we were saving that for a special occasion," said Dalry absently, staring up at the starkly-decorated cliffs.

"Doesn't the death of a god count?"

He looked sharply at her to see if she was joking. She was usually joking, and at the same time she was usually serious. It was a manner of tackling the world that experience had taught both of them. Sometimes a little humour was the only thing that cut through the pain to the truth.

The taverna they found still dabbled its feet in the sea, but on the far side of the river, hard up against what Annet identified as the Sand Lanes. The proprietor was a Palleseen expatriate browned enough to have been out here since before the war. After having shown a few rank badges and made a few special requests, they sipped the good tea and made plans. Annet had seen a map of the city, but it had been drawn by a Pal traveller of a century back, good for the general districts but not so much for detail. Now she made notes, based on what the tavernkeeper had said.

By this point they were both considerably more informed about the transformations the city had gone through. From the open veranda they watched the dynamics of the street. The locals in rough cloth issuing from the Sand Lanes to work at the docks or take up a shift in the mills. The Pals in uniform, plus what looked to be local Accessories – fit to raise an eyebrow – pushing through. Heading into and out of the Sand Lanes. Standing around the docks. A thin sprinkling for such a populous and busy city, but notable.

Dalry had asked about the Louse Monks, as it was a piece of local business he'd wanted to look into. The proprietor had chuckled. "Oh those sods are *out*. Still causing trouble up north, but not welcome around here, magister."

The old man had nodded, and his reserved expression could

at least have passed for Pal approval at one more superstition erased.

"It's all going to make things more difficult for us, I'm rather afraid," he said to Annet, after that. They had both seen this stage of things before. It tended to muddy the waters and lead to sporadic moments when being conspicuously in uniform could be bad for your health. Followed by moments when *not* being in uniform could be spectacularly bad for a lot of people's health, as the Pals pushed back. Bit of a no-win situation, really. When they'd embarked, on the Archipelago, the last word from Usmai had been peace, order and the Alkhand Oparan being generally positive towards the Palleseen. But that had been a whole two Alkhands ago, apparently.

"It's time," Dalry decided, "to go darken Angilly's door. She'll have answers, if we ask persuasively enough."

Gil in Mourning

"Following the events of the night of the 18th, order was subsequently restored in the city, initially utilising elements provided by Ventures under Fellow-Monitor Postry, subsequently with troops from the Peor garrison on loan from Sage-Invigilator Palinet. I will work with the new Alkhand on the topic of elements who supported the usurper Gorbudan to ensure that those who would be most obstructive to our continuing mission here are placed where they have no power to impede us. The Throne of Usmai has offered the usual concessions in return for assistance rendered and anticipated, as the new Alkhand's reign settles.

"Overall the mood in the city continues troubled but, barring further incident, I anticipate that it will calm over the next months. The Alkhalendi populace have reacted with predictable grief over their loss but a continuing atmosphere of public order and peace will allow them to see the benefit of the new regime. I am well-placed at the elbow of the Alkhand and can advise him of how to manage his new role to make the best use of his allies, and to steer him so that we, his allies, may be best requited…"

Excerpt from the dispatch of Sage-Invigilator Angilly to Professor-Invigilator Flockersly, following the installing of Alkhand Dekamran in Usmai.

It was the way she'd had to write it. There was a certain language expected, of a Resident's report to the Archipelago. The old man who ran Outreach would have wrinkled an eyebrow at poetry. Even then, she wasn't sure she'd quite gotten away with it. So hard to keep the feelings from soaking into the dry communique. The crisp little words of triumph. *We won. We got what we wanted. Hooray for perfection!* Not how she felt, but how she was constrained to report it.

Word, suitably triumphal, had gone winging its way off to Outreach immediately after the night action and the installation of Dekamran on the throne. The coronation had been a grim affair. The water of the pools where the Alkhand stood to be crowned was still stained by god-blood. The flow of the falls from above wouldn't clear it. And the actual divine *corpse*... She hadn't watched. Even for a Pal, brought up to hold such gross things in no high regard, just meat that people used to make offerings to, it had been too much to witness.

After which her life had become very busy with administration and petitions, all the burden of diplomacy entering a new phase. So many people wanting a piece of her, as if she hadn't won at all. As though actually getting what she wanted was one of those demon contracts where the demon had tricked you into wording your wishes precisely the wrong way.

And now this.

Loret, coming into her office, buttoned up tight. Not her uniform but her face. Pallid beneath the tan a month and a half in Usmai had given her. Saying the Inquirers were here for her.

Loret had something to fear from the Inquirers. Well, fine, Gil had worked out Loret had something nasty in her past, but honestly *everyone* had something to fear from the Inquirers. Even a Sage-Invigilator who had just – on paper – delivered the whole of Usmai to Pallesand.

Precisely what nasty thing Loret had in her past was something Gil had been trying to get to, honestly. Only with the whole fraternal war, and then the deicide, and the ungodly amount of fallout from both, further chances hadn't arisen. And Loret hadn't gone mad and stabbed anyone. Had just been the shrinking and rather ineffectual aide. Gil had spent a long time staring at the requisitions list attached to her most recent report because, while she was capable enough to manage most of the Residence business single-handed, enough was enough and she really needed an aide who'd had at least some basic Outreach training.

Probably Loret at least guessed. Probably the idiot girl thought the Inquirers were here for *her*, but nobody was going to send a Sage of Correct Speech out after a mere Cohort-Invigilator. They'd reserve that for someone of Gil's rank, honestly.

What did I do? What didn't I do? The mantra of every single officer in the Palleseen Sway when this little note crossed their desk. Gil wondered if she should buckle her sword on. And of course the answer to that was *No* because it was a stupid idea. Not as though she'd be challenging a Sage-Inquirer to a duel in response to some accusation of deviating from Correct Thought. Not appropriate at all.

After a few moments she told Loret to go get her sword and buckled it on. It made her feel better. Marginally more in control. And she was the Resident in a nation that had Pal boots on the streets, keeping the peace. Control was exactly what she should have.

She braced herself, when Loret opened the door to them, and then let out a startled breath because she knew them.

The old man she'd run into twice. Once when she'd still been working under someone else's jurisdiction, who'd sent her to go assist one Fellow-Inquirer Dalry, an 'enthusiastic seeker after knowledge', as he'd introduced himself. Which, with that rank, could mean a great many things. The second time, Annet had been with him and he'd had his Sage's badge, though Gil hadn't won hers yet. She'd been in charge of her own operation by then, and had ended up liaising with the pair of them a great deal. Dalry and Annet were those most unusual things within the Palleseen Sway: senior officers with a roving brief. Sometimes you needed an unorthodox approach so you could impose orthodoxy, after all. Outreach had built its reputation on just that, rewarding initiative that other departments would just have slapped down. Dalry and Annet had been something of a department unto themselves, as far as Gil could make out. Because he *was* an Inquirer, even though he mostly asked questions over tea rather than torture. And Annet was technically part of that big pool within Correct Erudition who studied the innovations of the imperfect world and decided how the stink of superstition could be scrubbed off so they could be useful. But the two of them were also scholars and they'd been working on the definitive history of the Palleseen Sway for a decade or more. Given all of their various hats looked like uniform kepis, you never knew quite which one they were wearing.

"My good friend," Dalry said, after the formalities. "How good to see our good, dear friend. Isn't it, Annet?"

"Dally, it is," Fellow-Archivist Annet agreed.

They stared at her like owls over tea and local honeycakes. And there was something up, and Gil – the professional reader of diplomatic rooms – could not tell who was in trouble and how bad it was.

"You've come in off the Archipelago," she asked politely.

"A bit of a slow boat," Annet agreed, equally politely, "but yes. You've done well for yourself here, Gil."

"Very well," Dalry said. "How good to see our good, dear friend doing so well. Isn't it?"

"It is," Annet confirmed. The air around them stretched very taut indeed.

She was too tired for it, in the end. The appearances were just too heavy to hold above her head with straight arms. "Look," Gil said. "Seeing as we're all good, dear friends, can we just skip to the part where you tell me which fingers you're going to break or something."

Dalry's owlish eyes actually widened by a good fraction of an inch. "Ah. Aha ha. Ah, no," he said. "I see. The, ah, old School song, yes. You know I've not been employed in *that* capacity for decades, surely." Actually shocked. Actually hurt, that she'd think it of him.

"I know you weren't *last* time I heard from you. I know that Correct Speech never quite retires anyone from that sort of thing," Gil noted. "But fine. If you're not here to put the screws on – on me or on *someone* – then what can I do for you?"

"You can... do, indeed, for us," Dalry, the Sage-Inquirer, the heir to such an exalted lineage, seemed to shrink a little inside his jacket. "Look, ah..."

Annet took the helm. "We need a little assistance."

Gil lifted her teacup with the air of someone always happy to help Correct Speech.

"To get out," Annet said.

Gil's tea stopped three inches from her lips. "... Of?"

"The Sway," Dalry said in a corpse's whisper. Looking, indeed, quite corpse-like. The urbane cheer sagging for a moment to show the face of a man who hadn't slept well in some time.

"You're not *in* the Sway," Gil noted. "Quite."

"Quite," Dalry echoed. "Although rather closer to the Sway than Usmai was when we set *off*."

Gil pressed her lips together. "What—?"

"I'm sorry to say that for rather personal reasons Dally and I need to make an urgent personal research trip to somewhere. Somewhere that isn't going to get added to the Sway or have a lot of uniforms on the streets any time soon. Which we'd hoped might be Usmai, but we have, well..."

"A fallback plan is, I believe, how a military fellow might describe it," said Dalry faintly.

"What in reason is going on?" Gil demanded of them. "Look, we are friends. I will help if I can. But this is... Is this some feud? Interdepartmental business? Did you flick the nose of the Commission?"

"What have you heard from back home, Gil?" Annet asked her.

Nothing but... But Loret being weird, basically. Just Loret whining save that, inside that whining, news lurked like a parasitic fluke. "What?" she asked. "Tell me. I mean I hear shortages. I hear something about a sickness they're isolating for. The war stretched everything, but that's all."

"The war stretched everything," Annet agreed. "The Archipelago is hungry, right now. But it's more than that."

"They discovered… a movement. Within the army. Within the islands," Dalry said quietly. "A cult. A cult that had taken root amongst the soldiers."

Gil cocked an eyebrow because that had *not* been in the dispatches. "It got stamped on, I assume."

"Some stamping occurred," Annet said. "But, by the time the Commission had put their boots on, it had spread. A lot of the soldiers coming home from the war had… ideas. Correct Speech was going mad trying to question everyone." A look at Dalry.

"I was present for some of the interrogations. As a historian, not an inquisitor. The Inquirers dug deep and turned up other things."

Gil didn't know what. Couldn't know. Felt the chill anyway. Like cold weather coming in off the sea.

"The old religion," Dalry said. "Fascinating, from a scholarly point of view. The Fisher King cult we tried so ardently to erase. So not just one cult but two, running through the army. Two very different ones, one pacifist, the other bloody to the elbow. The Commission in fits. Nobody knew how far it went. One of the cultists had a *Sage*'s badge. It got all very 'prove how loyal you are' back home. What with all the new ideas that had come out of the war."

Gil wasn't even wearing the tight collar of the uniform, but she felt it close on her throat anyway. Waiting to see how bad things would turn out.

"The Dead Companies," Annet listed. "The Left-Eye Brigade. The Unnaturals. Everything that finally broke the Loruthi. Except afterwards it all looked a lot like imperfection. And anything looking like imperfection was suddenly suspect."

"Which was where it became our problem," Dalry added. "Because of the book."

"The history?" Gil's mind went blank again. The pair of them had been at that bloody book for years. The definitive account of the history of Pallesand. "Wasn't that commissioned by the, the actual Commission though?"

"It was," Dalry agreed "Only..." A look between the two of them. "Only not so much, later. Not after everyone got so keen to wave flags for perfection."

Annet grimaced. "It's going to come as a bit of a surprise, I'm sure, Gil, but some of the things done in the name of the Sway weren't... very nice. Or fair. Or justified. Sometimes. And the more we researched our book, the harder it was to pretend that it was all... perfect. And then they started looking over our shoulder and seeing what we were writing and..."

"We had to get on a boat rather hurriedly, I'm afraid," Dalry explained. "Because by then it had got very bad indeed. I'm sorry to say. Very bad."

That phantom collar still tight about her throat. "How bad," Gil asked, "had it got?"

"The camps," Annet said flatly. Echoes of Loret's conspiratorial mutterings.

"The camps," Dalry agreed. "That was when we got out. When we saw what they would do. What they'd do even to their own instruments. Even after writing the history of all the acts committed in the name of perfection, we didn't quite appreciate how bad things were until then."

"Camps? For cultists?" And surely she should approve.

"At first," Dalry said. "Later, they had a... wider remit."

"A lot of people who probably didn't have much to do with either the healers or the Fisher King," Annet said. "Accomplices, dissenters, somebody's departmental rival. But you throw people into a camp with a bunch of cultists and treat them badly, probably everyone signs on with some sort of creed just to get a few friends. And the camps kept growing, and someone on the Commission just…"

"Ordered in the batons," Dalry finished.

On the Archipelago, Gil thought. *This is actually inside the borders of Pallesand.*

"They said it was fear of infection," Annet said. "That the camps were to quarantine a sickness brought back from the war. Everyone knew what was going on but not one document admitted to anything other than that. And even the soldiers they sent to clear the camps were… Not. Really. What you'd count as perfection. That's what's going on back home. That's what we would rather not be around. I'm sorry." As though what they'd been talking about was a trouble they'd brought to her door, rather than warning of a storm that would strike these shores no matter what.

She should have them arrested, she knew. They were dissidents, possibly traitors. But they were friends and they'd trusted her.

"What's your plan?" she asked them, and then, because that might still be an inquisitor's question and not a friend's, "What can I do?"

She wanted to sit Loret down, once the two scholars had left. Just order the girl to talk. But Loret wouldn't. And maybe Gil didn't want to put Loret in a vice, in case that other Loret came out. The one that had been sporadically useful to have around, but maybe wasn't useful any more now the fighting was done.

Gil had the dreadful sense of things flying out away from her. Things she'd need later. And it was only going to get worse because she was due to meet with Dekamran that afternoon. A private audience with the Alkhand. Exactly the sort of thing a successful Resident was able to demand. Exactly the sort of thing that Gil, the person, the woman who had made him the Alkhand for reasons that had nothing to do with policy, had wanted. Except, just like that incautious conjurer, she should have been more careful with her wishes.

*

She saw Dekamran on the throne first. The Alkhand, the White Petal Crown sitting naturally on his brow. She couldn't imagine Gorbudan wearing it so well. Three weeks into his reign, the water of the coronation pool still damp about his feet but the dignity of his manner belied his years. Nothing he'd learned overseas, nothing he'd been taught, just *him*. It should have been the moment of her triumph – as Pal Resident; as Gil, his friend. Except for the clothes. The yellow and the black, the colours of mourning. Three weeks now. But how long did you mourn a god, exactly?

He spoke to his petitioners. He'd made sure that at least some of those brought before him lacked deep pockets or rich sponsors, and he'd already dismissed two palace officials who'd sought to twist his requests to their own profit. Earnest Dekamran, almost desperate to do good and win the love of his people. Crashing through a complex forest webbed with self-interest and strung with feathered nests, so that those immediately around the throne whom he needed to rely on were already speaking sour words about him. So he heard this poor artisan's complaint, or that tenant farmer's, and ensured his underlings didn't bilk the beggars on their way to the throne. The gap between the solitary man in the big chair and the many, many hands who turned the wheels of power within the palace only widened. And, before, there had been Louse Monks standing in that gap, between the throne and the people. Because past Alkhands had been realists when it came to the love and devotion that the role demanded. Dekamran had no monks, nor any other bodyguard. And they had argued about that. Insofar as the Palleseen Resident and the Alkhand of Usmai could argue.

The last petitioner wasn't really a poor man. From the Sand Lanes, but a successful Artist, one of those demi-magicians who made the wooden animals fight. Haughtier than a man speaking to his Alkhand should be. His eyes sliding sideways past the throne to Gil. For a moment she had no idea what he had to do with her, but then it turned out that his workshop had been turned over by Pal soldiers, bearing the Alkhand's writ, and that when they had left with what they were entitled to, they had also taken away half the man's stock in magical trade. Because if there was one thing Pals were always hungry for it was magic. Hearing the list of what was taken, Gil could almost calculate how many tablethi someone like Drathel could boil it all down to.

And Dekamran – thus far so forthright, so wise – nodded, and hesitated. Visibly hesitated. His own eyes finding Gil amidst the court. He would have people look into the truth of the matter, he said. Not calling the man a liar but not accepting his words, as he had those of beggars and peasants. And the Artist would not call out his Alkhand, of course. And matters were not such that he might have smuggled a knife into the throne room to cross those forbidden waters and have at the throne. But there were madmen in Alkhalend, and there were desperate women, and those who had lost more than this, for less cause. One day someone would have the knife.

Dekamran dismissed the court then, and a servant manifested at Gil's elbow to say that the Alkhand requested the pleasure of her company.

Not one of the somewhat over-furnished audience chambers they'd once met in, to plot and carp and laugh. Instead, the Alkhand's personal shrine, its floor running with precisely-incised rivulets of water piped in from the waterfalls outside. The friezes on the walls were great marvels, Gil knew, but black and gold hangings obscured them. At one end, Dekamran slumped in a low chair, his feet cooling in the water as though the office and the duties had built up an oppressive heat in him. The throne should have dwarfed him but, now he was removed from it, he looked so much smaller. His shawl of mourning colours was clutched about him as though he was sick.

"Kama," she said. His eyes flicked to her and pinned her there.

"Gorbudan called me that," he told her. "I don't want anyone to call me that again."

"Dekamran," she said. And then, hearing the bitter edge in her voice, "Your Tranquillity, then." *We should be celebrating. We should he clinking glasses and drinking to the future. And now this. Because of a frog.* The Pal disdain for gods, and honestly, who met with the Pal Resident in a *shrine*, for reason's sake? An insult, and a barely veiled one at that.

He'd laughed about Kakrops, before. The Usmiat, admitting that, yes, to foreign eyes their religion must seem a big comical. The big frog. Ho ho ho.

They couldn't go on like this.

"Dekamran." She elected against 'Your Tranquillity'. Keep that much formality between them, she'd never get anywhere.

He watched her. A servant came in with ramaht. Good ramaht, but blunt, not fermented. Dekamran took one glass, delicate incised crystal like air between his fingertips. Raised it to her. A wan smile, even. But the wan-ness goaded her as little else could.

Just tell me how long, she wanted to ask. *Let me know when you'll be done with this morbid business and back in your own clothes and character, and I'll come back then.*

"I'll look into it," she said. "That last one."

That wan smile again. Aggravating.

"Although, read between the lines, the reason my – *your* servants were there at his shop was that he hadn't paid taxes. Probably for years. And yes, obviously they shouldn't have lifted more than that, but…"

"But it will keep the others in line," Dekamran finished for her.

"Well, yes."

"That those with the Alkhand's writ are thieves, and so it is better not to attract their attention?"

"Overenthusiastic enforcers of the Alkhand's will." A redefinition of the word 'thief' that efficient Pel barely supported.

And a spur of annoyance, because the Pal uniforms involved really had been worn by people with Dekamran's writ. The new Alkhand had found a great resounding vacancy in the palace coffers. At first it seemed that Gorbudan had taken it, and soldiers had been dispatched to Mantekor to take the place from his loyalists still holding out there. The story that had emerged, though, was more one of long and general neglect. Oparan, the melancholy, had not troubled himself with overseeing many aspects of his administration. There were plenty within the palace and without who worked out that one coin in the right pocket could save ten in taxes rightfully owed. For the last decade of Oparan's reign, the wealth of Usmai had been seeping away. And Dekamran had a lot of pledges to make good on, for those who had ushered in his rise to power.

It was how they did things in Peor now. It was a standard request in the Palleseen playbook. You want your taxes collected? We have all these uniforms just sitting about looking for something to do. Gil had brokered the arrangement herself, with Dekamran and Flint. And it had worked. Money was coming into the palace. Some of it. And some of it was going elsewhere. And all of it had to come from somewhere.

"I'll look into it," she said again. This tiny bandage, for one wound amongst a hundred. "Dekamran, I know Flint offered you a guard. A personal guard."

"He did."

"Right now, anyone could just… anything. Right there in front of everyone. Or at night, even. Gorbudan still has friends out there, who would rather no Alkhand than you. You have enemies."

"Would he lend me his demons, do you think?" Dekamran asked her. "Have them stand beside the Mirror Throne and outside my bedchamber. Surely none would dare raise a hand against me then."

And she had opened her mouth to say, yes, Flint would delegate Croskin's entire squad of Unnaturals if that was what

Dekamran wanted. Finally, a positive move, a sign of life from the miserable Alkhand! Except, just before the first words left her, she understood the sarcasm. "Just human guards, Dekamran."

"In Pal uniforms."

"Is it worse than the Louse Monks? They weren't Usmiat either. The throne has always relied on outsiders for protection." Biting back the standard Pal assessment of regimes where that was the case. Not like the Temporary Commission of Ends and Means had to hire Faraslandi mercenaries to stand outside the doors when they were in session, after all. "Don't you think it's time you changed your clothes?" Not Resident to Alkhand, just Gil to Dekamran. A friend advising another.

She saw the words strike. He actually flinched from them.

"I mean," she tried, "I've seen the royal wardrobe. There are a thousand outfits and twenty servants just idle." Making a joke of it.

"I will take your advice under consideration. I shall speak to the monks." Toneless. No friend in that voice for her. Barely the Alkhand either. And he hadn't given himself over to sorrow as his father had, not publicly. He saved it up for these meetings with her, it seemed.

The Usrani monks were all in the same stark colours, of course. But then it was *their* god. The one their whole tradition was devoted to. Understandable that they'd take it badly. "The monks," she said. Big, jolly Follo, Preceptor of the Usrani, was much before the throne these days. Still big, but when you took the jolly away it made him a massive, brooding presence that prickled the space between Gil's shoulder blades. You could hide a lot of knives in that man's mourning clothes, and she didn't think a baton-shot would bring him down, either.

"Dekamran, I've seen the monks. And you know what, they're still all over the city doing their thing. Keeping people fed, telling stories, teaching."

"I have had complaints from the villages around Mantekor," Dekamran said. She didn't need to ask what about.

"I'll look into it," she said. "Let me have details." Just whose livelihood the standard-issue boots had tromped through on their way to chastise Gorbudan's last supporters.

"I have had complaints from the mills, at Frava," he said.

"I'll look into it." And the mill owners at Frava had been cheating the throne for years and perhaps they could stand to have a few more complaints.

"My cousin, Damashili, her house was entered. Many things of value taken."

Something finally parted in her then. Some reserve of diplomacy finally emptied away. "She backed your brother," Gil said. "Some of those 'things of value' were stockpiled weapons, tablethi, money she was going to use against you. She has a son around age three who she'd put on the throne if she could. We're doing this for you, Dekamran. *I'm* doing this for you."

Will you grow up, it was just a frog.

She didn't say it. She actually had to review her own memory to ensure that she *hadn't* said it. But the words somehow flew from the back of her throat to the other side of his ears without her ever needing to give voice to them.

He smiled. Wanly. "You're right of course." Not about the frog. Not really about anything. But because she was the voice of Pallesand right now, and the throne had no monks to guard it and not enough money and a lot of subjects who were unhappy about the events that had placed Dekamran on it. And so it was politic for the Alkhand of Usmai to tell the Palleseen Resident that she was right.

She was abruptly right there, within arm's reach of him, just as you never were with the Alkhand. But where were the monks who might have stopped her? She was there, hands twitching to just reach out. Touch him. Hold him. Slap him. Something. Some action that would unequivocally break down the distance between them. "I would really like," she said, "for you to come to the Residence. Like you used to. Like things used to be."

He looked at her.

"I didn't do this for Pallesand." Spoken too low even though nobody was within earshot, because a Sage-Inquirer was in town and these were treason words. "I did this for you. Because Gorbudan would have had you killed. I sprung you from the House of Hard Angles. I gave you an army. All for you. And yes, because Gorbudan hated us *Kepishi*. And yes, because you're the better man for the throne. But because you're my friend, Dekamran. Because I couldn't bear anything to happen to you. And it didn't fall out the way I meant. You were there. Nobody went looking for any of that. But still... please."

And he just looked at her, and that damnable weak smile was like a knife and she wanted to scream.

Drathel's Fork

Fellow-Archivist Drathel. Not someone Gil really warmed to, but she has a likeable enough way about her when she's trying to get something. Correct Erudition, the Archivists' school, has a reputation for stuffy scholars and armchair generals, together with a whole spectrum of rather suspect types who try to re-tailor the cloth of superstition so it will match the uniform. Necromancers, lycanthropists, that sort of unsound business. You'd think the Archivists would be on the losing end of departmental squabbles more often than not, but the engine which drives their political capital comes from people like Drathel. The Decanters, because the world is full of magic; full of things that draw magic to themselves, or that persuade people to charge them up with power through propitiation and votive offering. Magic which could be more profitably put to use for the good of the Palleseen Sway. It's Drathel's job to get her hands on that magic, in whatever form the local industry produces it, and work out how to most efficiently reduce it down to crates of tablethi that are generally more convenient to ship.

The last time a pack of monks caught her at it, it had been the House of Hard Angles for her. There to wait for those assassins who had been patiently dogging her steps across most of Usmai. And here she was again, confronting a pack of angry men and women in ceremonial clothing and warning colours. Almost as if Drathel, of Correct Erudition, never learned anything.

Things had changed since that last time, though. Back then, Oparan had been on the Usmiat throne and, although Dekamran had been heir, the other brother had still been charging about making a nuisance of himself and giving licence to anyone who didn't want a Palleseen Decanter snooping about on their turf.

This time, when the angry monks finally tracked down where she'd got to within their big monastery, and found it was the worst conceivable place, angry was about all they could be. Rather than, say, vengeful, or murderous. She had a writ with the seal of the Alkhand on it, the new one who was a friend to Pallesand in all things. And while it didn't explicitly say she could creep down and spring the magic locks to their holy cellar to see what snackies they were keeping, it didn't say she couldn't. The wording, which she'd haggled over with the Resident for quite some time, was generous. And besides, there was a squad of soldiers kicking their heels up top who'd have some pointed questions if she didn't reappear.

And so the big lad, the great broad-waisted lead monk of this particular order, could only tell her, "You must leave."

"I was going," Drathel told him. "But seriously, what are you going to *do* with it? Tell me you're not going to eat it or something."

The shock on his face, the outrage, confirmed that all those wax-sealed pickling jars were indeed not for some secret monastic pig-out next holy day. They were for *something*, though. They had a ritual in mind, or they were trying to find one to fit the unprecedented circumstances. The sigils inscribed into the jars were complex and specific. Someone had been ransacking their traditions to preserve as much as possible of what lay within.

Which suited Drathel fine, because by doing so they were, as a side effect, preserving it for *her*. Terrible to let that much raw power just evaporate out into the landscape. What would all of those centuries of prayers have been *for*, then?

"Well, go on," she told the big lad to the folds of his bare chest and belly. "I mean, it's not like you can tell me 'These are the ancient ways. This is how we do it every time.' You're improvising. What's the plan?"

"What you take for a *plan*," said Big Lad, "what you take for *opportunism*, is respect. Kepishi, I would not expect you to understand."

Drathel looked up into the broad bowl of his face – intended to hold nourishing good humour but now just slopping sour gruel. "I've seen you lot all over. I know your deal. Good works, alms for the poor, all that. Creditable. You'd almost get away with it on the Archipelago, now the other business isn't relevant. If you could let go. If I thought you'd accept, I'd just make you an offer. You're not going to eat what's in those, why not turn it into something people can eat, hm?"

She knew there was no chance of them accepting, but she felt she had to make the suggestion. And just once it would be nice. Just once she'd like to have the High Devil-Eater or Grand Theurge or Lobster-Pope or whatever get this thoughtful expression on their face. Have them nod and shrug and say, well, if you put it like that, how much were you thinking of for all the candlesticks and thuribles and icons? But no, they'd rather keep cutting out hearts and ritually scarring each other.

But that was fine. She'd put out the hand of commerce to them and they'd wrinkled their holy noses at it. There were other ways, especially given which brother was on the throne and whose skirts he'd been hiding behind not so long before.

She look one last look at the cellar. The shelves with their ranks on ranks of jars. She didn't have the fancy magic lenses some of her more settled peers had scored, but there was an unguent she knew how to cook up, that stung like wasps when you rubbed it in your eyes but gave you something of the same sight. Through the tears, the jars lit up the whole room with what was inside them. And even the jars themselves would be a nice bonus, given all the wards and holy marks the monks had decked them out with. It was the motherlode of concentrated magic. Drathel, who had seen the insides of temples and sanctums and magician's lairs all over the known world, had never had such a bounty placed within reach of her acquisitive fingers.

Flint, she knew, was shaking down former Gorbudan supporters for their gold and jewels. For pennies, really. But that was because he didn't understand the meaning of wealth. *This* was wealth, the way Pallesand measured it. This was a Sage's badge for poor hardworking Drathel and the war chest for a whole new conquest for the Commission of Ends and Means. This was the glorious future.

Drathel grinned and nodded at Big Lad the head monk. "Be seeing you," she told him. She almost said, "Keep the old boy on ice for me," but that would probably be a quip too far and these religious types could be unreasonably touchy.

Up top, in the more traditional public parts of the monastery, she rejoined her escort and marched them out into Alkhalend. There they got to enjoy a small cup of sharp ramaht each while she made notes and juggled how she was going to get hold of that astonishing hoard of power. Because everyone in the city was still being so unreasonably sentimental about what had happened to the big frog, but nobody else had been asking, *Yes, but what did they do with the body?*

The tavern she'd picked hadn't been at random. Because people like Flint might eat a nation off the point of a knife, but Drathel was civilized. She used a fork, and that meant multiple tines to skewer morsels on. Drathel skipped some coins over to the owner to secure a private room upstairs. One with a nice airy screen that let you see out of the windows without being seen. The monastery, despite the monks' charitable habits, was in the good part of town where they could shake loose the better class of donations, so the tavern was nice as well. There were channels of running water cut into the floor, so everything was pleasantly cool despite the horrors of the outside. And somewhere below would be a pump eating up the local octagonal tablethi, to make this magic happen, but Drathel would magnanimously allow the waste so long as it made her more comfortable.

Her informant ducked in soon after, muffled up in a shawl and looking as suspicious as anyone could wish. A natural skulker, but more in the *away* rather than *towards* way of things, so not really used to clandestine meetings. Her face, when Drathel saw it past the hem, was pale and unhappy past the tan. Not a natural traitor either, but that was what you got when you paraded yourself past a professional Decanter after getting yourself messed up in something unnatural. You got marked, basically, and then you either got shopped to Correct Speech or rendered down for what was inside you. And that was probably going to be the end result, but Drathel was happy to play this particular fish – she smirked at her choice of imagery – on the line for a while, to see what entertaining contortions and leaps the girl could make.

"She got another private audience then," Drathel noted. "How private?"

Her informant stared loathing at her. "Nothing."

"You know for sure, do you?"

"She came back pissed off," the informant said. "So, nothing."

"Ah, frustration. Well, I know what it's like to want something and not have it yet. Relevant to our interests, in fact. I reckon I'll need some real leverage with her soon." And waited, watching.

The informant scowled back, volunteering nothing.

Drathel smiled, looked through the screen out at the sunlight. Lovely day for a spot of betrayal, honestly. "This place," she said, gesturing expansively at the unseen wider confines of the establishment. "The seafood is to die for."

The girl went still. Swallowed. "Correct Speech came to see her."

Drathel's turn to get serious. "What do you mean 'Correct Speech'? Correct Speech who?"

"Sage-Inquirer just off the boat. Someone she knew."

Drathel frowned, because that sort of visitor was someone she really should know about, and she absolutely didn't. Anyone like that would either arrive with their own people and make a big enough splash to get everyone wet, or else they'd be showing their papers to someone like Flint to commandeer a bully squad. When Correct Speech came creeping in to have an unannounced meeting with the Resident, something nasty was definitely up. Drathel reviewed her own recent past, years outside immediate supervision, running wild with Flint. Plenty of actionable decisions there. "You were in on the meeting?"

"Behind the door." Because if the Inquirers turned up then this girl would most definitely want to know about it.

"They mention me? Or Flint?"

A shake of the head.

"They here for you?"

A shake of the head.

"You going to make me *fish*, or what?" Drathel rapped on the table.

"They're going to the Grove," said her informant.

Drathel frowned. And of course the Waygrove was tangentially relevant to her profession, but there was a source of power she couldn't begin to know how to tap. Similarly, she didn't reckon Correct Speech were about to strap it to a chair and torture some answers out of it either. "Girl, you are not giving me enough to throw you back." Labouring the metaphor now because she was running out of patience.

Her informant closed her eyes. Closed her face. Wanted, visibly and clearly, not to be here talking to Drathel. Wanted not to be about to shop Angilly again, even more than she already had.

"They were on the run from back home," came the looked-for piece of backstabbery. "She helped them. Got them a local escort to the Alborandi place. They had… things. Fetishes or something. To get safe through the Grove to… elsewhere. Anywhere but here, they said. They… said things about home. What happened back home." A shudder. Though if Drathel was right about what this girl represented, probably nothing she'd heard had been a surprise.

Drathel patted her on the arm, not without sympathy. "Not so hard, was it? I'm going to be asking people for some big favours very soon," she told her informant. "You've given me some quality dirt so far, but you keep digging. Get me everything, and maybe we all forget just what you tracked into Alkhalend, hm?"

When her wretched informant had scuttled off again, Drathel composed her report. She'd been sending a great many reports recently. The Palleseen in Usmai had achieved a great deal, and Drathel had advance warning that the relationship between those two nations was due a serious renegotiation. Flint, blunt as he was, was just the sharp end of a wedge they'd be hammering on soon enough. When that hammer came down, Drathel wanted it to be tapping her securely into place, rather than just knocking her flat. Hence all the reports, filled with all the good work she was doing and everyone else's screw-ups, failings and character flaws.

After that, it was time to pay a visit to some old friends.

Most people lucky enough to get *out* of the House of Hard Angles never put themselves in the shadow of the place again. A Decanter's life inured you to a lot of those kind of shivers, though. So much of the world's magic ended up concentrated in unappealing shapes and places. And one thing she'd come out of the prison with was an understanding that there was a lot of power there. Not safe power, certainly. She didn't reckon you could just syphon those ghosts off and reduce them into tablethi. Ghosts were nobody's favourite source of power. There wasn't much to them individually, and they were very hungry. Leave a ghost alone and it would dissipate into the world. Even where the deceased's personality was driven enough to hang around it needed something to hold onto against the eroding tides of the world. An object, like the skull the old Alkhand had carried about. A person, the traditional possessing spirit that made necromancy so dicey. A corpse. Or a place. And everyone knew of some house somewhere where the dead resident had never *left*, but she'd never come across some place they'd stuffed full of ghosts like a pastry full of cheese.

North of the Garmoers there was another set of Successor States, and the withered little nut that was the Imperial Necropolis, last vestige of the Moeribandi Empire. They'd known more about the dead than anybody, and some day a proper scholarly delegation from Correct Erudition would go kick in some tombs and see what could be bled off it all. But here, right here in Alkhalend, was a leftover of their power, and Drathel confessed herself impressed. And hungry for it, because it didn't matter whose sacred text was scrawled over it all; once you'd rendered it down to tablethi it was all safely secular.

Last time, she'd been smuggled into the place under cover of night, given over to the grim-faced death monks who ran the place. Brought before the Under-warden, and what a fascinating man *he* turned out to be. Then whisked off to the cell that Angilly had eventually freed her from, somewhat grudgingly. As though Drathel doing her *job* was somehow an intolerable intrusion.

This time she marched her escort up to the door, seeing all the looks they were getting from the denizens of the Sand Lanes. And sure, Pal uniforms weren't popular anywhere, and you'd think the people around here would care less, having less to lose. A lot of muttering and frowning, though. A lot of clenched fists. And the Sand Lanes were where plenty of foreigners in Usmai ended up too, and maybe they had their own reasons for not wanting the Pals poking into their business. It all died down when they got to the House, though. It wasn't a place the locals wanted to go near.

It wasn't a place her escort much wanted to go near either, so she left them to sit and share a flask and their lunch at the door while she went in. Like with the monastery, she worked best alone.

The Moerends weren't going to be answering the sort of

questions she had to ask, and so she waved her papers at them until they gave up on the skull-faced taciturn act and took her to the Under-warden. And the House of Hard Angles didn't actually have a nice office for the man who nominally ran it. Because it had been intended as a mausoleum, not a prison. Even the Moerends just slept on straw mattresses in unbarred cells, a properly monastic tradition. And why did they want this outsider here to run the place anyway?

It was because he *was* Other. The House was crammed with maddened, imprisoned ghosts, a vast host of age-old trapped spirits. Most of them had been here for centuries, from the days when the Empire had actively claimed this place. She knew as much of the histories as anyone could uncover. Some scion of the Imperial line had designed this place as his tomb, and sent a thousand servants ahead of him into death, so that his eternal court would be well-stocked. Since when, the place had just accumulated more ghosts. Every prisoner who died here, every luckless visitor, the monks themselves. Probably even poor sods who died nearby in the Sand Lanes ended up drifting in and then couldn't escape the wards that glittered about the door and the walls. And none of this was necessarily useful to Drathel because ghosts were insubstantial and tricksy. Even crowded into this place like paupers in a ghetto, they wouldn't repay a Decanter's efforts. Unless...

Unless the Old Empire knew something that Pal science didn't, about harnessing ghosts. Which she rather suspected they had.

What she *also* knew was that the ghosts were a problem, sometimes. The House of Hard Angles needed a Warden, and the Warden was there to keep the ghosts in line. Notional head of some spectral civil service structure set up by the architects. The Warden was either some necromancer who'd been caught and thrown in there, inmate and Alkhand of the House at once, or they were something from the Grove. And it was amazing how often the Grove provided, when the need was there; not just somewhere for two academics on the lam to lose themselves. Portal Groves weren't unknown, but precious few places remained that still had working diplomatic relations with them like Usmai.

The Under-warden met with her at the end of a spur, several levels down. He was standing at the edge of that precipice, the narrow chasm that led down and down through every floor of the place. A channel for necromantic energy, Drathel understood. With the stinging stuff in her eyes she could see how everything was made to funnel inwards. Those old Imperial types had known what they were doing. If only *she* knew what they had been doing…

The man, the man with the ugly, honest face that came from nowhere in this world, looked at her. Just a man, and the wards had no power to keep him here. A fascinating and oft-discussed piece of theoretical necro-thaumaturgy: that the living spirit of a person and their ghost, post-mortem, were things of such provably different natures.

"I imagine you're close, now," she told him. "But not quite there. They built these bars strong. Believe me, I can see all the cracks where bigger men than you have tried to pry them apart."

His face closed the doors on her, but she had the measure of him. Just a man, after all. A man who cared about something, and that was always a mistake. That was just leverage, to Drathel. "You want to go home, don't you?" she prompted.

"Yes." The word, drawn from him without his consent. "We want to go home. We've been trying for… long."

"I mean, I'm not making trouble for anyone, helping you out. You're not going to go on a rampage because they locked you up. Back to the Grove, right?" As though she was writing the report, the one justifying her actions after all the terrible repercussions.

"Yes," he said again. And then it joined them. The thing. The Warden. Boiling up from below, feeding itself through the gap in the floor. Rising up like a serpent made of spindly legs. That head, compound eyes and flailing antennae and four crooked fangs like fingers. Drathel wiped a little more juice into her eyes and blinked until she could see properly. Not a ghost, not a demon, not anything within her purview. A thing from another world, and probably almost as terrible and alien there as it was here. Unnatural enough that the wards had let it in, but would not let it out.

The Under-warden lifted his hand to it, his face to it, as it loomed over him. Those ordinary, ugly, alien features of his was gripped by a terrible frustration and need. A need to be elsewhere than here, but not alone.

Drathel's professional take: if she could somehow get that *thing* connected to a few racks of tablethi she'd be almost as minted as she would with the jars from the cellar. It was *strong*, even though it was strong in that peculiar way that made it utterly vulnerable to the shackles of the House.

Sometimes you had to invest, rather than just hoard. She pulled out her bag. The trinkets and icons and odds and ends. More of the same, really. And it was Angilly's fault, because the Resident had brought her into this when she'd come begging donations for the free-the-Alkhand fund. She should have expected Drathel to be curious.

The Under-warden took the bag. Saw inside not just a handful of artefacts that still had power in them, but also the other bits and pieces. Copper wire from a jeweller's, some decent-quality crystals, brass cogs of various sizes. The sort of tat a Palleseen artificer might use in one of the new sciences. Because the Under-warden was a magician of devices and toys.

She'd seen what he was trying to build here. Probably it couldn't work, but it was the product of a magical tradition alien to her and she had no idea. She was just enabling him. In return for access. And probably she'd need to shut him down, in time. Their interests would clash and she, as surrogate for the inexorable march of the Palleseen, would have to screw him over. But right now he could get her access and she could get him materiel and so they had a deal.

"Good?" she asked, and he nodded. At his back, the horrifying segmented length that was the Warden coiled.

"So show me." And he did.

This was what the Moerends hadn't realised, when they lured the Warden into the House to be its new guardian, the slave and the master of the place. They were used to supernatural monsters from the Grove, to mad wizards. Creatures not normally accompanied by ordinary men who thought about things in ordinary ways. Again, Angilly was to blame for understanding that the Under-warden was so eminently bribable. If you could help him get towards his monomaniacal goal.

Deep inside the House, something very dodgy was going on. Not even the Under-warden's watchmaking nonsense, but something far more significant to wider Usmai. Drathel considered herself an expert in magical dodginess, having perpetrated it more than once. And right now someone was doing something of utterly surpassing dodginess right under the nose of the Alkhand and the Resident and everyone.

It was amazing how these ideas festered, over the generations and the centuries. How people who were just a part of the fabric of a place could just be fixated on *How much better things used to be when...* One more disease of the world that Pallesand, the modern, the enlightened, wasn't afflicted with.

Down there, the Under-warden showed her a crypt. And yes, the whole place was basically a crypt where the main guest, that long-ago Imperial dignitary, had never actually taken up residence, all those ghosts trapped for nothing. Except they'd made sure everything was ready, before the intended incumbent had ended up dying somewhere inconvenient, or lost out in a family struggle, or some such fate that meant they never arrived. And in the interim the place had just been... charging up. Like a building-sized tableth. Not as efficiently as Drathel draining some heathen idol, but that was still a lot of ghosts ready to power... something. Because this was it, proof positive that the old Empire really had been the business where ghosts were concerned. Proof of concept of how you could, with enough ghosts and an insane amount of forethought, preparation and sacred architecture, actually make the bloody things work for you.

A crypt, down there. A single sarcophagus at the ceremonial heart of the building. And she'd watched the Grand Moerend, His Quietude Arkanith, going in and out of the place, making prayers and lighting candles while a thousand ghosts looked on and – if they'd had it – held their breaths.

A grand ritual. An insane ritual. A rag of tradition left over from the old dead Empire that had collapsed in on itself and retreated into its own tombs centuries ago. Honestly, Drathel didn't think it would work for a moment. Arkanith was mad. All that work, both in the distant past and right now, just to concentrate a great mass of necromantic power where someone like Drathel could conveniently nick off with it. And while the Grand Moerend would doubtless howl at the sacrilege, she didn't reckon he'd be making a formal complaint to the Alkhand. Because if what he was actually trying to do got out, then Drathel didn't reckon the Usmiat would side with him, honestly, tradition bedamned. Nobody wanted the old dead Empire *back* any time soon.

Gil in her Cups

The thing about Flint was that he was a horrible person, really. But Angilly had looked in the mirror recently, and reckoned from the view that horrible people weren't in short supply. And Flint, Fellow-Monitor Postry, was someone who at least was mostly aware that was what he was, and didn't actually mind. Rather revelled in it, in fact. He was also an insubordinate son of a bitch by nature, amazing he'd ever secured a promotion in his life. Except that meant she could sit down with him and it wouldn't be awkward. The rank difference wouldn't stand between them like a wall they'd have to crane over to talk. He was uncouth, and he was unread, and he didn't know people back home. Basically just terrible, terrible company. But that was the sort of company Gil felt she probably deserved, after her audience with Dekamran. So, when the invitation came, to join Flint for some celebratory drinks, she reckoned she'd earned the punishment.

"Thought we'd have a serious siege, on the way in," Flint was saying, partly to her, partly to the handful of officers who'd clung long enough to his coat tails to end up here. "Mantekor, fortress of the Tiger-Crab, right? All the Alkh—the brother's holdouts. Except when we arrived they were trying to leg it. You never saw the like. Just a whole load of them, no fighting order, trying to have it away into the trees with their carts and baggage. And the baggage!" He grinned at her. "The war chest. What the lad hadn't spent of it. What his people had got their claws into."

There was a sample on the table, being picked at to pay for drinks. Gold coins, of various Usmiat vintages. A thick chain in the shape of an articulated serpent, with eyes of jasper. Rings, armlets, a handful of little onyx monkeys she thought were probably game pieces.

They were in a big private room at a taverna at the foot of the falls, and when the staff came in to refill everyone's cups they just dipped their hands into the pile in recompense. Everyone was getting rich today. A real redistribution of wealth.

Flint stood. "At least they boxed it all up nicely for us!" he announced, to general cheers and some hissing. Flint was several sharp ramahts ahead of Gil.

The hissing came from the newest addition to his command staff. At one end of the table a lizard propped itself up, blue tongue cleaning out the inside of a bowl. It was wearing a uniform jacket, badly tailored for its utterly non-uniform physique.

"These lads," Flint said, following her gaze, "are *keen*. They know whose pike to trail, right? This is Cohort-Monitor Ss*ss*ssy or something like that. I'm taking a whole load of these sons of bitches with me tomorrow."

"Lasses," Gil corrected absently. "Daughters."

"What?"

"Never mind. What's tomorrow?" The treasure was technically the property of the Alkhand, of course. And the part that wasn't was the property of the Pallesand state. But of course a fair amount would stick to Flint's fingers, and as far as she could work out that was essentially how Ventures was supposed to work. It substituted for having an operational budget to start with and motivated horrible people like Flint to go out and serve the Sway. The venal chisel placed to crack open places like the Successor States for further Palleseen investment.

Flint was making another toast, slopping drink across the

table as he thrust his cup into the air. Cheers and hissing. At the far end of the table, next to the lizard, Croskin mimed drinking, his presence adding to the general hallucinatory sense of things. Gil looked up into Flint's reddening face. Rubbery, honest, venal, crooked, cheerfully avaricious, no-one you wanted as an enemy, nor to lend money to. It was like there were a dozen men overlaid one atop the other, impossible to know which was the real one.

"You're like a card trick," she observed.

"I fucking am," agreed Flint, not understanding her in the slightest. The servants topped up everyone's cup but Croskin's, by mutual agreement.

"Demons," she said. "We're sitting drinking with demons. With *a* demon."

"Only the very best demon," Flint agreed, slouching back down into his chair. "Best I ever served with. Best to wear the uniform."

She wasn't drunk enough yet to find that funny. "They'll rake you over the coals for it."

"It's Ventures. We do things, in Ventures. If they work, maybe they become regular things. Why not demon troopers? Why not perfect a demon, if we're in the perfection business? Why not lizards in hats? All the great questions of our time, Gil. Look, you and I get to send a great trunk of money home on the next boat. Minus expenses, obviously. Have some expenses." He tried to shove some coins at her, which was a step too far towards the venal and she diverted them back to the drinks pile. "And Drathel reckons she can fuel the Archipelago for a decade with what she can scrape from the local temples and the like. So we're gravy. We're golden. We're heroes of the Sway. Croskin will probably make Companion in the next dispatches." He knocked back his cup just as the servant came back in. "Look, oi, matey." Then switching to a rough but serviceable jumble of Usmiat laced with Peost words similar-enough to be understood. "This is small sticks. Bring us bludgeons!"

Another handful of coins vanished into the servant's sleeve. They were charging Flint a premium, she reflected. But then the private back room was very exclusive. Plus nobody in Alkhalend really wanted to take Flint's money. Because he'd killed god.

Flint didn't seem to care. She shouldn't care. The pair of them would probably get a commendation in the next communique from Outreach. It was, after all, a big part of how the world was going to be perfected. Because you couldn't have gods cluttering up the place with their irrational demands and barbaric rites.

Kakrops hadn't seemed that irrational or barbaric, but you couldn't start making exceptions. Nobody on the Commission was going to settle for mostly-perfect.

The bludgeons arrived. Big wooden tankards filled with something that made the eyes water just to sniff. "Hus?" she demanded. "You drink hus?"

"You don't?"

"It's fish," she told him. "It's actual fish, fermented into alcohol." It was fish, rice and a particular kind of seaweed, but the recipe was quite fish heavy. The Cotto brewed it on their ships, which was usually where everyone would prefer it stayed. "I think it's a god thing for those pirates, actually."

"Well then that god can be last up against the wall," Flint decided, and downed half a mugful. His eyes bulged and he slapped at the table, making the coins jump and jingle. "Get it down you, Resident. Sage-Invigilator. Magister. Down in one."

"I will not." But she did manage a decent swig of her own. It was… indescribable would be the charitable word. It was sour. It was vomitous. It would probably taste better on the way up than it did on the way down, after her body had denatured some of it. It was passable. It was all right.

She put the half-full tankard down. Her mouth was rank with the taste of fish, but she could see why both Flint and the Cotto liked the stuff. It stripped away your civilized veneer of worries like it probably did paint. "What's tomorrow?" she said.

"Croskin actually drinks this," Flint said merrily. "I mean he won't drink water and he won't drink ramaht, but *this* is actually infernal-grade. He says if there was a way a demonist could send this stuff Below, we'd make a fortune from the Kings."

The demon had a tankard, and was suiting actions to Flint's words. The lizard side-eyed him, although that was an Ibaleth's default way of eyeing anything. The handful of junior officers were watching Steggers, Flint's second, as the man tried to balance a spoon end-on atop his knuckles. Betting the sort of money that no regular soldier's pay ever allowed. Barbarism. Imperfection. She felt abruptly excluded, by her own choices. She downed the rest of the hus and found her tankard topped almost immediately. The pile of treasure was dwindling, so Flint dumped another handful of old coins on it like someone inexpertly stoking a fire.

"Gil," he said, "Sage-Invigilator-Magister-Resident, if you don't mind me saying, you're a long streak of piss tonight. Crack a smile, won't you?"

She'd thought she had her smile on. The Resident's one, diplomatic and disconnected from anything deeper. Apparently when she'd had her head tipped back to drain the tankard it had fallen off. She stared at him.

"I just thought we'd won," she said, not entirely sure what she meant.

"We fucking won," Flint assured her. He grabbed the serpent necklace from the pile and waved it at her. "This is what winning looks like."

"Like a snake."

"Like being rich." A knowing look from a man she didn't wish to be known by. "I guess you were always rich. Fancy folks and the posh phalanstery, right? Some of us didn't have that. Some of us have this. Let me guess. Uncle on the Commission? Aunt's a Professor on the Archipelago?"

"I don't have an uncle on the Commission." A pause, before honesty reared its serpent's head. "I did have an aunt in Outreach. That's why I'm here."

"Come off it. Your dad's a big man somewhere. I know your type." Prodding at her.

"What's tomorrow, Flint?" More than one of them could change the subject. "Come on. You don't make your superior ask three times, soldier."

He smirked at her, grimaced, drank. "The Tesemer have all got together at that place of theirs. Their compound-monastery-menagerie thing."

"Ah."

"Yeah. I mean, they went pretty hard for the other lad, after all. I don't reckon they've all got together just to plan a real good birthday present for your boy on the throne. So we're going to pay them a visit. Receive their pledge of fealty to His Tranquillity. Sure they're anxious to give it."

"Going in force."

"You know it." And that maybe also explained the drinking. Not just a celebration after the sack of Mantekor, but to take the edge off the thought of the Louse Monks. Still not a crowd anyone should be keen to cross swords with.

They clacked mugs together. Flint read her expression. "My lads and lasses," he said, "my lizards and demons, we'll have them, if they bring it. Or we'll just have them. Not sure I want to give them a chance to bring anything. I have new toys to play with, Gil. You wouldn't believe the fun we'll have with those bug-fondlers." And, because he'd filled them with drink, she couldn't tell how hollow the words were.

The hus had flowed, slick and rank as the fish they'd brewed it down from. She'd knocked back her share. It was like a good battle-line of troopers. Put enough of it between you and the things that were troubling you, you could hardly hear the screaming. With her stomach sourly swimming in it, she'd been on the cusp of saying all manner of unwise things to Flint. She'd decided, around the fourth tankard, that she liked him. Not like *that*, but he was a decent sort. A man made good. And a good commander. A man who'd go to the wall for his followers. A man who led from the front. A man who could receive the salute of something like Croskin and not care about the creature's provenance. The Sway needed more officers like Flint Postry, she decided. And, on the back of that, very nearly ended up saying all sorts of things about just why she was a long streak of piss and couldn't get into the spirit of things. Things it was best he didn't know. Thankfully, by then, Flint was just about non-stop talking about himself, so she was spared the indiscretion. Though not the hus, because Flint had pressed a whole full jug of it on her as she left.

All those things she hadn't said were still crammed into her mouth and throat when she got back to the Residence, though. A wonder she didn't just blurt them out to the Usmiat servants who met her at the door and took her shawl. She told them to set out some tea and some sharp ramaht at her desk because she couldn't work out, right then, if she wanted to be more or less drunk.

The other thing that was in her office when she went in was Loret. The bloody enigma. The shrinking flower with the sharp petals. Loret, sitting on the near side of the desk, looking miserable. Loret, who'd already been at the Residence's ramaht stock, judging by the emptied bottle.

Not the first time a Resident's aide had been at the drinks cabinet, surely. But a bit brazen to just sit there when her employer came in. Having her there abruptly seemed enormously entertaining, a promise of some fun. If Gil wasn't having a good time then why should anyone?

"Cohort-Invigilator Loret, have you been *drinking*? This is unacceptable!" she demanded, with enough of a slur that it should have sounded like a companionable joke but somehow came out as a threat.

Loret said nothing.

"A bottle down already, is it?" Gil demanded. "Is *that* what a Cohort's ration is on the Archipelago these days? That's what they got you used to, is it?"

Loret said nothing.

Gil slammed the jug of hus down on the desktop. "Well don't think you're ahead of me."

Loret stared at her. Eyes red enough that maybe that emptied bottle wasn't the first. That made two drunk, armed women in a small room having a party, except Loret wasn't getting into the spirit of all this jolly fun.

"You're sending me back," she said. "You wrote. You're sending me back."

Gil blinked. Yes, she *was*. Because now she had a lot of extra responsibilities as the Alkhand's chief advisor, which meant she needed someone better than Loret as her bloody subordinate. But her bloody subordinate wasn't supposed to actually *know* yet.

"Are you reading my correspondence, Cohort-Invigilator?" And there was her drawer open on the far side of the desk, her filed copy of the letter she'd sent home sitting there. *Please, oh please might I have an adequate assistant here in this rather important post?* Expressed in appropriately formal language.

Loret met her gaze. And drinking in her superior's office was a disciplinary offence but reading the Resident's correspondence was arguably espionage.

"You're sending me back," Loret repeated.

Gil found that, yes, actually, she was rather spoiling for a fight, and if a throwdown with Loret was the only game in town, then she'd put up the ante willingly. She was going to get to the bottom of whatever the hell was Loret's deal. She dumped herself down on the superior side of the desk, slammed the drawer shut and broke the seal on the hus. The sour fish reek of it filled the room. She filled the ramaht cups with it, then the teacups as well.

"I've had enough," Gil told her frankly. "Of a lot of things, right now. You included." Took a deep breath to tear a serious strip off the girl, then shoved a cup over. "Drink. It's a local speciality. Let's fucking do this properly."

"I know it, magister." And Loret drank. Eyes widened a little, but no grand reaction. And she'd been with the Cotto, so maybe she did know.

"What am I supposed to do with you?" Gil demanded. And then she considered that, and said, "I mean you're just one thing of it. What am I supposed to do with any of it, exactly? Why is none of this going the way it was supposed to?"

What a good aide would do now, would be to note how drunk their employer was, and start tactfully suggesting that maybe the Resident should retire to bed and the conversation could be continued in the morning. Loret, not being a good aide, downed her cup in one go.

"I was at the palace," Gil told her. "It's a mess."

Loret looked at her, tight-lipped.

"Oh, I know," Gil agreed. "We won, like Flint said. We're well in, here. Back home they'll be delighted. Commendations all round. Usmai practically delivered in fancy paper with a bow. The crown absolutely dependent on us. Holds full of magic and gold. I mean, this is a triumph, you're right."

Loret, who hadn't said any of those things, drank more hus and watched her.

"You know who doesn't think it's a triumph?" Gil asked her. The words she'd wanted to say to Flint, but had retained just enough control to stop herself. But this was Loret. What did it matter? Talking to Loret was like throwing words down a hole. "Dekamran," she explained to her aide's stony face. "The man I actually *made* Alkhand. The man whose life I saved. Whose inheritance I won back. And he chose! I made sure he chose. He could have just… left. And I thought he'd be…" *Grateful. Happy.* "This was supposed to be our moment."

"You don't have to tell me this," Loret said. All that ramaht and two cups of hus, but she still sounded steady.

"I thought he'd…" Gil shook her head. "Loret, tell me, last thing before the boat comes for you. Tell me how I managed to mess things up so badly. What could I have done differently? Just this once, actually have some bloody residual trace of what it is to be an aide. Assist me. Advise me. Aid me, Aide Loret, in my moment of need. Because you cannot compose a formal letter and your handwriting is shit and you didn't read the brief and I cannot for the life of me understand why anybody thought you'd be suitable for this job. So tell me, Loret. Tell me something I need to know."

"You killed his god and you made him beholden to you for it," Loret said, then stared, a hand to her mouth as though she could retroactively stop the words coming out.

The enormous, the overwhelming, the positively regime-destroying spike of rage Gil felt, that had her on her feet and about to slap the girl, fell away almost immediately. She ended up standing but not sure why, staring down at Loret rather sadly. Sad about a lot of things, honestly. "Well I asked for that, didn't I?" she said vaguely.

"Magister. I won't go back."

"Oh, I've dressed it up. I've made excuses. If you've read it, you've read that. I've not sunk your career. Go and get some clerk's post and work on your cursive," Gil said.

"Magister." Emptying another cup of hus, putting it away far too fast for just some girl fresh out of the Archipelago. Her hand on her knife hilt. *Oh fuck I'm going to get stabbed by my own aide.* It seemed weirdly hilarious. It seemed very much like something she had coming to her.

"Loret," she said. Sitting again. Settling in for a bit of a rant, possibly one that would only be stopped by a stabbing. "Loret, I know when you're your age it all seems stupidly important. But it's fine. You'll get another chance. It's just a post that didn't work out for you. I'm asking them to send someone with a bit more experience, that's all. It's not your fault. It's on whoever looked at your records and thought you were aide material. You're too young. Usmai is too complicated. It'll be fine."

The knuckles of Loret's knife hand were white, flexing so hard it was amazing the skin didn't split. "Magister, no."

"Magister, yes," Gil told her. "Oh, sweet reason! Kids like you think every turn of the dice is life and death. Get some perspective."

She looked at the knife, trembling now, without obvious transition, in front of her face. Loret had her collar, or thought she had. What she actually had was Gil's Usmiat shawl, so when Gil slid sideways from the chair, Loret kept the garment but lost her. The whisper of Gil's rapier clearing its sheath was very loud. Her office wasn't exactly somewhere fit for sword-work, too much furniture and the walls too close. The knife was better than the sword. But Gil was better than Loret. The girl was all frenzy, no finesse.

"Hell, yes," she told Loret. "Fine. Yes. Come on then. Let's fucking do it."

The girl trembled, shawl in one hand, knife in the other like some obscure style of gladiator. "You don't know," she got out. And Gil had at least three chances to stab her, to use the sword's superior reach and simplify everyone's life. But the residual responsibilities of her position were still on her, suggesting that gutting her own aide in her own office probably wouldn't look good in the next report.

"Of course I don't know," she told the girl. "I mean, I'm just the Resident. Not like anybody tells me anything. Dekamran won't talk to me. Flint's got nothing but nonsense. And you. You with your only useful skill being that you're very quick with that knife you're showing me *sometimes*. And other times not so much. And you don't even seem to have any control over *when*. I mean, I've been in places I could use a good knife, Loret, but not one that only goes off half the time like a badly-charged tableth. What good is that? Just go home, Loret."

She could tell, around the point she said, *good*, that she was crossing some boundary. After that word, even as she continued to speak, the girl who stood on the far side of the desk from her wasn't her aide any more.

"I can't," Loret said very clearly, and then, "Life or death. It is. Life or death. In the camps."

Camps. Dalry and Annet, talking about camps. But Loret hadn't been in any camps. Nobody would send her an aide who'd been in some kind of… prison for… cultists…

"Camps," Gil echoed, suddenly trying to sober up because incompetence she could deal with, idiot youth she could deal with, but religion, right now, might be a step too far.

"You don't know," Loret said. "They don't tell you. The camps. Quarantine camps. That's what they said. Like we were sick."

Gil suddenly regretted a great deal, not least all the hus. "You're sick?" Except she knew what they'd been sick with.

"Nobody's sick," said Loret. "It's what they called it. When they put us there. When they found us out. And then they…"

"Loret, just get to the damn point!" Angry, aggressive, because that was easier than letting the girl fumble about for the words. Even setting the knife into motion again would be easier.

"I'm not Loret," said Loret. And every part of her moved for the stabbing. Moved to send her leaping over the desk, into the sword or past it, either outcome acceptable. Every part of her except the knife. Meaning nothing of her moved at all. "They killed Loret." Her face collapsed, tears running down it, teeth bared in agony. Every muscle of her vibrating as she fought herself and the knife. "They killed her. So I was Loret then. Because Loret had the papers to get out. They made me her. They gave me what was hers."

Gil blinked at her. Her sword had fallen out of guard, the tip scratching the desk's veneer. "What?" she managed.

"They. Killed. Loret," Loret said. Not Loret, presumably, except Gil couldn't stop thinking of her as Loret.

"Why?" she asked.

"Because," Loret said. "They. Killed. Everybody." Storms were in her eyes. Flames. Screaming. And then she was screaming. A single raw shriek of despair and rage and horror at herself. She dropped the knife, gripped the desk. Upended the whole weighty piece of furniture on Gil and her sword. Cups, bottles, papers filling the air. And gone. When Gil could get herself out from under the weight of bureaucracy, the front door of the Residence was flapping open and Loret had fled.

The Holes that History Leaves

Usmai, the great. Strengthened by its allies from the Grove, wise with the heritage of the Moeribandi, mightiest of the Successor States. The Alkhand of Usmai, blessed and beloved, whose word makes lesser regents tremble. When the Islermen made themselves into the Palleseen and cast away their old fishy god and its bloody rites, it was to Usmai many of their scholars looked. Half the words in their new-made language of Pel have Usmiat roots. The Tranquillity and elegance of the great nation, its wealth and tacit influence over its neighbours, were a great inspiration. 'If we remake our nation and society then perhaps we too can be as majestic as Usmai.'

And so, as the Palleseen spread their Sway across the world, at first slowly, but with growing strength and confidence and belief in the superiority of their ways, the glitter of Usmai remained in the minds of their leaders. Even centuries later, after Usmai had risen and fallen and risen again, within the fortunes of the Successor States. A special place in the thoughts of the Palleseen. A hazardous position to hold.

The Tesemer hadn't declared for him. A month, now, since his hasty coronation, and he'd thought they'd come round. The inflexible Tesemer, the proud Louse Monks with the bloody nose Flint's troops had given them, in the field and in the streets of Alkhalend. But Dekamran was the undisputed Alkhand now. The sole one. The only child of lost Oparan simultaneously alive and locatable. And so, despite all that had happened, the Louse Monks should have climbed down off their umbrage and bowed the knee to him. Proffered their centuries-old loyalty to the Mirror Throne, whoever sat on it, as they always had.

They hadn't.

Oh, they hadn't outright declared themselves rebels. But those monks who'd survived the fight had slowly gathered in the Tesemera, their fortified compound of a monastery, in the jungles north of the city. The place Dekamran had last seen from within his father's entourage, before moving on to the Alborandi and the Grove and all the terrible things that had happened there.

He'd sent messengers. They hadn't been decapitated at the gates, just informed that the Tesemer had no word for the throne. Just that. And it had been a month. It wasn't just that they were possessed of swords and beasts and batons, a significant military force that he had no direct control over, and felt at his back like the knife of an assassin. It was the place they held in the minds of his people. The terrifying, the indomitable, and also the loyal. Those the Alkhand trusted to stand beside the Mirror Throne. And when his father had fought his uncle, before Dekamran was even born, the Tesemer had declared for Sorthist, the Serpent's Fang, at first. That had allowed Sorthist to capture the young Oparan and blind him, and everyone thought it had ended then and there. But later, when Oparan had escaped and gathered his followers and turned the tide, when Oparan had Sorthist's spirit bound into the man's own cleaned and bejewelled skull, the Tesemer had bent the knee. Without shame or delay.

What is wrong with me, that they will not? I am Alkhand. Had Gorbudan so won their stony hearts that none other would satisfy them? Or did they have their own ambitions? Three generations ago, the royal bodyguard of Goshumai – savage archers from across the Garmoers – had installed some infant with only a drachm of royal blood on the throne. Made the child their puppet and ruled the nation for a generation, and for their benefit. Not even the most disastrous period of Gosht history. And a century before that, the throne of Lucibi had been auctioned off by the royal guard after their Dusarch had died without heir. The world hadn't ended. And a week ago, one of Dekamran's advisors had whispered in his ear that hadn't that much-removed cousin, that kid Jarushan, actually *joined* the Tesemer. Had his tongue cut out and everything, but so distant a royal scion that nobody had really cared. Except that meant perhaps the Tesemer really did feel they had an alternative to the Alkhand whose foreign allies had given them such a whipping.

They hadn't announced as much. They hadn't raised a banner. But they hadn't bent the knee, either. And so, in the end, he'd had no option but to send more than just a messenger to their gates.

Flint Postry and a significant contingent of troops would be turning up at the Tesemer compound even now, Dekamran knew. Turning up with the writ of the Mirror Throne to demand their obeisance. He wasn't holding his breath for it. Five centuries of loyal service and compact, between Usmai and the Tesemer, and perhaps today it was ending forever.

That was only one of his troubles.

Follo, the jolly man who didn't laugh any more, had requested another audience. The most respected and beloved man at court, perhaps. Always a jest to puncture the proud, a kind word to comfort the lowly. The High Ranin, Kakrops's chosen ambassador to the world. To look at him now was to see a ruin of some great monument. All that flesh was in its own mourning, hanging from the man in folds and creases. His face sagged as though detached from its skull.

He'd come to complain about the Palleseen. Of course he had. That was all people seemed to want to do. Except the Palleseen, who wanted to complain about everyone else.

Dekamran had dreamed of his older brother the night before. Gorbudan had said nothing. He'd been dead, lying there before the palace just as they'd found him. Instead of the angry, outraged look he'd actually died with, though, his expression had spoken direct to Dekamran: *I told you.*

Time would be the healer, Dekamran desperately believed. Time enough to consolidate his reign. To do enough good for people that they understood him as the Alkhand *of* the people, the man who made things better. A hundred small injustices that his ancestors had allowed to go on could be stopped. The Usrani could be given so much more to distribute to the Sand Lanes and the poor, even if it came from secular sources and without a divinity to bless it any more. Reason and enlightened thought could be made to clasp hands with Usmiat tradition to make a paradise of his nation. If he only had time. If only people wouldn't fight him over every little thing. And because they fought him, he must lean ever heavier on the Palleseen. While trying to blunt the excesses of those same Palleseen.

He hadn't even dared look at the accounts of his tax collectors. And true, his father had been lax, and there were Emorandi and temples and mills which had forgotten their responsibilities to the coffers of the palace. But giving responsibility for collection over to the Kepishi had not seen much of an increase in revenues to the throne, though his people complained constantly of how they were squeezed and fleeced.

The Palleseen. Not the Kepishi.

Follo had a new complaint, now. Of course he did. Scarcely a day arose without one. Save that this was a particularly bitter point. And Follo didn't shout or rage. That weight of sagging monk didn't thunder about the audience chamber. Just hung there and looked disappointed, and that was worse. "Do you know," he said, "what the Kepishi woman, the Archivist woman, will ask you for?" he demanded. And told Dekamran what, and perhaps the horrified look on his Alkhand's face was a little balm for the monk's spiritual wounds.

"Under no circumstances," Dekamran promised him. "Follo, you know me. You knew me as a child before I left Usmai. You knew me as a man when I returned into my father's and my brother's shadow. Nobody wished what happened. Not even the Palleseen, though many say it. Nobody will permit this. I will not. The Palleseen Resident will not. This woman, Drathel, she is a rogue. She does not speak for the Ke— for our allies."

The sad lines of Follo's clown face spoke only doubt. Dekamran couldn't blame him. What else could be said, though?

Dekamran was the last of his immediate family, to his knowledge. Gorbudan had died in battle, as was fitting for such a fiery man, but, before he'd done so, he'd rid Dekamran of their siblings somehow. Premath had taken his own life and been carried off by the skull-faced Moerends for their final rites, as he'd have wanted. And in letting them – in waiving the royal family's right to have the youngest son's body interred in the palace's mausoleum – Dekamran had won the support of the death monks, at least a little. And Enshili was gone. Had fled Gorbudan, or Gorbudan had her murdered, or... Nobody seemed to know. A handful of carved-up palace officials and Enshili just gone. Dead, was the official story, and sycophants keen to ingratiate themselves had placed the deed at Gorbudan's dead feet, even though nobody could say why the man might have wanted to do it. Dekamran's secret thought was different, though. Fled, he thought. Fled because she had never wanted to play the part of a palace princess. And so he searched for her, sent people to the houses of Emorandi families who might be sheltering her, but not too diligently. Yes he would welcome his sister if she returned, but right now he wouldn't blame anyone for wanting nothing to do with any of it.

He wanted nothing to do with any of it. But he was the Alkhand, so he had no choice. It was all to do with him. And once upon a time, being the Alkhand was what he had wanted.

After Follo had gone, Dekamran was left alone in the audience chamber. Oh, servants came and went, set down tea for him just as he liked it, hovered within earshot for the Alkhand's least request. He could have anything. Food and drink, poets and musicians, courtesans of whatever type or number he might desire. Alkhands had lived their lives for no more than that, and left the governance of their domains to palace officials and monks. But Dekamran had not wanted to be Alkhand for the hedonism, but to make things better. He'd returned home with a thousand ideas, but each of them could only succeed on the back of his people's consent and happiness. He was starting to feel that he had only their disdain, perhaps their hate.

And so he needed the Palleseen.

And he, *he*, the man who had been Dekamran before the crown and the emptily sacred words, also needed.

He'd seen her in the fencing circle, that first time. The new Pal Resident. This had been before the war, and before Gorbudan's fall from grace. He, Dekamran, just arrived back to find his mother gone and his father grieving. To find himself one son surplus to requirements at court, without friends. To find Sage-Invigilator Angilly, also freshly arrived and floundering. They'd found each other.

Friends. They'd become friends. Strangers in a prickly nation, even though it was his own. And she'd been playing catch-up to the Loruthi, and he'd been doing the same with dashing Gorbudan, the heir presumptive. Then the war had broken out and, despite Oparan's declarations of neutrality, the fortunes of both Pals and Dekamran had slid further into penury, while Gorbudan and the Loruthi had flexed their muscles and planned out the future.

Friends, in that extremity. With the old Alkhand failing, and Dekamran knowing that he should flee to save his skin because Gorbudan would not be able to simply leave him alone and whole, once the warrior prince became the warrior king. Knowing, but unwilling to flee because his ailing father needed him.

Good times. Despite the shadow of death or mutilation over him. Because of Gil.

Then he'd become the heir, Gorbudan banished for taking too many liberties, raiding the Palleseen mills across the Peost border. Dekamran's star in the ascendant, Pallesand winning the war, but Oparan still Alkhand and so there had been time. Time for many things. And, not being Alkhand yet, he had been free to drink and laugh with the Palleseen Resident. Free, even, to turn up at her door in disguise on the night she went to illegally duel, and kill, the Loruthi emissary. She'd needed him, and he'd needed her. Friends.

More than friends, when the Day of Milk and Flowers came. And then, after that permitted lapse, more than friends again. When he had needed a friend and more than a friend, and so had she.

And she'd been there for him, Angilly, when Gorbudan had thrown him in the House of Hard Angles. Dekamran's lowest ebb, when her friendship, her more than friendship, had been the sole thing left to him, and it had been stronger than all of Gorbudan's troops and supporters. Gil, his friend Gil, had carried him from prison to the throne, and yet when he had looked back at her, he had seen not his friend Gil, but the Palleseen Resident. The mastermind at the head of a great hierarchy of soldiers and clerks and a trail of ships with hungry holds stretching all the way back to the Archipelago. As though he'd held the warm hand of a living woman just a moment before, and now there was some wooden simulacrum in her place. Something a Beast Artist might fashion for their fighting games. A Kepishi machine where his friend had been.

And she looked at him, perhaps, and saw a gilden automaton, crowned and splendid. And cold.

There was one thing the servants couldn't bring him, and that was yesterday.

If it had been that simple, then… well, his father showed that melancholy was something befitting an Alkhand. Perhaps Dekamran could cut away that part of himself. Have sad verses composed. Listen to sour music. Just be Alkhand, govern, go on with the duties that history had laid on his shoulders. But he could not sever those strands because, absent the Palleseen

Resident and her compatriots, his rule would not last a day. No Tesemer, no Kakrops and half the Emorandi families already whispering amongst themselves. And every day another piece of outrage over this Kepishi tax collector or that Kepishi merchant, driving a wider wedge between Dekamran and his people. Meaning he must rely ever more on Kepishi uniforms to ensure that he and the throne remained in company.

He needed the Pals.

He wanted Gil.

It felt like a sickness, given everything else. It felt as though he should hate her. The architect of this razor-edged cell of a triumph. The victory that cut like knives, given him like a gift, with smiles. To find that his heart still pulled for her was unbefitting the Alkhand. Unbefitting a man. The tears that came to his eyes were not noble melancholy but some unsound weakness in him. Yet he could not rid himself of them. The Alkhand of Usmai was reliant on the ongoing support of the Palleseen Resident. Dekamran, the private individual of that name, knew such a yearning for Angilly, the woman. His friend. His lover. The woman whose goodwill he was utterly dependent on.

He sent the servants away. In doing so, he understood he'd made his choice.

One More Seat at the Table

Jack had been a priest, once, and a smuggler of gods in the Palleseen Sway. Enough to get him executed and, indeed, they'd executed him once but it hadn't taken. Oathan was a murderer, quite a notorious one in his day. Tally had been a religious terrorist setting fires across Jarokir after that nation's liberation *by the Pals. The Reckoner had killed a whole squad of Pal specialists using her arts, because healing was by no means the only purpose they could be put to. The Viper was... what she was, worse than all of the rest put together, literally by definition. And the boy was young in the ways of the world but there was a noose in the future for him, surely. A young villain like that.*

Basically perfect company, if you had horrors in your past you didn't want people judging you for.

They were sitting down to dinner at the Fever Lodge when the knock came. Their crooked little family. Oathan was cooking, because he was good at it. Had expanded his repertoire considerably since they beached up in Usmai and he'd got to play around with the local ingredients. His boy ferried dishes from the makeshift kitchen to the table. The big table they made from putting together the Reckoner's desk and the slab that Tally operated on and another rickety piece of furniture they didn't have any regular use for but that nobody ever got round to throwing out. There, in the big central room of the Lodge, that was surgery and fencing piste and anything else they could dress it up as.

An empty chair for Jack, who was off at his *club*, as he called it. The Difficult Wives Club. Oathan's joke. And Jack's club business was all their business right now. This plan of his, for when the boot came down and they needed to get out.

His difficult wife was lounging in her seat. Not that she ate, particularly, but her protégé did, and she was inordinately proud of having turned that girl's head. Trouble, Tally knew. Far too much trouble, and the only reason Caecelian was sitting there grinning at people was she loved to bring the trouble. She was waiting for Oathan to snap and bawl her out about it, demand she send the girl away. Because the Viper ate discord, and Oathan served up the most flavoursome argument just as he did the meals.

But he'd just simmered and stewed, and not caught fire over it. Not yet.

Her girl had the seat beside her. The Usmiat girl. The one nobody named. She'd end up with some suitable alias soon enough. Right now everyone was holding their breath to see if the kid was a fixture, or if some delegation from the palace would turn up and kick their doors in. Not as though any of them were ignorant over who she was.

Or maybe Jack was. Always hard to know how much of that vacant idiot act was real.

The Reckoner had put away her scales and was spinning a fork on her plate with her one good hand. The other was bandaged up after a patient had come in with a bag of coin and a smashed-up right hook. All very painful, even after Tally had done what she could to reset the bones. But the Reckoner healed fast. Right now Oathan had her on a dose of something that kept the pain in a distant room like a petitioner who wouldn't get to see the Alkhand for a week. Which meant she could enjoy the meal. Nobody enjoyed food like the Reckoner. You lived in a world of precise balances and bargains, you learned to appreciate the good things.

Tally herself had just taken her seat when the knock came. The boy, their usual doorman, had his hands full of soup tureen. She levered herself to her feet, cursing.

"Let them wait," Oathan called from the kitchen, "Unless they're actually about to *die* or something." As though turning up on the doorstep of a hospital about to die was just plain bad manners and they shouldn't have to put up with it.

"It's probably Jack," Tally said wearily, hauling her old bones out of the room and towards the front door.

"Why does he need to knock?" Oathan's voice pursued her.

"Because he's an idiot!" Tally shouted back. And it wasn't that. It was because Jack was polite, really. Ridiculously, shrinkingly polite. But the world was very rude, so that still counted as idiocy in Tally's book.

She opened the door to give any visitors the full benefit of her ill-temper and froze. A shabby Pal girl. Or woman, but standing with the inward-turned, shrinking look of a girl who'd been ill-treated. Filthy with mud and sand off the streets. The marks of someone sleeping in doorways and eating very little. But not, as she had been before, bleeding to death.

"I stitched you up," Tally remembered. "You're the… wait, aren't you the Resident's aide or something?" In which case their visitor was definitely dressing down.

"Please," the girl said. "I need… somewhere to go. And everyone out there hates Pals. And I can't… I can't be with Pals any more." She was swaying, tired. Certainly not fresh out of the Residence. "I've run away!" she spat out, like she was twelve years old.

Tally, who was past sixty, felt that the girl might as well have been twelve. This much youthful haplessness crammed into one body made her feel absolutely ancient.

Send her away. That was what you did, with girls turning up on the doorstep with neither coin nor actual injuries in need of fixing. Or, at least, the injuries this girl plainly had were beyond anything Tally's scalpel could cure, or the Reckoner balance away.

Sell her back to the Pals. That was what you did, when someone turned up who'd shrugged off the uniform jacket without official permission, because otherwise all those people who'd kept theirs on would be knocking, soon enough, to ask if you'd seen her.

Get rid of her. Because she was standing there like some new-minted deity whose portfolio was causing trouble to elderly expatriates trying to escape official notice.

Tally scowled, hating herself. And probably she *should* send the girl away to be someone else's problem, but she was a long way from selling someone to the army. Perhaps this counted as one last act of rebellion. "Fucking come in then," she said, more grudging than a three-generation feud.

Oathan was similarly less than delighted with the suggestion he should set another seat at dinner. "Piss off," was in fact his considered opinion. "We don't need one more lodger."

"I've got..." The girl was swaying, grey-faced. "Nowhere to go."

The Reckoner was staring. She had good eyes. They saw things most people would need two tablethi and a focusing lens to detect. "One more seat at the table," she said. "More than one lodger." Cutting through any mundane difficulties. "She was trouble when they brought her in before. More trouble now."

"Trouble we don't need, if she's run away from the Residence," Oathan said. The boy leaned in to him, the two of them thick as thieves when there was someone else to victimise. The big man nodded soberly. "The Cotto like you. Why not go to them?"

The Pal woman's eyes bulged at the suggestion. "You can't," she got out, a strangled whisper. "I can't. I don't want to be... Not that. Please. I can't go to them. I need to be free of... Of all of it. Please."

Caecelian leaned in to the Reckoner, murmuring. The pair of them were anatomising the girl, seeing more than anyone should be comfortable with. The eyes of the Viper saw what was there, whether humans were supposed to see it or not. They'd fashioned her well, when they called her up from the places she'd been born to.

How useful that might be, thought Tally sourly, *if only we could rely on her not just using her talents for causing problems.*

"Keep her," Caecelian said. "I like her."

Tally exchanged a look with Oathan. Anything the Viper liked was, de facto, venomous. And yet they'd agreed, when they set up here. She had a voice. She was one of them, a person. Not just the *thing* they'd made of her, back before.

But just one voice. Not enough to carry a decision. She met Oathan's gaze, agreed with it and drew breath to send the girl out into the Sand Lanes again. If anyone had the Fever Lodge's final word, it was her.

"She should stay," said the Reckoner, then applied herself to her plate, letting the food stand between her and anyone's questions.

Oathan inflated, stood, bunched his big fists, opened his mouth. Shut it again. Because the one person he wouldn't throw down with was the Reckoner. Not even for fear of the eldritch powers the woman absolutely had. But because she was almost always right.

"I mean…" he got out eventually.

"Just for a few days," the Reckoner said, around her spoon. "It won't be for long." As though she had seen some disease in the girl, that was about to reach its full flowering. A doom over their visitor's head. "You'll see."

Oathan hissed slowly through his teeth. "What's your name, girl?" he demanded, as his boy ran to fetch one more chair to fit about the table.

At the newcomer's panicked look, Tally snickered. "Oh don't worry. Nobody who lives under our roof goes by their real name. It's a whole thing, around here."

"Then," said the woman, "Then I'm Loret. I guess I'm Loret."

The Palleseen Hand

The long road from Pallesand to perfection was paved with broken stones. A complacent little bon mot *to trot out at the regimental dinner table. The suggestion that, even though the quality of the victuals was excellent, they were still nominally roughing it, out in the territories of the Sway. When originally penned, the writer had not simply meant rough going underfoot. Those broken stones had been palaces and temples, monasteries and halls of learning. The thousand wrong ways that ignorant foreigners could order and envisage the world. And the army would keep on marching until they were all stamped flat.*

Flint took his breakfast at a leisurely pace, because it wasn't as though a dawn attack would catch his enemy napping. A night attack had been out of the question too, as apparently these Bug-eaters could see in the dark. 'Bug-eaters' was his best translation of what his Peost Accessories called the Tesemer. They weren't fond of them. Flint reckoned he wouldn't much like them as neighbours either, honestly.

He was just finishing the pot of cold rice and salt meat when the Louse Speaker was brought before him. Or the Speaker for the Louse Speakers. He vaguely understood the term referred to some distinction or upper echelon within the monks as a whole, but decided he didn't really care what one pack of cultists called another behind closed doors. People like this, you either wiped them out or you didn't. You didn't get *interested.*

This one was a tall, lanky creature as so many of them were, wearing the loose robes and a broad-brimmed sloping hat. They had their falx with them. According to the lizards, you literally couldn't get them to put the damn things down. A whole honour thing that was just one more part of the whole question of *Why are these loons so difficult?* He made sure to keep his little breakfast table between them.

"This your knee, then?" he asked the figure. "I've the writ of the Alkhand in my jacket. The man you're all supposed to work for. Do we settle this the civilized way?"

The Louse Speaker regarded him coldly. When the man spoke, at first there were just clicks and scraping noises from him, the words then coming rough and rusty as though he resented using them. Speaking the local cant, not even that well to Flint's ear. And he understood, but his Peost was better, and so there was a whole charade of it. A monk used to speaking the True Language or whatever the hell they called their idiolect, talking in rusty Usmiri, and then Flint's own local turning that into Peost in his head, then speaking in the reliable gold of Pel to Flint. And after all that, no words worth the journey.

"He says they cannot renew their bonds of fealty without a Preceptor," his translator informed him. "He says they cannot appoint a new Preceptor until the moon is correct. Not the moon you see, but the moon as it was where they come from. Another moon. They ask the Alkhand to send for them once this is done."

"Yeah?" Flint asked, looking the Louse Speaker right in the pale eyes. "And how long's that going to be?"

Another exchange up and down the ladder of linguistics.

"He says they are even now making the required calculations."

Flint snorted. "Tell him the Alkhand works by the real moon and would be happy to pin a sash on whichever of them wants to be Preceptor. Or I'll do it, if they can't wait. Tell them the Alkhand isn't having a bunch of armed maniacs – monks, tell them monks – just sitting around within a two-day strike of the capital."

The translator said just that, as far as Flint could work out. He was a Peost with no love for the Tesemer – probably he'd been raised on stories of them as a kid, how nasty they were. Being able to talk down to them plainly went down well with him.

The Louse Speaker said something harsh and dismissive, and then went into more detail about just how harsh and dismissive he was being.

"He says there are tides and cycles that the writ of the Alkhand cannot overrule," the translator said archly. "Also he says that when a new Preceptor is appointed then the Alkhand must present himself at the compound in person to accept the service of his servants, because under no circumstances will they bend the knee to a – well…"

"Kepishi, right," Flint agreed.

"The term they used was less polite, magister." The translator sent a scornful look at the monk. "They speak through abominations, magister. There is no truth in them."

Perhaps it was just the tone, but what happened next suggested the Tesemer had sent out an emissary with a little understanding of Pel because the monk killed the translator. A single lightning strike of that falx, and the man's head gone from his shoulders. Flint fell backwards off his camp stool and rolled as his little table was cut in two. He heard the crackle of baton-fire.

On one knee, he brought his rod up from his belt, tableth already slotted. The monk was at full extension, his blade cutting down an Accessory who had put themselves between the falx and Flint. Two other human soldiers and an Ibaleth were already down around them, as suddenly as though their hearts had abruptly given out.

Flint spat the word and the rod sizzled in his hand. The bolt of fire struck the monk a glancing blow across the shoulder, staggering but not stopping the man. Flint saw the blade circle back for the stroke that would serve him the same way as the table and understood he was going to die.

Two more shots lanced through the monk's chest even as he thought it. A pair of his better sharpshooters getting their eye in now his own shot had held the monk still for long enough. The man still didn't go down but staggered, losing his poise, sword point dipping. Flint shot him four more times, getting the command word out with a soldier's blunt battlefield diction, as fast as he could say it. The tableth in the slot turned from gold to lead.

The monk was on his back, then, and most of his chest was craters. Dead, most certainly dead, yet Flint approached the corpse leerily. Unnatural sons of bitches. Who knew what they could do? Not necromancy, apparently. This Louse Speaker had spoken his last.

Curiously he used the tip of his baton to pry open the dead man's jaws. And shuddered, and closed them again. He hadn't quite believed the stories. The thing in there, broad, segmented, waving its little claw legs, was still alive. Let the fucker starve.

"Looks like we get to play with the new toys," he told his officers. "Get us in battle order. I'll ride with the Hand. I want this place off everyone's maps by dusk. And a commendation for the two who got shots into this sod. Heroes, the pair of them."

The Tesemera was a wood-walled compound. The buildings within weren't quite Usmiat, up on little stilts and using living trees for some of the supports. Rising high into the branches, with plenty of slots for archers and batons to get a commanding angle of fire. The Louse Monks were mustering in the big drill square they had in there. They'd have that nasty bug cavalry, he knew, and probably other nasty bug things. And those swords, a demonstration of which he'd just been a party to.

Needless to say, he wasn't going to be storming those gates any time soon. And honestly, he reckoned the Tesemer were the serious business when it came to charging about and attacking, but bottle them up behind walls, you'd robbed them of their best weapons.

From his howdah – a mode of transportation he was becoming rather fond of – he nodded to the lizard with the banner. She waved it enthusiastically, her whole body curved about the flagstaff for leverage.

The artillery began to advance.

He'd known, as soon as the first handful of these ogrodon things came over to Dekamran, that he would revolutionise war. He, 'Flint' Postry, here in this overseas backwater, would do something nobody else had done. And he'd seen carts and carriages. A mule team hauling some big engine around the field before setting it up. *Amateurs!* He had half a dozen pieces – his own Hand and the engines that turned tablethi fire into hermetic force to throw stone and lead. Each one was mounted on a hastily customised howdah, pointed forwards over the shield of the ogrodon's head. They advanced at the speed of the beasts, faster than any mule-drawn carriage, fast enough that the infantry behind were having to hustle to keep up. And the paths they took through the trees were narrow when they started, but the hustling infantry had nice wide roads after because that was another advantage of these big horn-headed monsters. And when they were close enough, Flint had the flag wave again and the engines spoke. The ogrodons did have to stop still just for that moment, both to absorb the shock of it, and so the shots didn't just punch holes in the jungle or the sky. But only for that moment, and then they could lumber on. And the things were doubtless expensive to keep, and you needed to have the lizards around for it, but weigh that against being able to put your engines wherever you wanted, and move them back and forth. Flint let out a whoop of sheer officer's glee when the artillery let fly a second time. The walls of the compound had already taken a couple of strikes, holding for now but they were closing the range. He'd just flicked their nose so far, in this one-sided punching match, but he was about to put some solid knuckles right to the face.

He'd had a letter arrive with the dawn. A rider from Alkhalend, one of his own Peosts. Drathel had commandeered them to get word to him. Since he could let the engines work now, he hunkered down in the howdah and pulled it out to read. The thunder from left and right didn't much dent his concentration, honestly. You lived through the battlefields of the Loruthi War, you got used to it.

Drathel had a bee in her cap about something, it seemed. Telling him he needed to get back to the city double-time, when he was done. Something 'for his advantage'. An opportunity he wouldn't want to miss, apparently. Flint had a cynical view of Drathel's 'opportunities'. Half the time they were get-rich schemes and half the time they were just trouble. For him, anyway. They were always get-rich for Drathel. He knew her type from long service. The specialists they put on a long leash, because you couldn't do that kind of work by the book. Magic out in the world came in a variety of inconvenient shapes, sizes and defensive capabilities, from unregarded burial sites to actual gods with a full complement of knife-wielding priests. There wasn't really a standard field manual for the roving Decanter. So probably there was some cache she'd found that she wanted Flint to come strongarm for her. Except... *The city's going to be seeing a lot of chairs moved around. Don't turn up late after everyone's found a seat. You don't want to be standing at the back.* And he knew *that* language. Officers' language, and neither he nor Drathel were your archetypal officers, the good family and the manners and the jostling for place behind the scenes. But they knew the cant. He understood what the woman was saying, and if it was true she was doing him a favour with the heads-up. He was her ally, and she wanted the tide to lift his boat in case she needed it for a sudden getaway later, was his best guess.

There was less bang going on than there had been a moment ago. He put away the letter and popped his head over the rail. The big artillery piece on the next ogrodon along had fallen silent, more as a victim of its own success than from enemy action. It had broken its improvised mounting, and now three lizards and two humans were setting about some emergency battlefield carpentry, which was absolutely a thing.

He heard shouts, then. Looking back, he saw that the Tesemer weren't just sitting on their hands and watching their walls fall over.

They'd snuck out their cavalry somehow. The hooklopers, those nasty shrimp things with the mantis arms. Only a score of them, but they'd come straight out of the trees and into the back of his infantry and made a mess of the rear ranks before veering off. He heard the whistles and shouts of his officers and statloi as they made firing lines further back, and then let the survivors of the rearguard flee behind them. Just as they'd drilled, over and over. Nobody panicking. The hooklopers passed back and forth, in and out of the trees, their riders snapping off shots with bows or long batons, but the massed fire knocked a few of them down and drove the rest away.

The lizard beside him snagged his sleeve with one two-thumbed hand, hissing like a kettle. The monks in the compound had taken this as their signal. They were coming out.

Most of them just had their falxes. Maybe one in four had a baton or one of those man-tall bows. They could *run*, though. Even into the artillery, they could run. Something kicked in him, a little afraid of them despite everything, a little impressed. Understanding that either this was the last thing he'd see, or that he'd be the last person to see this. Flint or the Tesemer, one of them wouldn't be around for tomorrow's dawn.

He slapped the side of the Palleseen Hand mounted on his howdah. A pair of Ibaleth had already fit its string of tablethi in place and were swivelling it to aim right into the thick of the monks. At the same time, the mahout hooked at the ogrodon with her goad and the beast picked up speed, lowering its horns.

A thing – a bug the size of a hawk – flurried past the rail at Flint's face, drawing a long line of blood down his cheek. He yelled with genuine shock and fell back as it grappled with him. For a splintered moment he saw the hooked arms of the little monster poised in front of his eyes. Then the soldier beside him swatted it away with his baton, cursing. The air was dancing with them, bedevilling the engine crews. A distraction, though. Easily crushed.

"Let 'em have it!" Flint shouted, and snatched up his own baton. Beside him, the Hand began its chatter, raking swift fire across the advancing monks.

Afterwards, he sat in the ruin of the compound and let a surgeon tend his face. Shallow, inconsequential. He'd done the responsible thing and had them leave him 'til last, because despite the odds the Tesemer had carved up more than a few of his people. The attack from behind, the windsaws, their marksmen, the sheer bloody-minded refusal to know when they were beaten.

He had a dozen prisoners. Out of maybe three hundred monks who'd seen daybreak. Four who had been left too injured to keep fighting. Eight who were very junior, new recruits. One of them looked around seven years old. None of them had the bug tongue thing of the leaders. And maybe a handful of monks had just gone into the trees at the end. Maybe a couple of their riding beasts. So say twenty, at absolute most. That was how many Tesemer there were left in this world.

There was another world through the Waygrove, they said. A world full of Tesemer, or whoever the Tesemer had originally been. Full of insect monsters too, probably. Flint had no intention of going there to see, and he strongly advised the

Tesemer to stay there because otherwise he'd serve them just as he'd served this lot.

Five hundred years, they said. Since the first Louse Monk-ancestors had come out of the Grove. They'd been a terror, back then. Fought the Usmiat and the declining remnants of the old dead Empire. Tried to take over all of Usmai and start their own Louseocracy or whatever it would have been. And failed, in the end. Found some way to bend their pride into becoming the Alkhand's premier warrior-guard instead. Five hundred years. And he'd been the rock they'd broken against. And he was still here and they were gone.

He read over Drathel's letter again. Before, in the howdah, he'd felt keen anticipation. Some sort of scheme was afoot and she was trying to save him a seat at the table. Now he read exactly the same words and felt a chill little wind of worry. Change was coming. That shouldn't have been a problem because people like him and Drathel were born opportunists. But sitting in the ruin of the Tesemer dream, he felt an odd feeling of things lost, things fleeting.

Around him, his people were filling sacks and boxes, everything of value that had survived the assault, everything that looked magical. Barrels of falxes with inlaid hilts and the elegant carved batons the locals made with such care. Coin and art and a lot of ornamental bug fetishes that Drathel would probably turn to dross to draw the magic out of, and good riddance honestly. Food and drink, even. Waste not, want not.

Flint crumpled the letter in his hand and tried to work out where such foreboding was coming from.

The Resident Plays Host

"The role of the Resident, as pre-eminent representative of the Palleseen state within a nation under diplomatic relations and yet to be brought into the Sway, is (1) to act as the chief point of contact, representative, advocate and guardian of those legitimate citizens of Pallesand within the territory (2) to act as gatherer, focal point and reporter of intelligence generated within or arriving at the territory (3) and of overriding import, to guide and influence the local society and political structure to better favour, reward and comply with the ordinances of Pallesand, and thereby move all such Residented territories the closer towards perfection…"

Outreach Appointments Manual, short form, as approved by the Temporary Commission of Ends and Means.

"Under no circumstances," Gil said, and passed the cruet. The meal had been dragging on for a while, four courses prepared by an Usmiat chef who understood Pal tastes. Slate House's main reception room didn't honestly get the dust off it that often. Back when Pal fortunes in these parts had swung lower, she'd hosted a couple of bitter merchants at most, commiserating about how well the Loruthi were doing or how the authorities did nothing about Cotto creeping on board Pal ships and stealing whatever wasn't nailed down. Now that she was the chief advisor to the Alkhand, and what peace was kept was kept by Pal uniforms, suddenly everyone was jockeying to be her guest. And you'd *think* they'd be all ingratiating and raising a cup of good Pal wine to her health, but it turned out that being given an unobstructed field just meant they could sight up on her with all their grievances. Yes, it was *better*, seemed to be the tenor of their talk, but was it really better *enough*? Shouldn't the position of Palleseen merchants and mill overseers be even *more* advantageous? Why, there was this one trivial disappointment that this particular cloth merchant had suffered several days ago and the man was still telling the story of it even though it felt like whole ages of the world had gone by. Under cover of which, Drathel had somehow evicted the tedious ship's master from Gil's left elbow and sat in his place. Whereupon she'd discovered that tedium was preferable, because Drathel had a request.

The Decanter swilled her wine reflectively, eyes on the vociferous cloth merchant as she spoke from the side of her mouth. "Come now, magister. Perhaps I've not stressed the *value* of what they're sitting on. Sitting on, mind. Not *doing* anything with. Sitting on, because they've got no idea *what* to do. This isn't some ancient tradition, some revered folkway. Can't be. They've not been in this fix before. So they sit. And it goes to waste. Just a word in the Alkhand's ear, that's all I'm asking. For the good of the Palleseen Sway, for the sake of our valuable alliance, so on, so forth."

"Drathel," and Gil had been sampling the wine, but very much within moderation because, when she'd cut loose a couple of days ago, it had cost her an aide, "No. Even you must understand the knife-edge the throne is on, with the city as a whole, after what happened on the… the Night. Get your way, there'd be riots in the streets."

Drathel shrugged. "I mean we've got all those uniforms. Shame to have them idle. Besides," eyeing Gil slyly, "isn't that all to the good? In the Palleseen interest? Get those angry people in the streets, who's the Alkhand going to lean on? Not going to be those bug-mouth gals, is it? I mean, that's basically the Outreach playbook, correct me if I'm wrong."

"You're wrong," Gil told her without hesitation, because Outreach also taught you how to lie well. "Nobody wins if the whole country goes on fire because some Fellow Decanter decided they wanted to push the sacrilege angle. In time. When we're more settled."

"In time," Drathel echoed. "You should see the letters I get from home, Resident. I get professors and secretaries to the Commission practically begging me. You don't know just how much it cost us to beat the Loruthi."

Gil thought of Tarcomir, her sword going into him. "I do. The answer's no, Drathel."

The Decanter leaned back in her borrowed chair. "Sage-Invigilator Angilly. Gil. I like you. I value you. You've done good things for Pallesand here. Delivered the whole country to us for the cost of a field battle and a little street-to-street fighting. Amazing stuff. They should be delighted with you, back home."

"Should be?"

"Will be. Because you know how it is. We go into a place two ways, battering ram or steal the keys. You stole the keys, and the battering ram, well, it's expensive to cart around. Takes far longer to recoup your investment when everything's in pieces. But the most important thing to do, once you've stolen the keys to a place and everyone's waiting expectantly outside, is you *open the doors*, magister. You don't just sit there in front of them like the Alkhand's hired gatekeeper, letting us in one at a time or turning us away." And, if Drathel was linguist enough for it, there was an extra jab there. Emorandi, the Usmiri word for the noble class surrounding and supporting the Alkhand. 'Gatekeepers' would be a fair translation. Those who controlled access, but with a suggestion of sycophancy. Of dependency on the man whose doors they camped outside.

"We are not in a position to take on all of Alkhalend when they hear what you want. Even after Flint gets back, we're not. And the Alkhand will *not* agree. No matter how much he needs us."

Drathel's expression suggested that, in that case, Gil wasn't asking nicely – or nastily – enough. When she made to speak again, Gil cut her off with a sharp gesture. She didn't like the woman's calculating look. Something of the wine merchant who feels a prized vintage has gone to vinegar in the cask. But it wasn't a topic she was willing to explore.

Because Drathel was right. Let her be honest within the confines of her own head, at least. Drathel was right, and this was what the Sway should be demanding. If Drathel's calculations were correct, she'd discovered a treasure of singular value in the Usrani monastery. Just, as she said, sitting there.

The thought of giving her what she wanted stabbed Gil like a knife. The thought that she was selling her nation short made her sick for the consequences. Her face remained absolutely sanguine. She knew it did. You didn't get to be a Sage in Outreach if your face was just a window on your thoughts.

"Tell you what," said Drathel after a reflective pause, "there's still time, probably. Let me file a proposal with Loret, about how we could play it. In writing, all on the up-and-up. There's a way we can all be happy, I know there is."

Gil didn't feel happy, and even the smile slipped then. "Loret's gone," she said.

Drathel went still just for a second, the news striking her harder than Gil had expected. "You dismissed her?"

"Yes." Somewhat after she'd left, but probably the letter home counted.

"Posthumously?" Drathel asked carefully.

Gil stared at her. "Are you asking me if I killed my aide?"

Drathel was being elaborately casual with her wineglass. "We both know she's… excitable."

"If you see her, tell her she needs to come back and at least get her things," Gil told her shortly. Not that Loret had many things to start with.

★

The dinner had gone on to near midnight, and Drathel's request wasn't even the most objectionable she had to deny. One woman, a mill-owner and ideologue, wanted her to start forcing the monks and priests out of the whole country already, as though Usmai was already firmly part of the Sway with a heavy garrison in place to keep Palleseen ordinances. One man, a maritime investor, wanted her to get the Cotto exiled. Or he wanted them all hung from their own yardarms but exile would do. Another man, whose trade and status Gil couldn't even remember, had a strapping young nephew and perhaps the Resident would want to meet him. She wasn't sure if the man was seeking his nephew's promotion or betrothal but neither prospect delighted her. When she'd finally cleared the lot of them out of the Residence it was with an appalling sense of relief.

I really don't like my own countryfolk as much as I should. Flint, damn him, was a rogue and a villain, but better company.

The servants had the room cleared with brisk efficiency – the full-sized staff the palace ensured she had at her disposal. She sat at the table as they worked around her. A maid scattered cool scented water onto her scarf and shoulders, because the night was humid and close. Insects battered at the lamps. If they were sent by the Tesemer to complain to the Resident of their demise, they gave no sign of it.

She pushed her chair back. Almost called for Loret, as some small matter occurred, the sort of menial missive she'd trust the girl to take down. But there was no girl, of course. She'd vanished into Alkhalend after some gabble about… not being Loret. Which possibly explained her patent unsuitability to the post of aide. And presumably some fuller explanation would shortly arrive, cued by her own letter trying to dismiss an imposter.

She was just getting sunk into morose speculation about what Loret's game had even *been*, given she hadn't exactly taken advantage of her cunning deception, when a servant had a message under her nose. Folded and sealed with blank wax. She took it absently and thumbed it open.

Send all your servants away, it said.

Her heart jolted.

Under no circumstances, obviously.

Out of the question. She was the most publicly visible member of a force that was currently making itself very unpopular across the city as it flexed its new muscles. The list of people who might mean her ill was extremely long. Not even just Usmiat names on it, in fact. More than a few Pals, probably, for whom things hadn't been *better* enough. An almost ridiculously obvious gambit for an assassin, to send a note like that.

Ridiculous.

She could feel a pressure in her chest, that interfered a little with her breathing. The Usmiat vest she wore seemed too tight, suddenly.

Send all your servants away. And she couldn't. How irresponsible. She wasn't just some loose agent in a city where the Sway had little leverage. She was at the height of her power, Alkhalend cupped in the palm of her hand, about to be proffered to the Commission of Ends and Means with a ribbon on it. Not a chance she'd fall for something like this.

She called the chief servants to her. "You can go," she told them. "All the staff, in fact. Go home. Come back for noon tomorrow. I don't need anyone for the morning."

They were puzzled, solicitous, but deferential. They left and, in their absence, the empty spaces of the Residence grew around her.

The old side door. The one she'd slipped out of that night, to go fight Tarcomir. Because a Residence needed a place to enter and leave from that wasn't immediately visible. The shadow hand of diplomacy, that everyone knew about and nobody mentioned out loud. The knock came soon after the last servant had gone.

She made sure she had her sword to hand, hung off the

fastenings of her vest. If it was an assassin, she'd make them work for their fee.

It wasn't. It was him.

She made a little sound in her throat and backed away, more swiftly than if he *had* been there with a knife and a cause. He was cloaked, dressed down, just as he had been when he'd come to see her before the duel. The difference being he hadn't been *Alkhand* then.

"No," she said, and he stopped at the very threshold. Before his face could turn, she said, "Come in. Quickly. How did you even—?"

Dekamran's smile, the self-deprecating one that had drawn her to him in the first place. When they'd met at the duelling circles. When he'd taken up the woman's straight sword to match her, because who was he then, except the spare son without a future? "It turns out," he said, "the Alkhand *can't* actually just sneak out of his own palace without anybody seeing. I've got about twenty of the palace staff down the street, waiting for my command. I am, however, in private conference with the Palleseen Resident about matters of state import."

"Are you?" She retreated to the big dining room, found the wine. Poured a couple of glasses and her hands only shook slightly. "Kam, this isn't right."

Again that taut moment. The ruler of the nation they were in, waiting to see if he was being rejected. Pausing in the room's doorway as though each threshold required its own invitation.

"I should come to you. At the palace," she tried, desperately. Put a glass down on the table for him. Like she was luring in a beast only semi-domesticated. Like her hands and her mouth were in the pay of different polities.

Again that smile. "If I sent all *my* staff away, people would talk. And if I didn't, they would *talk*." The way the Usmiat were, about these things. That everyone knew they went on, but they must go on behind closed doors, and unmentioned. And this *hadn't* been *going on*. Not since before the coronation. Not since the death of Kakrops had driven a wedge between the throne and the Palleseen, while also binding them irrevocably together.

"Gil," said Dekamran. Standing there in his borrowed clothes, like the Alkhand from the stories going about the city incognito to hear what his people said about him. Just that. Just her name.

"You – we – can't just," she said.

"I can't live with a wall between us," he said simply. "I miss you. The *you* I had, and the *I* I was, before. And so I come to you. Must I beg?"

Spreading his arms. Practically baring his chest. If she'd ever wanted to turn regicide, there would be no better time for it. Dekamran, the man who could have been the great enlightened Alkhand, if history had planted him in a soil to nurture such a man, and such an age. But instead he'd found this poison garden, and future histories would never know his virtues, and never be kind to him.

She moved towards those arms, and stopped. He had come to her. He would beg. She understood. Or understood one way of it. The Alkhand of Usmai would beg. Because she was not Angilly, the woman. Right now, right here, she was Pallesand, the empire. He was the man, come to beg the woman to take him back, despite everything and no matter which of them was to blame for what. He was the foreign ruler, offering what he could so that his people might be spared. A bitter taste came to her mouth. She tried to make it the first. She wanted so badly for it to be the first. For things to somehow be the way they had been, between them. But the gall was on her tongue because, whatever either of them wanted or intended, that second had moved into their relationship like a noisy lodger that couldn't be ignored.

If I take his hand. If I give in to him. If I lead him upstairs. Anything beyond the wine and a word and seeing him out the door. If I take what he offers, I am making a bargain on behalf of Pallesand. I am agreeing to keep denying Drathel's request, to push back against the merchants and temper the demands of my countryfolk. I am accepting a private tribute from Usmai. A bribe of flesh and joy.

She wanted to, very very much. She knew she couldn't. Dekamran watched her, sipping his wine. The man who needed his lover; the regent who must buy his nation's pawned wellbeing. She couldn't. She would still try to steer her course so that Usmai could retain its tattered dignity and pride, but she could not accept what he offered, just because she wanted it.

He looked so vulnerable. Any young man who has bared his heart to a woman who can just say no.

When she held him, it was just like before. His body, soft, comforting. The warmth of him. The way her chin fit into the crook of his shoulder. When she led him upstairs, into sovereign Palleseen territory and dodging all the border checks, it was just like before.

Mosaic: The Tide

The approach to the harbour of Alkhalend is complex at night, but if a visitor doesn't make the attempt then it's stand well out at sea or risk being driven into the wall. A series of lights are exchanged, between ship and shore, and the night shift of the dock stevedores scurry to find a berth of the right dimensions and launch a pilot. In this case the nature of the visitor is already pre-suspected. The dockers of Alkhalend's Water Lanes have their own longstanding codes and conventions but the newcomer is using Pal-standard lights. Not unknown even before the accession of the current Alkhand but, back then, an excuse to make a visitor wait until more obliging traffic was catered for. Right now, any vessel running Pal signals is best got into berth swiftly, because you never know how high the complaints might rise if you leave them waiting.

No surprise to the pilots, then, when there are uniforms at the railing of the *Salient*. A trim merchantman that would still have given any Cotto or other pirate a rude shock if they'd tried to take liberties. Despite their love of compartmentalisation, the Pals retain a long tradition of fight-worthy merchantmen on the seas that goes back to the old Fisher King cult. When a visiting vessel might turn trader or raider depending on the quality of your coastal defences.

The *Salient* rounds the fortified end of the sea wall. If it were the old Islermen come to call they'd be on their best behaviour in the face of those brooding ports and fortifications, but the

Pals have more efficient ways to take a town, Outreach, for one. Bringing influence in through the side door where the world might suspect, but can't know for sure.

At berth, the master of the *Salient* provides minimal detail to the dockside officials, relying on a precedent that Gil began after Dekamran's elevation to heir presumptive, and which has only been built on in the month since the man rose to the throne. Pal ships aren't searched, their cargoes neither impounded nor taxed. You take what they state at face value because the Alkhand won't protect you if they complain. Which they will. Local merchants and those from ports outside the Sway may curse the unfair competition, but they can whistle as far as the current regime goes. It isn't even the Alkhand putting his own royal thumb on the scales so much as every grade of functionary and bureaucrat knowing which side of the bread has butter on it.

The *Salient* declares only passengers, and these stay aboard for now, save for a mere handful of messengers. Men and women who go tripping across the face of the city hunting out a very specific handful. The chief visitor aboard wishes to update his intelligence before making more formal contact. To see if, at this eleventh hour, things have changed.

So it is that, before dawn, Fellow-Archivist Drathel is woken at her lodgings and hailed to go perfect her accounts before Sage-Broker Berkely.

Under other circumstances, another time or place, word would run hotfoot up to the Residence that a Pal vessel had arrived. Exactly the sort of thing the Resident should know. Gil is off her game, though, because that game changed fundamentally on Dekamran's accession. She has been full of a higher-level backbiting and turmoil that doesn't leave much room for subterfuge and tradecraft. And nobody at the docks or elsewhere thinks so fondly of her as to let her know off their own backs.

She can find out in the fullness of time. And so they let her sleep.

Other eyes do mark the visitor. Nearby in the Water Lanes, Hullseer Orhuhst, king of the Cotto – those within arm's reach at least – ponders the *Salient*'s arrival. He is pirate chief, ship's captain, first over the rail in a clash of timbers. He is also priest, votary, a life dedicated to the hungry maw of the shark god the Cotto venerate. This doesn't mean he's automatically opposed to the Pals. Sometimes they're useful. Right now, though, they represent a noose about the neck of ship-taking in this part of the seas.

Orhuhst casts some omens. Not the full ceremony, not the old way, which would involve tattooing one of his crew with sacred symbols, getting them out of their heads on hus fortified with jellyfish-derived mind-whack, sewing them into the skin of a seal and then trawling them behind the ship covered in blood until the sharks came. That's for holidays and, honestly, other places. God's all very well but it's not exactly an approved spectator sport around here.

The omens tell only of that noose tightening. The Pals aren't going anywhere, and perhaps he and his floating court will need to dance down the coast somewhere else, soon enough. Orhuhst has business in the city, though. There is the matter of the girl.

He knew her when she came to him, that first night. The moment her feet hit the planks of the Water Lanes he knew her, and a little offering of blood and ink and gall ensured her path crossed his. Someone special. Sewed up inside another Pal's identity like a sacrifice in a sealskin. Loret.

And now his voices tell him the girl isn't safely burrowed into the shell of the Pal Residence but out on the streets. He has eyes on her. The clan of foreign magicians and sawbones who have her are safe enough for now, but soon he'll have to take her. Open her up and let out what's inside her, if it's going to be like that. He will make contact. Not like the clan up at the Lodge are immune to a greased palm or a threat or a favour owed.

And now this. His omens tell him that at least a faint string or two, glistening red in the water, connects the *Salient* with Loret, as it does with many other things. The tide is changing, bringing in the sort of flotsam that can foul a hull.

Because they don't have the big things to worry about, the denizens of the Fever Lodge also hear about the *Salient* before Gil. A Pal ship putting in, crammed to the gills with troops, is news that has feet running to many quarters across the city. People who are very dearly concerned with just how tight the Pal hand is going to clench around Alkhalend. And nobody brings a couple of hundred troopers and some Accessories on a merchantman refitted as a troop carrier unless some manner of business is meant.

It's Tally and the Reckoner awake before the dawn for a very early breakfast, because neither of them ever learned the habit of sleeping in. Not actively conspiring, exactly, but there is most certainly a conspiracy underway. Jack's plan, that has him up at the House of Hard Angles all hours. Words only spoken outside the ears of casual visitors. And nobody's entirely sure about Loret. Right now she's just a barnacle on the hull of the Lodge and they may yet scrape her off.

The runner, a dockwoman whose son didn't lose a leg despite having it slip between two closing hulls, tells the news swiftly and carefully. A good observer in a part of town that sees a lot of traffic, she even identifies the Accessories as probably from Oloumann far to the north. Which Tally knows could mean all sorts of trouble, but just the official above-board Pal trouble is probably enough.

It'll complicate everything. More boots on the streets. The hands of the Pals gone from just gripping lapels like a thug to clutching throats like a strangler. A formal list of the wanted, deserters and fugitives all. Steps to bring Usmai formally into the Sway. Each and every option certainly possible, and only adding to everyone's trouble.

Tally turns to her breakfast kedgeree sourly. Three years in Alkhalend. Like a home to some of them, though maybe not her. To Oathan's boy, the only place he's ever known not run to the strict rhythms of Pal military order. She's seen him about the streets, nimble as a monkey, boasting and jeering and running away. Not that she ever had children or maternal instincts, but it made her smile a little, so long as nobody was looking at her. And Caecelian's girl, and maybe even Loret given time. They'd become quite the horrible multigenerational family with her as matriarch. Responsible, even though she'd never asked for it. Not entirely clear to her why, after they'd fled the army together, she'd ended up leader. The old Accessory, the former priestess, the cooling coal of what she'd once been. Probably because she was the only one of them who had any sense, honestly.

"When Jack's up," she tells the Reckoner, "he needs to get right back down to his club. Find out how ready that nasty son of a bitch actually *is*. If we can pull this stunt off at all. Or else we're fucking out, and he's on his own."

At last, Gil. Waking into vague memory. Sleep's fog, garnished with the ramaht they'd shared, then the wine he'd brought. The good stuff, from Stouk, that he knew she liked. Not believing, quite. Clawing at the boundary between dream and waking like someone fumbling through layers of curtains to get to the sun.

He's still there. In her bed, here at the Residence. Forbidden, by Pal ordinance and Usmiat tradition both. The Alkhand. Not the Alkhand. Just Dekamran, for as long as he still sleeps and the hand of responsibility lets go its grip of his face.

She rolls over, warms herself against his back. The softness of him, where a soldier would be taut muscle and maybe a scar or two from the lash. Puts her chin into the dip between his neck and his shoulder, where it fits.

We have done a bad thing, she thinks. Because it's preferable to, *I have done a bad thing and he has done a pragmatic one.*

The knock that comes on the heels of the sun startles her. She waits for the servants to stir, but there's silence. She dismissed them. Not to be back before noon. She's going to have to answer her own door.

She rises, robes, hauls a shawl over hair that needs time to get settled. Whoever her visitor is, they probably aren't ready for the basilisk stare she's going to give them.

The bright young woman in uniform at her door is basilisk-proof, offering the sort of official writ Gil's very familiar with. Gil's presence, as Resident, is respectfully requested in the wardroom of the *Salient*. A luncheon, a chance to give her report on the current status quo of Usmai, a gap into which a variety of other official purposes might be fit. Under the order of Sage-Broker Berkely, Correct Exchange, Valuations department.

Gil stares at it. Nods to the messenger, who probably assumes she's only staff and not the actual Resident actually answering her own actual door.

Gil retreats back inside.

She wakes Dekamran. Watches his face to see if those first moments will tell her any truth about the inner man and how he truly feels. Then stops, in case she finds out. Better to live with suppositions than die in possession of the facts.

"You have to go," she tells him. "Something's come up."

Dekamran sits up. Gives her that smile, the one she's desperate to be real and not just his polite face, his *keeping Gil sweet* face. "I mean," he says, "I think they probably need me for something, over at the palace. They usually do." Very casual. Just like things used to be, between them.

"What?" he asks, then. She has her polite face on. He can't see behind it.

"Are you…?" His hand up, but she flinches back before he can touch the glint on her cheek.

"I'm sorry," she says. She doesn't know what for yet.

She dresses herself after he's crept out to rejoin his escort – who probably suspect but can't *know* and that's the point. Maybe it was just a whole night of turbulent negotiations and not a boundary crossed. She's mostly made do with little to no staff. It was always how things were. Not having even Loret to hand to hold a mirror is a pain, but the Palleseen Resident is used enough to her near-Usmiat dress that she doesn't need a maid to help her into it. She splashes water across her shoulders and the back of her neck. A uniform jacket, tight at the collar and the cuffs, would be murder by midday.

That morning, she makes sure she's up to date with correspondence, in case any of it relates to the new visitors. A senior officer has just turned up on her patch. Sage-Broker Berkely might have clandestine orders from Outreach, or he might be here with Correct Exchange's latest dodge, or to oversee a new swathe of factories that someone wants to gift to Usmai, or he might just want to expand his exotic seashell collection. If it's the latter then Gil will scour the beaches herself, honestly.

As she steps out, she has a surprise visitor. None other than 'Flint' Postry, freshly returned from the ruin of the Tesemera. Stained jacket over his shoulders and shirt unbuttoned halfway to his navel. Wanting to know what's going on.

"Barely had two hours with a pillow under my head," he complains, as they wind their way through the streets together, "before some officious little twat with a Sage's writ is hollering me out from digs."

"Not my doing," Gil promises him. "And no idea. Still, always good to know they've not forgotten us, back home." That cynical soldier's smile between them, two people more than happy to be on their own recognizance.

The wardroom of the *Salient* is the most Palleseen place Gil's sat down in since she came to Usmai. Even Palinet's Residence over in Peor has a certain encroachment of local décor. Sage-Broker Berkely is fresh out of the Archipelago, though.

People leaving his presence tend to have the impression of a neat little man, like a filing clerk promoted past his station, none of which is true. He's taller than Gil, shorter than Flint, and quite long in the arm. A man made by nature to mug incautious night travellers in alleys or creep into second storey windows, placed behind a desk and taught double entry book-keeping. Correct Exchange is that branch of perfection that keeps track of weights and measures, coin and commerce. They count everything in the Sway and, of all the things they count, some small but important percentage finds its way to the islands.

His eye takes in Flint's almost defiant dishevelment, Gil's local dress. Berkely is in full uniform, as are his ship's master, senior aides and the Companion-Monitor who commands his sizeable escort. The windows of the wardroom are thrown open, and down the length of the table there are things that look like lamps, but whose tablethi-charge is devoted to cooling the air. It's still close and muggy in there, but Berkely's collar is done up right to the chin.

"Sage-Invigilator Angilly, delighted to make your acquaintance. Needless to say, I've read all your reports," he says pleasantly. His people pour spiced wine, the naval ration that tastes of orange – more the colour than the fruit honestly – but keeps scurvy at the stave's end.

"You're very kind," Gil says warily. "And I'm at a disadvantage. No word—"

"What you've done here, in so short a time," Berkely goes on as the soup is set out. A good Pal recipe, its surface a crispy skin. Gil recalls it from the phalanstery without much joy. Her palate has travelled widely and picked up more exotic tastes than Archipelago cuisine.

"To turn the regime and have them so dependent on us.

Honestly, I raise a glass to the pair of you. A masterstroke," Berkely says happily.

They match his raised glass, receive the general approbation of the table. There is another shoe to drop, and Gil reckons it's a heavy one. Right now this feels like death by a thousand compliments.

"Fellow-Monitor," Berkely addresses Flint, "before I forget" – he's not a man who forgets a thing, Gil is sure – "there's the matter of garrisoning. My people have been crammed aboard for longer than I'd like. Can I pass to you the responsibility of finding them space ashore?"

"Of course, magister," Flint says. "How, ah, long for, can I ask? Only I can shift some lads around but—"

"Well, permanently, of course," Berkely says. "They are the new garrison."

Gil and Flint don't exchange a look because, if they had, everyone would have marked and read it.

"Berkely," she says, because she's a Sage and he's a Sage and so it can be just names between them. "I think you've outsailed your own prep. What sort of a brief are we looking at?"

There is just the tiniest glint in his face. A man who knows exactly how fast he's sailed, and made very sure no little birds outpaced him. The other thing the Brokers do, that endears them to nobody, is auditing.

"Well then," he says, as though it's been a fun little game but that's over now. "The Commission of Ends and Means is, obviously, delighted at your progress here in Usmai. *Usmai*, after all. Not just some little tinpot kingdom of savages, but a bastion of elder civilization, and practically ready to join the Sway with barely a shot fired."

Flint shifts at that, because he and his put quite a number of shots out there, up to and including into a god, but in the grander Pal scheme of things apparently that doesn't really count as much more than harsh language.

"The administration is keen to move things on to the next

logical step," Berkely says. "Hence Valuations sent me over to assess what you've built here, make recommendations, get some wheels turning, you know how things are."

Gil nods pleasantly, Flint warily.

"So bunks for four hundred, if you would. Two hundred and fifty regulars and a hundred fifty Accessories who can probably just camp out somewhere. And after that I'd be very much obliged if you could show me around your own people. I've heard such things."

Flint nods, face that of a man wrangling difficult calculations. A number of locals are about to be evicted from *somewhere* to make room.

Gil opens her mouth and Berkely sidesteps her neatly by saying, "Ah, that was it! I knew something was eluding me. Your aide, Angilly."

She scrabbles for purchase on the conversation. "Yes, only I'd thought—"

"There have obviously been some serious errors back home, and I'm carrying Outreach's sincere apologies. Nobody seems to know how it happened. Some little bureaucratic mix-up." Berkely's face, the slight sheen of sweat completing the picture of a waxy mask, not living features at all. Behind the holes of his eyes Gil sees a great deal of knowledge about how things are back home that he is not going to make the gossip of the wardroom table. And if she butters him properly, or finds the weak point in his staff, she'll find out. She's seen the scraps Loret let fall and she's heard the two fugitive scholars. She very much needs to find out the latest from home. Because that home, that unknown place with its murky recent history, has spat out this new complication just as she was getting her own house back in order.

There's a young man at Berkely's shoulder. Very neat, enough that even the Sage-Broker looks a little shabby. Less a human being and more a drawing out of a manual on how to properly carry the uniform.

"Companion-Invigilator Samellers," Berkely introduces him. "Your new aide. Your *proper* aide. And amongst his duties will be apprehending whoever it was who was masquerading as your previous aide. All unknown to you." A very definite jab of criticism. *You, a Resident, and you never knew! Dear me!* Gil smiles pleasantly, seethes inwardly, not least because it's true.

She nods to Samellers, the immaculate. If she'd had a protractor and a set square, doubtless she'd find his answering nod to be within point two of a degree of the regulation standard. He is going to be, she can already tell, an obstructive little shit.

"That's very kind of you," she tells Berkely. "It's been a chore keeping Residence business turning over without help. And yes, I'd value a chance to sit down with you and Samellers here. I need to draft a final report, on the fate of my previous aide, and a little perspective would work wonders because it's all been a bit of a mess." Finding herself, curiously, giving the impression that the case file on Loret has been closed, possibly fatally, rather than flagging up that the mad girl is still running about the streets of Alkhalend with a knife.

Berkely waves the matter off as beneath the dignity of a Sage-Broker. "I'll let Samellers brief you."

"And for yourself, if you're here for the duration, I'll arrange a presentation at the Alkhand's court," Gil went on. "I'm sure Fellow-Monitor Postry can incorporate your officers into his structure. I'll commandeer a townhouse for you – you'd prefer closer to the higher echelons of Alkhalendi society, or to the industrial district? And then doubtless you'll let me know how the Resident can facilitate your mission here."

"Aha, hm," said Berkely. Just a noise, really. Just a sort of verbal tic that shouldn't have been able to convey any information at all. Least of all the very clear import of *Ah no, Sage-Invigilator, things are not as you suppose at all. This rug you stand on, allow me to give it a sharp tug.*

"I do apologise," said Berkely unapologetically. "I perceive I may have given an incorrect impression of my presence here. I will of course be leaning a great deal on your *local* knowledge, Resident." A stress, on that word, that abruptly made Gil very conscious of her dress, his uniform. Made her feel like she was a child caught by the phal matron in the middle of raiding a costume chest. Made her – in these clothes that were so eminently practical for the climate, and were rather beautiful, and that she liked – feel ridiculous.

"However," said Sage-Broker Berkely, and smiled very thinly indeed. If it were butter over bread you'd not taste it. "The *Commission*," he said, that dread body, that guided the Palleseen Sway and from which he derived his direct authority, "is *delighted* by the *progress* made in Usmai by this partnership of Outreach and Ventures." A man laying out an inarguable syllogism, step by step. "To the extent that Usmai has progressed beyond those early stages of contact where the writ of either Outreach and Ventures runs. The Usmai operation has now passed into the hands of Valuations, preparatory to the nation being formally *invited* to become a part of the Palleseen Sway. Your ongoing assistance will, of course, be invaluable in bringing this about, for as long as I have you. But doubtless there are other less-tamed shores in both your futures, in due course." Watching them. Lifting a glass. "To your success, though." The thing that Gil and Flint had both just become victims of.

Foundlings

Loret and Enshili, sitting up atop the second story of the ramshackle that the Lodge was part of. The healers spread their domain wide like a stain through the lowest floor, but not high. Given the architecture, though, no feat of acrobatics to find where a flat section of roof forms a makeshift balcony. There, after sunset, they sit side by side, legs dangling. Two daughters of the Lanes, girls come into possession of adulthood without prospects or hope, for all one's a scion of conquerors, the other a sister of the Alkhand. The district is full of scenes like this. Young fry of Alkhalend looking into the night for a divination that mostly only has the one answer.

"What is she, though?" Loret asked. "Really."

"You must know," Caecelian's girl said. "She says you Pals have no qualms about using her kind. Even over here, the new chief of soldiers keeps a stable of them. I saw them myself, the night it happened."

Loret nodded. "No. I mean, yes, I've seen… Not on the Archipelago, the islands, so much. Not *them*. We – they – keep them to the Sway, amongst the – the foreigners. But I saw them in action. They sent them in for – when we… when it happened. Not even the worst of it. But they didn't want to get their own living human hands dirty, in the end."

Caecelian's girl, not up on Loret's provenance, watched her.

"But I know they do what they're told. Contracted, isn't it?" Loret went on. How she'd wanted to talk to *anyone* for an age.

How she'd wanted to talk to Angilly, really. She'd wanted to be Angilly's friend somehow. The Resident with her sword and her determination, just striding about the city and making things happen. And if Loret had opened the door to her even a little, she'd have ended up confessing everything. Thrown herself on a mercy that maybe even existed. Angilly wasn't like the people back on the Archipelago. Loret had seen that straight off. But she hadn't dared shift that door more than a crack, and she'd got angry, and then... it had all come out the worst way. She hadn't been able to pull it off. She was weak and stupid and just... a waste. A waste of everything that had been shed for her and done to her.

"Not her," the girl said. Her voice shone when she spoke about her mentor. Loret envied her bitterly. "She got free. It was when I understood that, that I knew I wanted... this. This life. To be like her." Even though Loret was absolutely positive the girl could never be like *her*. "Because I had a lot of *things*, back before I came here. But I never had that. Just people telling me what I would be."

"Yes," whispered Loret. The girl glanced at her and she forced out the words, "Yes, I see." Like someone had punched her in the gut and she was trying to talk around it. Waiting for the moment to snap.

"My father," the girl said, with a certain emphasis that told Loret probably she should know who the girl's father had been, "knew what I was. And my brothers knew what I was. And all the other people, big men and women, they knew. So nobody ever bothered to find out. Only my littlest brother even cared, and he's dead. He made himself dead." The girl hunched forwards. "I helped him. He wanted it more than anything."

Loret nodded, judging nothing.

"With her, I'm free. Because if she can escape what the world had set for *her*, then I can. Anyone can. She was supposed to be someone's slave *forever*." They were talking in Usmiri larded with Pel where Loret's linguistics didn't stretch. *That* word had been imported from the Dead Empire, though, with the appropriate literal denotation. "Now she'll run for as long as she can, before anyone can chain her again. And she'll take me with her. We'll hurt. We'll be hungry. Our feet will bleed. But we'll still run. She can't love me." A sudden break in the girl's voice, as though, in that notional running, she'd hit rocky ground. "She says. Not me, not Jack, not anyone properly. But she says she'll try, for as long as she can. If she could love, she'd love me. I'm her greatest work of wickedness."

Loret honestly didn't follow all of that, but the overall tenor was plain enough. And surely demons couldn't love. It felt like something so obvious that nobody even needed to ask the question. Which maybe meant nobody actually knew the answer.

"Freedom," she said, "is wasted on some people."

The girl turned on her angrily but Loret's expression stopped whatever biting words had risen in her.

"I am here because I made bad choices," Loret said simply. "If I'd just done what was expected I'd be fine. I'd be happy, probably. Because I wouldn't know any better. If I'd been *normal.*"

The girl waited. This was the well Loret had been waiting to be opened in *anyone*, ever since it had all happened. Just this silence, this waiting for her to say. Angilly had never gone so far, full of her own business. Too much a part of the thing Loret had been fleeing.

"It was a cult," she said.

"I thought you Kepishi didn't do cults," the girl said, and Loret shut down again, feeling the well closed before she could recklessly hurl herself down it. And probably for the best. This was a girl with a demon as a mentor. Not someone you bared your heart to, surely. Every word you gave them would be a knife in their hand. Loret might as well write a signed confession and send it to the new Pal ship in harbour.

After a little space of silence, there came a light touch on her arm. She looked sidelong to see the Usmiat girl regarding her. *Go on.* As though this impromptu balcony was some magic space, where anything could be said without consequence.

Below, a patrol marched past, the worms that had been running through the spoiled apple of the Sand Lanes more and more since the newest Alkhand's accession. And more again since the new ship disgorged its complement. Men and women in that familiar dark coat she'd once worn.

"I was new in the army," Loret said, very carefully. Constructing her confession like someone working from plans without really knowing what the end edifice would look like. "It was the last year of the war. They were throwing everyone at the Loruthi. I was seventeen. They aren't supposed to send you till you're eighteen, but…

"I saw a lot of fighting. Just in a few months. And there was this statlos. That's like a…"

The girl's nod at the edge of Loret's vision showed she knew what a statlos was.

"Said we needn't fear getting hurt. We could sign up to something. Made it sound like it was… There was a pool, in the company. You put some of your pay in, and if someone got invalided out, they got a share. Or their folk, if they got killed. She made it sound like that. I didn't even realise it *was* a cult for an age. But there was a god. A god who would heal you, if you got hurt. Not straight-out dead hurt, but just about anything else. You signed a thing. To say if you were hurt, and healed, you'd belong to this god and do what He said." And she heard the old intonation come into her voice, speaking of the god she'd sworn to once. The reverence, the implicit capital, that Pel shouldn't have been able to support, but somehow did in this one specific case. He. God.

"Sign up to something," Caecelian's girl echoed, with entirely reasonable doubt. That didn't sound like god stuff, to her. It maybe sounded like demon stuff. What it actually was, was *Pal* stuff. A people who never found anything useful they couldn't boil down to words on paper. It was one reason why they kept winning.

"I signed. And this God, all He wanted of you," that same emphasis, and she hated herself for it. Even though she'd betrayed God in the end, she still couldn't stop herself, "was to not hurt people. That was what you agreed to. Once you're healed, you don't harm. Simple."

"So what happened when you were healed?" the girl asked. Absolutely hanging on the words, wonder of wonders. This sorry, sad, sordid tale of Loret's, flowering here in foreign soil.

"I never was," Loret said softly. "I never got hurt. The war ended. We went home. I saw it happen. Real miracle healing. I saw someone with their skull cracked open. I saw a leg come back. We all knew God had our backs, in the army. And the medicos, and the officers even. Not a word said, but people got healed and then they found duties that didn't mean holding a baton. It was like *everyone* knew. Like… this was the whole Palleseen Sway now. This secret that meant you got a second chance at life. We went home full of it. That statlos, everyone. Just full of God. And we found out that everyone hadn't known, but we were so full of it they soon enough found out. And you're right. We don't do cults, we Palleseen. It's like the number one thing we don't do. The thing we absolutely can't have going on, not even healing cults that mean our soldiers don't just die. Imperfect. Bad. Wrong. Because God doesn't have a rank badge and doesn't fit in the chain of command so we can't have people doing what He says.

"So they started sending people to camps. Just army camps at first, only you worked out that every company had God people in it. And then there were other people, not army people, and by then we were three to a bunk and it wasn't just an army camp. And they made sure nobody had a baton, not that most of us could even have used one, and the soldiers on the outside weren't those who'd signed up. And they weren't allowed to talk to us in case they caught it. They said we were sick. Like a plague. And it got worse. More people, less food. And then worse.

"We scared them. It was stupid, really. Of all the people in the world we were the last ones to be scared of. When the soldiers beat us, we didn't even fight back. Didn't even help each other. Couldn't. I saw someone who did. Just punched a soldier who'd been kicking someone on the ground. They died, the one who threw a punch. Their chest opened. Like a flower. Where the shot had gone in, that time before. That was when I saw how it was going to be. A lot of us did. Because they were scared of us, but soon enough they realised they didn't have to be. People kept getting sent into the camps but then they started taking groups out, too. People who didn't come back. And then worse."

Loret clammed up then, because she'd already spilled God's secrets, but that didn't mean she didn't have more betrayals in her. She'd betrayed the Palleseen Sway for God, and later she'd betrayed Angilly for Drathel, and in between she'd betrayed God, too. Turning coat felt like the staples holding her life together, and if you'd taken those moments of false faith from her history she'd collapse like a disjointed puppet.

The freedom that Caecelian's girl bemoaned, that the girl's mentor clung to, and that Loret had squandered at every turn. Only bad decisions.

She remembered the knives going in, with the assassins in the House of Hard Angles. Going into the attackers, going into her. Both sacred exchanges, but none of God's. Because when the fit was on her, she had no control over it, nor a thought for her own survival. Small wonder the Pals found cults so easy to crush, if putting on a robe and adoring an idol equated to losing all sense of self-preservation. She remembered stabbing the Louse Monk at that weird little monastery village, when Angilly had been attacked. She remembered the overwhelming rage that had risen in her at Slate House, that she'd fled rather than add the Resident to her tally. And these were not singular aberrations. She'd gone in to the elbows in blood more times than these. God had washed His hands of her in disgust. And other hands had caught her.

"In the camps, towards the end, when we all understood we were going to die," she told the girl, "other priests were there. Rounded up and thrown in with us. Not God's people. Not peaceful people. They said we could fight. They said their god loved it, the blood and the pain and the fear. I'd seen blood and pain and fear by then. Felt it. Been beaten. Seen the spaces where people had been taken away, before more people got thrown in to fill them. It would be me, soon. Eighteen. I was eighteen." It seemed a thousand years ago. "God had never healed me. He couldn't touch me. I said yes. To the new priests. Because if I didn't, then the blood and the pain and the fear would belong to the soldiers who were keeping us there. But if I did, they could be mine, too. Just a little."

They'd inducted her. The camp had been on a cliff, so there was nowhere to run. One night, in a storm, they'd taken her to the edge. Made her fall. Caught her only after she'd known it was too late for anyone to catch her. Cut her. Cut themselves. Made her taste a mix of their bloods and the rain. The salt of it. The rush of it. Not helpless. Not doomed to God's meek death. Sworn to a new master. The old lord of the isles. The Fisher King whose resurgent cult was rushing about the ankles of the Palleseen state like an incoming tide.

She tried to speak, to fully complete that betrayal, tell this girl the secrets of her other mystery. She couldn't, in the end. Not for fear of divine retribution or reverence for the sea-stinking sacredness of it all, but just because, what was it? Blood and fear and death, just like the soldiers brought. Except in the name of some ancient sea-thing, rather than for perfection. Amazing how little different it looked, from the shore.

Then there was movement below again. Not another patrol, but two figures coming briskly up to the doors of the Fever Lodge.

"That's Jack," Caecelian's girl identified, meaning the smaller of the two. "Come on. Let's see what he's got."

They kicked up from their seat. The girl's hand found Loret's arm, clasped, clenched. In her face were no platitudes, no *It will be all right*, no assurance that every action or event would be justified by gods or God or perfection or any of it. No admission that the world was anything other than a storm of chaos and misfortune. *Misery and wickedness*, Loret remembered her saying, as though it was a catechism to answer everything. As bad as the sea cult's blood-creed, surely, save that there was no room in *Misery and wickedness* for a master telling you what to do. That was Caecelian's freedom. Misery and wickedness from high to low, horizon to horizon. The thought of it sped Loret's heart a little, or else it was the girl's hand on her arm.

She had a vision, then. In that moment as they were about the scramble down. They came to her sometimes. It was a part of what she'd agreed to. One of those many bad choices. The stink of brine and rotting weed, a closure of the ears as though waters washed over her. A presentiment that, of the people she'd met on this shore, many would be dead before long. The tackiness of blood on her own hands.

Then the girl was pulling at her, and they skittered down and slipped inside on Jack's heels to see what was going on.

What brought Loret up short, inside, wasn't that the Fever Lodge's whole complement was assembled there. It was who Jack had ushered inside ahead of him. The big, bony man shrugging a cloak off, staring around as though he'd been invited to his own assassination.

"I thought," she said faintly, "that he was trapped. In the House."

She'd spoken very quietly but the haunted gaze of the

Under-warden clicked round to pin her even so, until Caecelian's girl had to literally stand in the way to free her.

"Not him," the girl said. "*She* is."

"What's going on?" Loret asked. They had one of the medical tables out, and papers over it, that Tally the surgeon was even now pinning down to keep them flat. *Maps*, she thought, because they were like officers planning an assault. Except what she saw there looked more like maths than maps. Circles and diagrams and calculations. And they were all there, too. The Reckoner, even Caecelian. A full-on assembly of Higher Orders.

"She," said Oathan, the big man who didn't like her, "is not a part of this." And true, most of them didn't like her much, but Oathan liked almost nobody, and her least of all.

"Neither am I," Caecelian said. The girl's mentor had been idling at the edge of the group, and Jack at least plainly thought that she *was*. He caught the woman's eye, raised his eyebrows, mummed at the table and the calculations.

"Only I thought," he said mildly, "you'd have, you know, insights." His weird, lilting accent, whatever distant part of the Sway he'd been conscripted from. "Fish and the sea, you know."

"A fish can tell you nothing of the sea," Caecelian said, not unkindly – Jack was just about the only person she kept her edge sheathed for, when speaking. "Being so much *of* it." She pushed off from the wall, tousled his mop of sandy hair in passing, and then looked to Loret. Caecelian looking straight at you was like being stabbed and feeling the meat and weight of you hanging off the blade.

"My apprentice likes you, for some reason," the demon said. "Come." Opening the door they'd just come in by, the cool of the night's breathing rolling in. Tally pinned down a final piece of paper before the stir of air could lift it from the table.

Loret didn't want to go anywhere with a demon. She did want to go where Caecelian's girl went. Who else did she have to cling to? And so, when the pair of them stepped out, she was in their shadow. The wretched one, the knife one, the serial betrayer of creeds. Fitting company for Caecelian, surely.

Behind them, Oathan snapped out, "Not you!" as his boy tried to absent himself too. And then then door closed on the lot of them like a trap. Save that Loret misunderstood which side of the bars she'd ended up.

Caecelian was good enough – at deception, false hopes, all the traditional demon things – that Loret had forgotten to be wary when it happened. They'd been shadowing and dodging Pal patrols, playing skip with the Sand Lanes' new custodians. Loret, formerly of the uniform, lost herself in seeing how the light of that lantern extended such a short distance; when you were holding it aloft yourself, it seemed that you could see forever, but really it just made the shadows deeper. They weren't even the only skulkers about that night. The Sand Lanes crawled with nocturnal traffic that the patrols never saw. Their course ran between drinking dens and houses of ill repute and midnight Taumachy arenas where ill-made wooden monsters made from a menagerie of discarded parts tore one another apart for fun and profit. Caecelian met with Beast Artists, paint and sawdust on their hands as they reassembled new combatants from the remnants of the old. She met with a big Pal man who was a smuggler, and whose eyes devoured her as he handed over herbs and tablethi for practically nothing. She met with a moustachioed bravo with an accent like Jack's who spoke in low tones of who was fleeing the Lanes and where they might be going. A hollow centre to their conversation, as of a point of the compass never mentioned but figured into everyone's calculations.

And then Caecelian met with the Cotto and Loret understood she'd been stitched up. They slipped down into a cellar that stank of rot and the sea, that must flood to the brim every high tide. A sacred place, she knew. It spoke right to her, in her heart, where she'd written her most recent betrayal of faith over all the others.

Hullseer Orhuhst and his court, a half-dozen of them. The woman with the sharpened teeth grinned at her, as glad to see her as the shark is the seal.

Loret tried to bolt, but Caecelian, who had absolutely been ahead, was behind her now, on the dank stairs, hand to her sword. And Loret's own was to her knife, clasped there just like a good cultist's should be. It was always knives, the way Pals envisaged the sinister and hidden forces of religion. And God hadn't had much use for knives save for eating with, but Loret's new master was more than willing to play to every Pal stereotype. He was, after all, the cult they'd known best, before they rid themselves of it.

"What is it?" asked the girl. Not in on it. Not betraying Loret The Betrayer to this new fate. Her own sword ready to draw, even, to defend she knew not what.

Caecelian looked at her protégé's hand. "Who would you draw for?" she asked.

The girl looked from her to Orhuhst, biting her lip. "Me," she said. "Against anyone. If I have to."

The demon woman laughed, delighted. "Good. Well, let's see if you have to, childling, and who you're fighting." Her eyes found the pirate king. "I brought her."

"You did." His barbarous accent, serving the neat, trim words of Pel like his ships would serve a lost merchantman.

"What is it?" the girl demanded again.

"Your new friend," said Caecelian, "stinks of gods. And fish. Which is its own particular flavour of wickedness, it's true. But it's a knife that has two edges, childling, and I want to know who it's going to cut."

Loret felt her arm clench. Orhuhst stood forwards from his fellows. He had a knife, too. He had a god, too. Not the old Pal god, obviously. Not the dark storm-and-sea monster they'd worshipped once, then grown sick of. Found too costly in blood and treasure and faith. The monstrous shark god the Cotto venerated was a world away from the Fisher King. Fish and fisher, after all, existing at opposite ends of ideology. Except it was all the same ocean. All the blood shed for either cult ran into it and mingled and mixed, along with every other horrible sect that howled to the moon and tides and held holy some kraken or leviathan, some set of jaws or pincers or tentacles from the lightless depths. And so, even though she was probably their enemy and their rival, she who had had the Fisher King's consecration poured into her was yet holy to them.

The thought of it made her queasy. She could still taste the salt and iron of it. When the camp had been surrounded. When they'd sent the Dead Companies in, because they wouldn't trust the living not to come out infected by one creed or another, the faithful'd had to choose. And there had been Loret. And then Loret had been killed, and there'd only been *her* to step into the shoes, take on the name and the papers and the hideous burden of sacrament. To smuggle all that sea-faith out of the islands.

"Yes," said Orhuhst. "She knows us. Special, to us. I thought it when she stepped off the boat. Helped you then, girl. Help you now."

"I don't want your help," she whispered.

Orhuhst grinned gold and murder at her. "Whoever does?" he asked. "Until the storm comes. The storm came for you, seachild. Did it not?"

She nodded. Didn't want to. Couldn't have stopped herself.

"A storm time," Orhuhst said. "A blood time. We need you, seachild. Caulk to our timbers. Stays to our masts."

"What are they going to do to her?" And Caecelian's girl drew her long skia from its sheath. Waiting for her mentor to hail her back.

"Will you see?" Caecelian asked her lazily. "What they do to her? The blood and the god of it? You don't have to. Come away with me, instead. This Pal creature you've just met, perhaps she will be dead soon. Then you don't have to care."

The girl looked at her, at Loret.

"This is what it means," Caecelian told her. "This is what it is like. To be like me. To care, and not to be able to care. I can't make you understand. But I am showing you."

"I don't want her to be alone," the girl whispered. Loret felt something breaking inside her. Like it had when she'd betrayed one faith for another. Not a promise of salvation. Still, more than she deserved.

Caecelian grinned. "Go trawl for your god," she told Orhuhst. "She's all yours."

The Value of Everything

The majority of Palleseen departments did. *The pieces of the machine, each to its small set task, up to and including the army, which* did *for foreign armed resistance on a grand scale. Some departments* knew, *a set of skills to be applied to a variety of tasks. Or else just knowledge looking for application, so that* know *could be turned into* do *as it had with necromancy or conjuration. Outreach* knew, *because every Outreach assignment was different. You couldn't learn the tradecraft by rote. A handful of departments, though,* administered. *Surely a tedious and inconsequential thing, a mere grease between the wheels of mightier engines. Save that it was* administration *that ran the Sway, without which* do *didn't get done and* know *remained unknown. Valuations* administered. *Specifically it came in behind the maverick* knowers *and ahead of the humdrum* doers *– including the army if necessary – and totted up all the accounts to determine just what was* known *and what must be* done.

Berkely had relocated to shore. A merchant's hall had been donated for his use by a clan of Emorandi who knew what was good for them and which way the wind was blowing. Still on the waterfront, with the *Salient* within signalling distance just in case, but definitely a foot in the door.

He'd seen a variety of Alkhalend's residents so far, some at his invitation, others petitioning of their own notion. The sharper of the Usmiats come to present gifts and indicate their willingness to play by Pal rules, properly tenderised and conditioned by all the good work that Angilly and Postry had put in. Opening lines of credit, suggesting mutually profitable arrangements, informing on rivals. The usual. It all went into Berkely's book, along with little diagrams of circles and connecting lines as he built a map of influence within the city. All very much within expectations. The model of a city half-tamed by circumstance and the hard work of Berkely's predecessors.

Other visitors had been Pals from within the city anxious to fit into any new hierarchy, or else foreign merchants and magnates not wanting to be left out. Either they were from nations within the Sway, in which case he could work with them within the usual limits, or else they were from nations yet to feel the benefits of Palleseen protection, in which case they might as well pack up and get on the next boat out because they were, Berkely considered, crap out of luck. He would use all of Pallesand's influence to ensure that anyone from beyond the reach of the Archipelago found Usmai a dry country to trade in, and maybe those lands would understand that accepting perfection really was good for your bottom line.

His latest guest settled down across from him, eyeing the wine. Berkely gave a nod and she poured a couple of light doses out, grinning at him. His look discouraged that, and the grin went back in her pack where she doubtless kept a variety of other commodities he wouldn't want to see openly traded across his desk. Ah, Decanting. Decanting *did* and also *knew*, which made it complex. It was also very much the lifeblood of the Palleseen economy, especially after the expense of the war. Cocky little shits like Drathel were clawing their way up the rank ladder all over if they could keep the lights on back home. Literally. There had been blackouts across some of the outlying islands at the height of the war because the same tablethi that powered the lamps had been putting holes in Loruthi soldiers via the army's batons.

"It's like this, magister." Drathel looked like she was physically restraining herself from putting her feet up on Berkely's desk. She already had one arm slung over the back of the chair, her jacket also. Not a respectful way to appear before a Sage-Broker, but that was Decanting for you.

"You heard about how the local cult came a cropper?" Drathel asked him.

"They have so many," he recalled. Really a painfully tedious quantity of monks. "You mean the frog, though?"

"Frog indeed, magister," Drathel confirmed. "Our valiant Fellow-Monitor Postry, who I passed in your waiting room, shot it up a treat. Laid down the law for the locals about just what kind of nonsense we'd accept from them. Being attacked by a giant frog not being included." Drathel drained the wine, eyed the bottle and retreated from it under Berkely's uninviting gaze. Her breed of roving Decanter would take anything not nailed down, in his experience.

"Thing is, though," Drathel said idly. "The Usrani – that's the frog monks – carved the old boy up and kept him. Morbid, I call it. But they stuck him in jars. That's a whole house-sized frog in about a hundred big stone jars, all sealed with wards and sigils. All anatomised – liver and lights and the lot. Godflesh, magister. And right, yes, big frog, what's the fuss? Except *godflesh*. I could refill every tableth on the Successor Coast with what's in those jars, magister. I could give you such a harvest of the good stuff that they'd be singing all our praises back home."

"I'm sorry to impose on your valuable time, Fellow-Archivist," said Berkely, "but Angilly has already made me aware of this, and…" The smooth words, but watching her with what he liked to think of as The Eyes of Correct Exchange. The ones that saw where the money went and how the scales balanced.

"I've done some calculations. Very much back-page-of-the-notebook given I've not gone up to my elbows in the jars yet," Drathel said, "but I reckon, conservative estimate, over a hundred thousand tab, all in. *Conservative* estimate, magister."

"You're not serious." She was serious, within limits. Every

Fellow pushing their agenda before a Sage would lard on the prospects, but Berkely reckoned the calculations of her trade was an area where the fly of Drathel's talk came down and folded its wings.

"Conservative," Drathel said, "means, with me, *at a minimum*. As in, *I guarantee you at least*."

"Well, duly noted," Berkely said. "Angilly has, as I said, alerted me to the prospect, but her reading of the situation is that making a play for it right now would destabilise the region. Regrettable local superstitions, to be tolerated until greater perfection, so on, so forth." One hundred thousand charged tablethi. Conservative estimate. "Unless…?"

"Permission to speak very freely indeed, magister." Drathel leaned back in her chair, meeting his gaze and not turning to stone even a bit. The very bold, ambitious Fellow.

"Permission to speak without the theatre," Berkely invited.

"Permission to speak without being put in your book there," Drathel went on. Apparently feeling she could dictate terms to her superior.

Still, a hundred thousand. And this was why you always had to make time for bloody Decanting even though they were such a mercenary shower. They were like those pigs you used to find the valuable mushrooms. So long as they still had a good nose, you didn't send them for sausages.

"Sage-Invigilator Angilly, our Resident," said Drathel, burlesquing a look of regret. "I have a tale or two, I'm afraid, to tell you. About her conduct, about her soundness, about just what strings are a-tugging at her professional judgment."

"You are making a formal—"

"I am not, magister, because I wasn't born yesterday and I know what happens to mouthy Fellows who start pointing fingers up the ladder. But I would like to speak now, without a word going in your book, and I would ask you to do me the credit of hearing me."

Berkely leaned back. He was a stern man. He was a man

who did things by the ordinances. He kept his jacket buttoned and his conduct within the precise trammels of approved limits. And he did all of this because he was, at heart, a brigand. In another life he'd have been picking over bodies on a battlefield, surprising travellers in a lonely pass, leaping over the rails of a raiding ship. And he'd have set his actions to precisely fit the mores of those trades, too. Just because he knew book-keeping and could carry on a polite conversation didn't mean he wasn't as fiercely acquisitive as any cutpurse or bandit.

"Well I suppose," he said, putting down his pen, "you'd better say what you have to."

Drathel had done her groundwork, he had to admit. Both her own observations, and information from within the Residence. Some of it was chaff, sure enough, not worth the weight Drathel gave it. So the aide was missing, maybe dead. The girl hadn't been a real aide, and she'd only have been executed if she was caught. So Angilly had killed the Loruthi envoy in an illegal personal duel? Honestly Berkely found that whole episode almost amusing, in a cringing sort of way. All very antique! Not exactly from the modern manual of diplomacy, but there *had* been a war, maybe Drathel had heard…?

Receiving two fugitives from Palleseen justice and letting them pass on without apprehending them, *that* was a disciplinary matter, true enough. Possibly Angilly would have a take on it that would let her squeak out of censure, though. Outreach had a lot of leeway built in.

And then the other thing. The morsel Drathel had been keeping back, knowing everything was small beans otherwise. If it had just been the duel and the aide and the two scholars, that would have left Berkely in a quandary, because he wanted the hundred thousand, same as Drathel. But while Angilly was technically subordinate to him in the Usmai operation now, she was still a Sage, and this wasn't enough ammunition to pierce that kind of plate. But the other thing. The damning, unprofessional thing.

"Really?" Berkely held himself steady. He felt a twitch of revulsion at the whole business. Not the act itself, because sometimes this was what Outreach did, when it was appropriate, when it helped the Sway. But at who seemed to have influenced whom, in the transaction. Whose interests were being looked after. Not Pallesand's.

"I mean," Drathel said with a shrug, "he's a nice-looking lad. I can see it. But he's got her tied in a proper knot, magister. It's not right."

It wasn't right. What it *was* was the door onto a hundred thousand tablethi, conservative estimate. Because it put all that earnest advice Angilly had given him in a very different light. All that tiptoeing around local sensibilities and maintaining the power of the crown.

"Local unrest, however," he noted. Because all these things could be true at once.

"Between Flint's people and your people and the ones we've got on loan from Palinet..." Drathel shrugged.

"And the rest," Berkely dropped in, and her eyes went wide for a moment and then came back sharp and calculating.

"I mean," the Decanter said, "we helped them cut their own balls off during their little civil war. Not like they've grown a new pair yet."

On her way out, he asked her to send in Fellow-Monitor Postry.

'Flint' Postry was in some godforsaken halfway state between the shabby creature Berkely had first seen, and a respectable soldier. Probably he'd turned up mostly in uniform but, sweltering in the waiting room, had slowly lost buttons and fastenings until various parts of it flapped off him. He hadn't shaved, either. A disreputable, unpresentable sight. But that was Ventures for you. You went into Ventures when you were hungry and broke. A lot of battlefield promotions from the war were ending up in that quarter these days, because otherwise you ended up with someone at your officer's table who didn't know how to hold a fork. Berkely recognised Flint, one brigand to another. Specifically, a brigand inside the house seeing one still lurking about the garden.

"Fellow-Monitor Postry, you've been making some use of your time."

Flint tried a small nod, correctly divining that the words could go either way. "Magister," he said, just like every soldier who doesn't know if he's in trouble yet.

"My own man has come back with quite a copious report on your military forces here. You've been improvising."

"Ventures, magister. It's what we do."

Berkely's nod conveyed that there was a time for what Ventures did and, insofar as Usmai was concerned, it was in the past. "These lizard creatures. Ibaleth?"

"Lizards, right." Flint was very tense, as though the ceiling might fall on him, or assassins leap from under the desk. A man who knows the ambush is somewhere. "Them and their monsters."

"The monsters cannot be separated from their… handlers?"

"Not that I could work out," Flint said. "And the lizard lads – lasses – they're keen. I mean, sure, they're lizards, but they know fighting. Don't have gods, so far as I could make out. Work with us. Work with the Usmiat. Worked with the Loruthi in the war. I saw them in action back then. Thought to myself, *I want one*. And here I am with twenty on the payroll, and a siege piece mounted on each. Magister…" Advancing like a man who fears the ground is mined. "You should have seen them in action. Getting your artillery where you need it is the real fuc— the real trick, on the field. Wins you or loses you. And they not only tootle them around like pins, but you just fire off the back of 'em. You can get a rolling siege line like they were just regular troops. Move and shoot, move and shoot." His enthusiasm was weirdly childlike.

"Well, granted," Berkely said. "I'm forwarding the reports. With your recommendation that we can fit them in as some sort of new class of Accessory. Obviously, they'll make their own call back home. Lizards. Not exactly uniform standard. But until we can master these monsters ourselves, or find a solution, they fill a tactical gap. So tell me about these Seraphi of yours."

Flint, emboldened by his success, pushed his forces forwards. "Good lads," he said. "You've got to understand how much these Peosts got pissed on. By everyone else and by their own people. You never saw anyone keener to get the uniform boots on so they could start kicking back."

"'Seraphi'," Berkely repeated fastidiously.

"I mean, it's what they call 'em," Flint said, feeling a sudden tactical shift. "The way they do things in these parts."

"Accessories," Berkely noted, "is what we call them on the Archipelago. And we do not deploy them as a regular army force close to home. For, I would hope, obvious reasons."

"Well sure, yes, normally," said Flint. "Only, there's a whole tradition around here. And they did good. Took the uniform and the training. Prospects, magister. We give 'em prospects better than just being a farmer. You should have seen 'em on the field. Held up under fire and—"

"Yes, yes," Berkely said. "And I appreciate that, once a territory is inducted into the Sway, then recruiting locals into peacekeeping Accessory positions is acceptable. But large numbers of local troops under arms in a territory that has yet to formally accept perfection is not safe. What if they desert you the moment, say, Palinet over in Peor raises the taxes? Or some idiot religious festival isn't observed. We cannot have troops that we rely on, save that we cannot rely on them to do certain things at certain times. That is not how the army works. It is not how the Sway is maintained. It is not safe. Your 'Seraphi' will have to be watered down. Contingents of them distributed elsewhere in the Sway. Or else we might have a mutiny that guts our entire armed force here, and then where would we be?"

"It wouldn't be a problem, magister," said Flint. Berkely

weighed him, waiting to see if he'd been corrupted by the locals like Angilly.

"Fellow-Monitor Postry," he said carefully. "You've done well for yourself, here. Well for the advancement of perfection too, obviously." One brigand to another, making it plain he knew just whose pockets the loot was in. "Your name has already been mentioned approvingly in dispatches. I am in a position to make a further recommendation. Ventures will, of course, be setting up somewhere else. The next territory on the map where the first few drops of Palleseen influence can be scattered, like ink into water." The hard life, starting from scratch in a place where everything was done differently. All of Flint's work to date credited to another's ledger in return for the uncertain prospect of loot and gain. "Alternatively, the Successor Coast will require overall military oversight under Valuations, and subsequently under a Perfector, when we adopt the territory formally into the Sway. Obviously, your existing experience would recommend you for the post." A future shorn of daring raids and caches of treasure, but with the steady prospects of security and prestige. The buttons on Flint's uniform doing themselves up, one by one, until he would look almost respectable. Not a future to be sneered at. Berkely had made the same choice, and now the jacket fit him very well indeed.

"I see, magister," Flint said thoughtfully.

"What do you see, Fellow-Monitor?"

"I see I'll have to make a list of which Ser— Accessory squads would be best to deploy overseas, magister. The more fractious ones." And if there was some guilt in him, some regret over the soldiers who had followed him and his promises this far, not a whit of it showed in his face. The transformation was remarkable.

"Well, that is entirely creditable," Berkely said. He said it in a way that had Flint halfway out of his seat before an admonitory finger sat the man back down again. "There is one other matter I noted, in my man's report."

"Magister?" That soldier's response, suddenly understanding he wasn't clear of the mined ground yet.

"One liberty you've taken that I'm absolutely certain will not be approved of," Berkely said. "I have consulted with my own specialist. She was horrified, honestly. Fellow-Monitor, why don't you tell me about these demons?"

Chains of Command

What is it to be Croskin, the demon? A philosophical point. What is it to be any demon? Are they like us, even as like us as they appear to be when manifested into the World Above? What exists, in the Realms Below, that is an individual demon? The terminology that conjurers have inherited from the semi-savage past, that of Kings Below, infernal fiefdoms, thrones and dominions, that is a human thing. A gloss put over a chasm of otherness *so that it might be understood. They are not like us, the demonists caution. Even those, like Caecelian, who are formed into so pleasing and human a shape are not like us. Perhaps those least of all. They are things of malign spite, deception and violence. That is why we, with the long spoon of a contract between us and them, can so successfully use them to further malign, deceitful and violent enterprises. They are brutes by nature, hence we make them labour for us. To treat a demon as something more would be to let it practise its malignity, mendacity, brutality, on us. Croskin's innards are reflected in his form, then: barbed, hideous, predatory. A shape caught between what he is and the purpose for which he was hauled from Below by the contract of his inept summoner. And now, owing to poor draughtsmanship, still here Above. Wearing the uniform. Following the orders. Commanding his subordinate fiends. What is it to be Croskin, thing of violence and resentment and enforced adherence to orders? Ask any soldier in the Palleseen Sway, they'll tell you.*

Croskin saluted. Not a natural series of movements for his physiology, but he'd practised. The jacket rucked up around his shoulders, strained across the bulb of his belly, rubbed at the base of his useless little wings where the slits down his back were. The hat remained improbably balanced on his swollen head.

"Croskin. Cohort-Monitor. Mate," said Flint. This was in the new place the army was now, since the Sage-Broker had arrived. One more part of the Usmiat city given over to the uniform. Croskin understood a conquest by sections as well as any soldier.

"Magister," Croskin croaked. He couldn't do parade-ground straight, really. There was a heavy-armed slouch built into the way he was made. He did his best, though.

"Croskin, mate." And Flint wasn't all right. Had been drinking. Early in the day for it, but not unknown for Flint. His eyes had red around the edges. And if this had been a meeting between demon and summoner then the demon would be looking for the thin edges of things, where they might get their claws in. Drink and demonists didn't go together. You had to be sharp. That wasn't how it was, though, between Croskin and Flint. They were subordinate and superior officer in the Palleseen army. The appropriate games of dominance and exploitation were wholly different in character.

"Magister," Croskin said again.

"You've done good," Flint told him. "Look, wait. Here. I've got this." Bringing out a jug of hus, that fish-liquor the boatmen made. The good stuff, brewed to rite and ritual at the right phase of the moon. The stuff he could actually drink to some effect. Not the alcohol, but the sacredness of it. A fine, sharp blend of sin and sacrament. Flint cracked it open, took a swig straight from the neck, then passed it over.

There were words – thoughts, concepts – that would pass between demons, equal to equal, superior to inferior. That wasn't how Flint would speak to a human, nor even *could*. The means of expression needed facilities the World Above couldn't even conceive of. There were ways Croskin had learned, to speak to humans. Not demon to conjurer, but soldier to soldier, soldier to officer, officer to soldier. Each skill painfully learned, alien to him, but masterable in time. None of them seemed to quite fit what was going on here.

"Magister," said Croskin. He'd almost said *Master* like the man held his leash, but it wasn't like that. Not with Flint. "There are more of the local boys. We can smell them. Give us the city and shovels, I can double our number. If you ask the new man, the Sage-Broker." Letting the human words and the way they were used roll around his snaggle-fanged mouth until each one could come out with the proper shape and intonation to be understood. Pel was, after all, designed to be easy to learn and say. A gift, for a brute-work demon like Croskin.

"Yeah, yeah," said Flint. "Good thinking. We should do a map or something. Work out what streets to tear up. Look, Croskin. It's been. Only." Flint took the jug back and swigged. A human, drinking where a demon's lips had been and not caring. And true, the hus would scour away even infernal spittle, but still.

"The new man," Flint said.

Croskin waited.

"The new man," Flint said again. Like the phrase was a closed door in a passageway he'd meant to run down.

Croskin waited.

"He's big on the rules," Flint tried, a diversion down a side-passage in the hope it would link back around.

Croskin waited. Like the fugitive at the far end of the hall, hearing the boots grow closer.

"Only, the way we've been doing things," Flint said. "I mean, it's a mess, really. A real botch job. Amazed it's held together this long. With the… everything. Hats. Uniforms. Batons. You know. It's not right, he says."

"It is for a soldier," Croskin told him.

There was a moment when Flint was going to break. A demon always knew. Temptation, that old hook. But it was temptation to do good, and opposing it were all the strong barbs the Palleseen army had in the man, of self-interest and advancement. Any demon could tell you that doing good never survived that kind of tug of war. Flint made himself harsh, jagged and hard like his namesake.

"You're not, though. I mean, look at you." Spitting the words out like stones. "Fucking… disgrace to it. How could anyone think, really…? One of *us*? Seriously."

Croskin waited.

"You can't. Look, it's been a ride, sure. But who were we fooling?" Abruptly Flint was *we* again, just for a moment, for the last time. Then there was someone new coming, and the man said, "Croskin, this is Fellow-Invigilator Wattery. She's a… she's, well…"

Croskin knew exactly what Fellow-Invigilator Wattery was. He could smell the stench of it, no odour stronger in a demon's nostrils. What the woman was to the *eye* was stocky, short, young; dark hair back in a tight bun. Looking Croskin up and down like a cattle breeder about to haggle.

"I mean this is cute," she said. "The hat, the jacket. What in reason, honestly? All of it."

"It worked," Flint muttered. "When Galversty died. He stayed. Bound to the Sway, he said."

Wattery had some papers in her hands. Her fingers, thumbs, left dents on Croskin's nature as they leafed through them. The untidy scrawl of Galversty's shaking hand. The dead man's abbreviations and idiosyncrasies that had somehow resulted in… *this* unnatural state of affairs. The one that had Croskin in a jacket and leading a squad of his compatriots. The one that had, by subjecting him to all the rules and disciplines of an army, made him feel free.

"This is incredible," said Wattery, her tone suggesting not in a good way. "If it was a building I'd condemn it. I mean this whole nonsense could collapse at any point. What was he thinking?"

Flint said nothing. Croskin said nothing, feeling her tug

and pry at the flimsy piece of legerdemain that kept him in the World Above.

"I give you an order, what do you do?" Wattery asked him, straight out.

"Magister, as a soldier I obey," he said. The demon, seeking refuge in legalities.

"As a demon?"

"I obey," Croskin said between his teeth.

"Because?"

"You are my superior officer within the army of Pallesand."

"And as a demon?"

"Likewise. Magister."

"Damn me, this is mad," Wattery said to herself. "You made him a Cohort-Monitor."

Flint shrugged defensively. "Had to give orders to the other demons, didn't he?"

"Oh yes, the 'other demons'. Who take orders from *him*. Specifically from him."

"Right. Yes. And?"

"Postry, there is literally nothing stopping this... *thing* from tearing out the throat of a trooper, any of your troopers, right now."

Flint frowned. "What?"

"You put this *thing* in the chain of command. It does what you tell it. But those humans *below* it have no defence against it at all. It could murder the lot of them and there's nothing in the contract to stop it."

Flint looked at Croskin, back to Wattery.

"If you'd promoted it – as you'd literally requested, Postry – it could have started on the Cohorts. This is a demon. You can't just pretend it's one of us."

"Yeah, but..." Flint waved vaguely. "I mean..."

"Yes?" Wattery demanded.

"He didn't," said Flint. "I mean, none of us do. I could. You could. We don't. We're soldiers. That's not how it is."

"For humans," Wattery said, looking like Flint was waist-deep in a pool of oil and she was trying to explain why he shouldn't juggle torches. "You, demon. While you're still bound by this fucking nonsense. You have other demons beholden to *you*, sometimes."

"Yes, magister," Croskin said. He was trying to look at Flint, but Flint wouldn't look back at him. Was looking everywhere but. "Twenty-seven current muster, magister."

"Then I will have twenty-eight contracts drawn up," Wattery told him. "And you will – I command you, under the strictures of this shitshow of a contract – assemble your host, and they will accept what terms I give them. Or else I understand the locals have a particularly effective way of keeping you from troubling either the Realms Below or the World Above, and I'd be intrigued to see it put into action. Is that understood?"

"Yes, magister," Croskin said between his teeth, with clenched jaw, eyes still sliding off Flint's turned-away face.

"Yes, *Master*," Wattery corrected and, because she insisted, and because of the terms, she could make him say it. If she'd wanted she could even have told him to smile as he did so.

Gil at the Edge

She compromised. That was what you did, in Outreach. Outreach was there to compromise with the imperfect until matters had been manoeuvred into a position where another department could move in. Like Valuations. That was how it worked.

She compromised. In a foreign place you did foreign things, sometimes. Because the straight razor of Pal ordinance wouldn't cut. Or would twist in your hand and slit your own wrists.

The people you had to deal with, in Outreach. Her mentor had been best friends with some kind of squid-pope on her first assignment. A man you could drink with, play cards with, have a laugh. A wit, a civilized character. Born to the Archipelago he'd have been the sort of senior officer who threw the best parties. In Farasland he'd murdered people for god on the holy days. But, you know, doubtless he threw the best sacrifices.

And the thing you had to remember, about the compromises, the way you had to wield the razor, the people you raised a ceremonial squid goblet with… The thing you had to remember was that this outer you, this compromised you, it wasn't you. *It was a suit of clothes you took off, when Valuations or the inquisition or the army moved in. And when you did, it turned out you'd been wearing the uniform underneath, all along. Every button done up tight. Except sometimes that double set of clothes turned out just to be much for all the sweat and passion of a place. What was left, then, when they made you take off the compromise?*

The next order of business, after the Allorwen who definitely wasn't getting his mill back, was Arkanith. Drathel blinked at that. She hadn't thought the old corpse-fondler would pry himself out of his crypt under the House of Hard Angles. But you were nothing if not a politician, when you headed up the Moerends in Usmai.

They were in a chamber in the palace, set aside for Berkely's use. Technically the Sage-Broker was waiting for an audience with the Alkhand, all very proper, but he was using the time to hold a court of his own. A lot of people wanted to come ask favours of, make accommodations with, or just generally be nice to the new Big Man in town. Including, apparently, His Holiness the Death Fetishist.

His *Quietude* the Grand Moerend Arkanith, Drathel reminded herself, and murmured to Berkely, mostly to stop herself inadvertently saying the other thing. While Angilly made things ready for the royal audience, Drathel was sitting at the Sage-Broker's elbow to translate local colour. Arkanith had turned up in immaculate black robes. A particular black, because of course the old Moeribandi had about a dozen near-indistinguishable shades. If she rubbed the stinging stuff in her eyes, she could tell the difference properly, read the stink rising off each one. Right now she couldn't be bothered with the watering and the squinting. It was one of the dignified and ceremonial ones, anyway, and wasted on Berkely, for whom it was just 'black'.

Arkanith had gone for just the ghost of the make-up, too. Not the full ornate skull stuff, but a pallor and the suggestions of circles about the eyes, the corrugations of teeth at his lips. Religious casual so as not to look barbaric before the Pals. Smart old lad.

Arkanith had a whole spiel, basically. He spoke, not even in Usmiri, but in Old Morib, the ancient Imperial tongue that she'd never heard used by a living soul outside of religious rite, though probably half the ghosts in the House still whispered in it. A younger Moerend translated it all into slightly stilted Pel. Professions of goodwill, basically. An offering of services. All friends here, magister, yes indeed.

"What is he?" Berkely murmured from the corner of his mouth as the speech went on.

"Depends how deep you dig," she said. "I mean, on the face of it they're the priesthood of the civic state religion, the old death cult of the Empire, and they're deeply invested in what happens to people after death and all that, which from our point of view makes them a Bad Thing. On the other hand, scratch the surface and how it's actually played out since the Empire shut its nut is that they're really more admin and public ceremony than actual god business. Civil service, basically, because they were a bunch of literate, educated people in place after the Empire's tide ran out. So maybe a Good Thing. Maybe something we could co-opt, work with. I mean, bureaucrats. Our clerks and whatnot would probably see eye to eye with them and be able to synchronise accounts."

"And dig deeper than that?" Berkely asked, because he was no fool.

"Bloody maniacs, magister," she whispered. "Or, at least, a kernel of them. The inner cult. Never forgotten back when they were top around here and everywhere else. If you could bring the Empire back tomorrow, with all the necromancy and everyone having to Go To Their Proper Death like it was an appointment with the dentist, then they'd do it like a shot. Or this old boy would. Don't be fooled by the act. Just because it's grinning doesn't mean it isn't a skull."

"And this is… allowed around here?" As though the Grand Moerend went at it with horses in the street.

"Magister, it is not known. That second level of things is how just about everyone sees it. Only your faithful Fellow-Archivist has been doing some digging, and just in time. But don't worry. I'm going to put a stop to his nonsense, most profitably. And like I say, it's an inner cult. Cut that out, the rest might be useful to get the paperwork done."

Berkely nodded at her assessment, nodded at Arkanith as he finished his screed. The old priest bowed, smiling, terribly obeisant. *Hail to the new masters! May you live a hundred years!* Drathel had to admire the old boy's nerve, honestly. Stand there in the jaws of the Pal dragon and just rattle it all off, while planning *that.*

Well, I'll fix your kettle, mate, she thought, smiling and nodding at the retreating priest. *After which, maybe we can salvage the rest of the tea service. Ah, here we are...*

Angilly stepped in. In uniform, this time, though still with a dampened scarf about her neck, and her hair done back in that fancy Usmiat style. The legendary compromise of Outreach.

"Berkely," the Resident said. "The room's yours." And was she tense? Drathel found she genuinely couldn't tell. She'd look for a hand to Gil's sword hilt, but wearing your sword in front of the Alkhand wasn't really the thing. To all exterior purposes, Angilly was absolutely at ease. Drathel admired that. Honestly, she admired a great deal about Sage-Invigilator Angilly, right up until the woman started digging her heels in about the silliest matters.

All this falling out, she thought sadly, *over a dead frog.*

His Tranquillity the Alkhand Dekamran was enthroned, attended to by a flurry of servants who came and went. Not the Mirror Throne and the grand court and a hundred lookers- and hangers-on, and just as well. Just the Alkhand making time for a private audience with his good allies, the Palleseen. Berkely made the appropriate bow, even. A little loose-limbed, a little of bandit disrespect to it, but more than a foreign potentate would normally get out of a Pal of Sage rank.

The pleasantries, next. The usual. And Berkely wasn't the sort of officer who revelled in this sort of inflatory nonsense, which Drathel was glad for. But he could master the talk. He was a polite brigand, as befitted an operation that was more talking your way over the doorstep than breaking the windows. On behalf of the Temporary Commission of Ends and Means he expressed Pallesand's enduring admiration and respect for the throne of Usmai, throwing in a line about how the ancient nation had been an inspiration to the formation of Pallesand. An ingredient in the greater perfection that the Pals were so keen to export with menaces. He expressed his condolences for the loss – *not* death, because these linguistic foibles were important – of the Alkhand's noble father. His regret at the sequence of events that had unfolded thereafter, and the actions that had been necessary. His joy that humble Pallesand had been in a position to restore the proper royal arse to the throne. Not in those words, obviously, but that was Drathel's inner translation, not under any circumstances to make it to her face. Berkely's assessment too, she reckoned. But the brigand could do up his top button and use the right fork when necessary, could do it with aplomb, even. And then the last line of the little speech. How Berkely was so very happy that the uniforms and boots of Pallesand were able to ensure that said arse *stayed* there, despite all the unrest of a rather mutinous and ungrateful populace. And some of that ungrateful mutiny was because a certain sacred cave was lacking a tenant now. And some of it was because those uniforms and boots weren't exactly subtle as they went about the city. And none of that stopped what Berkely was saying from being entirely true.

And he said it all in Pel, of course, because Pel was the perfect language and, now Valuations was in charge, one couldn't expect the representatives of Pallesand to go round talking some foreign nonsense.

Dekamran – Drathel kept thinking of him as *the boy Alkhand* and he was older than she was. Mid-thirties, surely. Still with the indefinable air of a kid dressed up in his dad's clothes, though. Not physically too big on him, but spiritually. He did his best, though, and being polite and urbane was something the lad was good for. He also spoke Pel, absolutely perfectly. He met Berkely's points one for one, giving gracious thanks for each, extending Usmai's own admiration and recognition back to the Commission like a fencer binding over his opponent's blade. Until all the rubbish was said, out of the way, the air cleared for business.

Angilly had a schedule of talking points, of course. Incomplete, as it would turn out, but still packed. A variety of small matters, essentially. Bureaucratic canapes. Individual Pals, army and civilian, to receive this or that post or concession from the throne. Disciplinary matters, that ship which caught fire after being searched for contraband by soldiers who strictly speaking hadn't had the authority to do so. Berkely smiled and Dekamran smiled and they rattled through it all like any two people in a meeting who just want to get things done without anybody's nose getting tweaked. With Angilly in the middle, greasing all the right wheels. Offering options where needed that preserved both the dignity of the throne and the privileges of the Palleseen. Eminently professional.

Which left just enough time for Any Other Business. Drathel was expecting Berkely to at least give her the nod. Maybe even cede the floor to her so that any fallout could land squarely on Decanting, but the man was more than that. The bandit didn't mind dirty hands. And maybe he'd been looking forward to it. There was a thread of *mean* running through Sage-Broker Berkely, Drathel considered, and he hadn't taken to Angilly.

"There is one other thing," he said, just as the Resident was about to tie the bow on the meeting. "I apologise, Angilly. If I could…?"

Angilly knew. Drathel, watching her face keenly, saw the instant of understanding. Mouth open to usher the man out before the Palleseen agenda could be advanced past the neat little lines she'd set out for it. Berkely held up a hand, the hand of the senior ranking officer with command of the operation. It stayed Angilly. Even in Outreach you were part of the service.

Some instincts were ingrained. You didn't shout down your superiors.

"Your Tranquillity," Berkely said, "we've discussed a great many matters pertaining to civil order. I am aware, of course, that your reign is measured only in the months since your victory over your brother." Amazing that, in Pel, the man could say 'your victory' in a way that sounded like '*our*'. "I have observed, and received reports of, considerable unrest. Elements who were loyal to your brother who have not truly accepted you. Those who believe there is some cousin or much-removed nephew who might be rallied to, in order to advance their own disruptive and greedy interests. I am, obviously, very glad to have strengthened our garrison here in Alkhalend so that your ongoing security on the throne might be ensured."

Dekamran said that, yes, that was obviously very good. Also knowing something was up, by Drathel's estimation, but not exactly what.

"For example," Berkely went on, "I am, of course, honoured by your granting me this audience. I am aware, however, that similar private audiences are granted to a wide range of petitioners. I appreciate this has been a tradition carried over from less sophisticated times when, say, some stalwart with a sword could reliably stand between the Alkhand and an assassin's knife. In these modern times, a fanatic with a charged rod concealed on their person is a serious threat at range. The Emir-Jarl of Farasland met his end in just such a way within living memory, shortly before that nation was accepted into the Sway."

Dekamran said that, yes, that was obviously very bad, although not something he felt would happen in Usmai.

"Obviously Your Tranquillity's safety and uninterrupted rule is of primary importance to us," Berkely said. "As is the continued maintenance of law and order on the streets."

Drathel watched Angilly's eyes flick between Sage-Broker and the Alkhand, looking for a way into the conversation.

"I am informed," Berkely said, "of certain high-profile and

valuable targets that would be a gift to any insurrectionists. Items of cultural importance that could be used by insurgents to rally around. Symbols, as it were, of the complaints Your Tranquillity's people might have, concerning the circumstances of your accession. It would be disastrous for them to fall into the hands of your enemies. Why, I'd look for fighting on the streets within the week." Overplaying it just a little, in Drathel's professional opinion, but maybe there was a place for theatre. "I think it best, therefore, that we take the protection of such artefacts into our own hands. For your safety."

Angilly tried to speak, then, and again the hand silenced her. In that pause, Dekamran said, "You speak of the body of god."

It was as though everyone's footing shifted at once. Even though the language was still Pel, it was such an *un*-Pal thing to say that abruptly the man seated before them was not Dekamran, the educated, the urbane, the civilized. He might as well have stripped down to a loincloth and painted his face, as far as Berkely was concerned.

"I understand that the Kakrops Jars are just sitting in a monastery at the foot of the falls, protected by nothing more than an order of non-combatant monks." And, now *that* had been said, Berkely's own veneer was peeling away, revealing all that ugliness within. "Seriously, Your Tranquillity, *anyone* could take them. It's within easy strike of the docks. The *Cotto* could just send a crew in. Any of the Emorandi families who still wish your brother was on the throne, or fancy their chances at starting a new dynasty. Some crooks from the Sand Lanes who'd sell to the highest bidder."

"These things would not happen," Dekamran said simply.

"Your Tranquillity," Berkely pressed on, "I've heard the reports of both Angilly and Drathel. We all know just what event it is that represents resistance both to our presence here and your rule. Anyone in possession of these deeply..." *valuable* "symbolic artefacts would be in a position to use them against you. We must take steps to secure them. For your own sake."

The damnable thing was, Drathel thought, he was absolutely right. None of the factions grumbling about the way the civil war had turned out had necessarily realised it yet, but you could do a lot worse than having the corpse of a murdered god in your possession if your major beef with the regime was god-murder. All very reasonable. Perfectly good reason to get a pack of soldiers into that monastery and in control of the jars while Drathel waited for the ship to make port with a hold full of blank tablethi. After which the Usmiat could have whatever was left, honestly. Once the godliness was drained from it and she'd licked the symbols off the jars.

"No," Dekamran said.

Angilly started forwards. About to argue with her superior, here in front of the foreign potentate. About, in short, to make herself everything Drathel had ever said she was, tear right through all those accusations and launch into outright treason. Stopping herself on the brink of the precipice. Instead, stepping over to Berkely's other shoulder like Drathel's counterweight. Bending low to murmur.

"Berkely, we have discussed this," Drathel caught. "For exactly the reasons you're giving, the jars need to remain where they are. The city respects the Usrani monks. While they hold the goods, we have stability. The moment people hear that *we've* marched in and laid hands on them..."

"With respect I disagree with your assessment," Berkely told her flatly, again sidelong. No admission of disunity before the foreigners. Dekamran watched the conference, jaw clenching.

"I've been here seven years," Angilly murmured. "I know Alkhalend. Better than your pet Decanter. Trust me on this."

Drathel rolled her eyes. *Sorry, Gil. Honestly I tried. I gave you every damn chance.*

"Yes," said Berkely. "You do *know* Alkhalend." Said in such a particular way that it was as though Angilly had fallen on her face right there. Remained standing. Face perfectly composed for the Alkhand's presence. But tripped. Fallen, inside.

"Sage-Invigilator Angilly," Berkely said, each word lancing from the corner of his mouth like shot from a sniper, "it is, I'm sure, a constant battle, in Outreach. To know where the boundaries of proper conduct lie."

Gil's eyes widened. Her hand brushed her hip, and it was most certainly a good thing she wasn't wearing the sword, for all concerned. As she opened her mouth to respond, Berkely spoke aloud, over her. "Your Tranquillity, as your *advisor*, placed here by the wisdom of the Commission, I state in the strongest possible terms that these relics must be secured, so that your rule may be supported and maintained."

"The body of god will remain in the care of the Usrani," Dekamran said. "It is not something for your soldiers to seize. I forbid this. All these other things you have had from me. From me, the grateful Alkhand who understands what service his friends have done him. But you cannot lay hands on the body of god. It is as simple as that." Not even a devout man decrying sacrilege, but a ruler knowing how his people would look on him.

"If only it was," said Berkely, a translucent sheet of sincerity stretched over a chasm of greed. "Alas."

Dekamran frowned at him. "You are in my palace, Sage-Broker, in my city, in my nation. I forbid this. I will have my people stand a hundred deep around the monastery."

"That would be a terrible thing," said Berkely, in the voice of a man who knows what massed baton-fire can do to a crowd a hundred deep. "Your Tranquillity, in the interests of your security, I must deny you the chance to make any unwise decrees that might negatively impact on public order. For it is your palace and your city and your nation, but right now the soldiers that surround you are Palleseen, and any manual of statecraft will teach that it is the control of force that, at base, permits a state to function. You do not control that force. Nor will you be holding audience with your nobles and generals and similar. For the better maintenance of order, I feel that access to the throne should be carefully monitored and controlled, and the Alkhand should be attended at all times by an escort. There might be assassins."

"You can't put the Alkhand under house arrest!" Angilly hissed.

"Well obviously I wouldn't dream of it," Berkely said pleasantly. "Protective custody is, I would say, the more apposite term."

Drathel saw her look from Berkely to Dekamran, face twisted. Trying to communicate without words, without breaching the decorum of her position. Knowing that whatever she did would be a betrayal. The career officer, the woman. And Dekamran's face, bleak, disbelieving. Focused not on Berkely, who held the knife, but on Angilly, who had served him up for it. Drathel rather thought she heard hearts break, in the silence.

A jolt went through Angilly, like being stabbed. She was going to leap into the abyss. Drathel held her breath. But then Berkely just said, softly, "I have some disciplinary matters to go through, regarding just what is and is not appropriate for a Palleseen Resident. Return to Slate House and await my word." And that was that.

When they left, there were already Pal soldiers at the door, the escort that Dekamran was not going to be rid of while he lived, if Drathel was any judge. That would accompany him everywhere up to the point when Usmai entered the Sway and Berkely was named Perfector. At which point, whether exile or execution, they'd escort him on one journey more.

Blood in the Water

Small wonder an island people see god in the sea and sky. Small wonder the sea and sky look back. Hard gods, bountiful gods, capricious gods, and their people shaped likewise. Until, in one case, those people were hard enough that they cast even their gods from them, and embraced a perfection that didn't leave them at the whim of tide or weather. Or in others, they sought greater communion with the depths, wrecks and bones and drowned hopes, and become something like the Cotto, or a hundred other cults and sects and mysteries. All the myriad currents of the sea.

The water rose to mid-thigh, cold, salt. The smell of it, half rotten, half clean, that way the sea had. Only wood above, though, not the sky. Here, in the Water Lanes of Alkhalend, you did these things covertly. Even on those isles the Cotto called home, you did them at night, at certain coves, watched only by certain eyes.

But traditions warped with distance. They'd made allowances. At the rail, looking down on Loret, there was Orhuhst. He was the priest, the captain, beloved of the sea, of course he was here. There was the woman with the filed teeth. She was the champion, beloved of the sea. There were some three other Cotto, each tattooed across most of their bared flesh, each ferocious, each one in some way beloved of the sea. But *she* was there, too. Caecelian's girl, about whom the sea cared not a jot. The Usmiat girl Loret had sat with, overlooking the night of the

Sand Lanes and what washed in and out under its cover. Just that girl, who'd heard her idiot story and not laughed.

The Viper herself was not here. It was beneath her, perhaps beyond her, to care what happened to one lost Pal girl whom the sea had its teeth in. But her girl had come. Not to intervene. Not to help. But at least to see. To know, if Loret died, that she was dead.

They were in the hold of a ship. In Loret's experience you didn't want this much water in the hold, but they had a kind of square pen within the bilges, and it was open to the sea. Beneath her feet, just a lattice of wood. Beneath that, communicating through all the square holes, the water. Beyond the water, all the rest of the world's ocean, all of it, sans barrier or division and to hell with the cartographers.

Below, attached to the lattice, were lamps that infused the water with a corpse-pale glow. Perhaps on the Cotto isles there was some luminescent fish, some sacred lantern. Here they were just Pal desk-lights with charged tablethi. You had to compromise sometimes.

They had painted her. She'd not wanted them to, and marred their neat lines, so Orhuhst had taken hold of her arms. Firm but not painful, a father remonstrating with a cherished daughter. "These things must be," he had told her, "and it will go worse for you if they aren't done properly." Pel words, chewed over by his accent.

"Will it hurt?" she'd asked him.

"Yes," he'd said. Grinned about it. As though the hurt was the point and she should be grateful for the reminder she was alive.

Painted her, red and black, fluked arabesques that were sea-wrack and eel-back and kraken all at once. The woman with the teeth had taken needles and put a single permanent flourish into her shoulder, ink from sacred cuttlefish from a sunken temple somewhere, no doubt. A wave-mark, like she was claimed by them. Just as she *was* claimed by them, or by something like them.

They had given her hus. The sharp, stinking fish-liquor. The sacred drink. She'd let it scald her throat. By then she was painted and inked, so why not drunk? Why not blunt it all before the end? Except, the more she'd drunk, the sharper she'd felt. Hyper-aware, eyes seeing too many colours ringing everything. As though she saw souls. Then the woman with the teeth had flicked hus into her eyes and she saw souls, through the streaming tears. Saw the sacredness flaring from the woman like clouds of red expanding against the glitter of sun on waves above. Looked at the girl, seen the crown on her brow, the blessings of a dead divinity. Looked at Orhuhst and seen him as though he stood within the circle of vast jaws.

They had stripped her down to just a binding about her breasts and her Pal uniform breeches hanging sodden about her, loose at the knee. She tried to look around for the girl, Caecelian's apprentice, but Orhuhst's voice rang out, *No*.

The shark had come. That was what her eyes were for. The shark.

Longer than she was tall, a lazy grey shadow in the dark water, silhouetted against the sunken lamps. Curving a course around her, one dead button eye regarding her with cold consideration.

It passed behind her. She stared ahead. The tip of a fin grazed the back of her knees as it turned and passed sluggishly back round.

Orhuhst cast something into the water. The woman with the teeth did. They all did, save Caecelian's girl. Colours, expanding, and the shark shuddered, recoiled from some, nosed hungrily at others, then circled back to Loret. More animated now. Hungrier.

Its nose pushed into her thigh, as though it was a fencing master testing her balance. Its flank scored along her calf and she felt its teeth. Not the killing teeth of its jaws but the thousand sharpnesses of its skin, scratching at her. A flick of its knife tail and it was round again and its jaws gaped.

She whimpered. Orhuhst called her name, or something, and

threw. Her hands received a jug of hus without her intervention. He mimed drinking at her. His face was flushed dark, his eyes wide. She broke the seal. She drank.

The shark bit. She felt the ring of its mouth, the faint prickle of its teeth, like ice needles. No pain, and it had put no force into her. Just gummed at her leg thoughtfully, a gourmet sampling the menu. It flicked away, turned at the edge of its square domain, returned.

She drank and drank again. The hus was sour, harsh, spiced. A ragged, whimpering sob came from somewhere in the room. Somewhere that sounded very far away.

"Now," said Orhuhst.

That sob again. Some weak girl who feared death and pain and all that. Loret was glad she wasn't *that* girl. That girl had been a miserable thing to be. Caring about all the hurt she might do. Trying to keep to the impossible demands of a God whose healing tenets seemed so very grudgingly given. And whose followers, when the Dead Companies had brought their batons to clear the camp, had not even defended themselves, nor yet one another. Had taken the deaths because to fight back would displease God.

Loret had displeased God. And, because God had never had cause to save her from anything, she had escaped God's wrath on a technicality, there being no mortal wound to abruptly give her back. She had fled God into the arms of the Fisher King's cult because at least they fought. Fought like demons, like madmen, like people who cared whether they and theirs lived or died. Unlike Loret's former folk. And so they'd given her a knife and they'd given her to their cruel, petty, bitter god. And it hadn't done anything more than prolong the clearing of the camp, but it had at least done that. And got her out. After the real Loret had died. Got her out with all their thoughts and prayers. Those vicious, ugly things.

She was on her knees, the water lapping at her chin. Shivering, because the water was cold, because the shark was there, because of what was going to happen. The fish passed by again, the well of its eye weighing her. Another sob, the last one, squeezed out by the chill, by the hand of the water about her chest. That other girl's sobs and whimpers.

Orhuhst was in the water with her. Kneeling down before her, the water halfway up a bare chest on which a hundred stories of the sea and its gods were written. All intermingled one with another because all the seas were one sea. The ocean knew no borders. He showed her the knife. It was very important that she see and understand the knife. A beautiful piece of work, that knife. The hilt was coral carved into a knot of tentacles, with the pommel as the octopus's sack of a body, the knots of its eyes a rest for the underside of the hand. The blade was a shell, six inches long, pearlescent, razory. Impossible that such a delicate thing should not have broken. Yet here it was, and somehow she understood that, if he had cut below them, the wood would give way first and dump them into the depths of the harbour.

"Seachild," said Orhuhst, and distantly Loret heard Caecelian's girl make some protest, some demand. So far away, though. Too far to be of any help, but good to know.

The shark circled, nosed her again, more eager now. Trailing divinity behind it in the water.

"You understand," said Orhuhst and she understood.

He put the blade into her just under the ribs. The very tip of it, delicate as a seamstress. And unseamed her, to the navel. She felt it like a line of cold silver. He'd lied. There was almost no pain at all. She felt cheated. Pain was her due, after all. He unseamed her, and the water about them flooded with darkness, the inward life of her rushing eagerly out to meet the sea, its close cousin.

The fingers of Orhuhst, in absurdly intimate violation, reached into her. Grotesque in their tenderness, for hands that had a hundred murders hanging off them. Hands that had strangled, slit, beaten, now almost trembling with care as he took what was in her. The symbolic faith of a slaughtered congregation. What they'd given her, along with Loret's papers, when they got her past the Dead Companies and away.

And she knew, very distantly indeed, that it was worse, or better, or just more, because somewhere within her were more faiths than that. That enough of the other god, of God, God the grudging healer, remained. That Orhuhst's midwifery had let that cloud out into the water too.

Oh god, she thought, and did not even know what she meant.

Orhuhst stood. Retreated, footing as sure on the submerged grate as it would be on deck. The shark arrowed in, from idle flick to sudden lunge without transition. She saw the articulation of its jaw, the space behind the ring of teeth expanding and expanding, the forward thrust of its gape. Very distantly, a girl cried out. Or two. Or just one.

It went into the shark. All of it. What Orhuhst had released. Not the blood. That was the ocean's due. The rest. The faith. The prayers to the Fisher King. Even the remnant of what she had been, when just not hurting other people had seemed so good a thing. Swallowed up into that maw, and then the shark's tail flurried past her, its whiplash tip slapping the opened edges of her abdomen as it left. Gone from the cage. Gone through whatever unseen gap had admitted it.

She let out a breath. A sound. Feeling was coming back to her. Not pain yet, but she could feel the two severed edges of the cut brush together, like new and unwanted limbs grafted on.

"Get the woman," Orhuhst's voice came to her, though she could no longer see where he was.

A new voice then. A familiar one. Seldom a welcome one. An old woman's. "So what, exactly, have you dragged me half across town for— Fuck me! What did you do?" Harsh, cracked Pel, jagged with the last stubs of a Jarokiri accent. Tally, the surgeon of the Fever Lodge.

"Stitch her," Orhuhst said.

"Why?"

"Or she dies."

Tally made a sound that suggested just exactly how much she cared about that, but Caecelian's girl called out, "Help her! They'll pay you. You know that. Just help her!" Sounding… agonised, actually. Sounding like it was *her* they'd cut open.

"Well bloody bring her up then!" Tally's voice spat.

"No," Orhuhst said.

"What?"

"In the water. In her water. It must be."

"Or?"

"Or she dies."

"You can't…" Tally said. "I can't be…" And then, "Do you know how many people piss in this fucking harbour?" An old woman who had once been a priestess and so could afford a little sacrilege on credit.

"In the water," Orhuhst said.

"Fuck me," Tally complained. There was splashing. Loret forced herself to look.

The old woman, in Loret's eyes, blazed. The last flourish of an old fire, for sure, but blazing still. Some foreign flame cult, kneeling now in seawater. The girl was at her elbow, holding her wallet of tools out.

"I can't cleanse the wound," she complained. "I can't heat my tools." Although as her fingers brushed the needles and the blades, Loret saw them glow and shimmer with inner fire.

"Sew her up," Orhuhst's voice came, "with the sea inside her."

"Fuck me," Tally complained again, but she set to work. It felt distant and cold, like ants on Loret's skin, the needle and the thread and the water. The girl's hand on her shoulder. The neat, clean stitches criss-crossing one another. A scar she'd have always, as though she'd been a mother with a breech-birth at her young age. Nobody would ever know that it was not life she'd carried for nine months, but faith.

They gave her more hus, as it went on, and Tally took a swig too, towards the end, to keep her hands steady against the chill of the sea. The sea that Loret still *felt*, as though no quantity of stitches could seal it off from her. The sea that ran forever around the world.

Enough hus later and she was in a drier place. A cabin aboard the ship, with a robe over her shoulders and baggy Cotto trousers swamping her legs. Shivering with a cold that came from many places and passed through her to many more, like all the currents did.

There was food, then. Tally told her not to eat it, but Orhuhst said she must. Hot food, spiced fish chowder. He had not touched her innards, he said, proud as any butcher in the exactitude of his profession. She'd not be leaking gravy onto the table. And laughed. And was serious, hands down flat.

"The wedding," he said, "is made."

Tally looked blank; the girl did. Honestly, half the Cotto there did. This was deep religion. The oldest of old ways and the newest of new. Experimental theology. Loret understood. The Fisher King was the old Pal sea god. The Shark Queen was the Cotto's sea goddess. Two identities for the forces of the wind and waves, sharks and reefs, rocks and storms. The shipkillers, the drowners, the providers, the carriers from shore to shore. But the ocean was without borders. Back in the day, the Fisher King's votaries had fought the Shark Queen's adherents, but now the Pals were scouring all gods from the shores of the world. So: a wedding, a union, a recognition that it was all the same sea.

"You, we owe," Orhuhst told Tally. "You and yours." And Tally had a pouch of coin, sure enough, but there were debts that metal couldn't pay. "And you, we owe," Orhuhst said, and gave her the knife.

The coral and shell knife. The ridiculously delicate knife that she knew she couldn't have broken with a smith's hammer. Not in settlement of the debt, even, which remained an open letter of credit with the sea and its faithful, but because, having done what it did, it was *hers*.

★

The news came to them by stages, as they retreated across the city towards the Sand Lanes. There was a new ship in harbour, that came first. A Pal ship, the sister of the *Salient*. The *Mordant*, it was called, fitted out as a battery ship, rails strong with siege engines. Of a range to threaten any ship in harbour, certainly, and the city too, in need. Just sitting out there at anchor flying the Palleseen flag. *Mordant*, as in a thing that fixes colours so they won't wash away.

Then the streets, along the dock front and into the ramshackle of the poor districts. More uniforms, more tension. Loret could manage only short distances before pausing, resting. Tally was talking about sending for a cart. Instead, she and the girl strung Loret between them, paused when she needed to pause. And, as they paused, listened to the news.

There were Pal soldiers in the Usrani monastery, they said. Moved in, shouldered aside the monks. To protect it, they said. To pillage it, others said. And no shot fired yet, no monk slapped, but not taking no for an answer, either.

There were Pal soldiers in the palace, they said. And some claimed the Alkhand had called them there, for fear. To protect it, the Pals said, as they seemed to say about everything they did. But house by house, street by street, the rumour crept about Alkhalend that the Alkhand Dekamran, last son of his house, was now to be reached only through petition to the Palleseen. His *protectors*. That he, in his palace, in his city, in his state and power, was little more than their prisoner.

All these things they heard, in different permutations and from many mouths, until finally Tally lost patience and spent some of her new coins on hiring a cart to get Loret back. Because the uniforms were more and more in evidence, and the people of the city were more and more fractious, and she was worried about a full-on riot any moment.

At the Lodge, they sat Loret down at one of the tables. Tally made some vague comment about rousing the Reckoner from her bed, but Loret snagged her arm. Shook her head. Couldn't find the strength to put it into words, but she knew that this wasn't a thing she could let anyone take out of her. It was *hers*, like the knife. And for a woman who'd had her front slit open, honestly she was feeling very well. Weak, sick, dizzy, in pain, but with the sense that by morning all of that would have transmuted into strength, the sea's alchemy taking place in that god-shaped emptiness within her. Honestly, what really scared her was what she might be capable of, when it was done.

Caecelian was there, regarding her. The demon woman who'd sold her to the pirates. The vehicle for the sea-gods' will. The sower of dissent. *Seeing* her the way a demon's eyes did, that saw what was there. Loret had no sense of what she thought, about how it had turned out. Whether a living Loret was a disappointment or just one more potential vessel for future misery and wickedness.

The Viper looked up at her girl. "Well?" Perhaps expecting shouting, finger pointing, *How could you…? Did you know what they'd…?* But instead, the girl said, "I need to go to the palace."

Caecelian's face split in a radiant smile. No human woman could have looked as venomous or as lovely as she did in that moment. The true nature of her was exposed like a wound. Like a flower.

"There's something I need to do," said the girl. And then, against all odds, diverting her gaze from the mesmeric joy of her mentor to look at Loret. "I'm sorry," she said. "I need to. I have to leave you. I'll… if I can, I'll come back. But I—"

"Tomorrow night," said Loret.

"What?"

"Tomorrow night, and I will come with you," Loret said, feeling like someone falling down a shifting slope, scrabbling for purchase but unable to stop herself. Not knowing what she herself, this new her, would do next.

"You can't—" said the girl, but Caecelian, whose grin had grown even more all-devouring and beautiful, said, "She can."

At her pupil's stare, the Viper bared her fangs again. "I, too, have business at the palace," she said. "Tomorrow night's business. The timing is perfect." *Misery and wickedness*, said her face. Inside Loret, something kicked in sympathy, for the sea had many moods and wickedness was certainly amongst them.

Gil at the Point

She's far from the first servant of Outreach to discover that the two boats she has her feet on are moving apart. Standard operating procedure is to have your weight-bearing foot on the Palleseen barque always. Which makes what's happening to her entirely her own fault, an experienced senior officer who should absolutely have known better. Who did know better, when it was happening. Because, kid herself all she wants, she always knew that Dekamran might be important leverage, even at the nadir of his swing. At the same time, the convulsions back home in the wake of the war, and the cults, and everything, have altered the nature of the regime she thought she was serving. So: it is not the same river, she is not the same woman. The result – being swept downstream by the flood – is very much the same.

"He's ready for me, is he?" Gil said grimly. The neat little card. Not Berkely's writing, but some clerk on his staff. The Sage-Broker requests her presence to discuss matters of operational discipline before his definitive report.

Cohort-Invigilator Samellers regarded her brightly, the manner in which he did everything. So new out of the factory on the Archipelago that turns out perfect little aides that the shine was still on every button. Outreach operatives weren't supposed to gleam. They needed to get their hands dirty outside the Palleseen Sway. Even straight out of the phal and with a stick up her arse about proper conduct, Gil never glittered like this sugar-spun son of a bitch.

"If there's anything I can do to assist in your preparations, magister," he said.

She stared at him balefully. Right now, at the frayed and flailing end of her career, she didn't feel any particular need to keep up polite appearances. "You can drop the act. You're his creature, obviously. I don't see the need to hand you the rope so the noose is neat."

The accusation didn't impact on his composure in the least. "I appreciate why you might think that, magister, and obviously I regret the friction that has arisen between you and the Sage-Broker. I can only assure you that, if I am your aide, I will conduct myself accordingly. Including not taking any action that might harm you. In fact, you should consider me incapable of doing so." And there was something in the way he said it, some weird stress, but her mind was so full of her own problems that she just passed over it. She, who had been the very doyenne of tradecraft once, uncovering dissidents and trailing cultists to their lairs. But her world had closed like a fist. Care had shrunk it. The thing you didn't do, in Outreach, in the military. Or not about anything other than Pallesand or your own career.

"It's not like I need a dossier prepared." She glowered at him with directionless hatred and he let it glance off his porcelain composure.

"I will, of course, accompany you to—" he started, and she jabbed a finger at him so fiercely she almost put an eye out.

"You will not. I don't want you there." That, at last, cracked him, just a hairline fracture. Offended, perhaps, at the insinuation. "Look," she told him, "I don't know how this will go. Sometimes these things are a sniper's work, sometimes an artillerist's. If the latter, you don't want to be standing next to me. Even fresh off the boat, you don't. You get me?"

"I see," he said neutrally.

"And anyway, if things go *really* badly, I need someone left standing at the Residence to keep shop." She tried to make a joke of it. Not like things were going to go *that* badly.

"I see," he said again. "Very well." As though it was a concession she, his superior, had wrung out of him. "Magister, your sword."

"Hmm?"

"It seems to me," said the man of the flawless decorum, "that it might not be wise or appropriate to wear your sword to your interview with the Sage-Broker. It sets a tone. Certainly, on the Archipelago, I would not have expected it."

Gil found the offending article was, indeed, scabbarded on her uniform belt. That her hand was about its hilt, even. Easy enough to undo the buckled tab that held it there. The *frog*, she suddenly recalled, being the technical name. Some tiny remembrance of Kakrops, being taken treasonously into her meeting with the man who was stealing the god's body. Perhaps that was what decided her.

"We're not on the Archipelago," she told Samellers. "Hold up the mirror. Actually, no, just set me in order, whatever's out. If you do half as good a job as you did with your own, they'll make me Professor and elevate me to the Commission, just on sartorial grounds."

He blushed, actually blushed. Adjusted a couple of her buttons and tugged at the hem of her jacket to compensate for the sword dragging one side of her belt. And then it was time.

The palace. Since his audience with the Alkhand, Berkely had relocated all Palleseen administration there. A not-so-subtle message. Already the Emorandi were finding that they had to impress the Pals with the importance of their petitions, and that any audiences were conducted under the eyes of men and women in charcoal-grey uniforms, batons over the shoulder. Batons, in the presence of the Alkhand. And those other petitioners, the meaner ones, found that the new Alkhand's practice of setting aside time for them and their sponsors had drained away like water spilled on sand, and barely a damp patch left to admit it had ever happened at all.

Pal petitioners, needless to say, received prompt attention. Most of the time their requests could be satisfied without even needing to trouble the busy, busy Alkhand.

There had been considerable disquiet on the streets, and for that reason the Palleseen guardians of order and the throne had taken possession of the Usrani monastery, and the throne room. Or at least that was the order of events recounted in the official reports back to the Archipelago.

"Sage-Invigilator Angilly," Berkely said. He was at a fantastically ornamented table, the surface a sheet of translucent rose crystal over an intricately carved scene of the Tesemer hunting with windsaws. The legs of the piece were worked into bestial legs, gilded, the feet spread like claws. She was vaguely surprised not to catch him in the act of peeling off the gold leaf.

"Sage-Broker Berkely," she noted. "I understand you wished to see me?"

"Well my apologies for disturbing all that good work you're doing for the Pallesand cause," he said sourly. "What, precisely, were you thinking?"

She regarded him, not feeling the enquiry deserved a response.

"I have a stack of reports on how you've been running your operation here," Berkely said. "Some that reached me before I shipped out, others that hit my desk after I arrived." His gesture suggested that the opulent piece of furniture he sat behind was his *desk* now. "I mean, you hear stories about Outreach, but this..."

"Sage-Broker, listen to me very carefully," Gil said, and her tone stopped his game dead. "I have done a great deal to transform Usmai from a nation actively hostile to the Palleseen cause into one that welcomed us, supported us and was beholden to us. In the short time since you have arrived, you've undone a good half of that. If you proceed with Drathel's idiot plan to render down the Kakrops Jars, you might as well set the whole country on fire. We killed their god, and I'd just about managed to keep our balance, after that. Stop it all sliding into ruin and insurgency. But, you do *this*, you're throwing it all away. Listen to me. Not to Drathel, who thinks only about what she can brag about in her next report to her superiors in Decanting. Listen to someone who actually knows how things are, on the ground."

His face told her she might as well have spared herself the breath. That the priorities of Valuations were much more in accord with Drathel's Decanting than Outreach's long games and pulling of strings. Not that she had, in all honestly, been quite playing those games towards the end.

"Angilly," Berkely said, "it won't wash. Not with me. Not with home. Not even with your old man in Outreach. If he's even still in his post as we speak. Wouldn't surprise me if he'd been parcelled off to retirement in the next dispatches, honestly. Outreach is under the glass, back home. All those cut corners look a lot like imperfection."

She thought of what she'd been told by Dalry and Annet, about how things were going on the Archipelago. Grimaced inwardly at how much worse all this might actually be.

If, that was, she was so very invested in Outreach and her career and the Archipelago. But right now that wasn't her personal priority, and to hell with the service.

"Berkely—" she started.

"What happened to those two history buffs, Angilly?" he asked lazily, leaning back in a fortune's-worth of chair so that the ornamented wood creaked. "The pair who came to visit you. There are papers out for their arrest. Surely you did a little due diligence? Only, a little whisper says you heard all that and got them up to where that demon gate thing is, so they could put themselves out of the reach of the Commission. Well, out of reach one way or another. Who knows what your odds are, departing through that door?"

"If you're referring to—"

"You know exactly who I'm referring to."

"Then any papers on them arrived after they'd been and gone. They are historians and researchers with a writ from the Commission." Angilly shrugged. "Is that seriously the pin you're using to fix me, Berkely? Is that what you'll offer as an excuse, when you and yours are thrown into the harbour by the Usmiat?"

"The Usmiat will grouse and tear their clothes a bit, and then get used to the new way of doing things," Berkely decided. "Because we have the Alkhand, after all. Their precious Alkhand, the only living child of the old one, the blind one. He's alive and on the throne and if they want both of those things to continue happening they'll know not to get ideas above their station. And soon enough there'll be another shipload of uniforms off the boat, and our friend the Alkhand will tell his adoring people how the very best thing for Usmai is that, in this dangerous and uncertain world, it becomes part of the Sway and accepts formal Palleseen law. And he can go retire to an estate somewhere with a couple of courtesans and a big bag of drugs or whatever the fashion is around here, after formally ceding direction of the country to the new Perfector. You know how these things go. Better than me, I'm sure."

"That new Perfector's going to be you, is it?"

Berkely spread his hands modestly. "Not for me to second-guess the Appointments Secretary to the Commission, hmm? Oh you look so sour, Angilly, but just fucking take this as an Outreach victory, won't you? Perfect end buys off a lot of imperfect means?" And that could have been it. He could have left it at that, a perfectly civilised end to the conversation that left her in a position where she had nowhere to go. Sidelined but semi-complimented, given a slice of the credit and told to eat it up like a good girl. Just exactly how things should have worked, Outreach passing the operation over to Valuations with a brisk handshake, and on to the next territory in need of softening up. And she wouldn't have left it there, obviously, but he'd dug a good hole for her, and climbing out of it would have been effort. Instead of which, he had to indulge himself.

"Of course," Berkely went on, one finger doodling idly on the crystal tabletop, "if you want, probably you could go join him on the estate, when we pension the lad off."

She found she had gone quite still. Just making a sort of interrogative noise. Not even a word.

"I understand," said Berkely expansively. "Outreach. You have to do these things. Strange bedfellows. I mean, I'd heard the phrase. Always thought it was a metaphor, but there we are."

"Berkely," she said, warning.

He met her eyes. She realised it was the first time he actually had. He had a way of looking at you that just took in the face, but never admitted to that human contact. Which was a blessing because, she now decided, human contact with Sage-Broker Berkely was not a thing to be cherished.

"Only I *thought*," he said, and the stress showed that, actually, he genuinely did care about this. He, the licensed profiteer, here to tot up the stock before taking over the shop for the receivers, cared. Saw what she had done and judged her. Disgusted, fastidious, hands drawn back so that the foreign muck couldn't get on his nice, clean, larcenous fingers. "I *thought*," he repeated, "you see, that when you lot lowered yourself to that kind of thing, it was so you could get *them* to do what *we* wanted. With your *wiles*, you know. Only what *appears* to have happened here, is that the Alkhand was such a boy in the sack that you're trying to stiff your proper masters to keep the randy son of a bitch happy and that seems to me to be exactly arse about face on how it's supposed to be." And was it jealousy of her, or of Outreach's airs and graces or just that Berkely was the sort of man who, given a higher chair, would never miss the chance to piss down on someone?

Not that he was wrong. The huge and unreasoning tide of rage and hatred that fell on her was far more about his accusations being *true* than anything else. She had compromised in her duty. She had forsaken Palleseen interests. She had loved Dekamran. To nobody's particular benefit.

When the sword came out, his eyes followed it. He lounged, still, but she reckoned his fingers gripped the carved arms of his fancy chair rather more tightly.

"Those words," she said tightly, "are not between departments, not Valuations to Outreach. Nor are they professional words from the operational chief to a subordinate. They are personal, Berkely. You and me." Shifting her grip so she had the sword below the hilt, hand about the first few inches of the blade before the honed edge started.

"Really, Sage-Invigilator," he tried. A smirk, he tried. A derisive look, to dismiss it all as histrionics.

"You and me," she said again. "A personal insult. Which you will withdraw now." And while, on paper, those words said or unsaid would change nothing of the official position between them, the concession would weaken him. Give her a handle on him, leverage to turn things about. You could not back down, one human being before another, without ceding significant ground.

He understood just as much. "You know," he said, "I don't think I will."

She found she was smiling. Because he'd had her on the rear foot all this time, like being forced backwards down a narrow corridor, but abruptly the walls around her had opened up and she could deploy the sort of footwork she preferred. "Well then." And she brought the hilt of the sword down on the tabletop.

She hadn't meant to crack it, but when the slab of rose crystal fractured like a spiderweb it was, she had to admit, a nice touch. Berkely certainly flinched. For a moment she had him. A man who could not compete with her in this arena. A man who fenced only through the papers of his account books, or wielded his authority like a bludgeon.

He stood smoothly, and for a moment she thought he would call for his sword right then. Give her the bloody satisfaction of putting some slashes in that uniform jacket, clipping off a button or two, seeing what colour Valuations bled. But it was his people he called for. Or rather, it was Flint. Now counted amongst that number.

Fellow-Monitor Postry, Flint to his declining number of friends, burst in with a handful of troopers at his back and stared. Seeing Gil, the sword, the shattered tabletop. Berkely, now standing, chair pushed back as though to get it out of her vandal reach.

"This doesn't concern you, Flint," Gil said flatly. "This is personal. An insult the Sage-Broker is about to swallow right back." And actually, all the better to have the witnesses. How else to make the man's climb down the sweeter?

Berkely summoned a smile. Just the ghost of one at first but he brought it back to the land of the living quick enough. "Oh no," he said. "No, no, Sage-Invigilator. I mean, I appreciate that the Commission has not outright banned the practice *yet*, but the most recent commentariat from their sessions has made it very clear that the business of duelling between officers is very strongly frowned on. Very strongly indeed." Smoothing down his jacket, tugging at the seams of his breeches, banishing the moment of genuine fright she'd given him. "Inefficient. Results in too many untoward injuries. And," burlesquing alarm at such an un-Palleseen thought, "rather smacks of ritual and ceremony. Practically a heathen custom. A little too much of the old ways, hmm? We do *not*, any more. We do not lower ourselves, no. Fellow-Monitor Postry?"

Flint started. "Magister?"

"I'm afraid the position of Sage-Invigilator Angilly has declined considerably during the course of this interview. Her explanations for her aberrant conduct have not only verged entirely towards the *deviant*, but she has offered violence to her superior." A hand towards the ruined tabletop, prime exhibit in evidence. "Under the circumstances, I don't think it's appropriate to just leave her at large with the facilities of Slate House at her disposal."

"Magister?" Flint repeated.

Berkely's expression moved to one of sudden inspiration. "You know, Fellow-Monitor, I do believe that there is an institution within the city that might assist us. It seems that the Sage-Invigilator has grown extremely fond of local matters, after all. Positively immersed herself in them, to the detriment of her duty. Perhaps you would escort her out of the palace and have her locked up in the, what do they call the place, the House of Hard Angles, isn't it? I don't think that she's fit to run around the city compromising our efforts. I really don't think we can trust her to keep her hands to herself."

"Magister?" Flint said again, eyes flicking from one Sage to the next.

"Take the bitch to the prison and throw her in," Berkely told him. "Direct order, Postry. Perhaps you'd be good enough to execute it."

"Flint," said Gil, as he turned to her. Abruptly her sword had flipped in her hand, the point towards him and his people. The three troopers clutched their batons uncertainly.

"Gil, don't make this difficult," he warned her. Reached, then drew his hand back sharply when that needle point flicked at him.

"Flint," she said again, trying by that nickname, by their familiarity, by their nights with the hus jar, with the easy talk, to get some leverage on him. But he was slippery, was Flint. All those shared memories just slid off him, and now the troopers had their batons levelled at her.

She could go for it, she knew. Batons in a tight space, not ideal. She could slit their uniforms, their throats. Kill Flint as he backstepped and waved ineffectual hands. Cut down her compatriots in cold blood to get to Berkely. A final lurch into treason.

"Gil," Flint said. "Come on. Sword down."

She didn't have it in her, she realised. Not to kill Flint, nor these three soldiers who had only their orders and a complete lack of context about what was going on. And in that moment of revelation they surged forwards and grabbed her, and Flint took her sword.

Terms of Execution

What is it to be Croskin, the demon? To have taken the contract, and the uniform, and found it freeing. To have found a new identity under the comically undersized cap, in the baton clutched in barbed paws. To have, for some brief span, a life. Not the strained existence of a demon under the exacting duress of a contract. Not the brute servitude of a subject to the Kings Below. Something freer. Something better. And demons have no faith, but does that mean they can't have something to believe in? A flag. A uniform. An adopted nation.

What is it to be Croskin, now? Betrayed by all these things. The fit of the uniform too tight, the flag twisted into a noose, the nation just a trapdoor to open beneath him. And demons are wicked things, fit only for vile service. Drive them, torment them, force them, shackle them. You cannot truly hurt a demon because they are walking injuries to the fabric of the world. You cannot wrong them, because they are by their very nature wrong. You cannot betray a thing made of lies. Misery and wickedness, as the words run.

What is it to be Croskin, promised a place in the world and then sold by the cause he gave himself to? Ask all those in the camps, before they were murdered. Ask every soldier sent to a stupid death by an idiot officer. Ask Gil, even now on her way to the House of Hard Angles. To be Croskin is to be bitterly disappointed with the way the world has served him, and to be so disappointed is the last scrap of his adopted human life they've left him.

He had assembled his people. His demons. His squad. All the things that Flint's people had unearthed, led to them by Croskin's keen nose. The prisoners of the Successor Coast's demon-hating past. Freed from jars and skulls and from beneath sigil-inscribed stones. Given a brief life of almost-freedom. And to a regular human being, a soldier's lot was constriction and service, but to a demon it looked a lot like liberty.

He had them lined up in this room in the palace, this cellar. A place for the royal wines and victuals. He'd made it his drill ground. His disparate creatures. The bird-insect-reptile-crustacean mashup forms that had been the very knife-edge of nightmare to locals of three centuries before, but now looked faintly ridiculous. Moth-eaten costumes unearthed from an ancient trunk. He'd straightened their jackets, those that could wear them. Done up the few buttons that would stand it. Stepped back, like any drill sergeant, to view his handiwork. Anything but uniform, but as good as it was ever going to be. One last flourish of the Palleseen colours. If he'd had a bugler in the squad he'd have ordered the funeral post. If he'd had a flag he'd have it half-mast out of respect for what was being lost.

Croskin the demon could not feel sorrow or loss, of course. Not in a human way. Any demonist would tell you as much. Which left him considering these sorrow-like and loss-ish things within him and wondering just what the hell they *were*, exactly.

No tears, of course. But a certain look to his dead, red eyes when Fellow-Invigilator Wattery came in to inspect the troops.

"Really?" she asked, faintly incredulous, seeing them all lined up there like the worst honour guard in the world. "Fuck me but you're taking this as far as it'll go, aren't you?"

Croskin saluted her. "Magister," he said. "All present and accounted for."

She didn't believe him. He saw her counting, until she'd reached the same figure Croskin had given her before. Twenty-seven demon troopers and he, Cohort-Monitor Croskin, reporting for duty.

She had a satchel, and in the satchel she had contracts. He couldn't see them but they were burning a hole in his mind with their presence. As though each time she moved he heard chains clinking. And he would have fought her. He would have torn her. He would have ripped her head off and howled hell down her neck. Save that she was his superior officer in the service, and he was constrained to do what she told him.

"It's about time we re-established some normalcy around here," Wattery grumbled. She had the first contract out. It was depressingly brief. You learned to be wary of the long contracts, as a demon, but you learned to be really wary of the short ones. A competent demonist knew you didn't need a thousand words, and you'd more than likely trip yourself up with them if you tried.

"The one benefit of this ridiculous situation," Wattery told her captive audience, "is that your current bindings mean you literally have to agree to whatever the fuck terms I throw at you, right? I tell you jump, you hit the fucking ceiling. So thank you to your man Galversty for that I suppose. He left you flapping about on the end of the line for far too long, but at least it's simple enough to reel you in. So fine. Twenty-eight individual contracts. None of this chain of command rubbish. Each of you bound to me, and back to the Kings when I'm done with you or you meet your end. None of this hanging about indefinitely pretending to wear the uniform."

"I am proud," Croskin said, "to wear the uniform."

There was the tiniest moment when he scared her, then. To hear such a thing from a demon. But then she remembered who was holding both the rank insignia and the contracts.

"You, here, now, Trouble," she told him. "You'll affix your mark to this, and bind yourself to me, superseding all past arrangements. And in doing so these others, who've bound themselves to *you*, will have that binding transferred to me, via all these other clever bits of paper I've got here. So I don't have to stand here like a fucking lemon while they squawk and chitter their way through it all. You got me? Gak."

Croskin paused. His eyes swivelled left and right, waiting to see what that *Gak* might summon. Its cause was quite clear, namely the blade that had introduced itself alongside Wattery's throat, drawing just a little blood, just a bead of it.

Its wielder moved, a fencer's sidestep, keeping that razory edge beneath the demonist's chin. Wattery's eyes went wide when she saw. Don a human face all she wanted, there was no way the Viper could hide what she was from a trained demonist.

Wattery made a little motion of one hand towards her satchel. Probably there were some solid anti-demon measures in there, sigil grenados or a warding fan. The sword moved. Another bead of blood. Wattery stopped.

Croskin watched. If Wattery told him to, he'd descend on Caecelian tooth and claw. But he reckoned she'd get precisely halfway through any such order before losing her rank and privileges to the blade.

"Where is your anchor, precisely?" she asked him. And she wasn't his officer and he wasn't bound to answer, but nor was he prohibited from it. "In limbo," he growled. "Precisely."

The Viper's smile was a terrible, beautiful thing. She took another step, putting herself beside Croskin, putting herself before Wattery, pushing a little on the hilt so that the demonist's chin went up. There was another there – no, two. A Pal human girl hanging back, looking like she'd crawled out of her own grave and part of her wanted to share the experience with the world. An Usmiat human girl right up at Wattery's back now, her own sword out and making sure the demonist didn't get any ideas about a sudden retreat.

"You have discharged my kin from your army," the Viper told Wattery. "Are these pieces of paper your cages for them? Are they *in* those cages yet? How unfortunate."

"They will go Below. If they are not bound," Wattery got out, moving her jaw the absolute minimum distance to let the words out. And it was true, of course. Croskin could feel the hunger of his home clutching at him. Unnatural, for a demon to be out of hell. Only the contract allowed it.

"Girl. Make yourself useful," Caecelian said.

The Pal girl stepped forwards, unwillingly, uncertainly. Croskin squinted. She was hard to look at. Like the sun on water. Something wrong with that one in a way that the Realms Below couldn't even have made worse.

She had a piece of paper. Little more than a scrap, really, torn out of someone's book. The handwriting was weirdly childlike. Croskin felt the pressure of it against his inner being, his very nature.

"Bind them to this, if you please," Caecelian said. "Release them to it."

Wattery's eyes were very wide. Not just with the sword's pressure. With professional alarm. "You can't," she said. "A demon. Make a contract."

"I was slave to an army conjurer for a decade," Caecelian said, with feeling. "Amongst my other duties I watched him draft contracts every day. To send my kin into your wars. I saw it done. I remember how the words work. Not just the way a demon knows them, the thin end of the lash, but how the handle feels too. I watched and learned, demonist. I know. Bind them. To me."

"No," Wattery said, and then whimpered at the slightest motion of the blade.

"To me," Caecelian said. "Or..." Reaching out with her free hand, her off-hand. "Can *I* just... is this a thing that you have kept from us for so long, that *we* can..." Because Croskin and all his people were hanging invisible in the air. Standing there, as physical as a demon ever was, but hanging there too, between one contract and the next, and she had a contract right there. As amateur a piece of work as anyone ever saw, but perhaps it was different between demons.

"Yes," he said. And, to the others, "Tell her, yes."

They muttered, chattered, gurgled, all the noises their physiology permitted them. Assent, in sounds human and bestial. *Yes.*

"No!" Wattery shouted. But there was no forbiddance in that *No.* No occult strength.

Caecelian let out an exultant cry, thrusting the crumpled contract up, and in that moment the demonist acted. Batted the sword at her throat aside. Took a savage gouge across her shoulders from the Usmiat girl as she leaped away. No cry of pain, though, just hands thrust in her satchel for a fistful of wards that would protect her, that would send any number of demons shrieking Below.

"Gak," she said.

Her head, and one arm at the shoulder, fell from the rest of her, as though abandoning the cause and the uniform and going to seek a separate future on the floor.

The Pal girl stared at what was left standing of Wattery – not standing for long, but for long enough that a weird note of comedy attended the subsequent collapse. The knife in her hand, the pearl-bladed one, swirled with clouded red as though the demonist's blood was diluting into an infinite sea.

"Good," said Caecelian, and though demons should know nothing of *good*, Croskin could only agree.

Master of All He Surveys

"... Once a nation has been either induced or pacified sufficiently to be inducted into the Sway then a formal administrative staff shall be assigned, overseen by a provincial governor taking the title of Perfector, and being of at a minimum Sage rank. In those territories inducted into the Sway through force the Commission's recommendation is that all non-collaborating remnants of the existing administration be removed, and accommodations to be reached with secular collaborators only, and then only if such accommodations strongly favour the furtherance of perfection. In territories inducted without recourse to force of arms then, while further leeway may be granted for the incorporation of existing secular civil structures into the new administration, at the Perfector's election, over-reliance on such measures is discouraged. In any event, any individuals remaining who might in future raise a legitimate (under prior legislature) claim to control or authority over the territory should be removed as soon as this may be conveniently achieved..."

Preamble to On The Practice of Provincial Assimilation as approved by the Temporary Commission of Ends and Means.

He had given it all away.

He hadn't realised. He couldn't even have said when it started.

Long before the new man, Berkely, came, certainly. Which

meant that, loathsome as Berkely was, Dekamran couldn't blame him. It wasn't the headsman who pronounced sentence, after all.

When precisely, then? When Kakrops had been killed by the Pals, in that fraught and desperate skirmish at the pools? When the frog god had died, but he, Dekamran, had let them crown him anyway. He, the bringer of ruin?

Before. Before, before.

When he'd stood before Flint, across the Peost border, and said 'yes' to the man's help in retaking his birthright? That was surely the point when the scales had tipped. Surely.

Before.

When Gil had freed him from the House of Hard Angles. Would his brother truly have killed him? Would he, if he could have heard Dekamran speak? Would he not have accepted an advisor, even one shackled to the throne and in arm's reach, as enemies might be kept?

When his father had turned away from Gorbudan, back when the old man had been Alkhand. Could he, Dekamran, have turned the tide then? Travelled to Mantekor. Reconciled with his brother. Or was he already in the river, being carried swift downstream towards the rocks and not realising?

When he had returned, just too late to see his mother walk away and take the mask of the Alborandi. When, because he did not want to hear the coloured version of events from all the self-interested parties who were there, he had chosen the one stranger who'd witnessed the event? Was that it?

When he'd first met Sage-Invigilator Angilly of Slate House, the Palleseen Resident?

A woman out of favour, because the Pals had been out and the Loruthi in. A man out of favour, because Gorbudan had been heir presumptive. Natural allies, each the underdog in their own field. Why not turn to company that understood?

And, because of that, when the Alkhand Oparan had finally lost all patience with Gorbudan's raiding and taking sides with the Loruthi during the war, against Usmai's declared neutrality,

Dekamran's rise had been Angilly's. His fate and that of the Pal fortunes in Usmai, inextricably linked. Until they grew so strong that they no longer needed him. And Gorbudan had said, so often, how the boy over on the Peost throne was just a puppet. And at no time had Dekamran ever thought, *That could happen here.*

He could almost feel the strings. When they brought people before him, for his judgment. When they brought things for his seal. And if his strings did not suffice to move his hands then they'd just seal the things themselves. As though his mute, unwilling presence sufficed to give legitimacy to their documents.

Right now, he had the luxury of the Alkhand's chambers. He could call for food, for drink, for poets and musicians, as his father had indulged his sorrows with. He had not. He ate sparingly, drank blunt ramaht, sat alone with his books or without his books. And the company he most desired was that which he could not, must not have. The Pals would have preferred a hedonist, he knew. A sot who lost himself in pleasures and left the burden of governance to his new friends. Who let them raid the wine cellars so long as they brought him back a bottle.

Outside his door were two Pal soldiers. They would answer him very courteously if he spoke to them. Taken on face value, though, they were the most ignorant men in the whole of the Pal garrison because not an answer did they have for any question he posed them. Nor would they let him walk abroad without holding him at his own door while they sent for an escort. For his own protection. Assassins, don't you know. Though, when he quizzed them on the nature of these assassins, their customary ignorance descended like a veil.

One day, he rather suspected, there would be assassins. When his ongoing presence in Usmai was neither necessary nor even useful. *Then* the killers would come, and the guards would not be there.

He went to the door, one more time. To reason with them. To demand that he be allowed to see the Resident. The person he should not under any circumstances be allowed to see, not by them, nor by his own pride. The person he shouldn't want to see. Given all that had happened, and her role in it.

He wanted to see her. He wanted to hear what she had to say. And she would have a way of explaining it that set it aside from *him* and *her*. She wouldn't be a part of it. Would tell him that, obviously, she couldn't *stop* any of it, nor yet reverse it. But that she was sorry for it. She hated it, that it had to happen this way. And, if Gil's sympathy was the only thing that the world could give him, he'd take it. He'd cling to it. As he'd cling to her, in the vanishingly unlikely event that he ever got the opportunity to. Knowing himself weak, and a traitor to his own people, but true to his heart.

At the door, the guards were not there. For a moment, cued by his earlier thoughts, he went cold with the thought that this was *it*. That they'd tired of him even more swiftly than he'd thought. The assassins were already here.

The air was metallic with blood. He put his head out and looked down the corridor.

He was wrong. The guards were there after all. They even had friends because there were three more uniformed bodies at the very far end. A spectre was stalking towards him. Her sword, her long, straight skia, was all-over blood.

He did not know her. Dressed in sackcloth and rags and a Palleseen hat, slashed and decorated with red like clothes brought out for a very particular festival. Wearing a hideous mask, like a demon's fanged face. He did not know her even when she stood right before him and stared up into his face. Not even when she took the mask off. Weirdly, it was the other one he recognised. The Pal girl standing at the far end of the corridor. Loret, Gil's aide.

His heart leaped, when it shouldn't have. No mercy from that direction. Except Loret had a knife and must have made some contribution to the bodies they'd littered the floor with.

"What...?" he got out.

"Dekamran," said the girl with the sword, and it was her voice he knew.

"Enshili?" he demanded. And then more, save that the questions, so many of them, all tried to come out at once, and so none of them did. He just gaped.

She grabbed his arm and hauled him, skidding in blood, to where Loret was. The Pal girl seemed in a state of shock. A hand to her midsection, a hand holding the knife as though she couldn't let go of it but didn't want it near her. Its rainbow blade was clean and murderous.

Enshili took him to what had been her own room, until she had left it. Past there to the little room with the loose window nobody had discovered. Her exit then, her exit now. Outside, in a little unattended spur of the Constellar Gardens, there was a killing ground.

The Pals fenced to the star, he knew. He'd trained that way himself. A six-spurred piste and the fight revolving about it, clashing when the duellists lined up with the lanes. In this little circular clearing about a fountain, a woman, something like a woman, had fought like that. Killed four men and two women. Stood, now, with her blade slanted across her shoulder, the steel still red. The water of the fountain ran cloudy.

She was very beautiful, this woman. Poised, fair, deadly. If Enshili had told him she was a goddess, he'd have accepted that, though only a goddess whose purview was bloody-handed and monstrous.

"She is the Viper," Enshili said. "She's my teacher. She saved me." From what? From Gorbudan? From the palace? From being Enshili? "She's a demon." Defiantly. Yet still fearing his reaction.

Of course she was a demon. Just as he had been saved from Gorbudan by the Pals, what worse thing could save him from the Pals save demons, the ancient forbidden thing the Moerends preached against. Dekamran stared. The Viper looked at him with contempt.

It was something he felt he'd earned. A demon's contempt. He had sunk low in the fortunes of the world, after all.

He should just go. Flee into the city. Flee into the countryside. Just flee. Except.

"Loret," he said, and the Pal girl jumped at the sound of her name. He knew the answer, of course, but he couldn't not ask. Couldn't not expose himself to the crushing disappointment of it. Could only say, "Angilly, did she…?" *Did she send you?* As though anyone in their right mind would send this mad-eyed murderchild to do their rescuing for them.

"Her?" Enshili spat. "The Resident? You don't need to worry about *her*. Your revenge is taken for you. They threw her in the House of Hard Angles just today. She's gone." Taking his arm, genuinely solicitous. "She can't hurt you."

He made a sound, like a sob, like laughter. "Then what?" *What even is there left?* "What now?"

They got him out of the gardens and down into the city. One patrol stumbled across them and Dekamran just stood and watched, a dead weight witness to his own salvation, as the Viper and her apprentice went for them with bloody intent. As Loret just stood there, frozen with a terror of – it seemed like – her own hands, until a Pal soldier stepped within three feet of her and she killed him. Cut his baton in two. Cut the tableth slotted into it in two. His arms, at mid-forearm. His throat. A single, fluid movement of her hand that she instantly tried to disown.

And then this. This low place, on the edge of the docks. The backroom of a tavern whose existence had never needed to stain his knowledge of Alkhalend until now. Brought here because that was where *they* were.

They were Follo, the Preceptor of the Usrani, and some of his people. The frog monks, the jolly dispensers of alms, who'd had nothing to laugh about since Kakrops was killed, and even less since the Pals had turfed them out of their own monastery a few days ago. *They* were a trio of Tesemer survivors, one of them short an arm, and a pair of Ibaleth that presumably found the current détente undesirable. *They* were a handful of Emorandi nobles who had most to lose from the Pals, and who had mostly supported Gorbudan when there'd been a Gorbudan to support. *They* were a knot of Cotto, tattooed and ferocious. *They* were a rabble of others. Ship-owners, Beast Artists, thugs from the Sand Lanes, a big Pal man and a skinny Pal boy, a Maric bruiser with a bristling moustache.

Dekamran stood before them. Their Alkhand. Their massed gaze withered him, but he had to say something.

"I have made mistakes," he told them. Not the most enthusing start but it was what everyone there was thinking. "I didn't see the poison of these people until it was too late. I trusted too readily. I'm sorry. I lacked the wisdom of an Alkhand. But I see now. That they must be resisted. Fought. Driven out." Too late, too late, both to learn wisdom and to fight, but what could he say? "I am your Alkhand," he told them. "The heir by blood." *Gorbudan dead in battle, Premath by his own hand. Only this dreg of royalty left.* Gorbudan, or his father, they'd speak fire and lightning. He had none to give. And neither Gorbudan nor his father would have made the errors he had.

Follo stepped forwards. The solid man, the huge man. A fixture of Dekamran's childhood. Always a funny story that taught a lesson as well. Always time for the younger prince nobody else had time for. To see that face downturned in grief was to see the world broken.

"Your Tranquillity," Follo said, "No."

Dekamran stared at him. "No? No to what?"

Follo's gaze slid downwards, unwilling to meet his Alkhand's eyes. "As you say, you have made mistakes. Not been wise. Your judgment, with the Kepishi. Your people despair. I do not believe that they will rally to any banner you can raise. Your name – I am sorry, Your Tranquillity, but you have eaten away at your name, one decision at a time, and now it will not bear you." He glanced at Enshili, who was glowering at him. "I am glad you are free. But you should leave. Leave the city, leave these shores perhaps. Place yourself beyond Kepishi vengeance. Beyond that of your own people too, perhaps. You have been too much with the Palleseen for too long. In the minds of your people, their colours are dyed fast in you."

"But then who do you have?" Dekamran demanded. "I am the heir, the last son. What distant cousin, what by-blow? I am here, Follo. I am the Alkhand. Let me serve my nation!" *I who put my own longings first.* "Let me go to war for Usmai!" *I who never directed a battle.* "Let me lead the charge." *I who never truly fought.*

Follo's massive, sagging melancholy told him, *But who would follow you?*

"There must be something I can do, to restore myself in your eyes!" Dekamran got out. There was an almost embarrassed shuffling towards the back. *Is he still here? Isn't it someone else's turn to speak?*

"I am not their creature!" he shouted. And surely that he'd had to be *rescued* from his own palace proved that, but he saw it in their faces. The next time someone in a Pal uniform offered him some choice, to save his throne or his country, what would he choose? Could they have faith that he would cast aside the one and keep faith with the other? He never had before.

The monk sighed. "I wish…"

"Wait," he said. Understanding, at the last. Stepping back, beckoning Enshili to him.

Tomb-Robbing

Like sea-gods to islanders and people of the coast, so death-gods to everyone, for obvious reasons. Sometimes one and the same, to those who truly understand the bottomless hunger of the waves and the depths. Not tax-gods. By the time taxation becomes relevant, the window for devising new gods tends to have closed. But death, most certainly. Because ghosts are real, and usually malign or miserable, so natural to seek out some psychopomp that can explain what terrors lie on the far side, that these lost spirits would rather cling on than be subject to. Or what chance occurrence holds them back from their reward. Necromantic gods, whose priests traffic in corpses and spirits; anti-necromantic gods, determined that the dead not be disturbed. But always death, that great fascinator worn in the hair of religion.

Drathel had perfected getting into and out of the House of Hard Angles by now. Because the Moerends weren't her allies and she didn't want to rely on the monomania of the Under-warden.

This was to be her final visit, she suspected. And, let's face it, not the most conducive place in the world. Nowhere you'd take a date. She was more than ready to wash her hands of it.

The main business of the day was deep down in the crypt level – the part of the House that most people didn't even know existed. *That place? It's a prison. Oh and there are ghosts. Why build a prison for ghosts? Well do you* want *just loose ghosts everywhere?*

Honestly, the logic writes itself. Or that's how Drathel, irreverent on a professional level, imagined the conversation. The thing she was certain of was that, to the overwhelming majority of Alkhalendi, it was just a prison for ghosts and people, and a place you didn't want to be in the shadow of. She reckoned that only she, Arkanith and maybe three lesser Moerends actually knew the true purpose of the place. *She*, of course, had worked it out from first principles because she was rather clever. They, or some Grand Moerend since the fall of the old Empire, had likely done the same. Or maybe the secret had been passed down over the many centuries since then, but she'd have thought someone would have tried this stunt before now, if so. And it wasn't a trick you could do more than once.

Before she descended, she needed to take a weather-gauge of the other nonsense that was going on, within the House. Because it was all go, in the House of Hard Angles.

Amongst her other professional skills, Drathel was a good sneak. Not mandatory for a Decanter, but if you were the advance kind that went out with Ventures and robbed temples and tombs, then it was worth picking up. She managed to dodge the occasional Moerend padding about the upper levels, and creep downstairs to where the Under-warden lived, and worked. It was the man's work that interested her. Because the crypt was the real treasure here, but she knew full well that the man had been assembling quite the trove of charged bric-a-brac for his own purposes. Mostly because she'd been the unwilling donor of quite a lot of it when they'd come to spring Dekamran from durance here. Honestly, that was property of Decanting and she wanted it back. Ideally, before the imprisoned lunatic could do anything unwise with it.

The Under-warden had a chamber at one end of the long slot running vertically through the building and deep into the earth. He'd chosen it, maybe, for its big blank wall, which he'd made his chalkboard. Literally: dusty white marks and sigils covered the wall. Drathel did not know the notation, nor even the characters. It was a scheme of writing and mathematics that didn't belong in this world at all. She felt she understood it, though, in principle. Calculations of stress and tolerance, descriptions of the flow of power. Decanter work, seen from the other side of the mirror.

The Under-warden was hard at work when she found him. He had a machine, or that was her best approximation at a description. His assembled magical tat was laid out in a kind of grid, and he'd wired it all together with copper. Always the magician's favourite metal, copper, mostly because magicians were cheap and gold raised eyebrows. Some of it was complex clockwork, springs and intertoothed gears. Some of it was invisible, just implied forces that would be conjured up should the whole miscellany end up powered. Then there were wires spreading out across the wall in a convoluted design that was spiderweb and sunburst all at once, each node and terminus annotated in chalk in that dense, blocky script. The Under-warden himself was standing back from it as Drathel crept into view. Down to his braces and shirtsleeves, clothes stained with oil and soot and a little blood, from where he'd needed to anoint various parts of his device.

It was fascinating. Drathel hoped enough of it survived that she could get a good look at it. She could see the pathways the magic would take, when he drained his little hoard. That was prentice work for a Decanter like her. Then she could see he'd linked everything up to – well, the House itself. The House of Hard Angles. This sprawling network of wires and sigils was a mere fingernail of the plan, because it involved the entire building. The Under-warden was, she suspected, working with the way the place had been constructed, suborning it. He'd looked very carefully at the sigils on the outer walls and the door, and the way the architecture was designed to funnel ghosts in and not let them out. And not just ghosts. A demon, stepping into the House, would not come out. And nor could that other thing. The Warden. His pet, his creature, his whatever-it-meant-to-him.

He was going to let it out, she guessed. Use this arcane fuckery to break a hole in the spiritual walls big enough for a cursed centipede monster to escape. Honestly, she felt relatively ambivalent about that. It didn't need to be a problem for her or for the Palleseen administration, and under other circumstances she might have said good luck to him. But what he was using to power the animal act of his little circus was *hers*. Plus, if he got his way, he'd spoil a few other pots she was boiling. Overall, the interference was substantial enough that she had decided to put a full stop into his sentence here in the prison.

Not right now, of course. Not she herself. She had no intention of going toe to toe with the Under-warden because he was a long-boned son of a bitch who looked like he murdered children for a pastime. But she had left special orders for a squad of soldiers to come down here and kick over the man's toys and take back all that good stuff. And yes, he was just one man. One man with a nasty pet, but a man nonetheless.

She watched him work for a little while. Seeing the man alternate between childlike absorption as he chalked his marks, to any artisan's hard focus as he looked at his work from all angles, sucking at his teeth and rubbing at the back of his neck. Then something rustled in the dark, the man's constant companion, and anyway, the soldiers would be along soon enough. She didn't need to be here, to see the Under-warden's hopes and dreams, all that hard work, scattered and kicked apart.

Sometimes you've got to be mean. It was a lesson Gil had learned, and plenty of others in Drathel's career. The cause of the Palleseen Sway and the cause of Drathel's Career had one thing in common. Sometimes you had to break stuff to help them along.

She'd thought about dropping in on Gil, while she was here. For old time's sake. But what would be the point? And Drathel liked to avoid feeling guilty wherever she could. Not like she was *proud* of screwing over the former Resident, but the woman had been in her way.

She took the next stairs down, and then the next, until she had retraced her path to the crypt.

She heard them before she arrived, the monks. A handful of cracked, reedy voices. Not Arkanith, because he was Grand Moerend and had people to chant for him. The few select death monks he trusted with this treasonous little secret.

The crypt space, the heart of the House, was shadowy, colonnaded, perfect for an intruding Decanter to creep about in. She had on a shirt with a few warding measures drawn on its collar and cuffs, and a tableth in the top pocket to keep it all humming along. When she walked, the scuff of her boots was deadened to nothing. When she stopped, the shadows drew obligingly about her. And not as though the monks were keeping a keen lookout for roving Decanters.

She could feel the power of the place. Hard to squeeze anything out of a ghost, sure, but there were a lot of ghosts here. And soon, if Arkanith had his way, considerably fewer. Or if the Under-warden had *his* way, the same result honestly. Which meant that Drathel would rather both of them ended up disappointed because if there were free magic snackies going around then, honestly, she wanted to be first in line.

As a by-product of its regular activities, Pallesand probably generated a lot of ghosts. Aside from the Dead Companies and the various necromancy sub-departments, probably most of them went to waste. Drathel had wondered, idly, if the House of Hard Angles could represent a new direction for Decanting. Ghost-mills, the mass processing of ephemeral remains to harvest the tiny wisps of power they contained. It all seemed vastly inefficient. Honestly, you'd have to be a mad death cult to even think of something like this. She didn't even know if the House of Hard Angles represented some longstanding Moeribandi tradition, or if some solitary mad genius-in-exile had built the one and only example here in Alkhalend.

Here in the crypt, she watched Arkanith go through his paces. Fascinating, really, to contrast the old priest and the

Under-warden several floors above. Both absolutely given over to their work, but so very different. The man up top was like an engineer. Experimenting, adjusting, chalking up his calculations. Drathel suspected that if she'd accused him of being a magician he'd have laughed at her, if he ever laughed. Arkanith, in contrast, was a creature of ritual. His process was not the spare, honed thing of the man above, but it had the advantage of following well-trodden paths. All those traditions and incantations, prayers and formal gestures were building on paths and patterns worn into the fabric of the world by co-religionists past, strengthening the old man's efforts by the magic of repetition, training the world like one might train a dog.

At the heart of the crypt, in a stone coffin crawling with death imagery, lay the corpse of Premath, third son of Alkhand Oparan. The younger brother. The dead one. Or one of the dead ones, rather. Hard to keep track of the Usmiat royal family right about now, although it wasn't something that was going to be a problem for long. And Premath had died, obviously, but he'd died in a very specific way. A sacred way. The death of the old emperors. Perhaps the first person to die like that in a very long time indeed. Drathel wondered how long Arkanith had been working on the boy, to push him to that. The third son, the one nobody really cared about, the weird one. Probably the kid had started off exhibiting a morbid taste for the old death cult. Premaran-as-was, the boy nobody had a use for. Finding a second father in the Grand Moerend who, alone of all the world, told him he was special and important.

All a bit sad, really. About to get a great deal sadder, because what Arkanith had planned for the dead kid wasn't going to come off either, and so dead Premath wouldn't even end up as a footnote in history. Probably, later, nobody would even remember that Oparan had *had* a third son.

She skulked closer, pillar to pillar. The corpse in the coffin was perfectly preserved, of course. The old Empire had perfected a melange of magical and practical means for that. In the sealed necropolis across the mountains there was a whole Imperial dynasty, withered but unrotted, sitting in the dark and thinking deathly thoughts. Or so they said. One day Drathel would lead an expedition there and turn the entire institution into charged tablethi and the world would take one more step towards perfection.

Arkanith's head snapped up. "Who is present?" he hissed. Apparently her stealth wards hadn't been all that. But she was in the very heart of sacredness. He did have a home ground advantage.

She stepped out into the open. Sauntered, really. Eminently casual. Feeling all her protections flex against the very nature of the place. Arkanith hissed at the sheer sacrilege of her. The three old monks stopped chanting, staring at her. All of them at least as old as Arkanith. A whole withering branch of the cult, at its very last ebb, making its final grab at relevance.

Around them, she felt the power build. Up above, the Under-warden was still working, but the joke was on him. All that he'd accumulated would just earth down here, the way the building was designed to. He'd be left with a tinker's wagon of copper wire and no exit for his precious monster. Except Drathel was about to ensure that Arkanith's own lunacy wouldn't see the light of day either. So many doomed schemes.

"I mean," she said, "what's the plan, exactly, Your Quietude? Turn up with the kid shambling about and mumbling and Usmai suddenly rallies to the old ways and declares a new Dead Empire?"

Arkanith stalked a step closer, bony hands clenching and unclenching. "I do not *need* their rallying. Do you think Death cares for popular acclaim? Premath was *chosen*. A child born to death. I will take him to the doors of the Necropolis. I shall knock, and they shall open. The Imperial Family shall adopt him. The first new Necromancer-Emperor in a thousand years, ready to reclaim his rights."

"A new age of death, sure, sure." It was depressing how many of these mad old cults basically trod the same inward spiral.

Drathel's ears popped, like she was underwater. The pressure in the crypt was growing, the ritual gathering up the skirts of its robes.

"And what?" she asked. "You think the Empire comes back because you get this lad on his feet again?" Up above the Underwarden was working, not understanding he was just going to be fuelling someone else's necromancy. Up above, though, her own soldiers would be moving through the House towards him, wards on their chests and batons at the ready. Drathel was tearing it all down tonight. Pulling the curtains open and letting the light of reason in on all this clandestine nonsense.

"I'm sorry to be the one that breaks this to you," she told Arkanith, "but nobody wants an empire of necromancers back. Probably not even actual necromancers, honestly. Not the ones I've met. I've read up on it. It sounds like a terrible idea. So it's time someone kicked over the castle you're building here, and it looks like it's me wearing the boots. And you know what? With you out of the picture, the rest of your lads can probably wash that skull stuff off their faces and actually be useful to someone. Put on an Accessory's uniform and help with the admin."

She was ready, when he went for her. And if he *hadn't* been balancing awesome cosmic forces in order to enact a forbidden ritual then probably he'd have been able to muster a bit more, here in the heart of his mystery. But his resources were somewhat tied up, and so her personal wards sparked a bit, and she felt the tableth in her shirt pocket get warm, but that was it.

She shot him. Aiming for the centre of the chest but the little rod wasn't the most accurate. There was a whole mathematics about focusing length and energy spread and the like, but what it boiled down to was Arkanith spinning away with a charred rosette under his collarbone. The other monks ran at her then, shrieking out their curses. Her shirt actually caught fire with the countermeasures, but she emptied the rod's tableth at them, killed two, then got the third with her *other* rod. Because the thing about Decanting was you tended to have a lot of tablethi and stuff lying around.

And silence.

Batons didn't work in the House. She'd seen that when Gil came to spring her. Being who she was, she'd spent a fun evening here experimenting with focusing runes and a military standard piece until she'd disproved that hypothesis. You just needed a bit of insulation, basically. Modern reason triumphing once again.

Up above the Under-warden was still working. Working up a head of power that wasn't going to go anywhere. A target on his back for Drathel's soldiers to aim at. She'd have his little stash soon enough, and his machine too, to examine, and his monster would haunt the halls of the House for as long as monsters lived. And without the sudden flash and fire of his completed work, without Arkanith's rituals, power would just keep sluggishly dropping down here. Oozing into Premath's cold body, she supposed. And eventually that might become a problem, in a necromantic sort of way, but Drathel was everyone's friend and was going to make sure that didn't happen. After all, she was a Decanter, and here was a corpse just saturated with accumulated magical energy. And once you'd got the power into a tableth, that did rather wash the death-stink off it.

She looked down at Arkanith, who was still shuddering. She pulled back her jacket. Over her smouldering shirt she had no less than three bandoliers, all heavy with uncharged tablethi. She made sure he saw them. Understood where all that sacredness was going to end up. You had to show people the error of their ways. It was practically Pal doctrine.

Mosaic: Housebreaking

He wasn't always happy, Jack. The last member of the Fever Lodge's expatriate crew. The one who people thought least of. For most of his life he'd been pretty damn miserable, in fact. God troubles; people troubles. The sheer frustration of having no leverage on the world. Small wonder now that, having actually achieved something, having won a little joy in the coils of the Viper, he's happy.

But not complacent. That's what a lot of people don't understand about him. Not insensitive to the injustices of the world. When he sees someone hard done by, Jack's instinct is to help. And not necessarily ask about recompense, but that's what Oathan and Tally and the Reckoner are for. Jack, happy, just wants other people to be happy too.

Which leads them all into very strange ventures. High stakes, high risk. The House of Hard Angles.

The Under-warden was never intended to be a scholar of the forces of the world. Certainly not of *this* world, which isn't even his own. Which he seems unable to finally part from, venture into the wood beyond the Grove as he might.

He sat down with Happy Jack once, and explained about his home, the place he and his monster got lost from, and that he has been trying to return to for too long. And Jack listened, and nodded, and grew paler and paler. A place of war, of weapons and ways of living beyond the worst nightmares of even the Palleseen. *Why go back?* Jack had asked, obviously feeling that literally anywhere else would be preferable. The Under-warden hadn't had an answer for him. *Force of habit* didn't seem persuasive, but perhaps that was all he had left.

Jack the Viper's beloved and the Under-warden. The founder members of the Difficult Wives Club.

He looks at his work, lit by Pal work lamps here in the bowels of the House. Checks his notebook, the scratched and scratched-through calculations. And every soldier got taught the essentials, back in basic training. You needed to know a bit about the toys that made the war go. He's working far beyond his brief, though. Self-taught, trial and error, trying to build something in *this* world that truly belongs in that other one. The terrible one. The one he's trying to return to.

When the soldiers come, the Pals, he's so frustrated with the whole business he almost sits them down and asks their advice. Maybe they have some new perspective he could use. They're not interested in it, though. They level their batons at him and tell him to get to his knees, to keep his hands where they can see them.

And you can't use batons in the House. Except he sees that their weapons are all prettied up with marks and sigils, and he understands that the prohibition isn't going to hold today. Well, fine.

The Under-warden stands there in his braces and shirtsleeves, hands up but still standing, just staring at them. Slightly incredulous, honestly. Because, yes, he's just one man, but don't they *know*...?

She explodes from the darkness, his monster, his wife. A frenetic flurrying of legs, and out of the midst of it her head, the reaching hand of it, fang-tipped. The Pal soldiers scatter. He hears their screams. The dying...

They're not dying. Screaming a bit but only that. Possibly they're more surprised at it than he is. The monster, his wife, veers away at the last moment. He sees the wards and symbols they have, flaring at collar and cuffs. The same symbols that decorate the walls of the House. Half the soldiers are knocked over like skittles, but those segmented coils, those venomous fangs, gain no purchase on them. They're on their feet the next moment.

The Under-warden is amongst them even as they gather. He is, after all, a soldier. The sword in his hand wasn't there a moment before. Its blade shines silver and it sears through flesh and bone, and magic wards too. One soldier he kills, the next he plays some trick with, so that the touch of the sword shorts out all the wards and protections across the man's jacket. Leaving him prey for *her*. She plucks the man from his fellows, hauls him into the dark. His screams echo through the House.

The Under-warden clips three fingers from the hand of the next as the Pal woman backsteps desperately. The next moment his eyes are raw from the flash, his ears echoing with the crackle of baton-fire in close quarters and he's on the ground. On the ground and an extraordinary amount of pain surging back and forth through him, trying to find a way out past the ward of his ribs. Shot. Three times shot. His sword is gone.

"Fuck me," says the squad's statlos. The soldiers have their batons levelled at the dark, not quite trusting the protections Drathel gave them. Then one of them kicks the Under-warden for good measure, and the statlos says, "Get the magic. Get the stuff. Tear this down."

Elsewhere in the House of Hard Angles: Gil.

She sits in a cell. Maybe the one Drathel was in, that time. Maybe even the one she freed Dekamran from. She's had quite the career in snatching people from the jaws of the House. Fitting she's ended up here.

Just as Dekamran himself did, she's been thinking back through all the decisions she made, that brought her to this point. The fruitless exercise of *Where was the moment I could have changed things?* It's not as though any magic in the world would let her stuff the sands back into the top bulb of the glass, after all. No mage nor god nor Pal perfection could ever turn back time.

All around her the House shudders and thrums with magical energies, duelling rituals and counter-rituals and the magical vandalism of Decanting, all fighting over the accumulated wealth of tortured souls the place is a vault for. Gil, no magician she, is blind and deaf to it. Plenty of mundane unpleasantness to take up her senses. Somewhere down there in the depths someone is screaming.

She has lost. Not to the Loruthi, not to Gorbudan, but to her own people. Not even a rare thing, for Outreach. Everyone ends up making one compromise too many. It's hard to walk the narrow path of Palleseen Ends and Means when you're in a strange place and have to make your own rules to live by.

When someone comes to the bars, she doesn't even look up. Some monk, probably.

It's not some monk. It's Loret.

Gil stares at the girl. The woman. Loret. Not Loret. In that moment, just a blank space in the shape of a human being that Gil could read absolutely anything in. Her former aide, the useless one. The runaway one. The mad one with the knife.

She has a knife – a new and rather fancy one. She looks, if anything, dangerously sane. The sort of sanity you could cut yourself with. She stares at Gil and Gil stares back because it doesn't feel like the sort of conversation she's in any position to initiate. Except Loret just stares, quite as useless as she ever was, even here and now, appearing out of the darkness of the House like her own ghost.

"I don't imagine you're on the books as Berkely's assassin," Gil says at last, eminently calm, as befits the unflappable diplomat. "But perhaps you're here cutting throats on your own account. What's it going to be, Loret?"

Loret bites a lower lip already ragged with it. She brings up the knife as though very keen that Gil gets a good look at it, before the end. A magician showing you how the trick is done.

She does the trick. A single pass of the blade through the air. Another. Not even very graceful, a bit awkward really. Making a bit of a mess of the angle, on the second move. The duellist in Gil kicks a bit, at the poor form.

The ringing of iron against stone is like a little tune, surprisingly musical. The sections of the bars, severed at either end, crusty with sudden ancient rust. Loret brings up the knife again, the pearl blade, without a nick or blemish, gleaming wet in the light. Water can eat through anything in time.

Gil tenses, waiting for Loret to come through that gap at her, wondering if there will be a moment when she can make a play for that impossible knife. But Loret just steps back, half into the shadows of the place, waiting for her in turn.

The Under-warden crawls across the floor towards his work, that the soldiers are dismantling. Around them, the darkness writhes with spindly legs, but impotently. Drathel has done her work well. Or well enough, at least. Which is when the others arrive.

Not exactly the world's most prepossessing intruders, to come threaten a squad of soldiers. Happy Jack, skinny little man, unarmed. The Reckoner, woman from who knows where, unarmed. Oathan, a Pal, and at least he's big. He gets most of the batons aimed at him.

"What have you done?" Jack demands. He runs over to the Under-warden and plucks at him. The man, wounded, maybe dying, tries to shrug him off. Tries to get to where the work is, to complete it.

One of the soldiers kicks Jack off him, a boot straight in the kidneys that leaves him gasping. They're shouting at Oathan, all the usual things. *On your knees, hands out.* He scowls at them, the hugeness of him, the gravity. But he's just a big man. He's not proof against baton-fire. Only the fact of his nation has kept him from being shot already.

It all does mean the Reckoner, just a slight woman whose glitter-touched skin is dull and unremarkable in this poor light, goes mostly unnoticed.

She sighs. There was a time when she was very concerned with keeping all the universe's accounts in order. That was how they'd taught her. Walk through the water, leave no ripples and your feet stay dry, that kind of mystic nonsense. It worked but, trying to teach the philosophy to others, it still sounded mostly nonsense to her. She used it to move hurts around. Generally to herself, where she could deal with them. A miracle healer who couldn't ever let go of her iron self-control or what might happen to the universal balance? And now she's mostly left that discipline behind because the universe is patently screwed on a variety of axes so why is it her problem? Now it's just taking wounds for cash and that's its own sort of balance.

"All right then," she tells the universe. Almost rolling her eyes at the transaction. Nonsense, really. A finger on the scales so that *there* becomes *here* and *yours* becomes *mine.* And honestly she prefers doing it with wounds, despite the pain, because that's what she knows best. But shoddy, hastily set-up magic can also slip down the gradient she creates, and at least it won't sting in the same way.

She glitters. Not her skin, but all the sparking protective wards. They dance about her hands, gutter, die one by one. The soldiers stare at her. It's such an understated piece of conjuring that the statlos doesn't even give the order to shoot her. Very lax. Why, she might have been drawing on some kind of dread powers or something.

Then the wards are gone, just bled away into the building magical charge that she, the Reckoner, can see very clearly all around them. Just one more reason to have a headache, really.

She wishes she hadn't come. She even left her candies back at the Lodge, and now her mouth waters for them.

The soldiers realise that the wards are gone from their clothes at around the same time the monster does. The darkness coils furiously and they try to bring their batons round but it wouldn't help and they're too late. Oathan and Jack don't watch, but the Reckoner's senses let her perceive in exquisite detail just what the centipede monstrosity does to each and every one of them. It's just one damned thing after another in here and she wishes she hadn't come.

Jack props up the Under-warden, calling him by name, demanding someone help him. Oathan is kneeling, now, fishing pots and vials from his pockets, snarling into his moustache. He forces something down the lanky man's throat, that will be good for pain, give a second wind of life. Enough for him to get out, get clear, and then maybe they can do something else for him. Except he won't go. Except he lurches to his feet, strong enough to throw Oathan back from him. Staggers over and practically runs face-first into the wall he'd been working on. Shaking hands reconnecting his wires. Turning to them, face ghastly with pain, streaked with tears. *Please, help me.*

Jack can find loose wires and twist them back into place, if it's obvious where they go. Oathan, as far as he's concerned, has done his part and wants nothing to do with any of it. And the Under-warden's hands tremble, hurt or cold. The potions are strong but they can't fight death, and death is an intimate of the House of Hard Angles.

"Please," the Under-warden gets out. "She needs to be free."

She being his monster, and what sane person would want such a thing loose on the streets of Alkhalend, but still…

The Reckoner sighs.

Deep below them, in the crypt, Drathel has her strings of

tablethi about the coffin. All ready for charging, to leave the body no more than a corpse. No more necromantic emperors, thank you. The world's had quite enough of them.

Something shifts, above. Her senses, the way the hairs of her arms and the nape of her neck prickle, the precise way the shadows fall on her eyes, the long experience of being a Pal magician in hostile places, they tell her a thing has come loose, in her plan. By now the intricate embroidery of the Under-warden should be pulled apart like cobwebs, and his pile of magic tat should be in the hands of her people. But that hasn't happened. In fact, with every heartbeat, it's not happening more and more. The man's ritual is still building and that is going to mess with her work down here. In ways she can't entirely predict, in fact, because the Under-warden and his methodology just don't play well with the way this world's magic runs. The man's a sledgehammer in a crystal cave.

Do I have to do everything myself? she demands of the universe, which answers *You'll wish you had.*

The Under-warden is struggling. The Reckoner can't take his wound. It belongs to a different world, won't even go on her scales. Tally's the one she really needs right now and Tally was smart enough not to come. Not to set one foot inside these cursed walls, honestly.

The Reckoner sighs. What she *can* do is see the design. The whole and efficacious design that the man, in his amateur botcher's way, has been trying to complete. As he wheezes and labours, she steps around him, corrects his maths, takes up the chalk and adds a handful of sigils, makes the final connections of the wires.

She looks at him, looks at Oathan and Jack. As though daring anyone to commend her for it. To make a scene.

The Under-warden sits back, his breath shallow and loud. The House of Hard Angles shudders.

Across the city, anyone with the slightest sensitivity to the uncanny knows. Headaches, nosebleeds, nightmares, visions. There is a hole for ghosts in the heart of the Sand Lanes and it has stood since anyone can remember, and in all that time not a spirit has squeaked out of it that wasn't housed in the body it belonged to. And now this. A tremor. A shudder. Cracks running abruptly up the walls – not physically, but spiritually. Because they built it well, those ancient Imperial necromancers. When they set out to make a ghost trap, to funnel dead power into some scion of the ancient line, they didn't mess around. Nor did they consider five, ten centuries too long for their plans to come to fruition. Like every empire, they thought they'd last forever.

In building well, they made their prison inescapable. No chance of a loose window, a side door, some gap or hole by which a determined spectre might squirm free. And all the various Wardens of the place, down the ages, were likewise caught by it. The creatures the rulers of Usmai had, by tradition immemorial, thrown or lured into those halls, to be guardians and defenders of their own jail. Up to and including the Under-warden's wife.

And so, if he cannot open a door to let her out, he has only one recourse left to him.

On their ships, the Cotto sea-priests choke on their hus. Hullseer Orhuhst stares at the waves and stars and takes this as a sign. That he should muster his people. That he must do what needs to be done. In the palace, the handful of magical specialists on Berkely's staff wince and leap up from their desks or out of their beds, but have no grasp of what's happening because they're too new in town and don't know the layout of the streets.

Two of those streets away from the House, Caecelian breathes the chaos.

"He's done it," she whispers, clutching Enshili to her. Feeling a vicarious triumph, that there's no chain large enough that it can't be broken.

The power from the Under-warden's stock is meagre, in comparison to the great weight of the House of Hard Angles. But so is a pebble, compared to the avalanche. You just need to know where to drop it, to start it all sliding.

Down below, Drathel feels it start to slide. Looks up, for a moment feeling in the pit of her gut that the actual physical building is coming down on her. Throwing up her arms despite herself, crying out.

The deluge descends on her. The purpose of the building, triggered awry, twisted out of true by the Under-warden's little wires, but still discharging through all the occult channels of the House. Up, sideways. Down.

She sees her tablethi turn, from lead to gold each one, faster and faster. A fortune in magic, filled to the brim in two breaths and a heartbeat. She tries to reclaim them with quick fingers but they're too hot. She can feel the power charging them and discharging straight out again, over and over, until they spark and dance and rattle. Until she burns herself on them. Until the buried crypt is lit bright as day by the spitting, jigging things. Filling and emptying simultaneously, and all that power…

Must go somewhere.

Must go everywhere.

Collapsing back, the Under-warden gives a harsh croak of triumph. Jack, Oathan and the Reckoner cluster close together as the dark whirls and seethes with the ascendant dance of his wife, his monster, his reason for being.

On the outside walls of the House, the wards go out like candles in a storm. The ghosts, all those thousands of knots of torment held unnaturally in being within the walls, they are consumed, they flee, they dissipate in air. They funnel down to feed the ritual. They evaporate. To Caecelian, to anyone with eyes to see, the night sky goes green-white for one instant, the stars displaced by ten thousand twisted faces. To demon eyes it's beautiful.

The sparks fizz, spit, stop. Drathel, on her back, sits up. Her head is ringing. Her body feels like someone's been over it with a hammer. But she lives, and so there's still hope and, ideally, a career to be advanced. She lurches to her feet and staggers over to the coffin.

Her tablethi are half-melted to the stone, the metal run into the grooves and inscriptions, gilding the ancient necromancy with a veneer of Pal perfection. Nothing that can't be pried free, in her professional opinion. And it is gold. Whatever has just been and gone through this damned place, it's left them nicely charged.

Not damned, she realises. Not any more. The stone around her is just stone. The great weight of it no longer drips with ghosts and torment. She feels a moment's regret, as though a wonder of the world has been brought down. But the Palleseen do it all the time and maybe she can take credit for this one, add it to her permanent record. It's worth a commendation back home.

Premath sits up.

Drathel, mid-pry, stares. His head turns slowly until he can meet her gaze. Greyish skin, eyes gone milk coloured, but still recognisable as the third son of Oparan. No need, now to paint the skull on, to give a reminder of death.

She swallows. She came here with a lot of protection about her clothes, but right now, all she can see are char and fray where her runes and wards overloaded and burned out.

It is an occupational hazard, say those who don't know the trade. It is a stereotype, say dismissive Decanters. It is a joke amongst Drathel and her peers. The intrepid robber of graves surprised by a corpse more lively than expected. It does not, of course, actually happen. Not to professionals. Not to Drathel.

She pulls away sharply, but the strings of her melted tablethi are caught about her wrist somehow, and Premath's answering lunge catches her by the throat. His fingers are like stone claws, like ice. She pries at them, but they are infinitely harder to get free than the slagged tablethi had been. Premath's dead eyes see only sacrilege and spoliation. He clutches and closes his chill fingers until there is nothing left living in his grip.

Gil and Loret just leave. The Lodge crew explained something of what they were doing to Loret, and why, but her mind was full of other things. Debts and betrayals, the ledger of her life. This thing she said she'd do, because she'd done so many wrong things that why should one more even matter?

"What's going on?" Gil keeps asking. Loret doesn't answer because, honestly, even if she'd listened properly back at the time, her understanding of the situation would probably be out of date by now. The walls around them seem to shake and blur. She has the constant sense of screaming, gibbering voices being sucked past her into oblivion. Once, a Moerend blunders into her, wailing, weeping. She shoves him away and just stumbles on. Until they reach the open door, and stagger out into a street in the Sand Lanes. At their backs the grim walls of the House of Hard Angles are dark, not a trace left of the wards that once blazed here like a wrecker's lamp for ghost ships.

One street further, they find Caecelian and Enshili. The Usmiat girl throws her arms around Loret. Abruptly all the terrible things, the ghosts and the horrors and the betrayals, seem justified.

Then the Viper grips her chin, hard as pincers. "Where is Jack?" she demands. And, eventually, Jack will hear that she asked, and smile a bit, because she can never tell him to his face that she cares. But there are moments like this which show that even a demon can.

"What's going on?" Gil demands again. Leaning against a wall, wide-eyed, staring about herself as though she doesn't recognise a brick or stick of this city she's lived in for seven years. "I need to get to Dekamran."

Loret releases Enshili. Looks at Gil. As though seeing her for the first time that night.

"Come with me," she says. "I'll take you to him."

"You have to go," says the Under-warden. Not to Oathan and the Reckoner, who need no encouragement. Not to Jack, who doesn't want to leave him. To *her*. The monster, his wife, coils above him, infests the dark, discolours the ceiling with her thicket of clutching limbs. She lets down her body like a bristling rope, her head questing close to him, antennae tracing the lines of his face.

"I've made a deal," he says, one hand gripping Jack's arm painfully tight, the other hand raised to her, resting along the line of her mandibles. "They made this happen. They got me what I needed. To break this place. To get you out. I said we'd help them. In the Grove. In the wood beyond. Keep them safe there. As you try to find home. But you have to go."

"Will she even remember, when you're gone?" Oathan spits, in the manner of a man who's put a lot of wealth and work into this, and sees the bill going unsettled.

"He's not going!" Jack shouts at them. "We'll get him out. We'll get him to Tally. Give him more potions. He's fine."

Oathan finds another potion, and then a twist of paper with some black salts in it that would get a corpse dancing for five minutes before it remembered it was dead. Dosage probably isn't an issue right now, honestly. He lets the man have the lot and the Under-warden necks it. Tries to stand. Can't.

His wife props him up. Coils about him, surges under his armpits and about his shoulders. Wraps him until it's like he's wearing a coat of legs. With the same delicacy as Tally performing surgery she sinks her fangs into his unwounded shoulder. He gasps, but it's a stronger gasp than before, the venom and the potions and the salts all living it up like it's the end of the world in his body and blood. When he speaks next, there's more wind to his words and he says not *You must go* but "Get me out. And then we'll all get out."

They get out. Lurching and limping as though the very stone of the building is coming down on them even though it's just the insubstantial avalanche of all those husks of ghosts, finally laid to rest.

Later, because it's a long walk from the bowels of the earth, one more figure steps out of the shell that was the House of Hard Angles. Out under the sky, looking up at the stars as though it's the first time he ever saw them, the Immortal Dead Emperor Premath leaves the scene of his own resurrection and wanders away. Wanders out of the city. Wanders north across the mountains to where the cold necropolis of his new kin awaits him.

Any Other Business

The Pals are on the streets in force. For those who've lived in an occupied city under the Sway or, worse still, have been with the Pal army, there's a distinct difference in character. If the locals thought that the increased patrols and the uniformed presence always at the corner of your eye was oppression, then having those uniforms right in their faces, the boots through their doors, has educated them. Around midnight an entire squad of dead soldiers was discovered in the House of Hard Angles. A discovery hastened by the resident Moerends fleeing the House, some of whom actually sought the aid of the Palleseen. Right now, therefore, a good slice of the garrison is going through the Sand Lanes and woe betide anyone out at night who looks suspicious. Or anyone making noise inside their homes for that matter.

The mounded and ramshackle construction of the Sand Lanes is not conducive to traditional Pal policing, however. Every door you kick down only leads to another. Every building is a maze. Either burn the whole district to the ground or give up on any possibility of seriously controlling it.

Deep within one such building, far from the shouts and the curses and the broken doors, the denizens of the Fever Lodge huddle close and do what they can.

Tally wasn't a miracle worker. Jack had faith in her. Had said as much, repeatedly, until eventually she'd turned on him and told him that he'd had faith in so many idiot things in the years she'd known him. His faith was an oft-pawned, lent and borrowed piece of merchandise, she said, and why should it matter a damn to her?

On the table, the Under-warden was still conscious. Which Jack knew wasn't Tally's favourite situation when it came to performing surgery, but she'd been with the army. It was hardly the first time. Operating under pressure was an old friend to Tally.

Operating under the shadow of the Under-warden's wife, not so much. And the ceilings of the Fever Lodge were low but that didn't mean the creature couldn't cling there, spread almost flat against the buckling boards, never still, a constant rustle and scratch as it shifted and settled its many legs. Its eyes, fists of glittering facets, were fixed on the man on the table. Watching as he groaned and gasped, and Tally pulled chips and fragments of bone out of his innards.

When it seemed that the pain would become too much, Oathan stepped in. Not to deaden the pain, because he'd done all the work he could in that direction, but to keep the agonised man *awake*. To perform acts of unmercy and ensure that the Under-warden experienced every slice and stitch of the surgery without falling into the void of unconsciousness. Because nobody knew what the monster, his wife, would do, if that happened.

Jack, whose own days of miraculous healing were long behind him, and who was grateful for it, stood by with swab and cloth, bowl and needle. Playing nurse as Tally worked swiftly and calmly, as a military surgeon must, and never once looked up.

Dawn was in the sky, unseen, outside, when she put down her tools. Dawn, and the patrols still out in force trying to find out what had happened, that had turned the city's vaunted prison into just a grand stone building one could put prisoners into. They never broke all the way into the Fever Lodge's inner chambers, though they kicked over everything in the first couple of rooms. And so, because nobody outside those chambers knew the truth, they never discovered it.

"Well," said Tally. Oathan, who at some point had simply gone to sleep, dread louring centipede wife notwithstanding, started awake.

"What?" he asked. Although, given they were all still alive and the monster remained quiet on the ceiling, the answer was plain enough.

"He'll live." Tally looked grey, haggard, a decade more on her this morning than there had been the evening before. It had been a long time since she'd put herself through that particular hell. Now, and only now, did she look up at all the segments and limbs and horror of it.

"He'll live!" she repeated, louder, in case the monster was hard of hearing. "Means you bloody better keep your end of the bargain. We don't do charity any more. Except for Jack and he's an idiot."

Jack, bag-eyed and swaying on his feet, collapsed down into a chair. The Reckoner brought a big bowl, one of Oathan's stewpots, filled with steaming water, and they washed away any of the blood that would come off without scrubbing.

The Under-warden blinked. "We will," he said, though only Jack, sitting at his head, heard him.

"Tonight," Tally said, daring anyone to contradict her. "Lay low today, get the hell out at sundown, before they make this place a part of the damn Sway."

"We need to wait," Enshili said. She was on the floor in one corner of the room. The Viper sat on a table, beside and above her, angular as a mantis as she hunched forwards. There was something about her manner that impacted on the happiness of Happy Jack. An unhealthy knowledge, a tension.

"Tonight," Tally repeated firmly.

"Wait for Loret," Enshili said.

"She's not one of us," the surgeon said. "She's the Cotto's. Part of that mad business they're involved in. If she goes anywhere, it'll be with them."

"I told her we'd wait," the girl insisted.

Tally's stare was four times as old as the girl and a thousand times more cynical. "Well la di da," the surgeon pronounced. "Only I hadn't realised you'd got yourself promoted to anybody giving a shit what you think."

Caecelian shifted. Just a very subtle shift, save that it grated the guard of her sword against the table. Tally looked at her, tired but giving no ground.

"You want to come piss in this glass, demon, you go right ahead. You think I don't remember some banishing rhymes from the High Fane?"

"All right then!" Jack declared hurriedly. "Why don't I fix us something to eat? Given that we'll be waiting until nightfall anyway. Given that none of this actually needs to be thrashed out and we're all just very tired."

"I'll go. You've got nothing left," said the Reckoner.

"Sod that. If anyone's fixing food, it's me," Oathan declared. "Or it'll just be bloody sweet buns and honeybread again." He levered himself to his feet. "Does that fucking thing eat?"

He meant the wife. The Under-warden didn't venture an opinion. Honestly, Jack reckoned he probably didn't want to know.

Oathan stomped away, shouting for the boy.

"Hey, no!" Tally shouted, as the Under-warden levered himself up on his elbows. The Warden herself uncurled down from the ceiling a little and she glowered straight back up at the creature. "What? He's just been stitched up. Unless you want all that hard work ruined." Actually facing down the faceless thing until it retreated back up to its massed coils.

"He wants me," said the Reckoner flatly.

Tally looked sour. "Well, of course he does. They all do." She made a disgusted gesture. "I mean—"

"I can't take it from him," the Reckoner said. "He's from

outside the world. The scales that he balances on, I can't affect. No more than I could *her*." A nod at the Viper. "But what?" She went over. "You know this, so what?"

The Under-warden beckoned her close enough to hear. Jack caught his voice, weak and thin. "For the fight. For the work. For getting us out, comrade. I owe you more than I can pay back."

The Reckoner's face went still. The way it used to be when she walked a tightrope with the universe and was never allowed to enjoy herself. "Nice to find someone," she admitted grudgingly, "who understands that." And another huge sigh, the way she did. "Well I owe the universe more than I can pay too. So somewhere we're quits."

Caecelian slipped from the table onto the balls of her feet, perfectly balanced. "It's time," she said.

Jack felt something twist inside him. "No."

She smiled at him and broke his heart, though honestly that was almost a daily occurrence. It was a fragile organ since it learned happiness.

"What?" Tally demanded of him. "No what?"

"I don't know," Jack admitted, "but No."

The Viper said, "I am going to fight. There is going to be blood and death on the streets of Alkhalend today. I will be a part of it."

They were all staring at her, until at last Tally said, "This is the Cotto's nonsense?"

"This is Alkhalend's nonsense," Caecelian said. "Chaos and the breaking of things. Drawing a blade against all chains. Down with the Palleseen Sway."

"They're not even *in* the Sway!" Tally hissed. "We're almost out. Can't they just—"

"Why you?" Jack demanded. Almost shouting. As close as he ever came to it, these days. "Why do you care about them?"

She glided over to him, touched his cheek, drew the fire out of him like a vampire of rage and strife. "I only care about bad things, Jack. You know that. Misery and wickedness. Misery and wickedness and one other thing. You know what matters to me."

He did know. In the silence of the night, the two of them together, he'd teased it out of her. Then wished he never had. Then tried his best to forget, to tell himself it was a problem for tomorrow's tomorrow. Not today. Not now.

Enshili was on her feet instantly, of course. Loyally by the side of her demon mentor. And Jack was about to volunteer. About to go enlist for a battle he couldn't possibly fight in. But she put a hand on his shoulder and told him *No*.

Oathan stormed back in then, having missed all of that. "Where has the damn boy got to?" he demanded. The others, clued in by more context, stared at him in alarm.

"What?" he wanted to know. Then understanding rose over his face like a tide. "No. The little idiot. Why would he—?"

His friends were going. His idiot friends from the Sand Lanes gangs, Jack thought. So of course Kilbery has joined them.

"I'm going to get him back," Oathan swore. "Little turd, always putting me to the bloody trouble. I'm going. Who's with me?"

Surprised, completely, when Caecelian and Enshili took him up on it. Unsurprised when Tally and the Reckoner didn't. And Jack wanted to. Jack would have done, but the Viper caught his eye and shook her head, and that was that.

Personal Accounting

Sage-Invigilator Angilly. An illustrious career with an ignominious end. Orphaned in a Jarokiri uprising. Left the phal for Outreach with more than adequate grades. An aptitude for work requiring more flexibility than most Palleseen departments. A swift rise through the ranks. Made Fellow ahead of her peers. Made Sage at the almost unthinkable age of thirty-two. A series of successful operations in and out of the Sway, instrumental in paving the way for Palleseen power, or in securing what others had already latched onto. Mentioned in dispatches and with approval. Finally, having taken over from a predecessor who had well and truly dropped the ball, she turned the situation round in Usmai. Transformed the nation from being pro-Loruthi with a simmering dislike of the Archipelago to being a staunch friend of perfection. Opening the doors for greater and more formal Pal authority to enter. Such a success story, and yet with such an end.

In the last of the night, Loret led Gil through the city. She'd thought it would be down. Into the Sand Lanes, into the maze of quays and ships. Instead, they crept past the very door of Slate House on their way upwards. One light burned in a high window. Sameller writing reports or reading her private correspondence.

"Where are we going?" Gil hissed at Loret's back.

"Where you want," the woman shot back.

"Loret, what happened to you?" Gil demanded. "Or who

even are you? What is going on?" Stopping in the shadow of the Residence as though the place could still lend her some symbolic strength. *My domain*. Except she wasn't the Resident any more. A fugitive from Palleseen justice, after all this time.

Loret turned. And *Who are you?* seemed an entirely apposite question. Since the girl had fled Slate House, after drunken violence and admissions and a good desk ruined, things had happened to her. She didn't shrink from the world the same way. Not as though she was safe from it, but as though she finally understood she couldn't be.

"Do you care?" Loret asked her. "Or is this just so you have something to sell, when they let you back in?"

"Harsh," Gil said. That damnable knife was in the woman's hand again. Perhaps it had never left. It looked like some ridiculous ritual piece a collector might pay a sack of coin for, save she'd seen it shear iron without slowing. "Loret— What do I even call you?"

Loret's look was pure disdain for a moment, as though she might come back with, *I am all the people you ruined whose names you didn't even know* or some such histrionics. Instead she said, "I'm sorry."

Gil blinked. "I mean, you turned up under false pretences and you were a terrible aide, but you just sprang me from jail so I guess we're even." Hoping desperately that *was* what the woman was sorry for. When she tried to speak again, to clarify the position, Loret just set off again. And fair enough, there was a leaden lightness to the air, and the sea below them had a luminous quality, like a tableth lamp that hadn't quite run out of charge.

She thought she'd worked it out, by then. Why they were going in what was, otherwise, an unthinkable direction. "I'll need a sword," she said.

"Probably," Loret agreed hollowly.

"I mean." Another turn. Passing the pools where a god had died. A flash of that night in Gil's mind, the rattle of the batons and the roar of Kakrops. "If we're rescuing Dekamran, I need a sword." Ideally also a hundred Alkhalendi loyalists storming the place, but a sword would be a start.

"Rescuing?" Loret sounded blank.

"Loret, if we're not rescuing Dekamran from Berkely then why in reason are we going to the palace? I mean, if Berkely wanted me dead he could've sent someone to kill me through the bars. Otherwise I'd think you were selling me out or something."

Loret stopped so that Gil almost ran into the back of her. "Ha," the girl said. "No."

"No selling out, or no rescue?" Gil prompted, abruptly feeling very exposed out here, very uncertain footing here on the paths up the cliffs, however broad and beautiful they were.

"No rescue," Loret said, and then, as Gil assumed the worst, "He's out. He's free. I'm taking you to him, like you wanted."

"He's in control of the palace?" Gil demanded.

"There's more up there than the palace," Loret said, and moved on, forcing Gil to dog her footsteps.

They made the Constellar Gardens before the troops started moving out. They hid in glittering bushes and behind topiaries as Berkely's uniforms began to march into the city. Gil knew that hustle. Something had happened that required an answer, but was short of actual armed insurrection. These were soldiers with the eagerness of those wearing the kicking boots, not the reluctance of those who might receive a kicking. A police action, therefore, and not a war.

"What's going on in the city, Loret?" she asked.

"Everything," the girl said, with a touch of her earlier uselessness. "They come for the jars today."

Ah. That. Gil hadn't read 'jar escort duty' or 'general uprising' in those squads hurrying down towards the main city, but perhaps she had been too long out of active service.

Loret led her deeper into the gardens and grounds, away from the palace. Dawn was still no more than an insinuation below the eastern horizon. A rumour that, perhaps, some time, the sun might return. And Gil understood where they were going.

"Loret, this is—"

"Yes."

"This is where we... The first place—"

"That first night," Loret agreed, over her shoulder. "I turned up at the Residence. You wouldn't tell me a word of what was going on. Dressed like an Usmiat, and not even mentioning who your smooth-looking friend was. And you brought me here. To this place." One of the many hidden spots within the garden. A place for trysts, and other things. The palace grounds were a maze of them. Practically the entire Emorandi class could pair off and find somewhere secluded if they'd wanted. But this place in particular was far from the eyes of the palace, whether Usmiat or Palleseen. This was where she'd killed Tarcomir, the Loruthi envoy.

Not her proudest moment. Though she had felt very alive, very real, when it happened. When it had turned out to be him dead, not her. In a life of tradecraft, false faces and diplomacy, sometimes you needed to feel real.

She felt very real now, with that life stripped from her. Her reality was all she had left. How she was, how she felt, as Loret brought her to her destination.

There was a gathering there, a score of people waiting in the last of the old dark. She saw the big, rounded figure of Follo, and a couple of Cotto pirates; a one-armed Tesemer; some Emorandi already armed and dressed for fighting.

Dekamran.

She gasped. If Loret had turned and stabbed her, there and then, she couldn't have felt it more keenly. She made half the distance between them in a rush, before the flex of the crowd pushed her away. The massed brooding disapproval of them.

"Kam," she said.

He was not in the full finery of an Alkhand, the impracticality of which increased sharply with distance from the Mirror

Throne. He was as she most remembered him. Just a man well-dressed, practical. Dekamran, whose face would surely split into that smile that lit it up so. Any moment, surely it would. That they were reunited. Now. Or not.

"Dekamran?" she queried. As though perhaps it was just a facsimile, a statue animated by some gifted Taumachist, rather than a man.

"Gil," he said faintly. Just one syllable but a lot of shaking in his voice. He wanted to go to her. She saw that very clearly. He wanted to throw his arms around her. And couldn't. As though there were bars between them still.

"I'm here," she said. "I'm out. I'm free. You're free. We can fight them." Not even specifying the *they*. Fight anyone. Anything that stepped between the two of them. Give her a sword and she'd cut down the lot of them.

"We will fight," Dekamran said slowly. In Usmiri, there was a linguistic distinction Pel didn't have. The *We* that included the one you spoke to, as against the *We* that was only the speaker and some others.

"Kam," Gil said. "Wait, no. I tried. I did everything." Hearing her own voice shake. "I didn't want any of this." And the words were simultaneously true and an absolute lie because how had she seen the future of it all, exactly? Some eternal limbo where Usmai was constantly tipping towards Pallesand and yet never falling into its maw? Where she could be simultaneously the good Resident and the friend of Dekamran. The more than friend. The lover.

"I am the disgrace of my people," Dekamran said. "I am the shame of my father."

"No," she said. Because he was her friend and so she would defend him, even against his own accusations.

"I have been blind," he said. "These are not your faults. I don't blame you. They are mine, only. But I have to correct them. I have to make up for them and show that I am worthy to be Alkhand. Or what am I?"

In her throat were the words that they could just walk away, both of them. He from the throne, she from the service. Find some place where nobody had ever heard of perfection. She'd give it away, for him. Wouldn't he, for her?

The answer to that was in his face. In the end, one of them chose duty, when her plans needed them both to be selfish, not just her. She felt her feet scuff, a back-foot fighting stance. A woman in a cell, still. Trapped by circumstance. "Kam," she said.

"I have to win my people back," he told her. "Fight me."

"What? No."

"Fight me, Gil. You duel. It's how you deal with things, when there's no other way. In Usmai, we understand that too. I have no other way, Gil. Fight me."

"I mean…" *I would kill you, Kam. I would cut you to ribbons. Tie an arm behind my back and a weight to one ankle and I would murder you in cold blood in any circle you chose.* "No, Kam." And, sudden, wretched inspiration. "We can't, anyway. Not the Usmiat way. The skia and the clavar, right? Never the two against one another. And you're hardly, you're hardly going to meet me like a, a Kepishi. So… No, Kam. I'll… go. I'll go. Or I'll kneel. Please."

"Well we can't just cross swords, no. Not by tradition," he said sadly. "And it needs to be done properly. But there is another way." And he plucked something from his belt and threw it to her. Her hands caught it automatically, even as she flinched away.

A rod. Ornate and spiralling, the beautiful local workmanship. Some ham-fisted amateur had chipped out the slot to take a Pal tableth. The killing word there was in Pel, so very easy to say in the heat of battle.

He had another himself. A matching piece with a gold octagon in the slot.

"It is done, I'm told. On these shores and amongst the Palleseen both. The modern way of settling these things. A new tradition."

She met his gaze. *I'm still the better shot. It won't help.* The rod sat in her hand with none of the life of a sword. Only the promise of death.

"Preceptor Follo, will you officiate?" Dekamran's voice cracked, as he spoke. Grief, and fear too. He had never been the warrior prince, after all. Not a man whose personal courage was sung about, as Gorbudan's had been. The soft brother. The one who was never supposed to become Alkhand.

She had a moment, then. A decade in an instant. A life where he had just *gone away*. Where Usmai had never seen him as a contender for the throne. Where his father had never switched to favour him. Where he had looked at Flint and the army and the choice Gil had given him, and said *No*. The expatriate prince, living comfortably somewhere in the Sway. Consulted, perhaps, on matters Usmiat. Allowed a pension. Allowed to live. She could have visited him, when her ship brought her to his shores. She could have…

"Kam," she said faintly. "Please."

The big, round monk rumbled, "Then it is to be five paces away from one another, that I shall count. Then turn and speak the words." Like a wedding.

They had to come close, this one last time, before they parted. Close, so that they could measure out the killing distance between them. In the light of the gleaming gardens she saw his lip tremble. The muscles of his jaw twitch. The fear of him. The soft man she'd only ever tried to protect from the world.

He met her eyes. He gave her that. Then Follo called on them to turn, so that the next time she saw him it would be to kill him.

She walked the paces like one in a dream. The rod, the gold weight at the heart of it, so inconsequential compared to a sword. And she could have controlled a sword duel. She could have managed it so that the wounds were glancing, fleeting. Honour without mortality. She had no control over the flash and fire of a discharged tableth. She was no trick marksman, to nick his ear or bloody his shoulder.

"Five," boomed Follo, and she turned.

There he was, ten paces away. How often she'd heard officers of the service complain, at how the short rods lacked the accuracy of a proper baton. *You have to get so close you might as well poke them in the eye!* Perhaps that would be it. They'd both spit out their words, blaze away, exhaust the tablethi, and in the end neither of them so much as singed. How absurd would that be? How welcome!

The moment hung between them. Neither spoke. The onlookers, witnesses to this new contract between the Alkhand and his nation, waited.

The word sat on her lips, tensed, poised to leap. From her to the tableth. From that to the rod. From the weapon to the heart of the Alkhand. There was a special roster somewhere on Outreach's books, they said, for Pals who had actually killed a king or equivalent. It was a matter for commendation. It could perhaps even buy her back into the service. *I put down the insurrection. I killed the Alkhand.*

She fixed her gaze on Dekamran's, eye to eye across that killing gap, and swallowed the word back down.

His lips moved. The flash seared her eyes in the same instant that his shot struck her and the world was lost to cleansing fire.

Mosaic: God's Flesh, Hell's Blood

When she bound them to her, over the corpse of the demonist Wattery, Croskin and his fellows asked, 'What are our duties?' Now that they had done this thing. This thing that Was Not Done. Demons bound to a demon bound to a demon in the world who was mistress of her own contract and acknowledged no master. The thing that would give any sane conjurer the screaming nightmares. 'What?' they asked. Because the Viper had them in the palm of her hand. They were her creatures, literally. She could have sent them onto the spears or made them her tame killers or had them labour and slave for her, as if she was one of the Kings Below.

She'd smiled at them, then. What else did such a one as she value, after all? One who had been a slave to the Kings, and then a slave and worse to a conjurer, and had been freed. Why else did she love Jack, but that he had engineered her freedom, and not taken up the leash himself, sorely tempted as he must have been? For what other reason did she torment the world and pick at its sutures, save that she was free to?

"Do what you will," she told Croskin, "shall be the whole of your law."

The mood in the city is grim. Dawn hasn't lifted it, just made it easier to see. Unlike a lot of the new blood, Flint's been kicking about the Successor Coast long enough to read it. The people of Alkhalend are pissed. Not just the regular pissed they'd been once they understood all the uniforms on the streets weren't just another bunch of Seraphi loyally following the Alkhand's orders. *Seriously* pissed. Because everyone knows that today the Pals are shifting the Kakrops Jars from the Usrani place at the foot of the falls onto the *Mordant*, out in the harbour. For safekeeping, obviously. To stop anything happening to the sacred remains of the dead frog. You know, just the way the Palleseen are notorious for caring so much about other people's beliefs and sensibilities.

He has his orders, though. Left to his own devices, the way it was when it was just Ventures over in Peor, he'd probably not be doing this. Agrees with Gil, honestly, about the wisdom of poking this particular hornet's nest with a stick. But it's not Gil in charge any more, and Berkely has made it very plain that Flint's fortunes are inextricably linked to Berkely's, and Berkely's are very tied up in a supposed hundred thousand tablethi hoard of godflesh, all bottled up in around five thousand extra tablethi of sacred jars. In short, the sort of haul it's worth risking a riot for.

Drathel better cut Flint in for a slice of the take, is all Flint has to say about it. Not knowing that, right then, Drathel is a corpse deep under the shell that was once the House of Hard Angles.

He has a pack of hard lads and lasses at his disposal, and a bit extra as well, not quite out of the Pal rulebook. First off are a core of his Peost Seraphi in their pale Accessory uniforms. They don't know what Berkely's decreed, concerning their future. The boat that's to come and take them to some distant part of the Sway far from Peor, and any thoughts they might have about home rule, hasn't arrived yet. Until it does, they're his loyal followers. They get to actually manhandle the jars, two to each weighty stone god-holder. Just in case Kakrops has any lingering curses for those who might disturb his final rest.

Some of the Usrani try to get in the way. That's what the people in the darker uniforms are for. Flint's regulars push down any monk who threatens to impede the de-jarring of their monastery. Not brutally. No kicking and nobody gets shot.

Firmly enough to dissuade anyone from being a hero, though. Let them go give alms and teach poor kids all they want, but the licence of the Usrani to get things done in the city ends where Pal writ takes up.

He has wagons, outside. Big ones with teams of four mules. More than that, they have an ogrodon. A bloody nightmare, getting the thing into the city. Another thing Usmiat tradition would rather he hadn't done, but who was counting? The wider streets are big enough for the massive beast, though, and he'd only crushed a handful of stalls and trashed a few shopfronts. The ogrodon's howdah will take a good share of the jars. They've even got a crane set up, to lift them in. Flint reckons that any ideas the locals have about swiping a few divine souvenirs won't survive contact with the monstrous beast's horns and stomping feet.

The monks stand around and wring their hands, but contribute nothing more to the procedure.

Out at the end of the sea wall, the *Mordant* has tied up. That's the plan. Under no sane circumstances is Flint going to try to get this circus through the labyrinth of the Water Lanes. Half of Kakrops would end up in the harbour by sheer mischance, whether or not the locals tried anything. But the sea wall is broad enough for an ogrodon and change, and he can parade through the big, mercantile streets of the mill district until he reaches the land end, and then follow its smooth curve to where the Pal ship awaits with a hungry hold. It's a good plan. Flint's very proud of it. No reason why it shouldn't come off without a hitch.

All loaded up with no more than some angry monkish muttering, and Flint gives the signal to proceed. He's up on the howdah beside an Ibaleth mahout with a quartet of sharpshooters should anyone below get rowdy. The Seraphi get the wagons moving in the dust of Flint's monster, and the regulars march escort beside and behind. A tight ship, basically. Good order and plenty of implied retribution should someone so much as throw a stone.

From the water, plenty of eyes watch them start their trek through the city. Knives are loosened in sheaths. Signals are awaited.

Two of the eyes belong to Hullseer Orhuhst, who has pledged his people to this venture in return for a variety of considerations, physical and metaphysical. There are a lot of Cotto in the Water Lanes of Alkhalend right now. Far more than anyone really realises, as they've been filtering in aboard this ship or that for the best part of a month. Orhuhst is quite the hand with peering into the tangled sargasso of the future. They don't call him Hullseer for nothing.

The Cotto have always been a presence, never a power, along this coast. Their strength on the waves and the unassailable islands they call home have meant that even the most powerful Alkhand or admiral has had to come to terms. Sometimes the terms the Cotto would prefer, sometimes terms that serve the land better, but they've never been conquered. Never made someone else's creatures. Orhuhst has seen the Pals, though. Understands them, now that Loret has come to him with her appendix of faith. Knows them for a people who don't let seas stand as a barrier to their ambitions. Let the Successor Coast fall to the Palleseen Sway and the Cotto won't be free much longer.

Strike now, then. Win friends, harm enemies, and gain this particular situation's unique benefits.

And, at last, the time has come. A new party, clumping onto the deck of his ship. Monks, Tesemer, Emorandi, Sand Lanes bravos, expatriate foreigners who'd hoped this was far enough to be out of the Pal shadow. All the allies the tide has brought in. There, in their midst, a man, pushing back his shawl, showing his face. Orhuhst reads the new lines there, the sorrow and the grief. They lend him a regal quality he had previously been lacking, in the Hullseer's opinion. Dekamran, the Alkhand, come to lead his people into battle.

"It's done then?" Orhuhst asks.

Dekamran nods grimly. They've given him some armour. Plated leather pauldrons and a four-mirror cuirass like the old war-leaders. "Your people?" he asks.

"Some here," Orhuhst says. "Some on the water. We're ready." And he's about to say *Boy*, to this man who never vaulted a rail or led a charge. But doesn't. If Dekamran is ever to truly be a man, today is that day. Orhuhst won't take it from him. Instead, he says, "Alkhand, the strength of the Cotto stands with you." Like an old story. And the Alkhand is too wise to listen to that sort of story, but everyone else there will tell their neighbour and word will race across the city.

"Look for my signal," Dekamran says. A faint, thin smile lends an icy light to his face. Not the cheerful, self-deprecating look of the second son doomed to obscurity, but the smile of the Alkhand going to war. "Believe me, you won't miss it."

As the continuing chorus of outrage from the citizens of Alkhalend shows, one does *not* ride an ogrodon through the streets of the city. Some of the mills that have just lost porches, hoists and goods yards were of Palleseen ownership, but Flint reckons it's all within his breakages limit if this cargo is worth what everyone says. So plain is it, in fact, that ogrodons are not a part of the city's usual traffic that, when he looks down an intersecting street and sees *another* ogrodon lumbering his way, he literally doesn't register it for a moment. A thing that can't be there, and so his eyes assure him it isn't until his mind catches up. By then it's almost upon him.

Dekamran is in the howdah of the ogrodon *behind* that one. Just because he's the Alkhand leading his people to war doesn't mean he has to be an idiot about it. He sees the lead beast break into a lumber, its whipping tail bashing in the shutters of ground floor windows. Flint's beast has been goaded forwards, so it's the following troops who take the brunt. A spackle of baton-fire dances about the charging beast's head and it lurches. Most of the shots meet only bone and armour, but a couple pierce through to the throat, the eye. It thunders into the ranks, no space between it and the walls and the wagons for the Kepishi to get out of the way. Dekamran: the screams, the bark of orders, the agonised bellowing of the beast, all come to him as from a great remove. His own mount is picking up its pace.

The wagons have halted. Soldiers clutch for their weapons. Either side of Dekamran's beast his people flood. They are not the disciplined ranks of the Palleseen army, but right then the disciplined ranks of the Palleseen army are dealing with the insertion of three great horns into their battle-line. The Pals swarm and shove and crunch together, trying to re-establish their order. The ogrodon ahead is down on its knees, shaking its head weakly, its scaled hide a constellation of red holes where the shot went in. Up on the howdah, a handful of Ibaleth shoot down at the enemy as the Pals pick them off.

Dekamran's people have batons, some of them. They have hacking clavars and long, needle-pointed skias. They have spears. Some have no better than clubs and knives. Some have been soldiers. Some have led soldiers. Some are veterans of all the scraps and skirmishes that are the engines of Sand Lanes hierarchy. United, this one day, in their desire to strike back at the Pals.

In the front ranks, Teerasla the Louse Monk opens her mouth and makes a sound like a rattle. The beast on her one hand leaps forwards and carves up the face of a Pal statlos, stabbing over and over with its bladed arms. She drags a clavar from its sheath and follows it, the point of the charge. Beside her, a thug that her people would have run off the streets at any other time. Beside him, a Maric expat driven from his city by Pal occupation. Beside him, an Emorandi duellist and poet, her sword ramming to the quillons in the gut of a soldier. Beside her, the city. Every scrap of the city that can.

The Pals recoil, waver. Cohort-Monitors and statloi bellow their orders. Some have run but most understand that unity is life. They form lines and squares, those on the outside facing off with truncheons and swords, those on the inside shooting, shooting, slotting new tablethi and shooting again. By now there is another flood of Sand Lanes irregulars attacking them from the alleys and windows on the far side of the street, but they hold. Veterans of the Loruthi wars, Peost Seraphi who've been under Pal orders for years in their own country. It will take more than this.

The first wave is thrown back with bloody losses on both sides. In the midst of the Pals they have the wagons moving again. Flint has used the bulk of his ogrodon to shunt the dead beast aside. The path to the sea wall is clear.

He ducks as an errant shot puts a hole in the side of the howdah. Gives his orders, to be relayed through the ranks. On the sea wall they'll be able to hold this rabble. Move forwards and stop for nothing!

The Usmiat insurgents see only a retreat and follow up, shooting, throwing stones and bottles and knives, clashing in brief, inconclusive scrums with the rearguard. The irregulars, the gangsters of the Sand Lanes, are running from roof to roof. Across the tops of mills and warehouses and factoras, taking potshots at officers or throwing rocks and barrels down on the close-packed Pals. In amongst them is Kilbery, the boy from the Lodge. The boy from the army camps and, before that, the orphanage. A baton in his hands that he stole from a soldier at the start. He knows how to use one, though. Grow up trailing the battalions and you can't help but pick up a bit of the trade. He lines up the weapon's length, speaks the Pel word and feels the baton quiver in his hands like a living thing. Down there a soldier, some soldier, one of them, drops into the sea of his comrades and doesn't resurface. He's killed someone, but it's a battle and it happens and he feels only a whooping excitement that he's a part of something greater, and by choice. It's never been like that for him before.

None of this can have escaped the attention of the Pal forces bivouacked near the palace. Flint has flagged for reinforcements anyway, just in case Steggers, up there, is having a slow one. There will be plenty more boots marching down the cliff path ready to deal out some civic pacification with extreme prejudice, and probably some of the squads that have been kicking barrows over in the Sand Lanes too. All he has to do is hold out, honestly. However, he'd also rather the jars made it to the ship intact, and when he gets close enough then the artillery aboard the *Mordant* can also be factored into his calculations. From the useful vantage of his howdah, therefore, Flint watches the fight that straggles back through the streets of the mill district. His people are taking heavy losses but they're holding together. Honestly the furious pressure the Usmiat are keeping them under is discipline's best friend right now because nobody has the option of running away. And so they drag the wagons onwards – the mules mostly dead by now, their traces cut – and make a snail's pace retreat down a street littered with the bodies of both sides.

Ahead, the walls of two warehouses give way to clear sky. The sea wall will shortly be his, and from there things should only get easier. No bastards in windows shooting down at his people. Good open ground for a firing line. Control properly re-established and by that time even Steggers should have gotten his boots moving and come down with some uniforms to finish this sorry business off.

One of the Ibaleth has been trying to attract his attention for some time, but it's all just hissing to Flint and he's ignored it. At last, it drags at his sleeve with a double-thumbed hand. Flint turns his attention from the fight behind to what's in front of him.

All along the curve of the sea wall the water swarms with little boats. Skiffs and junks and sloops, no two alike, barbarously painted. The piratical crews are already casting hooks up at the top of the wall, swarming up the ropes. Nobody can climb like a Cotto sailor. Flint makes a snap decision, and it's that the pirates will stop his people and stop the wagons but they won't stop the ogrodon. And the ogrodon is carrying a good share of the jars. Maybe not a hundred thousand, but if he brings forty thousand tablethi to the hold of the *Mordant* then that should be enough to look good when the reports are going in. Plus, he'll live.

The Ibaleth is hissing again. The Cotto are leaping into the front of his troops, hacking at them with hatchets and blades. Time to go, surely time to go. Except there are enemies ahead on the wall, now. Not pirates. Not locals. About as far from locals as one could get, honestly.

Flint's mouth, open for the next command, is suddenly very dry.

Orhuhst hauls himself up onto the wall and surveys his new domain. Dominating his view is the Pal ogrodon. Impressive beasts and, since not amphibious, he's not had much cause to face one before. Most of his people have made their ascent at its heels to go for the human soldiers. Holding them, getting in close where their firing lines won't do them as much good. There are locals craning out of every warehouse window and loading hatch, throwing and shooting or just screaming insults. At the back of the compacted column, Dekamran's people are doing solid work. The massed staccato of disciplined baton-fire has gone to tatters of individual cracks and snaps.

In the thick of it, Teerasla fights, sinking her steel into

every Pal uniform she can see. Her windsaw is her other hand, deflecting, striking, rending the eyes of her enemies. Beside her, scum from the Sand Lanes; nobles in their jewelled shawls. An animated wooden crab the size of a mule tears Pal soldiers apart with its pincers at the will of the old Beast Artist behind it.

At the back, Dekamran licks his lips. Not the warlord, after all. Not his older brother, or his father. Just some soft boy with too much education. The Alkhand, though. By formal coronation first, by the acceptance of his people more recently, in the moment that he killed his friend.

He shot Gil. He saw her punched from her feet with the force of it. No duellist could have asked for a better strike. In that instant he'd dropped the rod and tried to run to her. To beg her forgiveness, to say he was sorry. To undo what he had done, even though he'd done it to undo all those other things he'd done. But his people closed around him, acclaiming him, applauding him. He never even had that last moment with her.

Now he sees the Pals, his enemy, packed in, fighting one another's elbows, crushed against the side of the wagons, clambering atop them for space, only to make themselves targets for every window-lurker with something heavy to throw. Desperate, frightened men and women who can't get out.

If he showed Gil no mercy, how much less do they deserve?

"Give the order to part the way," he calls, and the word goes forwards. Then he tells his mahout to drive the goad in. The ogrodon stamps and shakes its horned head and begins to build up speed. Ahead, the Usmiat insurgents are melting away into side-streets and through windows, already primed for the move. For a moment the Pals think they're running away. A brief, murdered cheer starts up before they see what's thundering down on them.

Orhuhst, climbed up to the very last roof-end of the warehouses, sees all that. Nods approvingly. The boy's coming on and they'll make a general of him yet. Probably means Dekamran and Orhuhst will lock horns themselves someday, but that's for the future.

Flint makes a decision, then. He, the adventurer, the cheerful rogue who always looks after his people, understands that this time he won't. The bonds of comradeship that Ventures builds, between master and men, have been cut half through by the decisions Berkely had him take. He's already a thing apart from them. Easy to sever the last strands of that camaraderie. He's in Berkely's world now, where loyalty is something that only exists from below looking up.

"Get her moving!" he tells his own mahout. "Just go for the ship!" When the creature just hisses and snaps at him, he snatches the goad and lashes at the huge beast himself.

The ogrodon groans and shudders, lurches forwards, its head sweeping boxes and crates from the wall, even getting caught in the highest rigging of a Cotto sloop and snapping the mast.

Ahead, the enemy are advancing.

"Charge!" Flint says. "Get the fucker moving!"

Ogrodons will charge anything. Walls, forests of spearpoints, trenches. They stop for nothing, and their hide is proof against most of it. Anything of this world, they will lower their heads and lumber blindly towards.

The score and a half of figures standing in the ogrodon's way are from elsewhere, though. Misshapen, no two the same, but formed into a double firing line and still wearing scraps of Pal uniforms. Croskin's demons, and the ogrodon will not get any closer to them. The sheer reeking unnatural stink of them has it treading backwards, scattering the Cotto with its tail, threatening to trample Flint's own people.

He hears the barked order from Croskin, Pal-standard. The demons charge. On two feet and many feet, taking raggedly to the air, hurling themselves at the horns of the panicking ogrodon.

"Signal the ship!" Flint yells. "The ship! The..."

At the far end of the sea wall, the *Mordant* rocks at anchor. Even at this distance he can see its rails swarming with Cotto, a positive flotilla of little boats clustered around it. There's fighting on the decks, but the *Mordant*'s marines are all ashore. Berkely's people, whom Flint himself garrisoned. The beset vessel only has its regular crew. Though bodies fall back from the rails and he hears the distant crackle of batons, the *Mordant* is being overrun.

A hundred thousand tablethi does not, in Flint's personal book, balance the loss of his one life.

One of the demons, feathered, screeching, appears over the shield of the ogrodon's head, bringing its baton to bear with a second set of arms. The mahout shoots it in the beak and it drops back, but the rest are crawling over the ogrodon like a disfiguring plague.

Flint just goes. Takes a rod and his sword, hops the side of the howdah and skins down the straps to the ground. A Cotto makes a game try for him, but he discharges the rod into her face before it's knocked from his hand. His sword takes three ringing blows – not even intended for *him*, particularly, just the uniform. He has a mad idea that he could strip naked there and then, and walk unmolested through the battle to freedom.

Then the dart of a skia flays his ear and he reels back. His return cut wins him some space, but he's got nowhere to go, as much a prisoner of the battlefield as his people.

A hand seizes his shoulder, barbs and claws snagging in his jacket. Because he wears it open against the heat, he twists out of it, coming round to face his new enemy.

Croskin. Cohort-Monitor Croskin as was. The whole ape-bulky mass of him staring at Flint with red eyes. The hat, the damnable hat, still atop his puffed-out head.

Flint tries with the sword but Croskin just lets him cut, then crushes his fingers against the hilt until he lets go. The demon's long arms lash out and grab him, shake him till his teeth rattle like baton-fire. A moment later, with casual strength, Croskin hoists Flint into the air and goes up the nearest wall like a spider.

Over the top of the main battle, Dekamran sees the Pal ogrodon lurch and totter. Its cargo of jars sways. There is fighting aboard it, the remaining Pals trying to fend off the demons. *Demons!* But so many Usmiat ways have been trampled into the dust, why not that one? The main body of the Pal force is just a tight crush of bodies about the wagons now. The back one has already fallen, locals trying to haul it back up a street choked and mounded with bodies. The Pals surge back, trying to reclaim their priceless treasure. Trying to stop anyone undoing their sacrilege. The tide sways. Usrani monks, who had come to recover the body of their god, flee or get trampled or shot.

A boy, just a skinny Pal boy in ragged Usmiat clothes, leaps atop the wagon. He has a baton, discharging it into the faces of the Pals as they haul on the backboard. Then he has a knife, brandished in the air, the sun on it, absurdly heroic. He slashes at the ropes of the wagon. The jars begin to move.

Dekamran has the very best viewpoint for it. Seeing the faces of the Pals, even, as the great jars of godflesh start to slide towards them. The things they were so desperate to claim and now understand they didn't want at all. Not like this. Not all those hundredweights of stone and dead frog sliding off the back of the wagon on top of them. With that tide come the fighters, slicing apart their broken order. Dekamran sees the boy, the Pal boy, wave his little blade in the air and cry liberty.

He's gone the next second. A target too tempting for some Pal sharpshooter. Snatched away by the force of the shot and lost in the struggle of the crowd.

On the sea wall, Orhuhst has found a loyal Ibaleth – or at

least one that will agree to being loyal so long as he's around with an axe – to calm the laden ogrodon. The demons have gone to bedevil the Pals. At the wall's far end, the *Mordant*'s Pal flag has come down. His people have shown their characteristic enthusiasm for taking control of ships that don't belong to them, and the harbour sharks will feed well tonight.

"Get this thing moving," he tells the Ibaleth, speaking slowly so she can understand him. The Pals have provided him with both a conveyance for these priceless jars, and a ship to put them in. He sees no reason to waste all that careful planning.

Three streets behind the fight, Croskin comes down to the ground again. He's loped rooftop to rooftop, trailing demons like festival streamers. Now he pauses, the air still full of fighting, but removed, a party in the next room.

He puts Flint down. The man stares at him. Croskin sits on his haunches, adjusts his hat.

"Go," he says.

Flint, battered, disarmed, dishevelled, just stares at him. Not that he's begging the justice of being killed by Croskin, but Croskin is a demon. They're monsters. You don't expect table manners and poetry from them, and you don't expect this.

The pinkish-red eyes watch him, cynical, ancient. Croskin's raspy voice says, "She said, do what you will. And because we were soldiers, we fought." As many still fight, the air ribboned with shots and screams. "Because you betrayed us, we fought you. Because we are anathema to the Usmiat, most hated of hated, we made ourselves their allies. Because it would appal them. A stain on their souls they will never be rid of." Croskin chuckles nastily.

Flint gets himself sitting up, waiting for the demons to descend on him and tear him apart, here in this secluded street away from the action. A little diversion for the legions of hell.

"You sold us," says Croskin. "But before that, you made us like you. You freed us, and gave us ranks and tasks and *respect*. Like humans with humans, not masters with demons. You made me one of you, Flint." His name in the demon's mouth, spat out like a stone. "You gave us something we never had before, not Below, not Above, even though you took it back. So this is what I will. Go. Flee. Live. For old time's sake, Flint. For what we had."

"I'll go," Flint says hurriedly. "I'll run. You'll get no more trouble out of me." Flint scrambles to his feet and runs for it, getting two streets clear of the accusing gaze of the demons.

And stops. Honestly he doesn't know how many of these reversals he can take. His heart might not survive another.

Marching into sight right around the corner come Companion-Monitor Steggers and a whole column of reinforcements. More than enough to take the insurgents in the back and put an end to all of this.

"Magister?" Steggers asks, wide-eyed at the state of him.

Perhaps there's a brief moment when he holds onto the right thing to do. To have no part of it, however it goes. To do what Croskin told him, as the price of his preservation. Maybe that was what Flint from Ventures would have done. Flint the ambitious career officer has other priorities.

He starts giving orders, slotting neatly in at the head of the chain of command. He can redeem himself, with this unlooked-for gift. A swift, sharp raiding strike, like he led back in Peor. Take the Alkhand and his people before they understand what's what. Bring Palleseen discipline back to the streets of Alkhalend. Steggers only has a handful of squads, probably those out kicking doors in the Sand Lanes overnight. But with Flint's signature dash, it should be enough. Once the Usmiat start running they won't stop.

Kilbery knows this place. It's like home. The screaming and the acrid smell of medicine. A street, an alley overhung with cranes and the forward-thrust upper storeys of warehouses. A makeshift hospital, with the wounded laid out on blankets and sheets. The corpses, too. Usrani monks pass back and forth doing all that can be done. But not for him. His torment deserves a special devil.

The great mass of Oathan kneels beside him, working on Kilbery's leg. It's broken. He feels almost nothing of it, because Oathan knows his trade. A weird, floating clarity where the offending limb seems very far away. He watches the man's big hands set the bone-ends together, pressing and kneading them through the skin, and then a monk comes with a splint. Precious little talk between Oathan and the Usrani, the one speaking only bad Usmiri, the other not speaking Pel at all, but they both know their trade.

Oathan sags down, sitting. "I came to get you," he says. "Didn't get any further than here." Looking impotently furious with himself. His apron is smeared with blood, his fingers with five colours of unguent. It's like old times, back in the army. "Old habits," he spits. "I couldn't just..." And then the familiar shift, the way he alchemises any unwanted emotion into anger eventually. "What where you even thinking, you little turd? How's this anything to do with you? We're getting out. You know that. Tonight and we're gone from this pox-ridden place and clear."

Kilbery, with the weird detachment of the drugged, says, "No."

Oathan stares at him. "You will not bloody argue with me. The Pals have their teeth into this damn place now. We're leaving."

"No. The Alkhand has come back," Kilbery says.

Oathan plainly doesn't care if the Alkhand has turned green and caught on fire. "It's not our fight," he hisses to the boy. "We are none of them. They won't thank us and they won't want us. And the Pals – boy, you *know* how it goes. You and me both, we do. We saw it from the other side often enough."

Kilbery takes a deep breath. "It's my home."

"It is not."

"It's all the home I've got. I've got friends here. I live here. This is *home*. You're going to tell me I can't fight for it?" His face twists, astonished by his own boldness. Unmedicated, he'd just have grumbled behind the man's back, never thrown all this in his face. "You go. You run away. I'm staying. With my people."

Oathan goes red, inflates, the storm Kilbery's lived with all his life, about to break one more time. The boy balls his little fists, as though he's in any position to fight back. But then something goes out of the big man. Broad and huge and massive as he is, for a moment he seems very small and old and weak, just staring at the boy. Not his son, just some boy he picked up and made his apprentice and skivvy. And son, at the end. His son.

Then there's shouting from down the street. Oathan levers himself to his feet. There are more soldiers coming, fresh ones. Nothing's between them and the injured, and then the back of the embattled Usmiat.

Almost nothing.

Oathan's eyes go wide. "*Her*," he says.

The dregs, that's what they are. No real barrier that would hold against two solid salvos and a charge. Injured insurgents who can still walk and hold a weapon. A one-armed Louse Monk. A pair of Cotto somehow gotten lost from the waterfront. An old man with toy tigers snarling about his knees. A girl with a jointed serpent about her shoulders and an old woman atop a wooden crab the size of a table, come fresh from bearing the wounded in its claws. The biggest Pal man Flint ever saw, armed with nothing but his fists. A rabble that can't even form a solid line to stop him because neither flank will stand alongside the centre. Croskin and his demons. The anathema of Usmiat tradition, right there in the open and giving their allies second thoughts.

"Damn me," Flint says ruefully. "I reckon they're doing more good for us over there than they'd do over here."

"Magister," Steggers prompts, and Flint shrugs.

"I mean I guess we sweep the fuckers from the street and move in."

"Magister," says Steggers again. Fearfully, this time. Pointing. A woman has stepped forth from the enemy.

She is the most beautiful thing Flint ever saw. A man with an eye for women, no less, and somehow he never came across this paragon in all his days. Just walking across the killing gap separating the Pals from that ragbag of defenders. Wearing most of a Pal uniform herself, though worn with the shirt unbuttoned to a non-regulation degree. She meets Flint's eyes and smiles.

He knows what she is, then. That she's just like Croskin, under that flawless skin. That his eyes see what her nature tells them to see. She's poison. Nothing but poison.

She has stepped to within a corpse's length of him. Steggers is making dry noises. Flint is very aware he should be giving the order to shoot, right now. Scythe the vision down along with the rest of them. Just another Croskin with a nicer face. But she holds him. She holds Steggers. And, denied those two voices of command, the firing line of Pals just holds as though the instant before their assault has been pinched between the long nails of the woman's finger and thumb.

The Viper, Caecelian. A thing shaped by human malice to perform human wickedness and degradation. Cut loose in the world. Unleashed, literally.

Demons do not care for the things of the World Above. That's well known to demonists and scholars. The Kings Below confirm it. Why, if they did care, you might have qualms over using them so badly.

And not to gild the poisonous lily too much. Human grief and angst and torment feed her. She is a thing of pretty spite. Pain is her meat, sorrow her drink. But then she fell amongst humans who were surgeons and healers, who cut and burned and poisoned to make people better. Mixed messages from the world.

Enshili wanted to be here standing with her. Her creature, her acolyte. The Usmiat princess that Caecelian corrupted. The girl she freed. As it was with Croskin, she finds herself deeply invested in freedom. It has become her philosophy. And all too often freedom hurts far more than the safe close walls of obedience, and so much the better for that.

She was cruel to Enshili. *You made a promise to Loret, to be there when she came back. It was her or it was me, and you chose her. So I banish you from my side. If you would be like me, then you will be bound by your contracts!* Making it about pettiness and jealousy and vitriol, and not at all because she cared. Making the girl go stand at the back like a bad pupil.

Enshili was watching, now. Watching from the street where the wounded were. Any moment her restraint would give and she'd run out, and the shooting would start. So Caecelian needed to bring things to a close.

She nods. The other nods. In position. Taking no initiative, but ready to follow her lead. *We difficult wives, always causing trouble.*

"Misery and wickedness," she speaks into Flint's slack face and runs him through the throat, a perfect fencer's lunge. The man next to him – and she knows rank badges as well as any soldier – opens his mouth in alarm and she makes it his target. Her point through the roof of it and into his skull the sly way. Both officers down in an instant.

The other, her fellow wife, makes her move. And nobody had expected the thing to take up Caecelian's call to arms. Surely *she* would just hang about the ceiling of the Lodge over her wounded husband. But here she is, coursing like a nightmare over the roof and down into the midst of the Pals. Scattering them with the lashing length of her body, seizing on them with the fanged hand that is her face.

Caecelian cries out, exulting. The ragged line of defenders are running forwards: demons, Taumachists, thugs and invalids and all. She kills a Pal woman who's bringing a baton up. The weapon that discharges into her at near point blank range, she doesn't even see.

She kills the wielder anyway, her signature on a personal contract. Another shot takes her midway into the strike. She stumbles. Graceless, suddenly.

She is very sorry for Jack. He will be so miserable and she will not be there to feed off it. All that sorrow wasted.

Oathan pulls her out of the fray. Rough hands on a body that is fraying around her. The form she was given long before, when her master conjured her from air. The big Pal drags her away, lays her down. Enshili is kneeling beside her, screaming at her, weeping. "How could you! How could you!"

Caecelian reaches up, takes the girl by the ear and drags her head close. Kisses her, lips to lips, feeling threads of her unravelling nature pass one to another. Her other hand has found her belt pouch. Fumbling with the fastenings, these human things she has to mimic. Finding the paper.

She slashes the startled girl's cheek with a thumbnail and smears the blood across the new contract. The thing keeping Croskin and his people in the world. They need an anchor. She can't be that any more.

"Yours now," she tells Enshili, seeing the girl's brown eyes flicker red with the gift. She wanted to be more like her mentor, and that's the venom the Viper's put in her, just a spark of hell. "Go to Jack. Tell him." And the girl is still doing all that useless weeping and caterwauling humans are so fond of, and that's wasted now. "*Listen*," Caecelian hisses, gripping the girl's wrist hard enough to hurt. "*Tell* him."

Would he understand? Simple Jack, Happy Jack? Except he'd never been simple, and he wouldn't be happy either. He was a sharp one, under all the vacant smiles. He'd know.

Caecelian feels the last binding threads of her sunder, and takes her new freedom to hell.

Orhuhst supervises the loading of the *Jagged Hand That Feeds* – formerly the *Mordant* – when the call comes that he has a visitor. No regular caller either, but the very Alkhand, still atop his howdah and wearing his authority well. Like a suit of clothes he's finally grown into.

"It's done?" the Hullseer calls up from the deck.

"It is," Dekamran replies. "And the Pals up in the palace aren't coming down for now." A real concern, given the strength the Pals still have in the city.

"And if you have to smash down that fancy house of yours one day, to get them out?" Orhuhst asks him.

"Then I will build a greater one when they have gone," Dekamran says.

The Cotto laughs at that. "You and I," he says, "will not be friends forever. But let it be a year, ten years. Let us be old men when we come to blows. I like you, Alkhand."

Dekamran's expression suggests that makes one of them. The Pal woman is still heavy on his conscience. His eyes follow the sigil-inscribed jars being hoist into the *Hand*'s hold. Perhaps half the accumulated flesh of Kakrops, by weight. All that had been on Flint's ogrodon. And Orhuhst waits to see if this will be it. If the fragile alliance between land and sea will break even at this.

Dekamran understands, though. The political convenience, the theological significance. All that education has to be good for something.

"I wish you good sailing," the Alkhand shouts to him.

"Ah, we're here a little longer, if there's trouble." Orhuhst grins. "This much cargo takes some balancing and settling. Plus there's ritual. And some new crew to take on board. We'll pop some of these toys when the time comes." He gestures towards the Pal engines at the rails, that his people are just itching to play with. "You'll hear the bang of it. That's how the Kepishi do it, I think, when they give word from ship to shore. A *salute*." Savouring the Pel word.

In truth he isn't sure about the new crew. But the sea teaches you to live in hope, and that anything can be beached by the tide, just when you need it.

The Road to Everywhere

Behind every grand history, the dates of battles and the names of kings, there are a hundred small stories. The people that the scholars will never know and the bards never sing of. People just doing their best with the hand life dealt them. Their entrances onto the stage as unnoticed as their exits.

At the back of the wagon: Tally, the old Jarokiri surgeon. Beside her, head on her shoulder, the Reckoner had somehow slept through all the jolt and sway of it, a crutch over her knees.

Balancing them out, Oathan's broad buttocks were planted on the driver's seat. He flicked at the mule every time it tried to stop and crop at the edge of the path.

These few, fleeing the walls of Alkhalend. No matter whose flag ended up waving over them. The resurgent Alkhand or the Palleseen, it was war either way. They'd had enough of war. Time to move on.

And, because both war and Pallesand seemed more than capable of dogging their heels across the map, move on somewhere nobody has a map too, why not? Given the opportunity presented itself.

In the bed of the cart, in the middle, a man sat. Braces and shirtsleeves and breeches, remnants of a uniform that shared some principles with that of the Pals without ever quite agreeing with it. The Under-warden, face still creased with the pain of the wounds he'd survived. Because of him – what came with him – the surrounding trees were very quiet. No sound of beasts, no worry of brigands. Something large and swift and many-limbed festered through the fringes of the jungle, and woe betide anyone who decided to interrupt *these* travellers in their journey.

And beside the Under-warden, the other founder member of the Difficult Wives Club, recently disbarred from membership owing to circumstances.

Jack stared out at the dark and the jungle. Not Happy Jack any longer. He'd passed through Unhappy Jack, though. Gone through the weeping, the red eyes, the demands made of a God who wasn't there and wouldn't help anyway. Now a grim, tight-featured and brooding Jack was left. A hollow thing where that cheery little man had once been. The Under-warden reached out, clasped his shoulder. The familiar of monsters trying to impart human comfort. Jack's look was bleak, flat. Not hopeless. Almost worse because it wasn't hopeless, honestly.

"Can we not," Tally demanded, "make this contrivance go faster?"

Oathan grunted. Shoulders hunched, against her and the world. A man with his own woes.

"Only I could walk faster than this," she carped on. She couldn't, though maybe there wasn't so much in it.

"You could carry our gear maybe, too," Oathan threw over those hunched shoulders.

"I don't want a wave of goddamn walking wounded from the fighting to overhaul us and people start demanding I ply my trade," Tally snapped. "We had enough of that back in the city. And all the wrong damn people. I'm amazed we're not still fucking *there*. I'm amazed a whole new Pal army didn't turn up in the harbour while I was elbow-deep in some fucking insurgent's guts. Or worse."

A venomous look at Jack, but his new face was proof against them.

"You ain't going to buy her back with good deeds, Jack," Tally spat. "Just the opposite, if anything."

"Leave him," Oathan said. Tally's eyes actually bulged. Oathan, the monster, the beast, taking an injured party's side.

She subsided into silence as the wagon rumbled on.

Not long after that, they arrived. A place none of them had seen before, save the Under-warden and his wife when they came through the first time. The compound of the Alborandi. The masked monks who kept the Waygrove.

As the wagon drew to a halt, Tally watched them at work in the moonlight. Nondescript figures in simple robes, each with one of those eyeless, painted masks. More nondescript than should have been possible: look away and you could never quite be sure if you'd seen a given monk before, or not. Tear off all those masks, would she find the blind face of Oparan, the former Alkhand? Would she find the face of his wife, the long-lost Alkhani? Or would even those revealed faces have nothing in them that could be held in the memory? Would the oblivion that the Alborandi promised resist such brute attempts to pierce it?

Tally stared at them all narrowly, leery that some monk might trot up with a spare mask. "You had better be sure," she said, "you can deliver."

The wood beyond the Grove, the one that didn't exist in this world, but linked a hundred of them. It was not safe. That much, all the stories agreed on. Incautious travellers met bloody fates. There were monsters.

The Under-warden's face turned to her, expressionless. There was a flurry and a blur of segmented movement out there, reflecting in his eyes more than it should do, given the dark. There *were* monsters in the wood beyond the grove, but monstrosity respected monstrosity. His wife was their safe passage. The expensive magical tricks the two Pal scholars had relied on would not be necessary.

"Don't look at me like that," Tally said, hearing her own voice and sick of it. "It's why we helped you, after all."

"We helped because he was my friend and he was trapped," Jack said.

"That might have been why *you*—" Tally started, but then the Reckoner stirred, frowning. Opened her eyes and hissed in annoyance at all the noise.

"What? I was sleeping."

"We're here, anyway," Tally said with little sympathy. "I mean, assuming you're coming."

"I'm coming. Why wouldn't I be coming?" the Reckoner demands. "Who isn't coming?" Looking from face to face around the cart. "Where's the boy?"

Oathan's shoulders hunched tighter. "Stayed. To fight. The little idiot."

The Reckoner, who had left the city with a collection of other people's wounds and had been resting since, blinked. "So you…?"

He said nothing, and Tally knew it was because he didn't know what words might come out. He'd shouted, raged, threatened, insulted, raised a hand, then lowered it when the boy, when *Kilbery*, muscled right back. The boy, determined to defend his home. To do the right thing, like doomed young kids so often did.

Oathan goaded the mule forwards. They ground slowly through the compound of the Alborandi towards that other exit, the one where the trees seemed to bend together to grant an infinite moonlit perspective. Not one of the monks so much as turned a masked face towards them.

And eventually it was there, right before them, and Oathan yanked the reins to bring their beast to a stop.

A whispering rustle from behind them was the Warden breaking from the trees, so that when the Under-warden levered himself awkwardly from the wagon bed, she was there to take his weight. To coil beneath his armpits and bear him up. To wrap him in her cloak of legs.

It wasn't like the cart was going through the portal. Oathan groaned and sloughed down from the seat, began lifting packs from within. Packs loaded with rolls of surgeon's tools, stuffed with bags of candies and jars of honey. The big satchels, with the glassware, he left in place.

"I see," Tally said flatly. "War," she reminded him. "You said never again. Not your skills used to stitch battle wounds. Not after the army."

Oathan looked at her, brutal, a bludgeon of an expression. His features quivered like she was seeing him through water. His face crumpled like balled-up paper.

"I can't leave him," he said softly. "He's just a boy."

"I'm not staying with you," she told him.

"I'm not asking you."

"I'm out."

"You earned it," he said. Barely grudging and unpleasant at all. She hardly recognised him.

"Well fuck," Tally said staring into the trees and their weird perspective. "I guess it's *this* then."

"Who knows. Maybe it will be better." The Reckoner seemed weirdly optimistic about the prospect. Perhaps, given her peculiar trade, she thought she might be able to skip out on some debt she owed the world. Even the essential properties of the universe can be cheated, by a deft-enough hand.

"Come on, Jack," Tally said.

"I'm not going either," he told them.

"You bloody are," Oathan said, but Jack just shook his head.

"She's *gone*," Tally said. *Didn't* say, *You're well rid of her*, though surely she thought it.

"Where do they go, though?" Jack asked softly. "They go Below, Tally. She's there. Where the Kings rule. And I'm going to find a way to bring her back."

"You don't know the first thing about conjuring," she told him. "And whatever's *down* there, it won't be her. The stuff that was *her*, that you knew, that's rubbed off. It's just the demon left. Not the face, not the manner, no damn fondness for you, that's for sure. Jack, don't be—"

He held up a hand. Silenced her. A long time since he was able to do that. Or maybe Happy Jack had never needed to.

"Oh damn," Tally said. "You pair of bloody fools." And managed a kind of distasteful one-armed hug. The most she had in her. The Reckoner was more effusive, and more understanding, and hadn't wasted any breath trying to dissuade anyone.

It was the three of them for the woods, then. The four of them, including the Wife. Tally looked back just the once, as they walked in. Seeing the huge man, the little man, the wagon, all the burdens they bore.

Render Unto the Sea

"… Sage-Broker Berkely, discovered in his chambers this morning. The assassin had left the weapon in his body, doubtless to cause additional consternation to the staff. For the record, the item was a plain duelling sword of Palleseen manufacture, the significance of which I need not comment on.

At this point the situation at Alkhalend is extremely doubtful. With the Mordant *lost and the* Salient *set ablaze, the only options for the garrison are to sit within the palace grounds, which are indefensible; to march for the Peost border; or to wait for a relief force from Sage-Invigilator Palinet in Peor. This latter possibility is complicated both because coastal communications between Alkhalend and Peor have become unreliable owing to increased pirate activity, and because of the massing of forces loyal to the Alkhand at the fortress of Mantekor.*

I am unfortunately not in a position to order punitive action either against Mantekor or the populace of Alkhalend, nor do I feel it appropriate to request additional forces. Currently the Alkhand has extended an offer for our remaining forces to vacate the city without further violence, in return for an unmolested exit to Peor. While I appreciate that this may simply represent a preference on the enemy's part for an open field battle, I am minded to accept for the chance to preserve the lives of our people here. In this case I shall remain in the city in the hope that the Alkhand will make a civilized allowance for diplomatic staff in order to maintain a channel of communication…"

Report to Outreach from Companion-Invigilator Samellers,
Acting Resident in Usmai.

From the deck of the *Jagged Hand That Feeds* was only open ocean from horizon to horizon, Orhuhst decided it was time to pay their dues.

He had the crew stand ready, and the jars brought up from the hold. It was twilight, because dusk was propitious for certain ceremonies. His crew had marked out sigils on the rails and the deck, all the old sacred signs. He could feel the pressing presence of the divine louring down over them like storm clouds. The Shark Queen, yes, but the Fisher King too, her groom. And, through them, all the sea-gods, the storm gods, the powers of sudden violence, hunger and rage.

They hauled the jars up, one by one. His share of the flesh of Alkhalend's frog god. And perhaps some of the Usmiat would see this as a sacrilege, as much as the Pals turning it all into charged tablethi. Orhuhst knew better, though. This was what was due from one faith to another. This was the body of Kakrops being sent to a proper rest, not just coined into magical currency for the Palleseen.

The first jar was hauled up to the rail and unsealed. They looked to their Hullseer to take the final step, to consecrate with his hands this great sacrifice to the waves. But there were hands more holy. He looked across the desk and beckoned to the girl.

Loret – the name she still answered to. And probably the girl didn't want to be sacred to the sea, particularly, but it wasn't her choice. You didn't get to carry that inside you and walk away unchanged.

And she'd come on board, after all. Come with her friend, the other girl with the red demon eyes and the quick sword. The pair of them crewmates he was more than happy to find a berth for, even if they hadn't come with a retinue.

That retinue were crouched about the deck even now, watching what was going on. Understanding it more than a human might, because demon eyes saw things the way they really were. And the Cotto had no problems with demons. Not a part of those traditions that had the Usmiat imprison them and lock them away. If Loret's new friend brought along a consignment of demon marines to throng the rails in a boarding action, Orhuhst had no objections to that at all.

Loret had her hands to the jar now. She swallowed, maybe wondering how much more this daubed her with the bloody waters of the sea-gods.

"Do it, girl," Orhuhst said. "This is respect."

Down below, the water thrashed with the bodies of sharks, the lower congregation of the gods, eager to take part in the sacrament. Loret braced herself, tipped the jar. The first chunks of godflesh slipped over the rail and vanished into the churning sea. It wasn't the first time. The Queen of Sharks contained multitudes. She was a pantheon in herself. Whatever the Usmiat did with their share of their dead god, Kakrops would live again in the oceans. His crew brought out the next jar. Loret stepped back, ceding the honour. Orhuhst clapped her on the shoulder. Almost paternal in his approval. She flinched, but not as much as before. At her belt, the pearl knife shone in the last of the evening sun.

Much later, months later, elsewhere. Far north of the Garmoers, across the Successor Steppes. Here, the past lay heavy on the land. A handful of nomad tribes roamed nearby, but none came here. Not to the gates of the Necropolis.

This was where the ancient emperors had retreated to, centuries before. The old immortal necromancers of the Moeribandi Empire, when they lost the last of their interest in ruling a living world. The tomb that they closed from the inside. The living had no business here. The people of the steppes gave it a wide berth. Only faint traces remained of the great roads that had once led here from across the known world.

Premath, third son of Oparan, stopped and looked up at the sealed stones, reading a thousand warding glyphs there. Sensing a vast wealth of necromantic power within. Barred to him now, but he was patient. The dead were always patient.

He sat. He waited. Eternal, undecaying, the last scion of a long-dead Empire, locked out of their halls. He could wait forever.

Eventually they came, the company he was waiting for, marching in their charcoal-grey uniforms.

Author Note

This is not a historical work. The world this series is set in is entirely apart from our own and neither Usmai nor Pallesand is a real world nation. I have attempted to learn at least something from the lessons of history, however, and in this I have been very ably assisted by some particularly erudite podcasts. I would therefore like to thank Mike Duncan of *Revolutions*, and Anita Arnand and William Dalrymple of *Empire* for their entertaining and informative work, as well as William Dalrymple's book, *The Anarchy*.